VIGILANTE MOON

VIGILANTE MOON

A Novel of Old Montana

STAN LYNDE
Illustrations by the author

COTTONWOOD *Publishing*

Copyright © 2003 by Stan Lynde

First Printing, January 2003
3 5 7 9 8 6 4 2

COVER PHOTO
Virginia City, 1866
Courtesy of the Montana Historical Society

PRODUCTION AND DESIGN BY
Mountain Press Publishing Company

Library of Congress Catalog Card Number: 2002092938
ISBN 1-886370-19-2/cloth • ISBN 0-886370-20-6/paper

PRINTED IN CANADA

COTTONWOOD PUBLISHING
120 Greenwood Drive
Helena, Montana 59601

*To all who follow their dreams,
and especially to Eleanor, my mother,
who taught me that I could.*

Introduction

Vigilante Moon, a story of love and courage and sacrifice set in early Montana, has won a place on my bookshelf among my favorite novels. Stan Lynde is not only a great storyteller but a master of the historical west. He brings to this work a lifetime of research, a love of the high and wild world untouched by civilization, an artist's vision, and a poet's gift of words.

The novel, set in Virginia City in its heyday, is authentic. The historical characters, from sinister road agents to vigilantes, have been woven seamlessly into the story, and come vividly to life on these pages.

One can read this novel not only for its gripping story, but for the images of a bygone world evoked by the author. There is something beautiful about the settling of the West, something that lives even now in the breath and spirit of the American people. Stan Lynde has caught that essence, that soul of the people in this splendid novel.

This is the work of a man who loves the West, who has devoted himself to its history and legend all his life, and whose talents all come together here in a novel that will long be loved and remembered.

Richard S. Wheeler
Spur Award-winning author, and Winner of the 2001 Owen Wister Award

Preface

On August 21, 1863, "Colonel" William Clarke Quantrill led approximately 400 Missouri guerrillas on a raid against the antislavery town of Lawrence, Kansas. The raiders spent some three hours in slaughter, killing nearly 200 civilian men and boys in their teens. The raiders also looted and burned the town, destroying property worth more than $1,500,000. The raid was the single greatest atrocity of the American Civil War.

In 1862, Montana's first real gold strike took place on Grasshopper Creek, a tributary to the Beaverhead River, and the town of Bannack was born. By mid-winter, 1863, there were perhaps five hundred persons in Bannack. By spring there were nearly a thousand.

In May of 1863 a second, even richer discovery was made, seventy miles away at a place called Alder Gulch. The several "cities" that sprang up along Alder Creek housed some six thousand people by late 1863.

The gold camps attracted not only miners and merchants, but a population of gamblers, thieves, and murderers historian K. Ross Toole called "the West's most unsavory group of cutthroats."

The leader of these evildoers was a soft-spoken, charming man named Henry Plummer. With a gift for organization and a personality that appealed to men and women alike, Plummer got himself elected Sheriff and organized the outlaws into a band called the "Innocents."

Between the winters of 1862 and 1864 the "Innocents" murdered a known 102 victims, although the actual count is believed to include a score more. Although the number of "Innocents" varied, including minor thieves, spies, and hangers-on, there were twenty-four principal members. All of them, including Sheriff Plummer and his chief deputies, were hanged by Vigilantes between December 21, 1863, and January 11, 1864.

It is against this historical background that *Vigilante Moon* takes place.

ONE

A Separate Peace

"T HE OLD MAN is feelin' bloody today," said Bravo Santee. "He aims to burn Jim Lane at the stake and pee on his ashes."

Will Hunter twisted in his saddle and looked back along the ranks of hard-eyed guerrillas. Some four hundred Missouri raiders, most of them young and all of them killers, rode their horses at a fast walk through the dim pre-dawn light. Although the sun had yet to rise, the day already promised to be cookstove hot, and stifling. Dust puffed up at the fall of each hoof, fine as powder, then drifted back to earth. Long-haired boys with peach-fuzz cheeks and red-rimmed eyes sat their saddles with an easy grace, and Hell rode down on Kansas.

The riders had left their camp on the banks of Sni-A-Bar Creek three days before and had marched southwest through Jackson County across the scorched fields and smoking ruins that had once been the prosperous farms of their Missouri neighbors. They had crossed into Kansas ten miles below the border town of Little Santa Fe and turned west. Unobserved, they'd ridden past a Union Cavalry bivouac and had skirted sleeping hamlets in the darkness. Now they rode toward the abolitionist stronghold of Lawrence with malice on their minds and murder in their hearts.

At the column's head, resplendent in the cadet-gray uniform and gold braid of a Confederate colonel, rode the leader of the strike force and the "old man" of Santee's discourse, the notorious William Clarke Quantrill. Son of an Ohio schoolteacher, and feared guerrilla leader in the vicious, no-quarter war between Kansas and western Missouri, Quantrill held the official rank of captain in the Confederate Army. Assuming the rank of colonel had been strictly his own idea. On that August morning in 1863, the "old man" was just twenty-five years old.

"What are we up against in Lawrence?" Hunter asked. "How many bluecoats?"

"Damned if I know," Santee said, "but I don't reckon it matters much to the old man—this here's a *revenge* raid."

Yes, Hunter thought, another revenge raid. Vengeance had been his own motive when he'd joined Quantrill. How many such raids had he been a part of since then, he wondered. Fifteen? Twenty? More than he cared to recall, at any rate. Lately, he'd begun to wonder when, if ever, the bloody raids and counter-raids would end. An eye for an eye and a tooth for a tooth, he thought, must surely lead to a blind and toothless world.

"Either of you boys have a chaw?"

The speaker, a hawk-nosed youth with clear blue eyes and sandy hair, reined up beside Hunter and grinned. He sat his long-legged sorrel with an ease that spoke of a life spent in the saddle.

"Sorry, Frank," Hunter said, "I don't chaw. Afraid it might stunt my growth."

The grin widened. "Your growth could *use* some stuntin'," said Frank James. "How tall are you anyway, Will—seven foot?"

"Six-three in my stockin's," Hunter said, "but I wear thick stockin's."

Santee reached across the neck of Hunter's gelding and handed his tobacco plug to Frank James. "Both you boys are taller than *me*," he said, "but I figure it ain't the size of the dog in the fight, it's the size of the fight in the dog." Santee's yellow eyes turned sly; his grin became a leer. "Anyway, I'm plenty big where it counts—or so the ladies tell me."

Hunter's stare was cold, expressionless. He disliked both Bravo Santee and his brother Rufus. He considered the men skulkers and cowards. Most of all, he despised their vulgar talk about women. Frank James, too, ignored the crude jest.

James bit off a corner of the plug and handed it back. Tonguing the quid to his cheek, he said, "Reckon that's true about the dog. And it ain't how *old* the dog is, either. My brother Jesse ain't but sixteen, but he's a fightin' fool. I allow that boy would take on a buzz-saw and give it three turns head-start."

"Obliged for the chaw, Santee," Frank said, spurring his horse forward, "see you boys at the pig-stickin'."

Just a few miles away, Lawrence, Kansas, slept peacefully under scattered stars in the early hours of August 21, 1863. A sometime base for Union attacks on the settlements along the Missouri border, the town housed no federal troops that fateful morning. The civilian population began the day with no hint of the horror to come.

The eastern sky grew brighter. Stars dimmed and disappeared. Somewhere across town a dog barked. An owl glided on muffled wings back to its nest in a barn loft. On the outskirts of Lawrence a rooster crowed. Below the settlement, the Kaw River rolled along its rocky bed. Born of the warm morning, a soft breeze sighed over the rolling hills, rustling the leaves of ripening corn. In a small corral above the river, a horse lifted its head, tasted the air, and nickered.

Just west of Lawrence, "Colonel" Quantrill halted the column and called the leaders of his Missourians to a final briefing. When his men had gathered around him, the young guerrilla chief began with a speech that was part rallying cry, part self-justification. "Lawrence, Kansas lies just below us," he said, "and we have come here this day to take vengeance on the town and its people.

"As you know, some of your mothers, wives, and sisters were killed in Kansas City last week when the building in which they were imprisoned collapsed. Five heroic daughters of Missouri died that day, gentlemen. The cowardly Yankees took them from their homes and confined them in a structure not fit for habitation by hogs! And why?

What was their crime? The dear ladies were accused of sheltering and feeding their menfolk!

"We are here to avenge those dear ladies, gentlemen. Our mission today is a simple one: we will kill every male and burn every house in Lawrence."

Will Hunter and some of the other raiders had dismounted, checking their saddle girths and the loads in their pistols. Quantrill sat his horse proudly, his hands crossed before him on the pommel of his saddle. He was a smallish man with pleasant features, clean-shaven except for a small moustache and goatee. Beneath his wide-brimmed officer's hat, curly brown hair caught the early sunlight. There was, Hunter thought, nothing in the man's appearance to indicate the ruthless and feared warrior that he was. Yet there was an arrogance in his manner, an implacable confidence that drew men to him, made them accept him as leader.

For a long moment the marauders were silent. Hunter saw Cole Younger standing with his brother Jim, feet apart, thumbs hooked into his gun belt. Next to them, Frank James looked thoughtful as he leaned against the flank of his sorrel, the tobacco quid prominent in his cheek. Bravo Santee and his younger brother Rufus stood close together at their horses' heads.

Will Hunter frowned. His head felt light, and there was an insistent ringing in his ears. Somewhere inside his chest he felt as if something old, hard, and rotten was breaking away. When at last he spoke, his voice's calm tone surprised him.

"*Every* male, colonel?" he asked, "even the young'uns?"

"Every male who can hold a gun," Quantrill said. "Nits make lice."

The guerrillas swept into town like wolves upon a sheepfold, shouting the rebel yell, their pistols blazing. A United Brethren minister was among the first to die, shot through the head as he sat milking his cow. The clergyman jerked suddenly upright as the bullet struck, then toppled sideways into the mud of his barn lot. He lay sprawled, eyes wide and unseeing, as the raiders thundered past.

Racing into the settlement at a gallop, Quantrill's guerrillas drew rein and divided into individual groups, whooping and shooting, one band to each street. Quantrill himself dashed ahead of his men down Massachusetts Street, shouting his hatred for the town and its people.

"Kill! Kill!" he roared. "We must cleanse Lawrence—and the only way to cleanse it is to kill!"

He reined up, dismounted, and strode into the City Hotel, demanding that the terrified staff cook him a large breakfast. Another hotel, the Eldridge, was already burning. The guerrillas were shooting the men who rushed outside to escape the flames.

The Missourians dashed to the home of their hated enemy, General Jim Lane, but found only his wife and daughter in the house. They would later learn the despised leader of the Kansas Redlegs had narrowly escaped capture by fleeing in his nightshirt through a cornfield. The guerrillas looted his home and set it ablaze.

At the center of town a detachment of unarmed recruits dashed out of their tents and raced toward the river with the Missourians on their heels. Most fell before the revolvers of the raiders as they fled. A few managed to reach the river and plunge into the water. None reached the opposite bank.

All over town the slaughter continued. Men and boys ran for their lives, some leaping from windows or crawling beneath boardwalks and shrubbery only to fall to the merciless gunfire of the raiders. Others, unarmed and trapped, tried to buy off their attackers. The guerillas took their money and killed them anyway. Wives attempted to hide their husbands and mothers their sons, literally standing between the killers and their loved ones, but to no avail. The women saw their men and boys dragged away and butchered before their eyes. Corpses littered the streets. Always and everywhere, the homes and buildings of Lawrence were put to the torch.

Will Hunter rode aimlessly through the burning town, disgust and self-loathing growing inside him. For nearly two years he had been a member of Quantrill's raiders. He had taken part in battles with Union regulars and Kansas Jayhawkers, and he had ridden on raids in which civilians had died.

He'd seen ambushes, looting, and torture on both sides of the border; but on this bloody Friday, Will Hunter found himself viewing war and its horrors from the viewpoint of its victims. Something within him had changed. He took no part in the killing and looting, but rode aimlessly through the streets of the town. At length, he reined his black gelding to a stop, dismounted, and sat down beneath a maple tree's leafy canopy.

The swelling cacophony of sound struck his ears as he sat there—a clamor of gunfire, shouts and screams, and the crackling sound of flames devouring dry wood. Embers drifted down onto the grass where he sat. Smoke stung his eyes and burned his lungs. He watched, bemused, as a live coal burned a hole in the sleeve of the short woolen jacket he wore. Lifting his gloved hand to the sleeve, he rubbed the ember out. Hunter felt a great weariness and sadness that seemed suddenly too much to bear.

A strange lassitude had come upon him. He lay back beneath the tree, hands behind his head, and wondered if he was going insane. Maybe, he thought, it's worse than that—maybe I'm going *sane*. They put insane people in an asylum, he mused, at least they do in peacetime.

In time of war, he thought, they make them leaders of men—like General Jim Lane and William Clarke Quantrill, or Bloody Bill Anderson, who wore a necklace of human scalps and whose murderous band tied those same grisly trophies to the headstalls and bridle reins of its horses. Anderson, who had led his men in with the rest of Quantrill's killers this day, was somewhere on the streets of Lawrence, living up to his name and his reputation.

Hunter lay back and listened. He identified the sounds of revolver, carbine, and shotgun fire. He heard the choppy clatter of horses' hooves and the wild shouts of the raiders. He listened to the thunder of the flames as fire roared through the town. He covered his ears with his hands, but still he heard the cries of terror and the keening of the women.

To his surprise, Hunter found himself weeping. Astonished, he sat up and touched his fingers to his wet cheeks. His vision blurred by tears, he closed his eyes. "Tears, by heaven," he said aloud, "I don't believe I've shed a tear since—"

Abruptly, Hunter sat up, then got to his feet. His thoughts had caught him unprepared. For just a moment he'd dropped his guard, and the tormentor had broken through. By force of will he tried to divert his mind from the words that would finish the sentence, but it was too late. The words came, and with them the beloved, forbidden name. "—since the day I buried *Rachel*."

Aimless and unseeing, Will Hunter crossed the street. At its edge, the lifeless body of an elderly black man lay on its back, pink mouth agape. Hunter nearly stumbled over the corpse, avoiding it only at the last moment. Still lost in his thoughts, he stared at the dead man, confused.

And then, close by, he heard the scream—a high-pitched, wordless shriek. Muffled and cut short, it faded to a terrified whimper. Hunter looked up.

A small, one-story frame house stood not fifty yards away, curtains billowing out an open window. The shattered front door hung at a slant, secured only by a lower hinge. Rufus Santee's blue roan grazed on the sparse grass in front of the house. The scream came again, followed by a man's angry voice. Through the open window, Hunter caught a glimpse of a terrified girl struggling in the arms of a bearded raider.

Hunter walked past the roan and entered the house through its splintered door. He crossed the modest parlor, stepping carefully around the overturned furniture and broken glass, and pushed open the bedroom door. Rufus Santee knelt atop the bed, his squat, powerful body pinning a partially clad girl beneath him. His right hand gripped her long, blonde hair as his left hand fumbled with the buttons of his trousers.

"No, by heaven, you will *not*," Hunter said.

Santee's head jerked sharply toward the sound. "Hunter!" he said. "What the—?"

Will Hunter's blue eyes were as cold as polar ice. "You know Quantrill's orders. We don't make war on women. Let her up, Santee."

The girl twisted in Santee's grasp, her frightened eyes focused on Hunter. "Not likely," Santee said, "we're killin' men, boys, and niggers out there, and we're burnin' this whole damn abolitionist town. I aim to take my pleasure where I find it."

"I expect even the Devil draws the line somewhere," Hunter said, his revolver trained on Santee, "and I'll not let you abuse that child. Get up off her *now!*"

Santee's eyes narrowed. His knees still pinned his captive to the bed, but the fingers of his right hand slowly released their grip on her hair.

"You're crazy, Hunter," he muttered, "you've got no call to go up against me on this."

Santee lurched abruptly back away from the bed, his long-barreled Colt suddenly in his hand and aimed at Hunter. His move was fast, incredibly fast, but Hunter's gun spoke first, orange flame stabbing through a cloud of acrid smoke, the sound of the shot loud in the small room. Santee's body froze in mid-motion as if it had collided with an invisible wall. A small black hole marked his forehead as blood spattered out behind him in a ruby fan across the flowered wall-covering. Like a puppet with its strings cut, Santee's limbs suddenly went slack. His body jerked sharply forward as the invisible wall gave way, and he toppled to the bedroom floor.

Crab-like, the girl scrambled across the rumpled bed, whimpering like an injured animal as she tried to flee the violence and the horror. She huddled shivering against the opposite wall, eyes wide and staring. With her legs drawn up, she clutched a patchwork quilt protectively before her.

Will Hunter holstered his revolver and stepped back through the doorway. He removed his hat. "I beg your pardon, miss," he said, "I surely do. Please don't cry—it's all over now." Then he turned and walked outside.

On the streets, the carnage continued. Bodies lay sprawled in the street like cast-off dolls. Smoke from the burning town stung Hunter's eyes and caught in his lungs. Riders spurred their horses along the streets and alleys of the town, shooting as they rode. Looters, many already drunk, emerged from doorways laden with the personal effects of their victims.

Watching the butchery, Hunter stood for a moment outside the small house. Then he strode past Santee's grazing roan and across the street to where his own horse stood. Grasping the reins and a handful of the gelding's mane, he swung up into the saddle.

As Hunter turned his horse away from the little house, Jim Younger came riding around the corner on his lathered bay. Recognizing Hunter, Younger reined the animal to a sliding stop. He held a whiskey bottle in his right hand, and he swayed unsteadily in the saddle as the horse danced a nervous quickstep amid the smoke and flying embers.

"Hey, Will!" he shouted, "You ain't seen Rufus Santee anywheres, have you? His brother Bravo is lookin' for him."

Hunter's face was impassive. "Why, yes, Jim," he said, "he's in *hell*, I believe."

Having spoken, Hunter touched the gelding with his spurs and rode north, away from the stricken town. He didn't look back.

———◈———

"Show me, Jim," said Bravo Santee, "show me where you seen my brother's horse." From beneath Bravo's battered hat, sweat crawled down across his wide cheekbones, cutting tracks through the dirt and smoke that stained his face.

Outside a small brick house near the center of Lawrence, with his arms laden with plunder, Santee struggled to fit a pair of silver candlesticks into an already bulging saddlebag. Beyond a white picket fence the bodies of a silver-haired man and a ten-year-old boy lay together, their blood mingled in a common pool. Smoke and flame belched out through the house's windows. From somewhere nearby came the wail of a woman.

Bravo Santee was excited. Killing always lifted his spirits and made him feel powerful, godlike. This day in Lawrence he'd slain his share. Bravo had killed men out of a sense of duty, in obedience to orders; but he had also killed for pleasure. Like his brother Rufus, Bravo was a small man, barely five feet four; but with a gun or blade in his hand he considered himself the equal of any man, and better than most.

Jim Younger sat his sweated bay, watching Santee with amusement.

"Shee-it, Santee—you ain't ever gonna get all that truck in them saddle pockets. Put that loot in a towsack and tie it onto that ugly roan you ride."

Santee's yellow eyes flashed. "Damn you, Jim Younger, I never ast you how to tote my plunder! You goin' to show me where you seen my brother's horse or not?"

Younger shrugged. "I reckon," he said, "soon's you get through fee-diddlin' around."

Bravo Santee and Jim Younger found Rufus Santee's body where it had fallen, sprawled amid the broken glass and litter of the sleeping room. Twisted sheets lay atop the bed. Blood spattered the patterned wall-covering above the corpse. At the open window, a vagrant breeze stirred the lace curtains and sighed as it moved up the street. Bravo squatted on his bootheels, touching his brother's face. His own face was grim, his expression hard as flint. His pale, yellow eyes glittered behind their slitted lids. When he spoke, his voice was tight as a banjo string. "How d'you reckon this happened, Jim?"

Jim Younger shrugged. "You can read sign good as me," he said. "Rufus is in a lady's bedroom with his britches undone. I'd say he was fixin' to have his way with a Kansas female when somebody—maybe her—settled his hash."

"Twarn't her," Bravo said. "See? Brother Rufe had drawed his pistol—it's still in his hand. I'd say he got hisself interrupted."

"Interrupted by a damn fine revolver shot. The ball took him dead center in his forehead and left him cold as a wagon tire."

Santee's gaze was steady, intense. "Who do you reckon done it, Jim?"

"Hell, I don't know."

Bravo stood. Bright blood stained the fingers of his right hand. Carefully, he wiped the blood on his pant leg and lifted his cold eyes back to Younger's face. "Don't know, or don't want to say? You told me you seen Will Hunter walk away from this house."

Younger frowned. He'd never liked either of the Santee brothers much, and he was getting tired of Bravo's questions. "Didn't see him come out of the house; but, yes, he came from this direction."

"Did you ast him if'n he'd saw Rufus?"

"Yes, but I didn't hear his answer. He just stepped up on that long-legged gelding he rides and pulled foot."

"Sum'bitch kilt my brother."

"Maybe. And maybe Rufus had it comin'," Jim said.

Bravo walked to the window, his face impassive. "Don't make no never mind whether he did or no. Rufus was my blood kin. Will Hunter kilt him, and I'm bound to kill Hunter. Simple as that."

Jim Younger strode to the bedroom doorway, stopped, and turned back toward Bravo Santee. Distaste was plain on his face. "Do whatever you need to," he said. "Ain't no skin off *my* arse."

Atop a wooded ridge in Cass County, Missouri, Will Hunter drew rein and allowed his lathered horse to catch its breath. Dismounting, he squinted against the late afternoon sun, looking back toward Kansas as he recalled the morning's horror.

It was peaceful there on the ridge. Only the horse's heavy breathing and the distant scolding of a crow disturbed the stillness. Below, Hunter watched the Grand River reflect bright splinters of light as it snaked out across the valley floor. He closed his eyes, remembering.

Oh, yes, he thought, we sure as hell got our revenge today. We took out our hatred on a defenseless town, on old men, women, and children. We surely showed those Jayhawkers the way *civilized* warriors make war.

Weariness crept through him. Sadness lay heavy on his heart. He felt sluggish, dull.

Within his mind Hunter heard a small, calm voice. *You killed one of your own,"* it said. *You killed Rufus Santee.*

Hunter recognized the voice. It was a voice that came at odd times and without warning to invade his mind. It was a voice that came to accuse.

"One of Quantrill's own, not mine," he said aloud. "Santee was trying to rape a woman! He pulled his gun on me. I *had* to kill him."

Your gun was already drawn. You'd have killed him anyway, said the voice. *You killed Santee because of the woman, all right, because she reminded you of another woman. Santee died for your sins. You killed that poor fool because of your guilt.*

"I wish I could kill *you*," Hunter told the voice.

TWO

To Begin Again

LAMPLIGHT GLOWED orange in the window of the Martins' two-story farmhouse as Will Hunter rode out of the woods and onto the meadow beyond. The moonless night was dark as a mine shaft, and Hunter guided the lathered gelding across the pasture toward the house more from memory than by sight.

Across the way, beyond the barn and outbuildings, a cluster of cabins that had once been slaves' quarters stood, but lamplight gleamed only in a single ground floor window of the big house. Somewhere ahead, a dog barked, the sound sharp and ringing in the stillness. Hunter turned the gelding toward the front of the house and drew rein at the long porch.

"Stop where you is," boomed a deep voice. "We ain't gwine stand fo' no more she-coonery 'round here!"

Hunter raised his hands. A huge black man stepped out of the shadows, a large-bore shotgun held at the ready. "Speak up, you," the man rumbled. "What y'all be doin' here this time o' night?"

"Easy with that goose gun, Joshua," Hunter said. "It's me, Will Hunter."

The giant's eyes widened, straining to see in the dimness. He took a step forward, shotgun still trained on Hunter. Sudden recognition flashed across his face. His broad smile displayed an expanse of strong, white teeth. "Lawdy, mistuh Will, it *is* you!" he said. "Ah 'most took you fo' a Jayhawker!"

Hunter nodded toward the farmhouse. "Is mister Ollie at home? I need to talk with him."

Joshua's smile lit the darkness. "Yes, suh, he surely is! He's gwine be plum tickled to see y'all!"

"Mistuh Ollie? They's someone to see you, suh."

Seated at a roll-top desk in the keeping room of the farmhouse, Ollie Martin was working on his accounts by lamplight when Joshua led Will Hunter in. "Will!" he said, rising from his chair and crossing the room. "The prodigal has returned!" Shorter than Will by a head, Ollie Martin smiled up into the younger man's face as he gripped his hand. "It's been too long, son," he said, gesturing toward a large medallion-back sofa beside the desk. "Come in and set a spell."

Joshua loomed in the sitting room's doorway, grinning broadly. Ollie turned to him as Hunter took a seat on the sofa. "Fetch the good bourbon, Joshua," he said, "Will and I have catching up to do."

Minutes later, Joshua returned with a bottle and two glasses on a silver tray. He set them carefully on a side table and left the room. Ollie Martin filled each glass half-full and handed one to Will. "You look tired, Will," said Ollie, "tired, and thinner than you were."

Hunter raised his glass in salute and sipped the bourbon. "I am tired," he said, "tired of the killing, and tired of the hate. I've quit Quantrill."

"I expect you had your reasons."

"All I know is I can't butcher civilians and burn their homes any longer. There has to be more to living than dealing death."

"Last month some fifty thousand men, Yanks and Rebs together, were killed in just three days' fighting at Gettysburg. God knows how many died in the war today. Yesterday in Kansas, Quantrill's hellions butchered and burned a whole town. It wasn't a military action, it was a pack of mad dogs turned loose in a henhouse.

"I'm quitting Missouri, too. Don't know where I'm going yet, but it'll be somewhere clean and free, a place to start over. The far west, maybe."

Ollie Martin nodded. "There's a lot of people these days who feel that way. As for me, I don't believe I could ever leave this valley. My roots are here—mine, and Lucy's."

"Not mine. Not any more."

Ollie nodded. "No," he said slowly, "Not any more."

Ollie Martin was silent for a time. Then he said, "You need to let go of the past, Will. A man has to forgive himself."

"Can't do it, Ollie. I promised Rachel I'd protect her. I told her I'd keep her from harm, but I didn't. I left her alone to go drinking with my friends, even though she asked me to stay at home with her. Now she's dead because of me and nothing can change that."

"Rachel is dead because a pack of Kansas Redlegs raided your farm!" Ollie said angrily. "You weren't even *there* when it happened!"

"I *should* have been."

The two men fell silent once again. The ticking of the mantel clock was loud in the stillness. Ollie Martin downed his bourbon, refilled his own and Hunter's glass. When he spoke again, his voice was calm, controlled.

"Have you heard about the gold strikes up in the northern Rockies?" he asked. "Newspaper said prospectors took more than $700,000 in gold out of the Grasshopper diggings before the snow fell last winter. There's even talk of a new road from the Oregon Trail to the gold fields, supposed to cut 400 miles off the distance."

"Heard something about it," Hunter said. "They say it's the biggest stampede since the California rush. Storekeeper in Harrisonville said entire companies of soldiers, Yank and Confederate, have just skedaddled and lit a shuck for Idaho Territory."

Ollie looked thoughtful. "I hear it's big country out there. A place of mountains and distances, with a sky that goes on forever. A man might do worse, Will."

"Yes," Hunter said, "I expect a man could always do worse."

The older man closed his roll-top desk and stood up. "Right now, you need a hot meal and a good night's sleep," he said. "Lucy's gone to bed, but I'll have Joshua fix you a plate and find you a bunk. We'll talk more come morning."

Exhaustion fell on Hunter like a weight. He had planned only to stop briefly at the Martins' and move on, but the whiskey and friendship had warmed him, melted his will. He *was* hungry, he realized, and bone-tired. "I don't want to be any trouble," he said thickly.

Ollie smiled. "That's a helluva thing for you to say to *me*, Will," he said.

Will Hunter woke with a start from deep sleep, his hand grasping the Colt's Navy revolver beneath his pillow. He held his breath, listening. What was the sound that had awakened him? It came again, more clearly this time, a soft, rhythmic rapping. Tap-tap-tap. Then he heard Ollie Martin's low voice beyond the door. "Five o'clock, Will. There's coffee in the kitchen."

Hunter breathed again, remembering the raid on Lawrence and the killing of Rufus Santee. He recalled the long ride back to Missouri, reaching the haven of the Martins' farm, and spending the night under their roof. His mouth was dry, his voice sleep-thickened. "Thanks, Ollie. Be right there."

The kitchen lamp burned low, crowding the room with shadows. Ollie was adding wood to the cookstove as Hunter came in.

"You look better, son," said Ollie, smiling. "You should try sleeping more often—I think it agrees with you."

He poured a cup of coffee from the pot and handed it to Hunter. Hunter returned the smile. "Well, I feel better," he said, "but I reckon I still *look* like a border ruffian—all teeth, whiskers, and eyeballs."

"Figured you'd want to make an early start. I had Joshua grain and groom your horse. Lucy will be down to cook you breakfast."

"No. Please tell her not to bother. I need to be on my way."

"All right. What else do you need, Will?"

"I left some clothes—shirts, an overcoat—my dad's fiddle, and the cashbox."

Ollie grinned. "So you're finally taking what I paid you. I buy your farm, and you ask me to keep the money for you. For two years now, I've had custody of both your land and your cash."

"Guess I just trusted you more than the bank."

"Anything else?"

Hunter studied the interior of his cup as if he was trying to read the future there. "No. I was just thinking. I don't expect I'll be seeing you and Lucy again."

"You never know, Will. Maybe you'll strike it rich out west. You may come back after the war and buy another farm."

"Maybe. As you say, a man never knows."

Solid as a tree, Joshua stood at the foot of the porch, his big hands holding the reins of Hunter's saddled gelding. Even in the gray light that preceded dawn the horse looked well-groomed and trail ready. Hunter carried a scuffed fiddle case, an Army greatcoat, and a carpetbag. He tied them to the saddle and took the reins from the big man.

Turning, Hunter gripped Ollie Martin's hand and held it. Neither man spoke. Swinging into the saddle, Hunter reined the gelding about and rode away up the lane. Ollie watched him go until he vanished into the grayness, then turned and walked slowly back inside the house.

Morning fog lay tangled in the lowlands like cotton caught in brambles as Will Hunter turned the gelding off the Harrisonville road and into a sun-dappled clearing. Inside the clearing, a small country church dozed in the sunlight, its windows shuttered, its siding stained by rain and snow.

Hunter drew rein and dismounted. There are crossroads on the earth, he thought, places where the happenings of a man's life occur time and again. For me, this church is such a place.

He had listened to his father preach from its pulpit; he had been baptized into its fellowship. He had stood before its altar as bridegoom and had pledged Rachel his fidelity and love. He had looked into her eyes and had made his vows before God and man. Not content with that, he'd made other promises, proud, foolish promises. He had failed to keep them. Rachel had died and was gone. He had died, too, he thought bitterly, but had remained.

Behind the church, amid dogwood, crab apple, and redbud trees, headstones marked the burial ground. Hat in hand, Hunter walked carefully among the weathered markers until he came to the one he sought. It was a simple white stone with an equally simple inscription:

RACHEL SUE HUNTER

BELOVED WIFE

1843 - 1861

Hunter knelt before the stone and pressed his forehead against the cold marble. Eyes closed, he said softly, "I know you're not here, Rachel, but I'm going away. I'm leaving our valley. This seems like the place to tell you."

No, he thought, she is not here. If there is a heaven, and if anyone is in that place, Rachel is there. She'll never grow old, and she'll never again know hunger or cold or pain.

Without warning, the still, cold voice spoke inside his mind. *She died in pain, though, didn't she? She died in horror and pain and ugliness with no one to defend her, and your unborn baby died with her.*

The tears came then, and the longing. "I love you, Rachel," he choked, "I always will. May God forgive me."

Twenty minutes later, Will Hunter set foot in the stirrup and rode away from the church for the last time.

Of all the days in the week, Big Joshua loved Sunday best. Sundays on the Martin farm were mostly quiet times, times of peace and rest. The Lord, Joshua thought, made Sundays so a man could get himself centered and ready for the week. The big man stood in the doorway of the cabin he shared with his wife Sudie and their seven-year-old son Jethro, and looked out. "Lordamighty, Sudie," he said, "but ah surely do love a Sunday."

Behind him, inside the cabin, his boy Jethro sprawled on a bench, teasing a kitten with a piece of yarn. Joshua's wife Sudie sat at their kitchen table, snapping beans into a large bowl. She was a tall woman, the light gold of her skin in stark contrast to her husband's ebony sheen.

Smiling, she looked at his broad back and raised an eyebrow. "Uh-huh," she said, "reason you love Sunday so much is it's your day off. On Sundays you can just be your natural, shiftless self."

Joshua looked out across Ollie Martin's hayfields to the deep shade of the wooded hills beyond. The day was sultry and still, as if all nature had fallen asleep.

The big man turned, bowed his head, and came back inside the cabin. His broad smile answered hers. "Hush now, woman," he said, "I've been up and doin' since before daylight—got all mah chores done and most of yours."

Her smile widened. Sudie was funning him, feeling frisky. Seeing his wife in good spirits made Joshua happy. "You best not be lyin' now," she said. "Tonight's church service and they don't let no tale-tellin' sinners in, no, suh."

Joshua chuckled, the sound a rumble deep within his chest. "If'n they don't let sinners in," he said, "that church is gon' be mighty empty."

Taking a corn-cob pipe from the pocket of his overalls, Joshua struck a match on the stove top and lit up. "Thinkin' ah might go up to Sawyer's Pond this mornin'," he said, "See if ah kin maybe ketch me a catfish."

Across the room, Jethro dropped the piece of yarn. The kitten happily pounced on the prize, rolling with it and scratching furiously with its hind feet. Joshua smiled, glancing sideways at his son. Looking at Sudie, he winked. "Anyways, ah might if ah kin find someone to go with me."

Jethro dashed across the room and looked up into his father's face. "Me, papa!" he said. "Take *me!*"

Joshua held the boy close, smiling broadly at Sudie. "You?" he said. "Why, that's a *fine* idea! Now why didn't *ah* think of that?"

Across the table, Sudie beamed.

Sawyer's Pond lay still and cool in a broad hollow some two miles above the Martin farm. Fed by deep springs and meandering Sawyer's Creek, it was one of Big Joshua's favorite places. On that hot August afternoon he walked along the shade-dappled trail that led to the pond with little Jethro close at his heels. Joshua's blue-tick hound Cajun ran beside and before them, nose to the ground and covering five times the distance they traveled.

The trail grew steeper, climbing uphill through the woods. Tail wagging, long ears flopping, Cajun continued her ramble through the undergrowth. The afternoon grew hotter. The woods seemed to doze in a heavy stillness. Leaves on the trees hung motionless as if on trees in a painting.

At the crest of the hill the trail topped out onto a rocky knob, then descended in a long curve to the banks of Sawyer's Pond. Joshua stopped to allow Jethro to catch up. He held out his hand, smiling as the boy took it.

Then, sudden and loud in the stillness, he heard Cajun's deep baying bark from the trail ahead. Joshua frowned. The hound's clamor grew swiftly more excited, her barking more frantic.

"What has that fool dog got herself into?" Joshua asked. "Likely she's met up wif a porky-pine or somethin'." Holding Jethro's hand, he started downhill, calling the dog. "Cajun! Come here, now! Leave that varmint be, fool!"

Moments later, Joshua and Jethro broke out of the trees to find the hound standing tensely in the center of the trail. The hair on her neck and shoulders were stiffly erect. Head held low, the dog snarled, yellow teeth showing, and began her excited barking again. Joshua squinted, staring beyond the dog, looking for the source of its excitement. It was then he saw the stranger.

The man was small and wiry, and he slouched in the saddle astride a sweated roan horse in a clearing beside the pond. He wore a dirty shirt of gray homespun, high-topped boots over stained woolen breeches, and a narrow-brimmed black hat pulled low over deepset eyes. His shoulder-length hair was lank and greasy, and a short, bristling beard covered the lower part of his face. A quid of tobacco bulged his cheek. He shifted the quid, smiling at Joshua's approach.

"Afternoon there, Uncle," he said. "Mind callin' your dog off? I do believe that bitch is fixin' to eat me."

Joshua strode swiftly to Cajun and grasped her collar. "Yessuh," he said. "Don't know what's got into that fool dawg. Sorry, suh."

Joshua felt the tenseness in the hound's body. The animal strained, quivering beneath his hand. She had stopped barking, but a low growl rumbled deep in her throat. His head still bowed toward Cajun, Joshua studied the horseman from a corner of his eye.

The stranger continued to smile, lounging in the saddle, but there was no warmth in the smile. The man's pose, seemingly relaxed, was tense and guarded. He wore a pair of Colt's Dragoon revolvers and a sheathed Bowie knife in a belt at his waist. A short-barreled shotgun hung from the pommel of his saddle. Joshua searched his memory. He knew most of the men in the valley, but he had never seen the stranger.

Joshua reached down, touching his son's head. The boy clung to his leg now, eyes wide and staring. In spite of the heat, a chill swept through Joshua. His inner voice told him this rider with the cold smile was not on the trail by chance, but design. The stranger had searched him out.

His eyes fixed intently upon Joshua, the horseman raised a hand to his face. Thoughtfully, he stroked his beard stubble. "Don't I know you, boy?" he asked. "Ain't you Big Joshua, Ollie Martin's nigger?"

"Ah works for mistuh Ollie," Joshua said slowly, "but I's a free man."

"Of course you are," the stranger said. "All you coon-ass bastards seem to reckon you're free these days."

21

Hands on the pommel of the saddle, the horseman raised himself in his stirrups and spat onto the roadway. "My name's Bravo Santee, Uncle. I'm lookin' for an old comrade o' mine. He's a friend of Ollie Martin. Might be you've saw him lately—Will Hunter?"

Beneath the black hat, the stranger's pale eyes seemed to glow as he asked the question. "Uh—No, suh," Joshua said. "Don't believe ah knows any Will Huntuh."

"No? Why, that is peculiar. You see, Hunter and me ride with Colonel Quantrill's Raiders. Leastways, we did 'til Friday last. That's the day the sum'bitch kilt my brother."

Santee frowned. For a long moment he was silent. He shifted the quid in his cheek and spat again. "Hunter told me about you one time, Uncle. Said you was about the strongest nigra in all of Cass County. Looks like you surely could be, big as you are."

As if by magic, a revolver appeared in the stranger's hand. Joshua heard the sharp double click as the man thumbed the hammer back. "Thing is, Uncle," the man drawled, "no matter how strong you might be, powder and ball be stronger still. *Where is Will Hunter?*"

Joshua straightened, releasing his hold on Cajun's collar. Protectively, he drew Jethro close beside and behind him. "Ah done told you, mistuh—ah don't *know* any Will Huntuh!"

Suddenly, Cajun lunged at the horse and rider. Smoothly, Santee reined the roan to the left, raising the revolver as he did so. The roar of the gunshot and the dog's sharp yelp came almost simultaneously. Cajun's head exploded in a red eruption of blood and bone, her body flung twitching into the high grass beside the trail.

Quickly, Santee re-cocked the smoking weapon and trained it on Joshua. His voice was thin and harsh, like a file on metal. "I've no time for lies, Uncle!" he rasped. "That bug-eyed little pickaninny dies next! *Where's Hunter?*"

Joshua could feel his son's terror. The child was shaking with fear, crying now in shock and confusion. "Ah swears t' God, mistuh— ah don't know! Mistuh Will *was* at Mistuh Ollie's Friday evenin' late—but come Saturday mornin' he done moved on! Ah don't know where to!"

Santee's voice was cold, unfeeling. "Make a guess, Uncle. If I'd kill a good blue-tick hound, I sure as hell won't spare that little cuffee o' yourn."

Joshua swept the crying child up in his arms and held the boy close. "Please, mistuh—don't shoot mah boy! Ah *did* hear 'em talkin' Friday night. Ah was in the next room, but yessuh, ah heard 'em all right.

"Mistuh Will say he done quit Quantrill—say he's goin' someplace else, make a new start—he say maybe the far west. Mistuh Ollie asked him has he heard about the gold strikes in the Rocky Mountains—some place called Grasshopper diggin's—an' Mistuh Will say yes, he's heard somethin' about 'em. Mistuh Ollie says that's a big country out yonder. He says, 'A man could do worse, Will.' Ah swears to God, mistuh—that's all in the world ah knows!"

For a time there was silence in the clearing. Bravo Santee sat astride his horse, revolver in hand, his cold eyes fixed on Joshua and the boy. Head bowed, Joshua held the child close, waiting for the gunshot that would end his life, or his son's.

At last, Santee spoke. "I believe you, Uncle. Git on home now, and keep your mouth shut. If I hear you been talkin' about this, I'll come back an' wipe out your whole damn family. You *hear* me, Uncle?"

Joshua felt relief flood through him, and something else—shame. A sadness, bitter and familiar, drained his hope. Impotent fury rose in his throat, nearly choking him. "Yes, suh—thank you, suh," he said.

When Santee had ridden away into the woods, Joshua knelt in the trail, holding his son close, soothing the boy until his fear subsided. Then the big man straightened, walked to the tall grass beside the trail, and bent low over Cajun's lifeless body. Lifting the dog in his arms, he turned back toward home.

"Come along, boy," he said. "Don't you be cryin' now, Jethro. Ever'thin' be all right now." But it wasn't. As Big Joshua led his son along the trail toward home, he wondered how long it might be before he'd love Sunday again.

THREE
On the Trail

E PIPHANY BAKER was awake and dressed long before daybreak. She clutched her heavy woolen shawl tightly about her shoulders and surveyed the familiar scene of circled wagons beside the rutted trail, their sun-bleached canvas tops ghostly in the gray light. Epiphany stood in the lee of the Playfairs' third wagon—the one in which she slept—and listened to the groaning sounds the sheet-iron cookstove made as it warmed.

A gust of wind swept through the camp, chasing the woodsmoke and rippling the tall grass beyond the wagon circle. Epiphany inhaled. There was a chill to the morning that surprised her—the season was summer, late August. Then she remembered. The wagon train had completed the long climb over 8,000-foot South Pass only the day before. The travelers had celebrated and rejoiced. After more than three months on the trail, the wagons had at last crossed the backbone of the continent.

Epiphany turned her attention back to the stove. The coffee pot had reached a rolling boil. Protecting her hands with a towel, Epiphany removed the pot, poured in a cup of cold water to settle the grounds, and turned to watch the sunrise.

Just two inches under six feet tall, Epiphany Baker was slender and slim-waisted. She moved with a long-limbed, coltish grace. Her large brown eyes looked out upon the world with a curious boldness, as if eager to experience whatever it might hold. Pretty rather than beautiful, a thin scatter of freckles traversed the bridge of her small nose. The breeze that accompanied the dawn tossed her fine, flaxen hair. When the sun exploded above the distant mountains she greeted it with a smile bright as the dawn.

"Always a remarkable sight, isn't it?"

Epiphany turned to see Ramsay Playfair, her employer, standing beside the stove. His right hand shaded his eyes. He, too, was admiring the sunrise.

"Yes, always," she said. "Good morning, Mr. Playfair."

Ramsay Playfair took an enamelware cup from the camp box and filled it with coffee. "Won't be long now, Piff," he said. "We should be in Bannack within the week. The week after that I expect to have the store open."

Epiphany smiled politely. "I'm looking forward to seeing Bannack City," she said.

Ramsay Playfair laughed. "You may be disappointed," he said. "I'm afraid 'Bannack City' is only a crude, dirty little camp. Prospectors struck gold there last summer and promptly laid out the town. By winter 500 people had settled in the area. I'm told there are nearly 5,000 there now."

"Well, that's 5,000 potential customers," Epiphany said.

"Indeed. That's the way to think, Piff."

Ramsay Playfair wrapped his hands around his steaming cup, warming them. He was a portly man of medium height with a pleasant face and clever gray eyes. A born merchant, he and his brother Anson had built a small dry goods store into a hugely successful, three-story mercantile in downtown Springfield, Illinois. The brothers' business had profited greatly since the War began, in no small part because both Ramsay and Anson had managed to avoid Army service by hiring substitutes.

Canny businessmen that they were, the Playfair brothers knew how to recognize an opportunity when they saw one. They knew that those who sold to the miners often made the real profit from a gold strike.

While Anson held down the business in Springfield, Ramsay hired drivers and loaded wagons with merchandise. Accompanied by his wife Alice and their hired girl Epiphany, he had joined a wagon train bound for the diggings.

Ramsay finished his coffee and set the cup down atop the camp box. He held his hands palms down above the stovetop, warming himself. "We won't be moving out until noon today," he told Epiphany. "The oxen and mules need rest. That should give you time to bake some bread and get a little washing done."

"Speaking of livestock, I'd best go tend mine," he said. "Breakfast in a half-hour, Piff?"

"Yes, sir. A half-hour."

Epiphany prided herself on her baking powder biscuits. Working swiftly now, she put flour, baking powder, and salt together in a large pan, added warm water from the kettle, and turned the mixture out onto a floured canvas square atop her work table. Kneading the dough, she patted it until satisfied with its consistency, then pinched it into fist-size balls. Dipping the top of each dough ball in bacon grease, she carefully placed them inside a well-greased Dutch oven and set them in the coals of the campfire. Minutes later, she had venison steaks frying and a pan gravy prepared. Then she set out salt, pepper, apple butter, and molasses. Later, she would bake bread for the day ahead, but preparations for breakfast came first. Epiphany took inventory of the meal in progress, nodded her satisfaction, and waited for those who would consume it.

"My stars, Piff! You are the very soul of efficiency!"

Epiphany smiled. There could be no mistaking that cheerful, breathless voice. Alice Playfair, Ramsay's wife, seemed to live her life in a perpetual dither. Curls bouncing, crinolines held high to avoid the dew-wet grass, she came gliding toward Epiphany from the windward side of the wagons. "I had intended to help you prepare breakfast," she said, "but I fear time got away from me!"

"I appreciate the thought, Mrs. Playfair," Epiphany said, "but there was no need. Everything is ready."

Like a nesting hen, Alice Playfair hovered briefly above a battered wooden chair near the stove, gathered her skirts, and sat down. Epiphany smiled. She poured Alice a cup of tea and handed it to her.

"I know your day can't begin until you've had your tea, Mrs. Playfair," she said. "Why don't we have a cup while we're waiting for the men?"

"Thank you, Piff! I declare! Hiring you was the wisest thing we've done! How long have you been with us now, dear?"

"I was twelve when you took me in," Epiphany said. "I turned sixteen in January. That would be four years."

"My stars! Time passes so swiftly! You're not the little tomboy you were when you came to us—you've become quite a lovely young lady."

Epiphany laughed. "I'm afraid I'm still that tomboy at heart," she said. "As far back as I can remember I've wanted to be a boy."

"Really? Why?"

"Well, not really to be a boy, but to do the things boys can do. Boys have adventures! They take risks, get their hair mussed, their clothing torn, and do all kinds of exciting, dangerous things. Besides, they grow up to be men, and men, as we know, rule the world."

Alice Playfair sipped her tea. "Well, I for one am glad they do," she said, "I rather enjoy the protection of chivalrous men."

Epiphany said nothing, but smiled politely. She was well aware of Alice Playfair's views on the place of women in the world, and of their need for protection against all manner of imagined dangers. Although the travelers had seen Indians only twice since leaving Independence, and then only at a distance, Epiphany had heard countless campfire conversations regarding the perils of Indian attack. Some of the stories had been frightening indeed. She'd listened one day as Alice Playfair and several other women discussed the horrors they heard white women suffered when captured by savages. The ladies all agreed the only thing a decent woman could do in such a case would be to take her own life. Epiphany wasn't so sure.

The sound of footsteps broke her reverie. Epiphany looked up to see Ramsay Playfair walking toward her from the direction of their lead wagon. With him were Abner and Tom, the teamsters. Quickly, Epiphany set out the food and began to fill the coffee cups.

She smiled at Alice Playfair. "We really must continue this conversation later, " she said, "but now it's time to feed our protectors."

Over the next several days the Playfairs and their party, together with the other members of the emigrant wagon train, moved closer to their destination. They crossed desert country, dust billowing upward in a great plume from the hooves and turning wheels of the wagons, as they moved on to a crossing of the Snake River. Epiphany walked alongside the wagons as they traveled, as did Alice Playfair, staying upwind to avoid the choking dust. Tom and Abner drove the mules and oxen, and Ramsay drove the men.

On arrival at the Snake, the ferryman demanded what Ramsay considered an outrageous fee to take his wagons across. A number of the emigrants paid, but Ramsay Playfair refused, and with several other wagons attempted an upstream crossing.

The crossing went badly almost from the beginning. Ramsay's driver, Abner, became confused and turned the big Conestoga wagon out of the shallows and into deep water, nearly capsizing it. With the help of Tom, his other driver, Ramsay managed to turn the heads of the mules upstream and into safe water. Half-walking, half-swimming, the animals pulled the heavy wagon across to the opposite bank. Several boxes of mining tools and blankets were lost when the wagon's tailgate came open. Despite Ramsay's best efforts to recover them, they vanished in the swift current of the Snake.

Ramsay lost his temper with Abner. He accused the man of carelessness and of being drunk during the crossing. He called him a fool and a lout. Abner, of course, quit on the spot. He demanded his pay and took his bedroll and personal effects to another wagon farther back in the train.

Even then, Ramsay's woes didn't end. As the mules struggled up the opposite bank, the lurching wagon straddled a large boulder and cracked the front axle. He and Tom mended the crack with rawhide and iron braces. The repair carried them over the last great mountain pass and down to the valley below. Then, while crossing a swale between low hills, the big Conestoga's front wheels suddenly dropped into a grassy washout and the axle broke through.

Now, at an open spot in the trail that emigrants called "The Meadows," the wagon, loaded with merchandise for the store in Bannack, lay fallen on its nose, crippled and—temporarily, at least—beyond repair. Ramsay had gone to John Oakes, the train's captain, to ask for help. Oakes had been sympathetic, but less than helpful.

"I'm sorry about your trouble, Playfair, but I have nine wagons besides yours to think about. As captain, it's my job to see they get to Bannack."

"Damn it, John, what about mine? I'm between a rock and a hard place. I can't leave my goods behind, and I can't very well stay here with them while the rest of you go on!"

Oakes shook his head. "We can't wait for you. We're within two days of Bannack. These folks are in no mood to tarry."

Oakes walked over to the wagon, and on his hands and knees studied its undercarriage. Standing, he dusted his hands on his breeches, his long face somber. "Best thing you and your people can do is take your other two wagons and come on to Bannack with the rest of us," Oakes said. "You can hire a freighter there to come back for your goods."

Ramsay struggled to control his voice. "By the time they got here there'd be damn little left to haul," he said, "Either a train coming along behind us would claim it as salvage or Indians would loot and burn it. That merchandise represents a major investment, John—I can't afford to lose it."

"I'm sorry, Playfair."

"So am I, by God."

"Poor Mr. Playfair," said Alice, his wife. "He looks quite upset, Piff. I fear his meeting with Mr. Oakes did not go well."

Epiphany smiled. Alice Playfair never spoke familiarly of her husband as Ramsay. Alice was a formal kind of woman, Epiphany thought; who else would hold to the fashion of the day and wear a hoopskirt all the way from Springfield? Worse, she insisted Epiphany wear one, too, which made climbing in and out of the wagon several times a day something of a challenge. Still, for all of Alice Playfair's eccentricities, Epiphany liked her employer. Alice was cheerful, industrious, and kind. In all the time Epiphany had worked for the Playfairs, she had never heard Alice speak a harsh or unkind word to anyone.

The day was sunny with a cool breeze, and the women had taken advantage of the weather to do some washing. Epiphany scrubbed and rinsed the last of their sunbonnets, wrung them out, and placed them atop sagebrush clumps to dry. As Ramsay Playfair plodded toward them, Alice minced through the trail's thick dust to greet her husband, her hoopskirt giving her the appearance of a great, gliding bell.

"My stars!" said Alice, "you look like a dark old thundercloud, dear! What did Mr. Oakes say?"

"Say? Said he was sorry. No one has room in their wagons to carry our merchandise for us. Oakes suggests we leave it behind and pay a freighter in Bannack to come back for it."

Reading her husband's mood, Alice Playfair responded the way she felt he wanted her to. "My stars! I'm sure you told him we couldn't do that."

"I certainly did. I told him we'd leave the train and stay behind. He promised to send a freighter from Bannack as soon as he arrived there."

"But. . . is that wise? To remain here all by ourselves?"

"I think we must, Alice. We can't just abandon our goods by the roadside. That merchandise is our future. Besides, we have good grass, wood, and water here, and Tom has agreed to stay with us. Don't worry, my dear. It will only be three or four days at the most."

"I'm sure you're right, " Alice said, hoping he was. "Epiphany has made a fresh pot of coffee. Come and have a cup—it will cheer you."

The blue, shining mountains thrust up from the foothills, surprisingly sharp in detail even at a distance. They caught the late sunlight on their peaks and trapped cold darkness on their wooded slopes. Ramparts of the Rockies, they tumbled and jostled each other like careless soldiers, their ranks forming one more obstacle for the gold-seeker. Ahead, the emigrant road wound north into the foothills along the Beaverhead to Bannack City and the diggings at Grasshopper Creek.

Will Hunter topped a low hill and reined up beneath an old, wind-scarred pine. Hunter's lathered gelding, its sides heaving from the exertion of the climb, faced into the wind and closed its eyes. Freed from the restraint of its lead-rope, the packhorse lowered its head and began to graze. Hunter breathed deeply and shook his head. Never had he known such distance, such space. His friend Ollie Martin had heard it right—this was big country, big beyond the telling—open, wild, and free.

Hunter had ridden westward from Missouri along the Oregon Trail, mostly keeping to himself, sometimes traveling for a time with wagon trains. There were travelers aplenty on the trail that summer. Some headed for Oregon or California; but most, like himself, were bound for the new gold fields on the Beaverhead.

He had pushed west across Nebraska and Wyoming, following the Platte River. At Fort Laramie, he had rested his horses and replenished his food and supplies. He'd bought a new 15-shot Henry repeating rifle from a traveler who needed whiskey more than a firearm. Hunter understood the man's priorities. Sometimes, when the small, cold voice inside his head grew too strong, Hunter found solace in whiskey himself.

In the valley, the setting sun painted the trees and hillsides with golden light. Long shadows, deep-dark and velvet-soft, gave definition to the land. Below, across the Beaverhead, an aspen grove caught a rising breeze that set its leaves to shimmering. "As good a place to camp tonight as any," Hunter thought, and turned his horses downhill.

Daybreak came without fanfare to the Playfairs' camp. Clear skies at sundown had by morning turned overcast, and daylight came to the land slowly, in shades of gray. Awake as always well before dawn, Epiphany kindled a fire in the cookstove and put water on to boil. She had not slept well. Frightening dreams had left her with a vague sense of dread, although she could recall only the feeling and not the dreams themselves.

The Playfairs' wagons stood spaced along a sloping hillside just above the broad meadows that gave the place its name. The crippled freight wagon canted forward on its broken axle. Just beyond stood the wall tent, where the harness and tack for the teams was stored. The tent was also the place in which Tom, the driver, spent his nights. In a clearing beyond the creek, too tired to wander, the draft mules grazed.

Epiphany looked north, along the silent, empty trail, and sighed. How strange it was, she thought. For more than three months they had shared their daily routine with others. Mornings had been filled with sound—the voices of men, the ring of a hammer on steel, the braying of mules and the lowing of oxen. Mothers had called and scolded their children, and children had shouted to each other in their play. Now, just a few days short of their destination, she and the Playfairs were alone.

A rising breeze scattered the smoke from the stovepipe and rippled the canvas tops of the wagons. From somewhere up in the hills coyotes yipped an eerie lament. Epiphany drew her shawl tightly about her shoulders and frowned. The nameless fear that had haunted her dreams returned. Noticing the firewood supply was low, Epiphany walked up the draw toward a stand of lodgepole pines a hundred yards or so behind the wagons.

Down at the creek, Tom eyed the clouds. There was a heaviness to the air, and the leaden skies seemed lower than when he'd awakened. "Looks like rain," he told himself, "before noon, maybe." He squatted on the creek bank, filling a water bucket.

Ramsay Playfair had slept poorly. All the plans he and his brother had made back in Springfield now seemed in jeopardy. They had selected their trade goods carefully; they had been shrewd in their purchases. Ramsay had joined a well-run wagon train, and he had committed his fortunes and his energy to establishing a business in the gold fields. Now, after months on the trail, a single, foolish accident had left him stranded. He was two days short of his destination and dependent for relief on the word of John Oakes, the wagon train's captain.

As if all that were not enough, Ramsay had awakened that day with stomach cramps. He stood at the rear of his wagon and grimaced as the pain slithered through his belly like hot snakes in a mating ball. He felt a sudden urgency in his bowels. Stiff-legged, he hurried toward a nearby patch of brush just uphill from camp.

Inside the wagon, in the bed she shared with her husband, Alice Playfair opened her eyes. Ramsay was gone, she realized. Always an early riser, he typically left their bed at least a half hour before she did, but on this morning she was concerned. Her husband had been restless during the night, his sleep fitful. He had seemed to be in some discomfort. "What's the matter, dear?" she'd asked, "Don't you feel well?"

His answer had been curt. "Bellyache, that's all. Go to sleep."

Now she lay awake, remembering. She hoped he wasn't coming down with something.

The Bannocks struck at dawn, a raiding party ten warriors strong. They rode out of the trees below the creek, stampeding the grazing mules and sweeping on toward the Playfairs' wagons. At the creek, Tom heard the running horses and the first high-pitched war cries and spun to face the attackers. He dropped the water bucket and drew his revolver just as an Indian in white buckskins rode him down. He had time to fire one futile shot before the warrior's lance ran him through and left him dying by the creekside.

Unarmed, Ramsay stumbled out of the brush above the wagons. He was stunned by what he saw. Warriors had reached the lead wagon; some were already rummaging through its contents. At the creek, a dismounted raider straddled Tom's dying form and jerked his head up by the hair. Ramsay saw the quick stroke of the knife and heard Tom's anguished scream. The storekeeper stumbled downhill in a shambling run toward the wagons as the warrior stood erect with his grisly trophy and howled his war cry.

A young Bannock in a full warbonnet, his face painted half black and half yellow, whipped his pony toward Ramsay at a run. At the last moment the warrior turned the animal sharply, touching the white man—"counting coup"—with his bare hand as he passed. Ramsay tripped, fell to one knee, and regained his feet. The Bannock raider turned the pony again, guiding it with his knees as he nocked an arrow to his bow and fired. Ramsay's body went down thrashing in the high grass, both hands gripping the arrow that pierced his throat. The young warrior shot him again, and then twice more, before he dismounted and drew his scalping knife.

———◈———

In her bed inside the wagon, Alice Playfair heard the raiders' war cries and the galloping hooves of their horses. When she heard Tom's gunshot and his agonized scream, she peered out from beneath the wagon's canvas cover. Down by the creek lay Tom's body, sprawled and bloody in death. Horrified, Alice stared as the Indians rode through camp, their faces painted for war and their bronzed bodies glistening even in the morning's gray light. Where was her husband? Had the raiders killed him, too? What of Epiphany—where was she? Alice trembled. Her worst fears had come to pass. She recalled the conversations, remembered the unthinkable torment she'd heard was the fate of female captives of Indians, and she panicked. Quickly, Alice sat up in her bed and jerked her husband's heavy revolver from its leather. Grasping the weapon with both her small hands, she pulled the hammer back to full cock just as the face of a Bannock raider appeared at the wagon's tailgate. Alice's discussions had prepared her well. Eyes tightly closed, she put the pistol's muzzle under her chin and pulled the trigger. The sound was loud inside the wagon, but Alice didn't hear it.

<hr />

Within the lodgepole grove, Epiphany turned at the sound of running horses and the cries of the war party. Horrified, she watched the leader of the warriors kill Tom at the creek. She stared, unable to move, as the raiders rode on to the wagons. She saw the young Bannock kill and scalp Ramsay in the high grass not fifty yards from where she stood.

She felt strangely divided. Her mind gave the order to run, to flee from the danger, but her body remained frozen in place inside the trees. She was both repelled and fascinated by the violence. The young raider mounted his pony again, the animal rearing, and whooped his war cry. His feathered warbonnet trailing behind him as he rode, he descended the slope at a gallop, then turned and thundered back up the slope again. Watching from the lodgepole grove, it seemed to Epiphany the warrior was coming straight for her. At last she broke free of her trance. She bolted from the trees, running hard for the brush-filled coulee that led to the creek. The movement was her undoing, because it was then the warrior saw her.

FOUR
Deadly Encounter

I N HIS CAMP among the aspens, Will Hunter squatted on his bootheels before a small fire and watched daylight come. Tethered by their stake ropes, his horses grazed contentedly on the tall grass beyond the trees. Hunter watched them with a contentment of his own. He felt rested and refreshed. Below, the emigrant road traversed the valley floor, leading on to the diggings. Soon, he thought, he would reach Bannack City.

From a rawhide pannier, Hunter took out a partial slab of bacon, sliced off several strips, and placed them in a blackened skillet on the fire. He put the rest of the slab back in the pannier. He had just turned back to the fire when a movement of the horses—or, rather, their lack of movement—caught his eye. The animals had stopped grazing. Heads held high, they stared north along the rutted wagon road, ears erect, nostrils testing the wind. Hunter took the skillet off the fire and slowly stood, looking north along with his horses, listening.

The sound of the revolver shot was clear, though faint. Hunter slid the Henry repeater from its scabbard and levered a cartridge into its chamber. Carried on the north wind, he heard the distant high-pitched cries of the war party. Somewhere beyond the bend in the road, one mile, maybe two, there would be trouble and death. Hunter strode swiftly through the grass and bridled the black gelding. Minutes later, he was in the saddle and racing north.

Skirts held high and her hair flying behind her like a flag, Epiphany raced for the brushy draw. The young warrior turned his pony sharply and rode to cut off her escape. Two of the other mounted raiders saw the running woman and joined the chase. Fear drove Epiphany. She cursed the foolish hoopskirt that hindered her flight; she prayed she would not stumble.

The world seemed a tip-tilted blur of earth, trees, and sky. Her lungs burned with the exertion of her running; she gasped for breath. Epiphany felt the earth shake beneath her as she heard the horses coming fast behind her. The brush seemed an impossible distance away.

Suddenly, a pony was alongside her, and a brown arm encircled her waist. Epiphany felt herself jerked off her feet and thrown across the withers of the galloping horse. Then, abruptly, the animal jolted to a stop. Still holding her, the warrior dismounted and Epiphany felt her feet touch the earth again. Gripping her hair with his left hand, the warrior forced her head back. Epiphany looked into the wild, half-black, half-yellow face of her attacker and struck at it with all her strength. Her clawed hands raked at him as she desperately fought for her life. Teeth bared, the warrior struck her hard in the face and she sprawled full-length in the grass at his feet. Epiphany heard a ringing in her ears; she was dimly aware of the other raiders riding toward her. Then she closed her eyes and fell away into darkness.

Will Hunter drove the thoroughbred hard along the wagon road, riding into the wind and fast closing the distance between himself and the war cries. The sound of a second revolver shot reached his ears, more clearly this time. He turned the big gelding off the trail and up a low hill to the east. Lunging into the steepness, the horse fought its way to the hill's wooded crest. Hunter drew rein, the Henry repeater in his hand as he dismounted. He took in the scene in a glance—wagons spaced along the hillside, the scalped and bloody body of a man at the creek, the looting Bannock raiders, the arrow-pierced corpse of a second man. He watched as a bonneted warrior on a painted pony raced downhill, shouting his triumph, then turned and raced back toward a lodgepole grove.

Suddenly, Hunter saw a woman break out of the trees, running toward a brush-filled coulee. The warrior turned his pony, riding after her. The Bannock leaned out and swept the woman up, then dismounted. Hunter nestled the rifle's stock into his shoulder and found the warrior in its sights.

The woman was fighting back, Hunter saw, struggling to free herself, fighting for her life. He hesitated, finger on the trigger, waiting. Too chancy, he thought, might hit her. Other Indians were riding toward the warrior and the woman now, she fighting, clawing. Then the Bannock struck her. Hunter saw her fold into the grass like a dropped blanket. He squeezed the trigger.

The warrior staggered, spun about, and pitched headlong. Hunter swung the Henry's muzzle onto the next Bannock and shot him, too. The others broke then, making a dash back toward the wagons. "They haven't seen me," Hunter told himself, "they don't know yet where I am. I'd best make hay while the sun shines."

The warrior in the white buckskins raced away from Hunter, zigzagging his pony. Hunter levered the Henry, fired, and missed. He mentally corrected, took aim, and fired again. The bullet struck the Bannock high in the back and tumbled him onto the wagon road. As the rest of the war party fled across the creek and away toward the distant trees, Hunter fired five more shots as fast as he could chamber the rounds. "Don't expect they've run into a Henry repeater before," he thought, "likely they think there's a dozen men up here. They won't be coming back any time soon."

Hunter slid the rifle into its scabbard and mounted the gelding. Beyond the creek, the fleeing Bannocks had vanished into the timber.

Hunter turned his horse downhill toward the high grass where the woman lay, face down and unmoving. Dismounting, he knelt and touched her shoulder. She was young, he noted, younger than she'd first appeared. Her hair was the pale color of straw, disheveled now but soft and shining in the gray light.

"It's all right, Miss," he said. "They've gone." Gently, he turned her over.

Hunter caught his breath. The girl's face was fair, with pleasing features. He closed his eyes, then looked again. Was his mind playing tricks on him? How like that other face hers was—the same small nose, the soft, full mouth, the random freckles. Hunter lifted her from the tall grass, cradling her against him. No, he thought, her face is not the same, not quite—but very like, yes, mighty like.

Epiphany's consciousness returned. Eyes still closed, she came awake slowly, with difficulty, as one climbing out of a deep well. Memory returned in pieces—the killings, the Indians, the warrior with the black and yellow face. Someone was holding her! Struggling, she fought to free herself. She opened her eyes.

"Easy, miss," Hunter said. "You're safe now. The Indians are gone."

Epiphany ceased her struggles. Eyes wide, she looked into the face of the man who held her. It was a strong face, she thought, rugged yet kind. The man's voice was gentle and reassuring. Epiphany found she was unable to control her body as she began to shake violently. Unbidden, her tears came. How foolish, she thought. The danger is past, there's no reason to cry now. Hunter held her, stroking her as a man might comfort a child. Gradually, she stopped trembling. She dried her tears. Softly, in that place of violence and death, a gentle rain began to fall.

Beside the wagon that held her bedding and possessions, underneath a canvas fly Hunter had rigged, Epiphany sat and watched the rain. The patter of raindrops on the stretched canvas soothed her and helped turn her thoughts away from the morning's horror. Hunter had carried her to the wagons, had wrapped her in a quilt from her bed, and had left her clutching a steaming cup of coffee beneath the makeshift shelter. He had found Alice Playfair's body in the wagon and had carried it into the wall tent. He had done the same with the bodies of Ramsay and Tom. Then, taking down the rope from the forks of his saddle, he had dragged the corpses of the three Bannock warriors up the hill and left them atop the ridge.

He kept a close watch on Epiphany as he worked. He was pleased to note she showed no further signs of shock or hysteria, except one. Wherever he went and whatever he did, he felt her watching him. She followed his every move, her brown eyes fixed on him. Only when he briefly left her sight, did she seem to grow agitated. When he returned, she relaxed once again.

When he finished his tasks, Hunter ducked under the fly and slapped water off his hat. Squatting down and facing Epiphany, he said, "My name's Will Hunter, Miss. I happened along while you were having trouble with those Bannocks—killed three, the rest ran."

"I. . . I'm Epiphany. . . Epiphany Baker," she said, "I work. . . worked . . . for the Playfairs. I saw the Indians kill Tom and Mr. Playfair. I suppose they killed Mrs. Playfair, too."

"Yes," Hunter lied. What the hell, he thought—in a way, they did kill her. "I'm camped maybe two miles back," he continued, "I'll need to go fetch my packhorse and outfit and bring them here. Will you be all right for awhile?"

"Yes," she said, "I think so. You. . . you won't be long?" There was a pleading behind the girl's brown eyes that begged him not to go, but her voice was steady.

Hunter smiled. "Not long," he said, "there isn't much chance the Indians will come back, but just in case—" Hunter pulled one of his Colt's Navy revolvers from the leather and handed it to Epiphany. "I suppose you know how this works," he said. "It's a good thing to have with you while you're waiting."

Epiphany nodded, placing the weapon inside the folds of her quilt. "Yes, thank you," she said. "Our driver Tom taught me to shoot, but I probably wouldn't be able to hit anything unless it was very, very close."

Hunter stepped out into the rain and swung up on the gelding. "In that case," he said, smiling, "wait until it comes very, very close and *then* shoot it." Moments later horse and rider had disappeared into the rain and the mist. Never, Epiphany thought, had she felt so alone.

The rain had tapered off to a sullen drizzle by the time Will Hunter returned to the wagons. He came riding at a trot, the packhorse following, and slowed the horses to a walk as he neared the camp. Beneath the canvas fly, Epiphany stood beside the cookstove. She smiled as Hunter drew rein, a bright greeting that touched him and brought his own smile in return.

Hunter tied his horses to a wagon wheel and walked up the slope toward her. She poured a cup of coffee and handed it to him as he ducked under the makeshift awning. She told him in words what she'd already said with her smile: "I'm glad you're back."

She had cooked breakfast during his absence, Hunter noted. She had even baked biscuits in the dutch oven. He was impressed. He had not been certain how the morning's violence would affect her. "She is both strong and able," he thought, "the girl is tougher than she looks."

When Hunter finished his breakfast of biscuits, bacon, and beans, he pushed his plate away. Epiphany and he sat facing each other across the small camp table. "You're a fine cook, miss," he said. "I am obliged."

"You saved my life today," she said simply. "The least I can do is feed you."

Hunter sipped his coffee, then set the cup down. "May I ask you something, Miss?"

"Of course, anything."

"The people who died this morning, were they family?"

Sadness clouded Epiphany's face. "No. I worked for them. They were Ramsay and Alice Playfair from Springfield, Illinois. The man the Indians killed at the creek was our driver, Tom. I don't know his last name."

"Maybe he had none," Hunter said. "Sometimes a man leaves his old name behind when he's making a new start."

Epiphany stood, her eyes downcast. She removed the plates from the table and placed them in the dishpan. "The Playfairs planned to open a store in Bannack City," she said. "Mr. Playfair's brother, back in Springfield, was his partner."

"And you, Miss, what are your plans? Will you be going on to Bannack?"

She met his gaze. Looking into her eyes, Hunter saw the hurt and sadness he'd expected. But there was something more—a strength, a resolve, that surprised him. "Yes," she said, "I have nothing to go back for. I came here to make a new start. I have a feeling you did, too."

Hunter smiled. "Sometimes, " he said, "we have only two choices— make a new start, or quit. I am not inclined to quit."

By two o'clock the rain had stopped. Sunlight broke through the tattered clouds and painted the land with brightness. A west wind sighed as it moved through the pines and down the valley, ruffling the grass. "Even the day has decided to begin again," Epiphany thought.

At a level place just below the lodgepole grove, Hunter dug the graves. By four o'clock he had finished his work. One by one, he brought the bodies to the graves and laid each to rest. Epiphany painted each name on a board taken from the camp table. She gathered wildflowers for each grave. From his father's well-worn bible, Hunter read the familiar words: "I am the resurrection and the life. . ."

The rhythmic ring of the shovel, pounding in the headboards, provided the death knell.

They sat together, the servant girl and the border ruffian, watching the long twilight descend. Pursued by coming darkness, the dying light retreated from the valleys to the hilltops, and then swiftly climbed the mountain peaks. A breeze swept up from the creek, stirring the ashes of the campfire and bringing a glow to its coals.

With the coming of dusk, stillness descended on the valley. The songbirds ceased their singing, and the wind faded and died away. Hunter took his horses to water and returned with a scuffed leather case that he had taken from his pack. Seating himself cross-legged beside the wagon, he opened the case and took out a gleaming, highly polished violin. Something about the way he held the instrument touched Epiphany.

For a moment he just looked at it in silence. Then he turned to her and smiled. "This was my dad's fiddle," he said. "It's been a few years since I played it, but—would you mind?"

"Oh," she said, "please do."

He applied rosin to the bow, then spent a few moments tightening the pegs and bowing as he tuned the instrument. Placing his chin on the rest, Hunter drew the bow softly over the strings and sent the first strains of *Little Annie Laurie* drifting out across the valley. At first, Hunter's playing was hesitant and uncertain, as his mind and hands sought to reclaim their old skill. Then, as he moved through the melody toward its conclusion, his confidence grew and he finished the song with the high, sweet notes and sure resolution of its final passage.

Epiphany closed her eyes and leaned back against the camp box. She had kept herself busy during the day doing what was necessary, keeping her mind from the violence of the morning. Now weariness fell upon her like a weight. Her limbs felt heavy, her eyelids seemed to have developed a will of their own to close, and she longed above all to find rest and renewal in sleep. Beside her, Will Hunter seemed to read her mind.

"Why don't you go along to bed, Miss? You've had a hard day."

Epiphany stirred, opened her eyes. "Yes," she said thickly, "I think I will. I don't know how to thank you for all you've done."

"There's no need. I'm glad I happened along."

"I keep seeing that Indian's face. . . half black, half yellow. His eyes. . ."

"It's over, Miss. Everything's all right."

"But. . . what if they come back in the night?"

"They won't."

"But if they do. . .?"

"If they do, I'll be here."

Hunter stood. Taking her hand in his, he helped her to her feet. Holding the lantern high, Epiphany made her way unsteadily to the wagon where she slept and climbed inside. For just a moment she listened as Hunter played the lilting first notes of *Beautiful Dreamer*, then she burrowed beneath her quilts and fell into a deep and dreamless sleep.

Hunter returned the fiddle to its case and stared into the flickering flames. He had come over twelve hundred miles to begin a new life, only to find his old life waiting for him. Sickened by killing, he had this day killed three men, shooting one of them in the back. Yes, he'd had no choice; he'd killed to save the girl. Some men gave little thought to Indians killed, or they claimed as much. "Injuns don't count," they said. "They're no better than varmints."

Kansans talked that way about Missourians, Hunter recalled. Pro-slavery men sometimes spoke that way about slaves, and even more so about abolitionists. It seemed a man always had to think of his enemy as something less than human so he could put him to death with a clear conscience. Well, maybe others could do that, Hunter thought, but I can't, not any more.

He would take Epiphany out on the road to Bannack in the morning, he decided. They would take two wagons and leave the freight wagon behind, as that fool Ramsay Playfair should have done in the first place. Ramsay's decision to leave the train and stay behind with his goods had cost six lives all told, including his own and the Bannocks, and had nearly cost a seventh.

Hunter had told Epiphany the Bannocks wouldn't come back, but the truth was he didn't know whether they would or not. They might return with a larger force. They might come back for revenge. They might attack us on the road as we travel. Well, if they do, I still have the Henry. I reckon I'll just have to shoot a few more of them. "Oh, yes," he thought, "I surely am tired of killing my fellow men. Isn't it a wonder the way I keep on doing it?"

Sunshine woke Epiphany the next morning. Startled, she sat up in her bed and looked outside. Since the wagon train left Independence, it had been her responsibility to arise each day before dawn and prepare breakfast. How *could* she have overslept? Epiphany threw aside the bedcovers and reached for her clothing. Then, in a rush, she recalled the events of the previous day—the attack by the Bannocks, the killing of Tom and the Playfairs, her own headlong flight and capture by the warrior.

She remembered the stranger, the man called Hunter, and his kindness and his strength. He seemed a man accustomed to violence, yet she sensed a great tenderness in him as well. Since childhood, she had noticed people's hands. She remembered Hunter's—strong, yet curiously gentle. He had working man's hands, calloused and brown from the sun. His long fingers tapered not at all, but were square to their tips. Hands that had killed the Bannocks were the same hands that had held and soothed her. Hunter's hands had made her a shelter from the rain and they had calmed her with soft music from a violin.

When she was a child, Epiphany recalled, her mother told her that a guardian angel watched over and protected her. Here in this place, Will Hunter had been her protector, but he was an unlikely angel. Muscled and lean, he moved with a lanky grace Epiphany realized was unusual in a man so tall. His collar-length hair and short beard were black and shot with gray. He carried twin revolvers and a Bowie knife in a belt at his waist. His manner was guarded and aloof. A sadness in his eyes hinted at an old and private pain.

If anything, Hunter reminded her of a timber wolf she'd once seen at the zoo in Independence. Confined to a small, barred cage, the animal had ignored the spectators, restlessly pacing the boundaries of its prison in a perpetual, loping walk. Epiphany had sensed the wolf's desperation and had felt both fear and pity. If only I could release it, she'd thought, and let it out of its terrible prison. Perhaps it would not know it was me who let it out, she thought—neither know nor care—but it would be free.

Quickly, Epiphany poured water into a basin and washed her face and hands. She combed her hair, donned a homespun work dress—no more of that hoopskirt foolishness while on the trail, she thought—and stepped out of the shade behind the wagon into the light. The stove was cold, but Hunter had built a campfire and had made coffee. Beans simmered on the coals in a dutch oven, and biscuits from the day before warmed in a covered pan.

A mule brayed. Shading her eyes against the brightness, Epiphany looked down toward the creek to see Hunter striding toward her. Behind him, eight harnessed mules stood tied to the willows at creekside. Hunter smiled as he approached. "Good morning, Miss Epiphany," he said. "You look a bit more rested than yesterday."

"I should," Epiphany said. "I must have slept ten hours or better. I didn't even hear you build the fire."

"I was up early, hunting mules. Last night I decided we ought to hitch two of the wagons and go on to Bannack City. I'll drive the Playfairs' wagon and you can follow in the other."

"What about the supplies in the freight wagon?"

"We'll take what we can. You told me someone's coming to pick up the rest."

"Yes. The captain of our wagon train, Mr. Oakes. He said he'd send back a wagon and a teamster. I should make a record of what we leave behind."

Hunter helped himself to the beans. "First, some breakfast. Then we'll load the stove and the camp tools. You can take inventory while I hitch up the mules."

———————◈———————

Hunter and Epiphany were still six miles from town when they met the southbound wagon. Two men—a barrel-chested teamster and an older man—occupied the wagon seat. They greeted Hunter with a careful nod when they passed on the road. Looking back, Hunter saw the teamster rein up suddenly.

He heard Epiphany's voice from the wagon behind him, even above the rumble of the wheels, and stopped his own team. "Mr. Oakes," Epiphany said, "it's me, Epiphany Baker! I was with the Playfair party!"

John Oakes stepped down onto the rutted roadway and approached Epiphany's wagon. "Yes, Miss Baker," he said, "I told Mr. Playfair I'd send a teamster back for his wagon. Where is your employer?"

Tears glistened in Epiphany's eyes, but her voice was steady. "Buried back at The Meadows, where you saw him last," she said quietly. "We were attacked by Indians two days after you left. They killed Mr. and Mrs. Playfair and our driver Tom."

For a moment, John Oakes made no reply. He took his hat off and stood, looking silently at the ground. His face reddened, and his hands shook. Raising his eyes to Epiphany, he said softly, "Oh, my dear. I'm so sorry. Were you harmed?"

"No," she said, "but nearly so." She raised her eyes, looking beyond Oakes. Hunter had walked back to where they stood. "Mr. Hunter's arrival was a timely one," she said. "He killed three of the Indians and protected me."

"I was camped a mile or two south," Hunter said, "I heard shooting and rode over. It was a Bannock raiding party, ten warriors, and I dealt myself in. I was too late to help the others." Hunter offered Oakes his hand. "Will Hunter," he said.

"John Oakes," the older man replied. "I tried to warn Ramsay about staying there alone, but he was stubborn. Wouldn't listen."

"A man makes mistakes," Hunter said. "Sometimes the penalty is greater than he could have imagined."

Oakes nodded. "We'll bring Playfair's merchandise back to Bannack," he said. "Will you and Miss Baker be staying there?"

The question surprised Hunter. After all, they had come many days and hundreds of miles to reach the gold camp on the Grasshopper. "Why, yes," Hunter said. "Where else would we go?"

Oakes smiled. "While we were on the trail this summer, prospectors hit an even richer strike just seventy miles beyond Bannack—a place called Alder Gulch."

FIVE
Alder Gulch

A S THE STEAMBOAT *Prairie Belle* approached Fort Benton, its great stern wheel churned the muddy waters of the Missouri into foam. Ahead, on the levee, a cannon belched a greeting. The steamer's whistles answered with a shrill reply.

On the riverboat's crowded lower deck, Bravo Santee celebrated his arrival with a last swallow of whiskey and tossed the empty bottle overboard. "Journey's end, by damn," he muttered. "It's taken us six weeks steamin' upriver to git this far, but that bottle may float back to St. Louie in three."

Santee was more than a little drunk. He squinted against the river's glare. Six river packets tied up along the mile-long levee, now crowded with people waiting to greet the *Prairie Belle*. The old American Fur Company fort stood farthest upriver. A scatter of twenty or so log buildings made up Fort Benton's single street. Bull trains rumbled through town and climbed the gray bluffs beyond, hauling freight and mining supplies to the gold fields. Along the levee, roustabouts handled cargo. Townspeople watched and waved as the *Prairie Belle* coasted toward its mooring.

Bravo Santee stood on deck with the other passengers as the distance to the landing narrowed. He watched as the faces of the on-lookers grew clearer, more distinct. There were hunters and wolfers,

49

long-haired mountain men, mule skinners and bullwhackers, and Indians in blankets. There were gamblers, hardcases, solid citizens, and sporting women.

Santee felt no curiosity about the town or its people. He had come 2200 miles up the Missouri on business of his own. He had no time for sight-seeing. Somewhere in the mountains to the south, he hoped to find the man he'd come to kill. Until he tracked Will Hunter down and avenged his brother's death, Bravo Santee had little interest in anything else.

He had paid 150 dollars at St. Louis for deck passage. Cabins on the *Prairie Belle* went for 400, but Santee figured the deck passengers would reach Fort Benton at pretty much the same time the cabin class folk did, and save 250 dollars besides. Santee had slept on the open deck in fair weather and foul, he'd cooked his own food, and he'd helped load when the steamer stopped at wood camps to take on fuel. He'd watched the landscape change from sprawling flatland to the rugged breaks and white cliffs of the upper Missouri. Twice, he'd seen buffalo along the banks, and one morning he had shot a fine mule deer buck at water's edge.

Twenty-four times since leaving St. Louis the *Prairie Belle* had nosed onto sandbars, but the captain was an old hand on the river and accepted the aggravation as a part of the day's routine. Usually, he simply swung the boat around, reversed the engine, and dug a channel through the bar with the boat's big wheel. When that strategy failed, he resorted to "grasshoppering"—dropping the long, heavy spars at the bow to the river bottom and lifting the boat over the bar with block and tackle, cable and capstan, in a series of lurching hops. Nights, they tied up along the bank. Even the boldest of pilots had no wish to risk a night passage in a river filled with shifting sandbars, floating snags, and ever-changing depths.

The other passengers had made music, danced, and socialized during the hot summer evenings. Above, on the cabin deck, the high rollers and the well-to-do passed their time at bar and buffet, attended by white-coated Negro waiters. They ate, drank, and boasted. Smoke from their cigars filled the cabin and fouled the air. Gentlemen played poker at felt-covered tables across from hard-eyed professionals. The gentry amused themselves. They took their ease. They dawdled. They passed the time.

Bravo Santee, however, did not. Years before, his Pa had hammered the lesson into him: when hunting coon a man needs to fix his eyes on the critter's track and keep on a-pushing. No time for day-dreams, Pa had said, no time for food or rest. There was time only for the job at hand, for running mister coon up a tree and fixing him in the rifle's sights. There would be time aplenty for socializing and soft living when the coon was in the pot.

Santee had kept his eyes on the coon. He had bode his time. He had drunk a little whiskey; he had sized up the other passengers. He had cleaned his weapons and put an edge on his Bowie. He had stayed clear of the gamblers and the whores. He had minded his own business.

Now he had reached Fort Benton. A few more days and he'd be at the diggings. Somewhere in the gold fields he believed he would find Will Hunter. Santee would tree his coon and kill it.

Santee picked up his saddle and carpetbag and slung his blanket roll over his shoulder. The *Prairie Belle* docked at the levee, and passengers hurried ashore. Santee elbowed his way into line and walked the staging plank across to the levee. It was good to be back on dry ground.

Dust billowed up behind the wagons and drifted away on the wind as Will Hunter and Epiphany Baker topped a low rise and looked down on Bannack City. Tough, raucous, and busy as a beehive, the town sprawled along dry hills in a sagebrush-studded valley. Rough-hewn buildings faced each other across a street crowded with freight wagons, bull teams, mules, and horses. Nearby, miners worked their claims along meandering Grasshopper Creek. It seemed to Epiphany that nearly every foot of dirt in the gulch had been, or was being, excavated. Placer miners plied their rockers and sluices along the stream, quartz miners were tunneling into the hills on either side of the creek. The sounds of these laborers carried clearly on the wind.

Epiphany set the wagon's brake, wrapped the reins around its handle, and climbed down. Hunter's black gelding and packhorse followed the wagon he drove, tethered to the tailgate. Epiphany spoke gently and touched them as she stepped past them. Stopping beside Hunter, she shaded her eyes against the setting sun and took a long look at the town and the rugged hills behind it. "So that's Bannack City," she said. "After coming all this way, I suppose I expected something more. It really is just a rude, ugly camp."

Hunter studied the scene through half-closed eyes. "Depends on your point of view. Some of those miners down there think it's the most beautiful place on earth. They will continue to, as long as the gold holds out."

"Mr. Oakes said the strike at Alder Gulch is even richer," Epiphany said. "I'm in favor of going on."

"I agree. We can spend the night here and start out early in the morning. John Oakes said he'd store the supplies from the third wagon here in his warehouse. You can arrange to have them sent on later, if you wish."

Epiphany said nothing, but stood at the side of the road, looking at the town. A gust of wind swept up from the valley floor, scattering grit against the wagons. Epiphany squinted her eyes, while both hands held down her skirts against the gusts. Her sunbonnet hung behind her head, secured loosely at her throat by its strings as the wind tossed and tousled her fine, flaxen hair.

Hunter's throat grew tight. Standing there in her homespun dress, slender as a willow—how much she looked like Rachel! For two years I've tried my damnedest to forget, he thought. Now I'm reminded every time I see this youngster. He set his jaw and looked away, back toward the valley. "Well," he said roughly, "let's move on down there. These mules won't drive themselves."

The sun dropped behind Bannack Peak and touched the clouds with flame. Sunlight lingered briefly on the high places, but Bannack City, spread out across the valley floor, was already sunk in shadow. Here and there, lamplight began to appear in the windows of buildings. The town lay more than a mile above sea level, and as Hunter and Epiphany turned their wagons downhill the cold came instantly with the departure of the light.

Epiphany was right, Hunter thought. Bannack is a rude, ugly camp, but at least it has begun to take on a more settled look. Here and there, brick buildings stood staunchly, and two-story frame structures now graced lots where rough-hewn log and slapdash board-and-canvas had lately ruled. The buildings were unpainted, Hunter noted. The entire camp had begun to take on a weathered, decaying look. Main Street boasted three hotels, seven restaurants, three bakeries, a grocery, an assay office, and a hardware store.

The side streets offered a variety of businesses designed to meet the wants and needs of the gold-seekers. These included a generous number of saloons, brothels, gambling halls, and hurdy-gurdy houses, each one dedicated to lightening the prospector's heavy burden of gold dust and nuggets.

Hunter and Epiphany parked the wagons on a grassy flat north of town and watered the horses and mules. It was nearly dark by the time they corraled the animals as a cold wind swept up the valley. Hunter shrugged into his Army greatcoat and Epiphany donned a sheepskin coat that had belonged to the Playfairs' driver Tom. "Alice Playfair would not have thought it fitting for a lady to wear a man's work coat in public," she said, "but it's warmer than my own."

"Comfort beats vanity every time," Hunter said. "May I buy you supper in town, Miss Epiphany?"

"That would be wonderful. It's been a long time since I've eaten a meal I didn't cook."

"Oakes told me Bannack has a sheriff, a man named Plummer. If you don't mind, I'd like to see him first. I need to tell him about the Indians and the raid on the wagons."

Epiphany nodded. "Of course," she said, "may I take your arm?" She smiled brightly, admiration apparent in her large brown eyes. She looks at me as if I'd hung the moon, he thought. The girl is grateful, that's all. I must not allow her to think her feeling for me is more than that. Hunter nodded and offered his arm. Epiphany took his arm, moving closer as they walked toward the lights of Bannack's busy main street.

◈

They found the sheriff eating supper at the Bannack Cafe. Sheriff Henry Plummer sat at a table near the stove, his back against the wall. As Hunter and Epiphany approached him, suspicion flickered briefly in his eyes. The sheriff's glance quickly measured Hunter and faded to a cold and guarded stare. Then he turned his gaze to Epiphany.

"Sheriff Plummer?" Hunter asked. "Sorry to interrupt your meal, but I need to speak with you at your convenience."

"Indeed," said Plummer, his eyes still on Epiphany, "there's no time like the present. Won't you join me?"

Hunter drew out a chair across from the sheriff and seated Epiphany. "I'm Will Hunter, " he said, extending his hand, "and this young lady is Miss Epiphany Baker. We're new to the diggings."

Plummer's hands were small, Hunter noted, almost feminine, but his handshake was firm and dry. Turning to Epiphany, the sheriff accepted her proffered hand and bowed over it, his cold gray eyes on hers. If his eyes were cold, his smile was warm enough, and his voice soft. "A great pleasure, Miss Baker," he said, "beauty is a rare commodity in a mining camp; thus, doubly welcome."

In response to the sheriff's signal, a stoop-shouldered waiter with the sad eyes of a bloodhound approached the table bearing two china cups and a coffee pot. He filled the cups and scuttled away toward the kitchen. "Now," Plummer said, "what can I do for you?"

Briefly, Hunter recounted the events at the Playfairs' camp. He described the attack by the Bannock raiders and the killings. He related his own part in the incident, of riding to the sound of gunfire and war cries, and killing the three warriors. He told of the burial of Ramsay, Alice, and Tom, and of taking Epiphany under his protection. "We met John Oakes on the road yesterday, heading that way with a teamster," Hunter said. "He'll be bringing the merchandise from the freight wagon here to Bannack."

Throughout Hunter's account of the raid, Epiphany sat quietly, sipping her coffee as she watched the two men. The sheriff was younger than Hunter, she decided, perhaps in his late twenties, slender and handsome in his dark business suit and necktie. His hair was a chestnut brown, his face narrow and pale, and a thin mustache graced his upper lip. Only the three-inch scar on the left side of his face marred his features, Epiphany thought—that, and the cold, gray eyes.

Plummer leaned across the table and touched her hand. "I'm sorry to hear of your troubles, Miss Baker," he said. "Please accept my condolences. You were fortunate indeed that Mr. Hunter was able to intervene on your behalf." Glancing down, the sheriff carefully laid the used silverware across his empty plate. He wiped his mouth and fingers with a napkin and laid the cloth beside the dishes. Raising his eyes to Hunter, he said, "The Bannocks are still troublesome at times. I appreciate your informing me of the incident."

From a vest pocket, Plummer produced a small silver watch. Opening its cover, he glanced at the timepiece and snapped the case closed again. "Time to make my rounds," he said. "I have enjoyed our meeting. Tell me—do you two plan to remain here in Bannack?"

"We're thinking of going on to Alder Gulch," Epiphany said, "but I do hope we'll meet again."

"As do I, Miss Baker," Plummer said. "I've recently been elected sheriff of that mining district, too, so I'd say the prospect is a likely one. I wish you luck in whatever you choose to do."

Plummer stood, his eyes on Hunter. "Clearly, you are a man of action and boldness," he said. "Come and see me when you're settled. I can always use a good man."

Looking at Epiphany, the sheriff touched his hatbrim, strode to the counter, and paid his bill. At the door, he turned back briefly, smiled a thin smile, and stepped out into the night.

They seated themselves once again at the sheriff's table, Epiphany nearest the stove. The sad-eyed waiter quickly cleared the table and set it again, then stood poised to take their order.

"We've got beefsteak and biscuits, venison chops and biscuits, or Irish Stew and biscuits," he said. "Might still be some rhubarb pie left, too."

Hunter grinned. "Good thing we like biscuits. What will you have, Miss Epiphany?"

Epiphany's eyes sparkled as she smiled at the waiter. "I think I'll have the Irish Stew," she teased, "and maybe some biscuits, if you have any. A piece of that pie, too, and coffee."

"Suits me right down to the ground," Hunter said. "Make it two."

As the waiter shuffled back toward the kitchen, Epiphany huddled into the sheepskin coat and moved closer to the stove. "Heat feels good," she said. "That wind out there has teeth in it."

For a moment she watched Hunter in silence. The light from the oil lamp made her eyes seem even deeper. "I have a favor to ask, Will."

"Anything, Miss Epiphany."

"That's the favor. Could you please not call me Miss Epiphany?"

The question caught Hunter off balance. "Why—yes, if you'd rather I didn't. What would you like me to call you?"

"My friends call me 'Piff.' It seems, more personal, somehow—friendlier."

He smiled. "Well, I certainly have no wish to appear unfriendly. Piff it shall be."

The waiter returned with their order. Epiphany thanked him with her eyes and began eating with gusto. Watching her, Hunter thought, That's another thing I like about the girl—her honesty. Everything she does, she does without pretense or affectation.

He asked, "Have you thought about what you'll do when we reach Alder Gulch, Miss—Piff?"

She lowered her eyes. When she replied, her voice had a serious, even sad, tone. "Find a place to live, of course, and work. I need to send a letter to Anson Playfair—tell him about his brother and sister-in-law. That won't be easy.

"I clerked for the Playfairs in their mercantile back in Springfield," she said. "At first I thought I'd ask Anson if I could open a store here with his merchandise, but I've decided against that. I'm really not a shopkeeper.

"I might open a restaurant, perhaps a small bakery. Miners are hungry men, and too busy to do much cooking for themselves. I do love to cook.

"When we reach Virginia City I'll try to find a buyer for the wagons, mules, and supplies. I'll send whatever money they bring to Anson and keep five per cent for myself. Do you think that's fair?"

"Sounds right to me. I think it will to Anson, too." Hunter smiled. "You could keep the stove and the cooking utensils as part of your five per cent. I expect you'll do well."

Epiphany finished her stew. Her eyes on Hunter, she asked, "and you, Will—what will you do?"

Will shrugged. "I really don't know. I guess it depends on what we find when we get there."

He looked up. The waiter was coming toward them. Carried high in his left hand was a tray containing two wedges of pie on china plates. Watching the man approach, Epiphany smiled her bright smile once again.

As the waiter served the pastry, Hunter studied Epiphany over the rim of his coffee cup. He thought, There is *one* thing I intend to do when we reach Alder Gulch—and that's keep an eye on *you*, youngster.

The place had been named Alder Gulch after the dense alder thicket that filled eight miles of the incredibly rich gulch, but fire destroyed the thicket in a single night shortly after the placer's discovery. Latecomers—if they thought about it at all—would wonder whence came the name.

The gulch ran all the way down from Bald Mountain to the fast-flowing stream the Shoshone called *Pas-sam-a-ri,* or Stinking Water. It featured seven settlements—Pine Grove, Highland, and Summit above Virginia City, and Junction, Nevada, and Central below it. Virginia, built near the mouth of Daylight Creek, was the queen bee of the settlements. The biggest and the brightest of the camps, and she set the style and the pace of life in the gulch.

Epiphany's entry into Virginia City was a memorable one. She sat cross-saddle behind Will Hunter on his black thoroughbred, her hands about his waist as the gelding wove its way between the ox teams and freight wagons that thronged muddy Wallace Street. After the still nights and days on the trail, she was unprepared for the noise of the camp. Bullwhackers and muleskinners shouted at their animals. The crack of their whips were like pistol shots as they drove their teams through town. From somewhere up the street the sound of gunfire exploded onto the morning air, whether deliberate and deadly or exuberant and reckless, Epiphany had no idea.

The music of strings, horns, and hand organs blared from the doorways of the Hurdy-Gurdy houses, accompanied by rough laughter and the clomping of miners' boots on plank floors. Two men, locked in bare-knuckled battle and trailed by shouting spectators, burst out through a saloon's doors onto the street. Epiphany nearly lost her balance as Hunter sharply reined aside to avoid the brawlers.

Bearded miners, buckskin-clad adventurers, burly teamsters, aproned store-keepers, soiled doves in silk, gamblers, and gunmen crowded the streets. Epiphany heard snatches of conversation as they rode past, some of it in languages other than English, and much of its meaning a mystery to her. "I panned that feller out, but I couldn't raise a color."

"Took me a bath, then I placered the tub to pay the barber."

"Lived in a wakiup over on the Grasshopper, but I been fresh-airing since I came here."

Looking up the gulch, Epiphany could see what appeared to be thousands of tents, cabins, and rude brush shelters strewn for miles along the creek bank. Miners worked every inch of their claims in search of paydirt, and great heaps of gravel stood as monuments to their progress.

Still clinging to Hunter's waist with her left hand, Epiphany covered her nose with her right as a vagrant breeze brought the odors of the camp to her nostrils. She caught the scent of woodsmoke, of whiskey and beer, of animal waste, and something else. Thousands of people worked, slept, ate and drank in the camp, and the outhouses of the gulch gave reeking testimony of the growing population.

Beyond the sights and smells that stormed Epiphany's senses an impression took root within her mind and became a decision. Like the miners who burrowed into the earth, like the gamblers and merchants who prospected the prospectors, Epiphany saw adventure and opportunity there in the gulch. She looked at the bustling chaos of Virginia City and knew she'd found her place of new beginnings.

A block off Wallace Street on a slight rise stood a two-story frame building bearing a sign that read simply: ROOMS. In the yard, a buxom woman pinned sheets and towels to a clothesline. Hunter turned the gelding uphill and drew rein before her. "Ma'am," Hunter said, touching his hatbrim, "your sign says 'Rooms.'"

The woman shaded her eyes against the sunlight, looking up at Hunter. "I know what it says. I paid a sign painter thirty dollars in clean gulch gold to paint it for me."

She was a handsome woman, Hunter judged, in her early thirties. Her rich auburn hair was caught up in a bun at the nape of her neck, and her face and arms were brown from exposure to the sun. "Wanted it to read Room and Board," she went on, "but the sign painter wanted another thirty to paint that so I advised him to go to hell."

She smiled then, brushing a strand of hair from her eyes. "Far as I know, that's where he went. You folks looking for a room?"

Hunter nodded. "The young lady is," he said, "unless your prices are as high as your sign painter's."

"There are higher rates than mine in the gulch and there are lower," the woman said. "I charge twelve dollars a week, room and board."

Grasping Hunter's hand, Epiphany slid off the gelding and onto the ground. She approached the woman and held out her hand. "Epiphany Baker," she said, "your new boarder."

"Lily Rae Bliss," the woman said. "Welcome to you, hon."

Hunter turned the gelding back toward Wallace Street. "I'll fetch your traps from the wagon, Piff," he said. "Be back directly."

Lily Rae placed her hands on her hips and looked up at Hunter. There was mischief in her green eyes, and her smile was saucy. "You surely are a tall one, highpockets," she said. "I believe you could hunt geese with a rake. I know it isn't polite to ask, but do you have a name or did you leave yours back in the States?"

Hunter returned her smile. "I left one or two things back there," he said, "but a man's name is the flag he flies under, and I brought my own. I'm Will Hunter."

Lily Rae's smile was warm as August. "A pleasure to meet you, Will Hunter," she said.

Hunter leaned low across the pommel of his saddle and took her extended hand. "The pleasure is mine, Lily Rae," he said.

SIX

A Lady's Honor

E PIPHANY'S LODGING turned out to be a neat room with a south-facing window on the first floor of the boarding house. The room contained a white-painted iron bed with a hand-made quilt for a coverlet, a small oak wash-stand, dresser, and chair. A vase lamp with a painted floral shade stood atop the dresser, and a braided rug covered the floor beside the bed. A small heating stove and wood box completed the furnishings.

"No visitors in your room, but you're welcome to use the parlor. It's down the hall just off the dining room," Lily Rae said. "Outhouse is around back, next to the woodshed. I serve breakfast at eight and supper at six. I don't provide a mid-day meal, except by special arrangement. There are six other boarders here, all men, and I do prepare lunches for three of them. They're a good lot, but it'll be a pleasure for me to have another woman to talk with. I'm glad you're here, Epiphany."

Epiphany's fingers trembled as they brushed the patterned quilt. She sat down upon the bed. "It—it has been so long since I slept beneath a roof in a real bed." she said. "For the last three months I've mostly slept under a tarp in a wagon or a tent. Sometimes, when the weather was good, I slept out under the stars. So much has happened since we—since I—left Springfield. I—"

Remembrance of the Bannocks' raid and the deaths of Tom and the Playfairs came back to Epiphany in a rush of sounds and images. Somehow, Lily Rae's kindness, the tidy room, and the feeling of having come to a place of safety and rest overwhelmed her. She had been brave, she had been strong, she had persevered. Now the floodgates opened; her tears came suddenly, unbidden, and uncontrollable. Lily Rae held her close, her strength both comfort and permission. "There, there, hon," she crooned.

Moments later, Epiphany abruptly stopped crying and pushed herself back out of Lily Rae's arms. She produced a handkerchief from the pocket of the sheepskin coat and dried her eyes. "I–I'm sorry," she said. "I don't know what's got into me. I wasn't raised to break down in front of strangers."

"Hell, hon," said Lily Rae, "most of us weren't raised to break down at all. We were all supposed to be good little girls and boys, and never bother folks with our feelings. Damn nonsense, like a lot of what they taught us. I figure the reason the Lord made more than one human being was so's we could share with somebody."

Lily Rae leaned close, her smile tender as she looked into Epiphany's eyes. "Tell you what," she said, "why don't I put the kettle on? We can have tea in my kitchen and talk for a spell. What do you think?"

Epiphany dried her eyes and blew her nose. Meeting Lily Rae's gaze, she smiled a shaky smile. "I'd really like that," she said.

For nearly two hours the women sat facing each other across a small kitchen table. They drank tea from delicate porcelain cups with matching saucers. Lily Rae identified them as the sole survivors of a tea set that had seen too many moves over too many rough trails. As the women shared the tea, they shared their stories.

Epiphany recounted her life in Springfield as household servant and clerk to the Playfairs. She told of her weeks with the wagon train, and of the morning raid that took the lives of Alice, Ramsay, and Tom. She wept again as she described the killings and the way she'd run from the young Bannock. Haltingly, she spoke of how he'd ridden her down and captured her. She saw again his half-yellow, half-black face and his wild eyes. She remembered her terror and the desperate way she'd fought him, and she told all that.

She told of regaining consciousness to find Will Hunter holding her. She spoke of his gentleness and his strength. She spoke of their time together as they traveled first to Bannack and then to Virginia City. "Now," she said, "I need to find work. I need to earn a living."

"You'll do fine, hon," said Lily Rae. "You've got spunk, and you've got character. I know, because I have those qualities myself." She poured another cup of tea for them both and carefully set the pot down again.

"There are women here—all kinds of women—running businesses, selling butter and eggs, and operating laundries. There are widows, grass widows, old maids, and youngsters like you. I know a girl who's clerking in a store for no money at all. She's making her living from the spilled gold dust she sweeps up every evening. Of course, there are the Hurdy-Gurdy girls and the fancy women, making money the easy way—which oft-times turns out to be the hardest way of all.

"A mining camp is a hard place for a woman alone," Lily Rae continued, "I lost my husband Frank a year ago over at Bannack. We lived on our claim up the Grasshopper. Road agents robbed and killed him in broad daylight while he was coming home from town. For a while there I thought I'd die, too. But a person doesn't die of a broken heart, no matter what the novels say. The truth is, a person generally has to *live* with a broken heart, and that's harder by far.

"Miners took up a collection for me—I believe most everyone on the gulch chipped in. I sold our claim, moved here to Virginia, and started this boarding house. I expect to do well and prosper because I won't accept any other result. If I'm any judge—and I believe I am— you'll do the same. You're smart and you're tough, even when you think you're not, and you're not the type to quit."

Lily Rae lifted her cup in salute. "There's one thing more," she said. "You have me for a friend, Epiphany. Here's to friendship."

Epiphany's smile was bright. "To friendship," she said.

The day dawned cold and brisk, the air transparent as crystal and the distant mountains sharp-etched and clear. Seated before a small campfire above the gulch, Will Hunter warmed his hands over the flames and marveled at the view.

The mountains overlooking the gulch—the Tobacco Roots and the Gravellies—caught daylight on their peaks and upper slopes, waking and warming to the sun's touch. The clarity of the air misled the eye, making distant places appear close. It seemed to Hunter he could clearly see every rock, tree, and blade of grass in the valley.

Below, in town, woodsmoke rose from chimneys as the camp began to stir. Sunlight flowed over the hilltops, gilding the cured grasses and scrub cedar. Birdsong heralded the day. Hunter leaned back against a wagon wheel, breathed deeply, and closed his eyes.

There was something about these northern Rockies, Hunter thought, that made a man feel he could do anything, be anything. The land seemed fresh, newly minted, with all its future before it. Somehow that made a man believe in his own new beginnings as well.

As was his custom, Hunter had rolled out of his blankets an hour before sunup. He had dressed quickly in the chill air as false dawn lightened the skies. Out of habit, he buckled on the gunbelt that held his knife and twin Navy revolvers, then he hesitated. For a moment he stood motionless in the lee of the wagons. Since the day he'd joined Quantrill in the summer of 1861, the weapons had been as much a part of him as his hat. Slowly and deliberately, Hunter unbuckled the belt and laid it on his bedroll. Those guns belong to another life, he told himself. I'm through with killing. A man doesn't build a life with tools designed to deal death.

He had slept well. The cruel dreams which sometimes disturbed his slumber had not troubled him for weeks now, nor had the mocking voice of the accuser that lived within his mind. Memories of Rachel, of Missouri and bleeding Kansas, still came at odd moments to haunt him; but they came less often than before, and for that he was grateful.

He was grateful, too, for the renewed confidence and hope he'd seen in Epiphany. He had delivered her trunk and personal effects to

Lily Rae's boarding house the afternoon they arrived in Virginia City, but it was two days later before he saw her again. Hunter had spent those days exploring the gulch, visiting its communities, and talking with its miners and merchants.

During that time he had formed a plan, and he wanted to share his thoughts with Epiphany.

He was surprised by his feelings. For most of his life, Will Hunter had been a loner, a man who preferred the solitary life. He had few close friends, and there had been no woman in his life since Rachel. It was not that he disliked people, he told himself, it was just that he felt little need for the companionship of others. Still, he had to admit, he missed seeing Epiphany.

Back in Virginia City, Hunter bought a dark blue flannel shirt and a pair of Levi's canvas pants at a dry goods store on Wallace Street. He blacked his boots, dusted his hat, and treated himself to a bath, haircut, and shave at a barber shop. Then he rode up to the front door of Lily Rae's boarding house and dismounted.

Epiphany met him at the door with an excited squeal and an embrace that both embarrassed and delighted him. Lily Rae took his hat, and Epiphany led him into the parlor to a settee beside a marble-topped table. She seated herself across from him, bright as a bird and full of chatter regarding plans for her restaurant and her future. Through Lily Rae she had heard of a cabin on Idaho Street that might be for sale. She hoped to see it as soon as the owner could be located.

Hunter said little because Epiphany did most of the talking. Teacup in hand, he sat, slightly uncomfortable amid the parlor's ornate furnishings, taking pleasure simply in watching Epiphany. She had arranged her hair in a chignon, ornamented with ribbons caught up in a silver net. The scent of her perfume drifted across the space between them and caused Hunter to recall springtime in Missouri and the fragrance of blooming verbena.

Epiphany wore a pale blue, satin street dress with a crinoline; and her brown eyes reflected the lamplight as she spoke. Abruptly, she stopped, and caught her breath. "But here I've done nothing but talk about my plans," she said. "I haven't let you get a word in edgewise!

What about you, Will—have you given any more thought to what you're going to do?"

"Yes, I have, some," he told her. "I spent the last two days riding the gulch and talking to prospectors. No doubt about it, Piff—this Alder Gulch strike is about the richest there's ever been." He leaned forward, his forearms on his thighs. "But most of the miners who are doing well in the diggings are the professionals," he went on. "Some of the men I talked to have followed the gold trail from California to Pike's Peak to Idaho, and they know their trade."

"I'm no prospector," he said. "I'm a farmer, and a Missouri mule man. This camp is a long way from the supply centers, and winter's coming on. The gulch is going to need freighters—men who can handle wagons and mules. It's a job I can do."

Epiphany frowned. "But where will you find wagons and mules?" she asked. "Do you know someone who has them for sale?"

"Well," Hunter said with a grin, "*you* have wagons and mules. Would you consider selling them to me?"

"The Playfairs' wagons!" she exclaimed. "Of course! The wagons and teams that brought us here!"

"And the wagon and mules we left at the meadows, if I can repair the axle and find the animals. What do you say, Piff?"

Epiphany smiled. "Ramsay's brother Anson doesn't know it, but he just sold you his wagons and mules," she said. "I'm happy for you both."

Late the next afternoon, Hunter had just left Ulberg's Livery Stable when he nearly collided with John Oakes. "Will Hunter!" Oakes said. "Just the man I wanted to see. I looked for you in Bannack."

"Sorry, John," Hunter said, "we stopped there, but didn't stay. Remember? It was you who told us about the strike here at Alder."

"I remember. Brought the goods from the meadows, like you asked. They're at my warehouse in Bannack. Won't know for sure 'til we check Miss Baker's inventory, but everything seems to be there."

"Any sign of the Indians?"

"No. The wagon is where you left it, and the graves haven't been bothered. Been plenty of emigrants through there, though."

Hunter grinned. "Looking for the golden streets of El Dorado, just like the rest of us," he said. "I'll be over this week to pick up the goods."

Oakes squinted against the sun as he studied Hunter's face. "Word is all over the gulch about the way you rescued the Baker girl. I'd like to buy you a drink."

Embarrassed, Hunter looked down at the boardwalk between his feet. He shook his head. "I only did what any man would," he said. Raising his eyes to Oakes' face, he smiled. "But I won't turn down a drink," he said. "Lead the way."

The two men walked together along the store fronts and cabins that made up lower Jackson Street until, on a corner at the top of a low hill, they came to a saloon called the Mother Lode. The log building had a false front finished in milled board siding. Two large windows flanked the doorway, and a raised gallery ran the length of the saloon's front. Below, standing hipshot in the black mud, saddlehorses drowsed at the hitchrail.

As Oakes and Hunter climbed the steps to the gallery, they heard a familiar voice. "Will Hunter and John Oakes. Good afternoon, gentlemen."

In the deep shade of the saloon's board awning, two men stood together. As Hunter's eyes adjusted to the dimness, he recognized the sheriff of the district, Henry Plummer. "Afternoon, Sheriff," he said.

Oakes nodded. "Howdy, Henry," he said. "Afternoon, Jack."

Plummer was dressed as Hunter had seen him in Bannack, in a dark business suit, hat, and cravat. Over his suit he wore a long canvas duster, its bottom stained and mud-spattered. His companion was a tall, broad-shouldered man with black hair. Beneath a battered hat, the man's eyes were cool as he appraised Hunter. He wore a long, blue Cavalry overcoat trimmed with beaver fur. Beneath the open coat, Hunter saw that the man carried a holstered revolver and Bowie knife on a wide belt secured by a brass "U.S." buckle. A loose silk kerchief, tied in a square sailor's knot, hung about his neck, and his knee-high riding boots sported big-roweled Spanish spurs.

"Meet one of the gulch's newer residents, Jack," Plummer said. "This is Will Hunter, the man who killed those three Bannocks at the meadows. Will, meet Jack Gallagher, one of my deputies."

Gallagher gripped Hunter's hand, his eyes intent. When he spoke, his breath smelled of cheap whiskey. "Heard about you," said Gallagher.

"I was fixin' to buy Will here a drink inside," said Oakes. "Can I offer you boys the same?"

"Thanks, John, but I've had my limit," Plummer said.

Gallagher grinned at Oakes. "Hell, I ain't got no limit," he said. "You can buy me one."

Henry Plummer placed his hand on Hunter's shoulder, drawing him aside. "You and Jack go ahead," he told Oakes. "I'd like a few words with Will here, if I may."

When Gallagher and Oakes had gone inside, Plummer turned back to Hunter and smiled. "I enjoyed our meeting in Bannack," Plummer said. "I've been wanting to talk to you, Will."

Hunter tried to read the sheriff's face. The man's smile was friendly, but there was no expression in his gray eyes.

"What about, Sheriff?" Hunter asked.

"I was wondering what your plans were. Do you expect to follow the gold miner's life?"

Hunter hesitated. "No. I thought I might go to work hauling freight."

"Hard way to make a living," Plummer said.

"Maybe, but I've got a strong back, and I can handle mules."

Plummer removed a cigar from an inside pocket and bit off the end. "There are easier ways," he said.

The sheriff struck a match and lit the cheroot, drawing deeply and puffing until the tip glowed red. "I told you in Bannack I could use a good man. Are you interested?"

Hunter frowned. What was the man asking? And why this strange dance? "I'm not sure what you're asking, Sheriff," he said. "Are you offering me a deputy's badge?"

Again, those cold eyes fixed on his. "There are a good many men making a great deal of money in this country," Plummer said, "we're entitled to our share."

"That may be," Hunter replied. "I guess I'll try to earn mine as a teamster."

"Strange," Plummer observed, "I took you for a fighting man. Saving that girl the way you did, those ivory-handled Colt's you wore at Bannack. I'd say you've seen action aplenty back in the States. Am I right?"

"Could be I've seen too much. I'm here to try another way." He felt anger, like bile, rising at the back of his throat. His voice had a metallic edge.

"My mistake," Plummer said, smiling, "I meant no offense."

In the doorway, behind the sheriff, Hunter saw Gallagher watching them. Turning, Plummer said, "Hello, Jack. Looking for me?"

Gallagher stepped out onto the gallery, his eyes on Hunter. His tone was surly, belligerent. "Lookin' for *him*," he said. "Don't get to talk to no damn hero every day."

He stepped forward, glancing at Plummer as he passed. Hunter saw the sheriff nod his head, then look away. "Smart, too," Gallagher said, moving closer. "Rescued that cherry piece o' fluff from the Injuns and kept her for himself. I bet she sure as hell ain't a cherry any more."

Hunter's hands flashed to his waist, found no weapons. A roaring grew inside his head like the sound of a waterfall. Even through the whiskey's fumes Gallagher had caught Hunter's move; his eyes widened as he grabbed for his revolver.

Stepping in swiftly, Hunter hit Gallagher with a solid left hook that snapped the deputy's head and sent his hat flying. The man's gun was out of the leather and coming up when Hunter caught him full on the nose with a hard right and clubbed him to his knees with a second right-hand blow. Gallagher dropped the revolver, grabbing for the gallery's rail to keep from falling. Hunter kicked the weapon out into the street.

The Bowie knife flashed from its sheath, coming up in Gallagher's right hand. Hunter caught the deputy's wrist and brought his knee up sharply into the big man's groin. Gallagher's eyes bulged. His mouth opened in pain. Still holding the man's wrist with his left hand, Hunter struck him hard in the face with his right—once, twice, three times.

The big deputy dropped the knife. He clung to the railing, blood streaming from his nose and mouth, his eyes glazing. He tried to regain his footing, but his legs pumped spasmodically and his feet kept slipping on the gallery's planks. Hunter grasped the man's hair and picked up the knife.

Naked fear was stamped on the deputy's face as Hunter brought the blade before his eyes.

His breath coming in ragged gasps, Hunter's rage spoke through clenched teeth. "If you ever—speak filth—about the young lady again—I'll cut out your lying tongue—and feed it to the dogs!"

Gallagher slumped to the gallery floor, groaned, and lay still.

His blood still high, Hunter turned to face Plummer. The sheriff met his gaze, his stance relaxed. "Jack tends to overstep a bit sometimes," Plummer said. "Some men shouldn't drink."

Behind him, in the doorway of the saloon, John Oakes stared wide-eyed at the fallen deputy. Hunter drilled Gallagher's Bowie point-first into the planks at his feet and stepped away. "Drunk or sober, he needs to watch his mouth," he said. "Miss Baker is a lady."

———◈———

Plummer watched, his gray eyes narrowed in thought, as Hunter and Oakes walked away up Jackson Street.

At the railing Gallagher pulled himself up to a sitting position and shook his head. "Damn you, Henry," he muttered. "Push him, you said. Sum'bitch damn near kilt me."

"Yes," Plummer said, "as a fighter, the man is a huckleberry above a persimmon. I wish I knew more about him."

Two miners walked out through the saloon's doors. Careful to keep their faces expressionless, they averted their eyes as they passed the deputy and descended the stairs to the street. A third, smaller man slid quietly out of the shadows near the door. He looked up at Plummer with sly, yellow eyes. "I kin tell you plenty about that 'un, Sheriff," said Bravo Santee.

SEVEN

The Storm Within

WILL HUNTER WALKED silently beside John Oakes along the boardwalk, his face dark and angry, his blood still high. "I never did get to buy you that drink," Oakes said. "Seein' you whip that blowhard Gallagher makes me want to buy you a barrel."

Ahead, on the corner, a long, sod-roofed building bore a sign that read "Miner's Rest Saloon." Oakes led Hunter inside and up to the bar. A few men stood drinking there, but moved away when they saw the expression on the tall man's face. "Two whiskies, barkeep," said Oakes, "the best you have."

The bartender set a bottle on the bar. "Valley Tan," he said, "made by Mormons down in Salt Lake."

Oakes nodded. The bartender filled two glasses. "The Saints won't drink themselves," Oakes said, "but they don't mind sellin' the stuff to us soulless gentiles." One elbow on the bar, he lifted his glass to Hunter. "To righteous wrath and a lady's honor," he said.

Hunter drank. The whiskey went down smoothly, warming his throat and belly. He drained the glass and set it carefully back on the bar. "I'm obliged, John," he said. "Let me buy you one."

The bartender refilled their glasses. Oakes lifted his and studied it thoughtfully. "You're new to the gulch, Will," he said. "There are some things you need to know."

"Such as?"

"Such as—there seems to be an organized band of killers and thieves operating here. Miners are digging riches out of these mountains that would make King Midas throw a jealous tantrum; but when they try to take their gold out, both they and their treasure disappear."

"That's the sheriff's problem, isn't it?"

Oakes glanced nervously around. The miners and the bartender had all moved to the far end of the bar. His voice was low, almost a whisper, as he said, "Some people think the sheriff *is* the problem.

"I guess what I'm sayin' is—if you're fixin' to give any more lessons in manners to Henry Plummer or his men you might want to put your guns back on and grow eyes in the back of your head."

Hunter leaned his elbows on the bar, staring at the bottles and glassware on the backbar. "I came a long way, looking for a place I could take my guns off," he said.

"You ain't found it yet, son," said Oakes.

———◈———

Back at the wagons, Will Hunter took his horses to water and moved them to better grass. Night was falling fast. Dark clouds loomed above the mountains, and a cold wind flattened the grass and scattered the yellow leaves of the cottonwoods. The canvas wagon sheets slapped and popped on their hardwood bows. The ashes from his cold campfire rose with the wind like a ghost from a grave. Hunter stood, his back against the wagon box, and watched the manes and tails of the horses blow in the gale. The weather, wild and restless, matched his mood.

The voice inside his head spoke: *How nice that you've turned your back on violence. You wanted to kill that man.*

"I could not tolerate his damned lies about Rachel."

Don't you mean Epiphany? She's not a child, she's a woman. She's not Rachel. She's not your unborn daughter. You can't keep punishing other men for your guilt.

"Will I never be free of you?" he asked the voice.

I don't know, replied the voice. *Will you?*

There was sleet in the air now, wind-driven crystals that stung his face and rattled against the wagon. At their picket pins the horses, sensing snow, turned to face the storm, heads low and eyes closed.

Hunter closed his eyes as well. He moved to the leeward side of the wagon, huddled against the wind's buffeting. Images formed inside his mind, pictures of Rachel, his wife. In memory, he saw her laughing in the twilight, close beside him on the porch of their cabin. He recalled her eyes, warm and deep with passion, in the long sweet nights of their lovemaking. He remembered the way her face glowed when she told him she was bearing his child. He remembered Rachel at the cabin that last day, hiding her fear as she watched him ride out on the road to Harrisonville. Finally, he saw Rachel as she lay cold in death in the high, wet grass by the spring house– forever dead except in memory, forever living except in flesh.

Hunter groaned, the sound lost in the howling wind. He tore open his bedroll, removed the belt that held his knife and holstered revolvers. He buckled the gunbelt about his waist, donned his Army greatcoat, and strode to where the black thoroughbred stood facing into the wind. Minutes later, Hunter had saddled the horse and was riding away from Virginia City into the fast-falling darkness.

Back in Missouri, riding with Quantrill, Hunter had searched for a way to deal with the memories that haunted him. Many of his comrades had sought to exorcise their devils through lust and drunkenness, but that had not been Hunter's way. Instead, he had mounted the fleet black thoroughbred, riding wildly through the night, leaving his demons–for a time, at least–behind him.

At those times he would give the gelding its head and ride flat out through the wildwood, feeling nothing save the wind's rush and the powerful animal beneath him, until he found a measure of peace.

The thoroughbred seemed to sense his mood. Hunter felt the animal's muscles stretch and ripple beneath him as it bolted before the wind and raced over the broken ground. Sagebrush and greasewood, stirrup high, slashed at his boots. Black trees–cedar and jackpine–loomed suddenly, then swept away in the darkness. Hunter leaned forward in the saddle, out over the gelding's neck, urging still greater speed. Was he running from something or going to something? He neither knew nor cared.

Away from the lights of town, darkness came fast. Hunter could see little of the terrain they traversed but still he drove the thoroughbred on at break-neck speed. Snow began to fall, great wet flakes that stuck to his face and blinded him. He raced past tents and cabins, more felt than seen in the darkness and thickening snowfall. A dog barked close at hand, the sound sweeping away behind him as he rode. Twice, Hunter felt the gelding abruptly check its pace, gather itself, and jump some obstacle only it could see. Each time, the horse came down running, and galloped on before the gale.

The thoroughbred turned uphill, lunging and slipping on the rocky, snow-covered ground. Even above the roar of the wind, Hunter could hear the horse's labored breathing. Then they reached a crest. The gelding plunged over the top and downhill, sliding and checking. Suddenly, the animal lost its footing—Hunter felt it falling and jerked the reins hard, hoping to bring its head up and avert the fall, but it was too late. The thoroughbred somersaulted, head over heels, and Hunter felt himself catapulted into space.

The earth shot up to meet him. The shock of his landing rocked him with unbelievable pain. A bright red haze exploded behind his eyes. Then darkness embraced him. In that embrace, Hunter found peace.

Thad Mitchell opened his cabin door and looked out. The squall that swept through the valley overnight had left broken branches and a skiff of snow in its wake. The day dawned clear and still, the rising mists above Alder Creek luminous in the sunlight.

Thad had turned twenty-two on the sixth of May, but he'd been a prospector and miner since his seventeenth birthday. He'd come to the Beaverhead diggings at Bannack just in time to join nearly 700 other men in the rush to the new strike at Alder Gulch. He had staked his claim at a bend of Alder Creek three miles from Virginia City.

At the time, mining law allowed each prospector in the Fairweather District to claim 100 feet of the creek from rimrock on one side to rimrock on the other. A short time later, however, a large group of miners from the Kootenai country arrived to find the creek fully located, and they protested loud and long. "Claims should end at the center of the stream," they said, "that's how it's done in California."

Their argument prevailed. Other prospectors who had arrived too late for the original stampede—and there were many—agreed with the Kootenai contingent. A miners' meeting adopted the California method, halving the size of the existing claims. The number of miners along the gulch doubled, and Thad Mitchell lost half his original claim. The Alder Gulch strike was incredibly rich, however, and the young veteran took the reduction in his stride. In the five months since the initial discovery, Thad cleared over $10,000 in gold dust and nuggets.

Most of the miners along the gulch gave scant attention to their living quarters during that summer. The majority were young men hoping to quickly strike it rich and return to their families before winter set in. They slept in caves, tents, brush shelters called 'wakiups', and under the sky with no shelter at all. The men had come for gold, and they worked their claims with single-minded determination.

Thad was no less determined than the others; however, because he had spent one winter in the Colorado gold fields and another in Idaho, he had a healthy respect for Rocky Mountain weather. Early that summer he had begun to build a small but sturdy cabin, working an hour or two each evening until he completed the structure. He bought a small stove, and planks for a door from the area's new sawmill. He built his own furniture—a chair, table, and bed—and even purchased and installed a four-pane glass window for the cabin's front wall. Now he stood outside the door, felt the chill morning air, and congratulated himself. His cabin was snug and warm. He could survive winter's worst.

Thad closed the cabin door behind him and walked downhill to a jackpine thicket above the creek. He moved into the trees until he came to a canvas-covered haunch of venison, suspended from a sturdy tree limb. Thad unwrapped the tarpaulin, cut himself a generous steak, and rewrapped the meat. Below him, bright sunlight reflected off the surface of Alder Creek. In the stillness of the morning, Thad heard the soft chuckle of the water as it rippled over its gravel bed. He indulged a favorite fantasy; he imagined the water was calling him. "Today, today," the waters seemed to say, "maybe today you hit the rich pocket. Maybe today you make the big strike." Thad smiled and turned to return to the cabin. It was then he saw the horse.

The gelding stood atop a low hill, head held high, its eyes fixed on Thad. Restlessly, it tossed its head, pawing the earth with its right front hoof.

The horse's black hair was matted and unkempt, and the animal wore both saddle and bridle. On its off side, a rifle scabbard hung empty from the saddle's forks. The animal's long legs and topline and its small, well-formed head told Thad that the gelding was a thorough-bred. The stiffness of its gait as it moved a few halting steps told him the animal was in some distress. Bending slowly, Thad placed the veni-son steak on a shaded patch of snow and walked toward the horse.

"Easy, boy," said Thad. "It's all right. I just want to help."

The gelding tossed its head again and nickered, but stood its ground, waiting as he approached. Thad reached out, stroking the animal's neck with his right hand. Gently, he grasped a bridle rein with his left. His voice was low, reassuring. "Good boy," he said, "easy now."

He led the gelding toward the creek, watching the movement of its legs as the animal walked. Except for the stiffness he'd observed, the gelding seemed to have no serious injury. There was mud and grass on the saddle and in the gelding's mane. It was obvious to Thad that the horse had fallen while running hard. "What happened, big fel-low?" he asked, stroking the animal's mane. "Where's your master?"

At the top of the hill, Thad found the tracks. Plain in the new-fallen snow, they told their story. A fast-running horse had raced at top speed over the rocky, broken ground. The horse had lunged uphill, its tracks deep, gouged-up clumps of rock and sod marking its path. The animal had reached the hill's crest and descended, slipping and sliding. Sud-denly, it had stumbled, falling hard. It had then regained its feet and limped several yards before stopping.

The slope was steep, snow-covered, and shaded by scrub cedar and jackpine. Morning light filtered through the branches, dappling the incline. A flash of brightness caught Thad's eye. Still holding the horse's reins, he knelt and brushed the snow away. Sunlight glinted off the brass receiver of a Henry repeating rifle. Thad wiped the weapon with his hands and slid it into the saddle scabbard. Carefully, he led the horse down the slope, alternately watching his footing and searching the broken terrain ahead.

Twenty feet downslope, Thad found the man's body. It lay face-down in a low depression, partially covered by snow and sprawled amid a boulder-strewn patch of sagebrush. Kneeling, Thad turned the body onto its back. Bright blood stained the snow around the man's head, and a ragged scalp wound gaped above his left temple. His hands and lips were blue and cold to the touch. Bending low, Thad laid his ear upon the man's chest, listening. Faint and irregular, he heard the heartbeat. "I wondered when I saw you," Thad said aloud, "whether I'd have to doctor you or bury you. For now, at least, it looks like doctoring."

Bracing his feet, Thad bent low and hefted the unconscious man onto his shoulders. Slowly, Thad straightened his legs and stood erect, testing the man's weight. Then, carefully and deliberately, he began the walk down the slope to his cabin. Once there, he slipped the latch and swung the door in, bending low to clear the doorway with his burden. At the rear of the cabin's single room, Thad's bunk was built into the wall. Cushioned by pine boughs atop a lattice-work of ropes, his bed consisted of wool blankets and quilts inside a canvas tarpaulin. Thad laid the stranger on his bed. He undressed the man, covered him with the bedding, and built up the fire in the stove.

As the cabin warmed, Thad rigged a clothesline in the corner above the stove and hung the stranger's wet clothing upon it. Then he put a kettle of water on to boil and re-heated the coffee. He placed the man's gunbelt on the table and frowned. The revolvers were Colt's Navy .36 caliber, their ivory grips yellow from age and handling. The chambers were fully loaded and capped. Thad found a powder flask and percussion caps inside the man's greatcoat. He slipped the Bowie knife from its scabbard and tested its edge. The blade was razor sharp. "You're quite a mystery, my friend," he said. "Whoever you are, you surely go loaded for bear."

Thad stepped outside to find the thoroughbred waiting beside the cabin. He unsaddled the gelding and wiped the animal down with an old flannel shirt. He led it to a south-facing slope below the cabin and hobbled it on good grass near the creek. On his way back, he split an armload of wood and carried it inside. Pouring warm water from the kettle into a basin, he drew up his only chair and sat down beside the stranger. Thad began to cleanse and bandage the man's scalp wound.

In Virginia City, Epiphany and Lily Rae turned their rented buggy uphill and drew rein in front of a vacant log building. Epiphany told herself she must study the building with an analytical eye, but her resolve was in vain. Her bright smile told Lily Rae that Epiphany's emotions had triumphed over her critical judgment. Obviously, her young friend loved the cabin at first sight.

Built into a hillside above Idaho Street, the structure sat atop its rock foundation and looked north across the rooftops of Virginia City to the hills beyond. About forty feet square, the structure contained two glassless windows, a dirt floor, and an open doorway facing the street. Its sod roof gently sloped both ways from the ridgepole to keep the weather out.

Seated beside Epiphany in the rented buggy, Lily Rae Bliss turned the carriage horse uphill and drew rein at the cabin's doorway. A tall, guant man with unkempt hair and beard came out of the building and doffed a well-worn hat. He seemed nervous, abashed by the presence of the women. When he spoke, he failed to meet their eyes.

"Good day to you, ladies," he said. "Name's Cootie Blake. This here's my place."

Epiphany stepped down from the buggy. She smiled, extending her hand. "Epiphany Baker," she said, "thank you for agreeing to meet us."

The man took her hand briefly, then released it. He ducked his head, looking down at the boardwalk between his boots. Awkwardly, he fingered his hat. "Commenced buildin' the cabin back in July," he said. "Went to prospectin' and never finished her."

"You do fine work," Epiphany offered. "You've obviously built cabins before."

"Yes'm. Back home in Michigan."

Epiphany looked inside the cabin, visualizing the tables, counter, and kitchen that would make up her restaurant. She turned back to the lanky prospector. "What is your asking price, Mr. Blake?" she asked.

"Well, ma'm, fact is I don't like to let 'er go atall. Wouldn't, if I didn't need me a grubstake." Blake scratched his beard thoughtfully. After a pause, he said, "I reckon I'd take four hundred."

"I imagine you would," said Epiphany, "but I'm told the going rate for a building this size is no more than two hundred and fifty. That is my offer."

"Why, I couldn't sell her for that, ma'am—I'd need three-fifty at least."

Epiphany looked thoughtful. She was silent for a moment. Then she said, "Very well, Mr. Blake, I'll give you three-fifty if you'll put in a good floor, glass windows, and a proper door."

It was Blake's turn to ponder the offer. "We talkin' gold, ma'am, or paper?"

The question surprised Epiphany. "Why, I hadn't thought," she said. "Does it make a difference?"

"Why, yes, ma'am," Blake said, "it surely does! Lincoln Skins—paper money—ain't worth nearly what gold is. And gold from differ'nt places has differ'nt values, too! Silver Bow gold runs $13.50 to the ounce, Bannack gold maybe $14.50, and Blackfoot gold $16.50. The purest gold of all is from right here in Alder Gulch—it's worth a full $18.50 to the ounce.

"So that's what I'll take. Three-fifty in clean Alder Gulch gold, and I'll put in a floor, windows, and a good door for you, ma'am."

Epiphany glanced at Lily Rae, who nodded her approval. Offering Blake her hand again, Epiphany smiled warmly. "Then I should say we have a bargain, Mr. Blake."

They finalized their agreement at Dance and Stuart's store on Wallace Street. Walter Dance, one of the owners and a friend of Lily Rae's, was also a miners' judge. Under his supervision, the parties executed their agreement. With money received from the sale of the Playfair merchandise to Judge Dance, Epiphany bought enough clean gulch gold to pay Blake $250 for the cabin and lot, with an additional $100 payable on completion of the improvements. A deed was drawn and signed by both parties, Epiphany's signature in her neat school-girl hand, Blake's represented by a careful 'X.'

After Blake left the store, Epiphany thanked Judge Dance. "I hope the money will change Mr. Blake's fortunes," she said. "He seems to have had poor luck."

"Indeed," said Dance, "but I'm afraid his bad luck is largely occasioned by his love for gambling. He sold his claim a month ago and lost the money in a high-stakes poker game. Blake is an excellent carpenter, but a poor gambler. At any rate, he'll do a good job of improving the cabin. Who knows? Perhaps some day he'll even leave the cards alone."

Outside, the women climbed into the buggy and drove off up the street. Epiphany could scarcely contain her excitement, and Lily Rae smiled at her friend's happiness. "Where to now?" she asked, "How shall we celebrate?"

"Oh, Lily Rae—I can't tell you how happy I am!" Epiphany said.

"Owning a business has always been my dream! Let's stop by Will's camp and invite him to join us!"

"Good idea," said Lily Rae. "How about supper at a good restaurant, with wine and all the trimmings? Unless, of course, you'd rather have dinner alone with the handsome Mr. Hunter."

"Don't be silly!" Epiphany said. "Will is—Well, he's a friend, the same as you are."

There was a twinkle in Lily Rae's eye. "The same? Well, maybe not *quite* the same."

"Well, no. . . maybe not the same. . . that is, not really," Epiphany said, plainly flustered. "Oh, you know what I mean."

Lily Rae turned the carriage out onto the road that led to Will Hunter's camp. Beside her, Epiphany felt the heat in her face and knew she was blushing. Grasping one of the uprights that supported the buggy's top, she turned her face away, but too late. Lily Rae had heard her stammer and had seen her flush. "Oh, yes," said Lily Rae, "I know what you mean."

They found Hunter's camp in order, but deserted. The canvas-topped wagons stood close together near the top of a barren hill, harness neatly arranged along the wagon tongues. Hunter's packhorse grazed nearby, greeting the buggy with a high-pitched whinny as the women topped the rise. Near the wagon, rocks rimmed a cold campfire. Fresh snow still lay in patches from the night's storm, but there were no tracks. The black gelding was gone. It was plain Hunter had not been at the camp that morning. Where *was* he?

Despite Epiphany's disappointment at not finding Will Hunter, she and Lily Rae celebrated that evening over supper at a Nevada City restaurant called Frenchy's. Nevada City was only three miles from Virginia City, and, as Lily Rae accurately observed, "that was about as near to Virginia as Nevada would ever be." Frenchy's advertised itself as "the most refined and elegant dining in Alder Gulch," which was probably true, as far as it went. The restaurant had board walls and a canvas top. It boasted red-and-white checkered tablecloths, linen napkins, brass chandeliers, and a puncheon floor. Reasonably clean-shaven waiters in white shirts and ties took the orders and served the meals.

The proprietor, the one and only Frenchy, visited each table to receive the praise, or sometimes the complaints, of the diners.

Epiphany's only complaint was an unspoken one—Will Hunter wasn't with them on this, her special day. She knew he'd been busy since their arrival in the gulch; for that matter, so had she. She had made a list of the Playfair's remaining inventory, including the wagons and mules. She had established the inventory's value through discussions with Judge Dance and other merchants.

With Lily Rae's help, Epiphany composed and wrote a letter to Anson Playfair that included both a business proposal and an account of the tragic deaths of his brother Ramsay and sister-in-law Alice. Epiphany had sent the letter to Springfield by way of the stage to Salt Lake only the day before.

It had also been with Lily Rae's help that Epiphany had found the cabin she intended to make her restaurant, and she had particularly wanted to share the occasion of its purchase with Will Hunter. She laughed and toasted the future with Lily Rae and affected an attitude of gaiety. Throughout the evening, however, her thoughts kept returning to the tall Missourian and their time together on the trail to the gold camps.

She recalled the way Hunter had held her in his arms after the raid at the meadows, and the quiet strength he had shown in the days that followed. She saw him in memory in the flickering glow of the campfire and heard him play again the sweet strains of *Little Annie Laurie* on his fiddle in that place of violence and death. She remembered his hands, brown from the sun, long-fingered and strong, and the gentleness of his touch. His shy smile, the deep sadness she sometimes saw in his eyes, his loping walk that made her think of the captive wolf she'd seen as a child—these were the memories that occupied her mind. Where was Will? Where *was* he?

EIGHT

The Way of the Wicked

WILL HUNTER returned to consciousness slowly, like a man rising to the surface from the bottom of a pond. He was cold, chilled to the depths of his being, and he wondered, "Is this how it feels to be dead?"

"Fool!" his mind replied. "The dead feel nothing."

"So we're told," he thought, "but I don't suppose a man can know that for certain until he dies."

He was confused, weary with a lassitude beyond fatigue. A great trembling shook him. Hunter became aware of a pulsing pain just behind his eyes. It was all he could do to keep from crying out. Where was he? Eyes closed, he stopped fighting. He allowed the pain to have its way. He tried to think and to remember.

Gradually, the way fog lifts from a meadow, remembrance came. He recalled the quick, savage fight at the Mother Lode, the blood lust returning. Memories of Rachel came back, the old, deep hurt recurring. He thought back upon his wild ride in the night. He recalled the horse falling, the sudden, blinding pain, and the darkness.

Hunter lifted his head and opened his eyes. Was it the pain that made thought difficult, or had he somehow grown dull-witted and slow of mind? His reactions dragged; his limbs felt leaden and clumsy. Again, he shivered, pulling the blankets close around him.

He saw that he was inside a cabin. A young man in a red-checked wool shirt stood across the room, warming himself at a small cookstove. Hunter tried to speak, but his throat was dry, his voice a husky rasp. "Where. . ." he croaked. "Who. . ."

The young man turned away from the stove, his smile open and warm. "Easy, friend," he said. "You've had a bad fall, but you're going to be all right."

The man poured boiling water into a large tin cup. Hunter breathed in a strong astringent odor. "Sage tea," the young man said, carrying the steaming cup toward the bed. "It will warm you inside and out." His arm supporting Hunter's back, the young man brought the cup to his lips.

Hunter drank deeply, downing nearly half the tea before stopping. He found his voice, "Who. . . are you?" he asked.

The young man smiled. "Thad Mitchell," he said. "I found you sleeping in a snowbank this morning, using a boulder for a pillow. Figured I'd bury you, but you weren't quite ready."

Hunter closed his eyes, remembering. "My horse. Did you. . ."

"He's all right. Just a scratch or two. I took your saddle off and hobbled him down by the creek."

Thad was silent for a time. Then he said, "I saw your tracks. You were riding at a full gallop last night when your horse went belly-up. You were riding as if the devil was on your tail."

"Maybe he was," Hunter said. He opened his eyes. "I'm glad the horse is all right," Hunter said. "It's not his fault his master's a damn fool."

Thad lifted the cup again, and Hunter drank the rest of the tea. He lay back. "Good." he said, "I'm obliged."

"Get some rest," Thad said. "I'm going down and check my sluices. When I come back I'll fry up some steaks."

Hunter had drifted off to sleep again before Thad reached the door.

———◈———

In a small private room at the rear of The Glory Hole Saloon, Henry Plummer poured three fingers of whiskey in a glass and slid it across the table to Bravo Santee. The two men were a study in contrasts. Plummer, sheriff of both the Bannack and Fairweather mining districts, was neatly dressed in a checkered shirt, cravat, and black business suit. His face was smooth and clean-shaven except for a small, neatly trimmed mustache. His manner was that of a gentleman.

Santee was small and wiry, with cold yellow eyes and dirty, shoulder-length hair. His teeth were broken and irregular, stained by the constant use of plug tobacco. He slouched back in his chair in an attitude that somehow managed to mix servility with arrogance.

"Now then," said Plummer, "you said you can tell me about Will Hunter."

"I kin tell you ah came all the way from Missouri to kill the sum'bitch," Bravo replied.

"That is unusual," Plummer said. "Most men come here to get rich."

"Gettin' rich don't interest me a hell of a lot. Money comes easy to them with the guts to take it. I'm here to even a score."

"And what might that be?"

"Hunter kilt my brother."

"Did he have a reason?"

Santee's yellow eyes flashed cold fire. "Reasons don't signify. Man kills my brother, I kill the man. That's the Santee way."

"You're not telling me much about Hunter," Plummer said. "Where did you know him?"

"On the Kansas-Missouri border. Him an' me rode with Quantrill."

"That tells me you can fight. So you rode for the South?"

"Hell, no. Rode for Quantrill. Quantrill was my chief."

Plummer shrugged. "I'm chief here," he said. "How would you like to ride for me?"

"Wouldn't mind, mebbe. Long as I get to kill Will Hunter."

"If you work for me, you'll do what you're told," Plummer said. "When I tell you to do it. You'll ride good horses, you'll have women, whiskey, whatever you want—the best the diggings can offer. As for Hunter, he's yours; but not until I say so. Understood?"

Santee downed the whiskey in his glass in a single swallow. For a moment he studied Plummer's face. Then he pushed the glass across for a refill and shrugged. "You're the chief," he said.

George Ives sprawled naked amid the tangled bedclothes and dreamed of his boyhood back in Racine County, Wisconsin. In the dream he roamed the woods near his family home with a wooden gun and a dog named Nappy, hunting make-believe grizzly bears, Bengal tigers, and men.

Beside him in the bed, Josie Mulhare propped herself on an elbow and studied him by the flat, gray light of morning. In repose, Ives's face had a boyish, innocent look. The bold, knowing eyes were closed. Lips that formed the smile that moved her—lips that charmed and chilled, flattered, and cursed her—were relaxed now, slightly open against the pillow. Even in the dull light his blonde, disheveled hair shone like the fine gold he brought her.

Josie swung her legs off the side of the bed and sat up. She drew her silken wrapper across her bare shoulders. She poured herself a glass of whiskey from the bottle beside the bed and drank, feeling the liquor's warmth spread to her chest and belly. Josie smiled. "Real whiskey," she thought, "I dance every night with men who pay for whiskey, but buy only cold tea. I deal in false whiskey, false affection, and false desire. Only the gold is real."

"Except with George Ives," she thought. "With George it's always been real—the gold, the whiskey, the affection, and the desire." Once or twice a month, Ives came late to her door and asked to stay the night. She liked it that he asked. No matter how tired or low she might be, seeing Ives made her heart skip like a schoolgirl's. She would always be there for him, and he knew it.

Josie had turned twenty-five just the week before, but she had been a sporting woman since her seventeenth birthday. She had worked mining camps from California and Nevada to Idaho Territory. By day she danced in a house on Wallace Street; at night she entertained men at her small cabin behind the dance hall. Like the others along the gulch, Josie had come to the diggings for the gold. She had also come because George Ives was there.

She had met George in California five years before. He'd been a wild young miner then, and she'd been the star attraction of the best parlor house in town. When he had exploded into Josie's life, Ives had not yet embarked on the life of crime he would later pursue. By the time he'd moved on to a job herding—and stealing—government mules in Washington Territory, Josie had found herself hopelessly in love with him. She knew that to admit the fact would make her a laughing-stock of her profession. One of the oldest jokes among the working girls was the sporting woman who fell in love with her client.

They had met again a year later in a gold camp called Elk City, back above the Selway. Ives had graduated to a career in banditry by then; and Josie was still popular, if no longer the camp's star attrac-tion. Later, when word came of the rich strikes at Bannack and Alder Gulch, Ives had followed the gold, and Josie had followed him.

Ives stirred. He sat up, stretched, and yawned. He felt light-headed and disoriented; at first he couldn't make out where he was. A dull ache throbbed behind his temples, and his mouth had a dry, cottony taste. The air in the cabin was stale, the odors a sour blend of whiskey, carbolic acid, cigar smoke, and cheap perfume. Eyes still closed, Ives groped for the bedside table, felt the woman beside him, and remem-bered. He fumbled for the whiskey bottle, found it, and drank deeply.

"What time is it?" he asked.

"About seven," she said, "you slept well, lover."

"Damn," said Ives, "I'm supposed to meet Henry at seven-thirty. Where's my pants?"

Josie bent, picking up Ives' clothing from the cabin floor where he'd discarded it. She handed him the garments and padded across to the small kerosene stove that heated the cabin. His coat, hat, and revolver belt were draped over the back of a Windsor chair. His muddy boots stood on the floor beside it. Ives dressed quickly, pulled on the boots, and buckled the gunbelt about his waist. The coffee was hot. Josie poured a cup and smiling, handed it to Ives. He sipped, made a face, and emptied the cup into the slop jar.

"It's a good thing you're a whore," he said, "because you're too damn dumb to even make decent coffee."

Her smile froze and her face grew taut. She was accustomed to insults from men, but Ives's words could still cause her pain. The warmth faded from her eyes, and Ives saw that he had hurt her. Eyes narrowed, he studied her face. It was a mistake to look at her in the morning, he thought. A man ought to just take his pleasure and go his way by night. In the cold daylight he saw the dark rings beneath her eyes, the crow's feet at their corners, and the deep lines at the sides of her mouth. "The poor bitch is getting old," he thought. "That claim is just about played out."

Ives produced a buckskin poke from his vest pocket and placed a gold double eagle on the table beside the bed. "You're a fine piece, Josie. Be seein' you," he said.

According to the clock behind the bar, it was 7:28 in the morning when George Ives walked through the front door of Cy Skinner's saloon on Cover Street. Henry Plummer stood at the bar, drinking coffee with a small, wiry man Ives had never seen before. As Ives closed the door behind him, he heard Plummer say, "Pay me." He watched Cy Skinner, behind the bar, curse and slap money into the sheriff's outstretched hand.

"Damn you, George Ives," Skinner groused. "Your goddam punctuality has cost me money."

Plummer smiled his thin smile. "Cy bet me five dollars that you'd show up late this morning," Plummer said. "I told him you'd be on time."

Cy Skinner had been a saloon keeper and associate of Ives and Plummer at least as far back as 1861, during the rich placer strikes on the Salmon River. He and Plummer had known each other since they were fellow inmates at San Quentin in 1859. Skinner was also a thief, a killer, and a pimp. He had established his Elkhorn Saloon at Bannack in the early days of the camp's gold rush. Later, when miners made the even more fabulous strike at Alder Gulch, he had opened a second saloon in Virginia City.

Skinner poured Ives a cup of coffee and slid it across the bar. "Josie must be losin' her touch," Skinner said. "Used to be, you'd be at her place all night and 'til noon the next day."

Skinner wiped a spill from the bar, careful not to look at Ives. "Of course, it could be you ain't the stud you once was," he said, "or maybe you slipped out while she was sleepin' so you wouldn't have to pay her."

Ives grinned broadly. He sipped the coffee. "Hell, Cy," he said, "I don't pay women—women pay *me*."

Over the rim of his cup, Ives studied the stranger beside Plummer. The man was short, barely five feet four, bandy-legged, and lean. He wore high-topped boots, a gray Confederate jacket over stained woolen breeches, and he carried a pair of Colt's Dragoon revolvers and a Bowie knife on a wide belt about his waist. Beneath his narrow-brimmed black hat, the man's long hair was the gray color of dirty dishwater. The stranger stood stock still, hips thrust forward and thumbs hooked into his gunbelt. Only his sly yellow eyes seemed alive.

Ives set the cup down and looked at Plummer. "Well, Henry," he said, "You sent for me."

"Meet Bravo Santee," Plummer said. "He's going to be riding with us. I want you to take him over to the Rattlesnake and get him situated. He'll be a roadster on the Bannack side, at least for now."

Ives nodded. He looked down at Santee and offered his hand. "George Ives," he said, "welcome to 'The Innocents'."

George Ives and Bravo Santee rode out of Virginia City in the thin light of an overcast morning. Above the Tobacco Roots the sun was a pale glow behind the cloud cover, like a worn spot in a garment. The two men turned their horses onto the road, meeting both riders and men on foot. They rode in the billowing dust of a string of freight wagons. At Central they found the road busy as a boulevard, choked with wagons, riders, and pack strings. The traffic thinned but little all the way to Junction, where Alder met Granite Creek.

Ives slowed his horse to a walk and reined in beside Santee. "Henry told me to fill you in on the way things work around here," he said. "This is the short version. The prospectors in the gulches try to keep their gold, and we try to take it from them. They try to ship their dust and nuggets back to the States. We try to intercept the shipments. There's only seventy or so of us, but we do pretty well because we're well-organized.

"Henry heads up the outfit. Bill Bunton, down on the Rattlesnake, is second in command. George Brown is our secretary. Cy Skinner is fence, roadster, and spy. We've got spies in all the settlements. In Virginia, "Clubfoot" George Lane has a shoemaker set-up at Dance & Stuart's store. When he hears a miner is about to send his gold out, "Clubfoot" passes the word on, and we send roadsters out to ambush the shipment."

Ives drew a silver case from inside his coat, removed a cigar, and offered the case to Santee. Santee shook his head, taking instead a tobacco plug from his pocket and biting off a corner. The men rode on in silence as Ives struck a match and lit the stogie. When satisfied the cigar was burning well, he turned back to Santee. "Henry is a hell of an organizer," Ives said. "He put his first outfit together back on the Salmon, and it worked well. It's working even better here."

"It doesn't hurt us any that he got himself elected sheriff of both the Bannack and Fairweather mining districts," Ives said, chuckling. "Old Henry's the nearest law in a thousand miles, and he's our leader."

Ives looked intently at Santee. He had expected some reaction to his words—a comment, a question, even a nod—but Santee stared straight ahead, his face impassive, his expression unreadable. Ives shrugged, accepting the man's silence, and turned his own eyes back to the road before them.

As the canyon deepened, the road turned rough, breaking out on Ramshorn Creek at Daly's Roadhouse. From there, the two men turned their horses down the valley of the Stinkingwater, crossing the river at Baker's ranch. A short distance further, they passed Dempsey's ranch, a relay point for the new stage line. After Dempsey's, the road became a trail which climbed to the bluffs beyond the river and wound west across a range of low hills.

Ives was lost in his own thoughts. He had almost forgotten the small man riding beside him. He was suddenly startled out of his reveries when Santee spoke.

"This mornin' you said, 'Welcome to the Innocents.' What did you mean by that?"

Ives pulled his thoughts back, trying to recall their earlier conversation. "'Innocents' is the name of our outfit," Ives said. "We're all 'Innocents.' Our password is 'Innocent.' We take an oath to stand by each other, to be loyal, and to do what Henry and the higher-ups in the outfit tell us to do. The penalty for disobedience is death. If a man reveals the outfit's secrets, or betrays a fellow member, some of the boys will track him down and shoot him on sight. Our purpose is to acquire plunder, by whatever means is necessary."

Santee rode in silence for a time. Then he said, "If there's seventy-some men in the outfit, you damn sure can't know every man by sight when you meet him. How do you get around that?"

"Two ways. The boys wear their neck scarves tied in a special square sailor's knot, like this one," Ives said, showing his own scarf; "and they wear mustaches and chin whiskers."

"*You* don't," said Santee. "You're clean-shaved as a choir boy, and I expect to be the same. Ain't wearin' no damn mustache and chin whiskers."

"Unless you're *told* to," Ives said coldly.

"*You* tellin' me to?"

"Suppose I am?"

Again, Santee fell silent. He frowned, working on the question. In war, a man obeyed the orders of his leaders. Back on the border, he had obeyed Quantrill. In return, he had been permitted—had even been ordered—to kill, destroy, and plunder. Santee decided the requirement was reasonable, a proper bargain. "If you are," he said, "I'll grow my whiskers any way you say to. But I druther not."

Ives laughed. "I'm easy," laughed Ives. "Wear your damn face hair any way you please."

Fourteen miles from the Stinkingwater they rode past Copeland's ranch, going on to Stone's Roadhouse where they rested their horses and shared a noon meal of venison stew, fry bread, and beer. At mid-afternoon they reined up at Bill Bunton's ranch on the Rattlesnake and turned their horses out.

NINE
Past and Prologue

W HEN WILL HUNTER next awoke in the cabin on Alder Gulch, he found that the pain in his head had greatly lessened. The paralyzing chill and the deep fatigue he'd felt earlier had subsided. His mind had cleared; and, best sign of all, his appetite had returned.

The cabin was warm. In the corner above the cookstove, Hunter saw his clothing draped over a line. His hat and coat hung on a peg near the cabin door, and his boots stood on the floor beside the woodbox. Hunter raised himself on his elbows, scanning the room. Something was missing. Nowhere in the small cabin did he see his gunbelt, or the holstered revolvers and knife he had carried. He noted with cynical amusement the anxiety their absence produced, and re-membered his short-lived resolution to put the weapons aside. He recalled the brief, savage fight with Gallagher at the Mother Lode and the way his first response to the man's insult had been to reach for his guns. He remembered his words to John Oakes that same day:

"I've come a long way, looking for a place I could take my guns off." And he remembered Oakes' reply: "You ain't found it yet, son."

Hunter stiffened. From just outside the cabin door came the scuffling sound of booted feet on gravel. The sound stopped. Hunter held his breath, his eyes on the door. The latch slowly lifted from its slot, and the door swung inward. A blonde young man carrying a dozen sticks of firewood stepped through the doorway, smiling. "Good!" he said. "You're awake. Don't know how you feel, but you sure do look better."

Hunter felt the tension drain from him. He had been holding his breath; now he breathed again. He recognized the young man as the man who had bandaged his head wound, who had given him sagebrush tea and his own bed. What was it he'd said his name was? Ted? Todd? No, *Thad.* That was it, Thad Mitchell. Hunter smiled. "I'm feeling better, too," he said, "better, and grateful for the care."

"It's not over yet," Thad said, dropping the stove wood into the box. "I promised you venison steaks, and that's just what we'll have—as soon as I can heat up a skillet." After adding fresh wood to the fire box, he greased a heavy black iron skillet and placed it atop the stove. "Picked up a few spuds earlier this week," Thad went on. "We'll fry them up to go with the steaks. Storekeepers are asking a dollar a pound for spuds, when they have them." Thad's grin was open, friendly. "When they *don't* have them, I guess they're free."

Hunter sat up in bed and grinned. "It's plain to see this is a first-class hotel," he said, "so if you'll hand me my clothes, I believe I'll dress for dinner."

After the meal, the two men drank coffee together outside the cabin and watched the shadows lengthen along Alder Creek. Beyond Thad's claim, other miners worked in the late light and occasionally called out to each other across the way. Here and there along the gulch, campfires flickered as men prepared their suppers. "That was a fine meal," Hunter said. "I'm in your debt, Thad. I wish there was some way I could repay you."

"You could tell me your name," Thad said, "unless you'd rather not."

Hunter laughed. "It's no secret," he said. "My name is Will Hunter. I've only been in the gulch for a week. Now can I ask you a question?"

"Fire away."

"I was wearing a pair of Navy thirty-sixes and a Bowie knife when I had my horse wreck. Do you know where they are?"

Thad took a long sip of his coffee before he answered. "A man can't be too careful these days," he said. "Thought it best to put your weapons away until we were better acquainted. They're in the cabin, on the peg beneath your coat."

Thad looked thoughtful. "Will Hunter," he said, repeating the name, "Will Hunter. Say! Aren't you the man who rescued the girl from the raid on the Playfair wagons? The one who killed the three Bannocks?"

"How did you hear about that?"

"Miners' telegraph," Thad said. "There's not much that happens in the district that doesn't get passed along as news. You *are* the man, aren't you?"

"I was almost too late," Hunter said. "If I'd showed up sooner, three others might be alive."

Thad smiled. He offered his hand to Hunter. "I'd like to shake your hand," he said, "and apologize for what I thought you were."

Thad's grip was firm and dry, Hunter noted. He liked the young man, he decided. He liked his open, honest way. "And what," he asked, "did you think I was?"

"There are other men in the gulch who carry two guns," Thad said. "Men who kill without thought, men who take what they didn't earn. Every gold camp has their kind, but they're worse here."

"John Oakes said something along that line. Said the rough element here is organized, and that they somehow get word when gold is shipped and intercept it. I said, 'That's the sheriff's problem, isn't it?' Oakes said, 'Some people think the sheriff *is* the problem.'"

"That kind of talk is dangerous," Thad said. "Word gets back to the wrong people, and the talker disappears."

For a time Hunter was silent, weighing the young miner's words. Then he stood, stretched, and looked below at the grassy patch beyond the gravel where his hobbled gelding grazed. "Thought I'd walk down and see how much damage I did my horse," he said, "and apologize to him."

"I'll go with you," said Thad. "Show you my claim."

The two men walked together down the rocky slope that led to Alder Creek. Hunter's thoroughbred stood beside the swirling waters, head high, watching their approach. Catching their scent, the horse nickered softly, the sound a deep rumble in its throat.

Hunter strode through the grass to where the animal stood, reached out and stroked its neck. "Hello, old soldier," he said. "You're looking well, no thanks to me."

Gently, Hunter's fingers stroked the thoroughbred's long back, carefully probing its fetlocks and pasterns. He removed the hobbles and lifted each foot, examining the gelding's hooves. Satisfied, he replaced the hobbles and gave the animal a solid pat on its rump.

The openness and vulnerability on Hunter's countenance surprised and moved Thad as the older man turned to speak to him. "Again, Thad," he said, "I'm greatly obliged. I hope I have the chance to repay you."

Thad grinned. "Well," he said, "I can always use a friend. Working a claim all day, every day, a man misses having people of character to talk to."

Thad's grin became a full smile. "I figure a man who apologizes to horses must surely be a man of character."

Back at the cabin, Thad and Hunter sat outside around a campfire and watched the first stars appear. Along the gulch, other campfires blazed before the cabins, tents, and brush shelters of the miners; and lanterns glowed dull orange at ridgepole and rafter.

"There are plenty of good men in these diggings, but the roughs have gained the upper hand," Thad said. "Almost every week there's word of another man killed or robbed by road agents, and the bad ones seem to be getting bolder."

The young man's face seemed more mature in the firelight. He looked thoughtful, somber. "Henry Plummer came to Bannack a year ago in the company of a loudmouth named Jack Cleveland," he began. "They seemed an unlikely pair at the time—Plummer was well-dressed, well-spoken, and popular—a born leader, people said.

"Cleveland was a surly drunk, a skulker, and a bully. Before long, it seemed there'd been some kind of falling-out between him and Plummer. Cleveland made threats, and the bad blood built. Then one day Cleveland pushed too hard and Plummer shot him down—put three balls into him and left him to die.

"Hank Crawford and Harry Phleger, two decent men, took the dying man to Crawford's place. Hank took care of him as best he could until he died three hours later. The next day Charley Reeves and Charley Moore, two of Plummer's friends, shot up an Indian camp over a runaway squaw Reeves had bought from the Bannocks. They killed the old chief, a baby, and a Frenchman named Cazette. Two other men heard the ruckus and came to see what was going on. The boys shot and badly wounded them, too.

"Henry Plummer had already left Bannack—said he was afraid the townsfolk would string him up for shooting Cleveland. Reeves and Moore lit out on foot just after he did, also in fear of the rope.

"Volunteers caught and brought them back to Bannack for trial. Plummer was tried and set free—people figured he'd shot Cleveland in self-defense. Everyone in Bannack knew the other two men were guilty. The camp wanted to convene a miners' court, but Reeves and Moore demanded a trial by jury, figuring they could bluff a jury. Turned out they were right. Their friends yelled, swore, fired their guns in the air, waved their weapons under the noses of the jury members, and threatened their lives if they found the boys guilty. The miners lost their nerve. The vote was eleven not guilty and only one guilty!

"The jury voted to banish the killers instead. A miner's court revoked that sentence, and the roughs began their takeover of the diggings. They believed they had the decent people buffaloed. They believe it even more today. Who's to stand against them? Sheriff Plummer? He became sheriff after he ran off Hank Crawford, the former sheriff. Nearly all of Plummer's friends and deputies are part of the rough element."

The campfire had died to embers. Thad fell quiet, stirring the dying coals with a stick. He added fresh wood to the fire and watched as the flames blossomed and lit the night. Somewhere, far in the distance, a coyote sang.

"Some said Plummer hired deputies like Jack Gallagher, Buck Stinson, and the like because he couldn't get anyone else to take the job. Some thought otherwise. Most of us couldn't be bothered. We were too busy working our claims, minding our stores, and hauling freight to worry about such things. Then they struck gold here at Alder Gulch and the prospectors—me included—stampeded over from Bannack.

"The hardcases—the bully-boys and killers—only got stronger. Now they control this entire region, from Bannack to the settlements here. They're robbing travelers in broad daylight. They're intercepting gold shipments, holding up coaches and wagons, and killing men for the money in their pockets.

"Plummer appointed four deputies to keep the law in Virginia City. Three of them are thugs and hardcases—Buck Stinson, Ned Ray, and Jack Gallagher—and one was an honest man—Don Dillingham. The first three planned to rob a miner who'd made a rich strike and was taking his gold out.

Dillingham threatened to arrest the plotters. They sneered at his threat, and he marched off to a miners' court being held that day on another matter—a claim-jumping case, I think.

"The other deputies stopped him just outside the court and shot him dead—right in front of nearly a hundred miners! The court tried the three, found them guilty, and sentenced them to hang. Many of the prospectors went back to their claims, but the toughs gathered in force. A crowd of drunks, rowdies, and whores from Skinner's saloon showed up, calling for the killers' release. Things got pretty confused—witnesses left, the judge left, and somehow the sentence got changed to banishment. The three rode out of town, but none of them left the area. The toughs had won again."

Thad stood, looking up at the night sky. Scattered across the blackness, clear and bright stars spangled the night. Beyond the distant mountains, a wan moon had risen. In the distance the coyote sang again.

"I tell you all this," Thad said, "so you'll know the way things are here.

"I've worked hard on my claim, and I've done well. Like every other miner, I know trying to take my gold out can get me killed. So I wait and hope for change. I still believe change will come, but I don't know how or when."

A cold wind sighed up the gulch, bringing a chill to the night air. The coals glowed fitfully and faded as the gust passed. Hunter had been whittling on a piece of alder wood while Thad had been talking. He snapped his pocket-knife closed and tossed the stick onto the dying embers.

"Brings to mind a passage of scripture my dad used to quote," Hunter said, "from Matthew 24: 'For wheresoever the carcase is, there will the eagles be gathered together.'"

"A golden carcass," Thad said, "and killer eagles."

———◈———

Morning dawned clean-edged and bright along Alder Gulch, the sunlight striking diamonds from the frost-rimed grass at the edges of the creek. Ice crystals formed like lace where the waters met the creek's bank and sun-bright vapor hung radiant above the stream. All along the gulch, miners emerged from their cabins, tents, and wakiups. They built their fires, cooked and ate their bacon and beans, and descended to the gravel piles that marked their claims. They studied the drift of bar and bedrock, shoveled dirt into rockers, long toms, and sluices. Fueled by hope and dreams of fortune, the miners bent to their labors and began another day at the diggings.

Above the creek, Thad Mitchell leaned against the woodpile beside his cabin and watched Will Hunter apply brush and currycomb to his gelding. In the two days and nights Hunter had stayed at his cabin Thad had come to like and admire the tall Missourian. He sensed a guarded melancholy in the man that seemed designed to keep others at arm's length.

Hunter swept the brush and comb in long, smooth strokes across the thoroughbred's ribs, belly, and flanks, paying particular attention to areas touched by the saddle and girth. He completed the grooming by thoroughly wiping the animal with a soft cloth. Then he lifted the saddle onto its back, and tightened the cinch.

"Watching you brush out that horse is like watching a mama cat groom her kittens," Thad said.

Hunter laughed. "We have been together awhile," he said. "I find he generally treats me well if I return the favor. We're both from the "show me" state of Missouri, so we need constant showing, I guess."

Hunter stood at the animal's shoulder and looked thoughtfully at Thad. He said simply, "I'm in your debt, Thad. Much obliged, until you're better paid."

Thad held out his hand and Hunter took it in a strong, firm grip. "You're welcome any time," Thad said. "The latch-string is always out." Hunter replied with a nod, swung into the saddle, and rode out for Virginia City.

———◈———

When Hunter drew rein at his own camp, John Oakes was waiting. He stood in the lee of the Playfair wagons, squinting against the sun. He grinned as Hunter stepped down. "About time you came home," Oakes said. "I've been up here four times in the last two days looking for you. You weren't here."

Hunter's grin matched the older man's. "That's probably because I was someplace else," he said. "What can I do for you, John?"

Oakes seated himself on a nail keg beside Hunter's fire pit and rubbed a gnarled hand across his beard stubble. "You can hear me out," he said. "I've got a business proposition for you."

Hunter stacked pitch pine and kindling inside the fire pit and struck a match. Shielding the flame from the wind, he set the wood ablaze. "I'm listening," Hunter said. "I'll put the coffee on."

He filled the blackened pot from the water barrel and placed it on the windward side of the fire. Then he sat cross-legged in the grass and looked across the flames at Oakes.

"I'm a freighter," Oakes began, "always have been. Freighted back in the States. When I decided to come out to the gold fields, I headed up the train that included these wagons of yours." Oakes removed a briar pipe from the pocket of his sheepskin and filled it with tobacco from a leather pouch. "Thing is, I'm figuring to expand. I'd like to buy your wagons and mules."

Hunter added wood to the fire. "I don't know, John," he said. "I was thinking of doing some freighting myself. Maybe we could work together."

Taking a burning splinter from the fire, Oakes lit his pipe and sent a stream of smoke out into the wind. "Maybe," Oakes agreed, "but that brings me to the other reason I've been looking for you.

"Two friends of mine—Albert Hess and Bill Fitzhugh—have made good strikes up near Summit. Between them, they've taken nearly five thousand in dust from their claims since June. They heard I was headed for Salt Lake with a string of freight wagons and asked me if I'd take their gold out for them.

"I told them no. Reason I can't take their gold out is the same reason they can't. Road agents get wind of every shipment that leaves the gulch, and they hold up the carrier. Whether Albert and Bill try to take their dust out on horseback, ship it out by stage, or send it with my freight outfit those damn killers will get it."

"Where's the gold now?" Hunter asked.

"Locked up in the safe at Dance and Stuart's store," Oakes said. "Walter Dance allowed they could leave it with him for the time being."

The coffee pot had begun to boil. Hunter moved the pot to a flat rock and poured in a cup of cold water to settle the grounds. "I sympathize with your friends," he said, "but what does their problem have to do with me?"

Oakes' pipe had gone out. He took a branch from the campfire and lit it again. "Back in Florence in '62 some of the boys found a system that worked," he said. "They hired a few good men who knew how to handle horses and weapons and sent their dust out with them."

"I still don't see—"

"What I just said about those men at Florence pretty well describes *you*.

"You're a good man and you know how to handle weapons. That leggy thoroughbred you ride has to be one of the finest horses in the territory. From what I've seen, you're not afraid of a blessed thing."

Hunter poured two cups of coffee and handed Oakes one. "I told you, John, I've had my fill of fighting," Hunter said. "I'm not the man you need."

"I told Albert and Bill you are," Oakes said. "They've agreed to pay you $250 each, if you'll do it."

Hunter frowned. "I said no, John. Get someone else."

Carefully, Oakes placed his cup on the ground. "Like who? There is no one else. The men in the gulch have noticed you, Will. They know about your stand against the war party at the Meadows, and they've heard about the way you took Gallagher down in front of Plummer at the Mother Lode. They have you pegged as a fighting man—someone to stand between them and the roughs."

Hunter's voice was brittle. "They have me pegged wrong," he said. "I carry no badge, and I'm no man's hero! I'm sorry, John, but the answer is no."

John Oakes stood up, pounding out the ashes from his pipe on the palm of his hand. "I'm sorry, too, son," he said, "I guess I had you pegged wrong, too."

Oakes turned to walk away, stopped, and looked back at Hunter. "I'll be at the Virginia Hotel until noon tomorrow in case you change your mind."

"I won't."

Hunter watched John Oakes ride away through the windblown grass toward the distant bustle that was Virginia City. The day that had begun in bright hope had changed with the conversation. It now seemed dreary, and spoiled, somehow. Hunter felt his anger ebb, changing to something very like depression. Oakes had no right to ask that of me, he thought. I want only to mind my own business and allow others to do the same.

You did need Thad's help, said the voice inside his head; *but you're right, of course—it is well for a man to receive help, but not to give it. You're wise not to.*

Shut up, he told the voice, I've had enough of you, too. I made the right decision.

If that's so, said the voice, *why do you feel so guilty?*

TEN

When Men and Mountains Meet

WILL HUNTER had only been away for two days, and yet it almost seemed Virginia City had doubled in size. Freight wagons, pack-strings, and foot traffic thronged Wallace Street as he threaded his way up the thoroughfare on the black gelding. Burly teamsters off-loaded boxes and crates from a high-sided wagon in front of Dance and Stuart's. A beer wagon loaded with barrels clattered past on its way to re-supply the town's saloons. The drinking places, hurdy houses, and gambling halls were wide-open and boisterous even at that early hour; and new frame buildings stood proudly on their lots in nearly every block, appearing as if by magic, like mushrooms after a rain.

Hunter turned the thoroughbred off Wallace and up a side street to Lily Rae's boarding house, drawing rein at the front door. He loose-tied the gelding, climbed the front steps, and rang the bell. Lily Rae answered the door herself, smiling when she saw him. "So you're back," she said. "Come in, Will."

Hunter doffed his hat, ducking his head as he stepped through the doorway. "Good morning, Lily Rae," he said. "It's good to see you. Is Epiphany in?"

Lily Rae cocked her head slightly to one side, appraising Hunter with her frank, steady gaze. Beneath her apron she wore a green-checked gingham dress that set off her hazel eyes, and her hair shone like burnished copper in the morning light. Hunter thought again what he had when he first met her: "What a handsome woman."

"Piff is over at her new building on Idaho Street," Lily Rae said. "She bought it day before yesterday from a man named Blake."

She looked at Hunter intently, then lowered her eyes. She seems troubled, Hunter thought. Then she looked at the bandage that covered his forehead, and her eyes grew soft. "I see you've been injured."

Hunter's hand made a deprecating gesture. "It's nothing," he said. "My horse fell with me. My own fault."

"Come into the kitchen," she said, taking his hand. "I'll have a look."

"There's no need," he protested. "Don't trouble yourself."

"Do as I say," she told him, and he knew there was no use in arguing. Meekly, Hunter followed her to the kitchen and sat down at the table. From a cabinet beside the stove, Lily Rae produced bandages, cotton balls, scissors, and a bottle of alcohol. She placed the items on the table and sat down beside Hunter. She removed the old bandage from his head and examined the wound. "Just as I thought," she said, "that cut isn't closing the way it should. It's going to need stitches."

"Please don't trouble yourself, Lily Rae," Hunter said, embarrassed by the attention.

"I may not be a doctor," said Lily Rae, bathing the wound with alcohol; "but between caring for my late husband and tending the hurts of my boarders, I've become a fairly skilled medicine woman. One of the things you men seem to do best is get yourselves hurt, and somebody has to repair the damage. Now I'm going to pour you a glass of whiskey. Then I'm going to sew that cut so it will heal properly.

"The only way you can prevent that is to get up right now and bolt from this house, and I can't believe you'd be that rude."

Hunter laughed. "You win, Lily Rae. Bring on the whiskey."

With forearms on the table, Will Hunter closed his eyes as Lily Rae closed the wound above his temple with needle and thread. The whiskey had warmed and relaxed him, and he submitted to her care with gratitude. "I'm glad Piff found her building," he said. "I'm sure she'll do well."

"She'll be happy to see you," Lily Rae said. "She wanted very much to share her find with you."

Lily Rae was silent for a time. Hunter felt her deft fingers and endured the needle's sting, the tug of the thread. At last when she was finished, she replaced his bandage with a fresh one.

"Be careful with her, Will," Lily Rae said softly.

Hunter opened his eyes. Lily Rae was watching him, her expression serious. "I believe Epiphany fancies she's in love with you," she said.

Surprise and confusion were clear on Hunter's face. He opened his mouth to reply, but was unable to find the words. "That can't be true," he said at last. "I didn't. . . I never encouraged her. . ."

Lily Rae leaned across the table and touched his hand. "I didn't for a moment think you had," she said, "but you rescued her and protected her. You've become her shining knight. Now she thinks she loves you. There's no accounting for a woman's heart."

"I do care for her," Hunter said. "I suppose I think of her as a daughter, or a favorite niece. But I certainly never—"

"I know, Will. I'm sorry if I was blunt. Sometimes I tend to be too plain spoken by half, but I felt I had to tell you. I know neither of us wants to see her hurt."

Hunter stood. He held his hat before him, looking down at his hands. "Of course not," he said, "thank you for telling me. I'm glad she has you for a friend."

Lily Rae smiled. "I'm glad she has you for a shining knight," she said. "Take care of yourself, Will Hunter."

———◈———

Hunter turned the black gelding up Idaho Street at a trot, his thoughts troubled. "I did not intend this," he thought. "I gave her no reason to think of me that way."

The voice that spoke inside his head asked: *Are you so certain? Perhaps she sensed that you have, shall we say, certain feelings for her?*

"Damn you!" thought Hunter, "I nearly killed Gallagher for making that suggestion!"

Because he was wrong, asked the voice, *or because he was right?*

"I don't think of Epiphany that way!"

You may deny it, but you do. Sometimes you do. Be honest.

"All right, maybe sometimes I do. She looks so much like. . . That is, she is an attractive young woman; but, by heaven, I would never do anything to hurt her."

Whatever you do now will hurt her, said the voice.

"Then," Hunter thought sadly, "I'll just have to find the way that hurts her least."

Epiphany brushed a strand of her fine, blonde hair from her eyes and surveyed the interior of the cabin that was to be her restaurant. Cootie Blake had been as good as his word; the cabin now boasted a solid door, glass in both front windows, and a plank floor. A tavern keeper named Mortimer had recently surprised the Gulch by dying a natural death, and his widow had sold the saloon's furnishings and returned to her relatives back East. From her Epiphany had acquired three circular tables, twelve oak chairs, and some shelving. Planks placed atop barrels had become her lunch counter, and the stove and utensils from the Playfair wagons provided the essentials for equipping her kitchen. She had talked to Blake about building a partition between the dining area and the kitchen. He had agreed to do the job and take meals at the restaurant as payment.

Epiphany was pleased with what she'd accomplished, but eager to see the work finished and the restaurant open for business. She needed a better stove, a range with a warming oven and reservoir if she could find one. She needed more shelves and bins in the kitchen, a pie safe, dishes, curtains for the windows, tablecloths—the list seemed endless. Epiphany saw her restaurant not as it was, but as it would be. In her imagination she saw the customers—miners and freighters, businessmen and clerks, hungry, hard-working men—sitting at her counter, at her tables. She saw them eating the meals she'd prepared, heard their compliments, and received their payment in the glittering gold of the gulch.

The vision inspired her, but she knew that making her business a success would take careful planning and hard work. She had never been afraid of work. She had worked hard since she was a child. This time, however, her labor would be not for others but for herself. She would build the future she'd long dreamed. Alder Gulch offered her opportunity, and she intended to capitalize on it.

She walked to the cabin's open door and looked out. Virginia City was a booming camp. In time the town might become a great city, a place of commerce and prosperity. Her friend Lily Rae had warned her that mining camps had uncertain futures; they might flourish for a season, then fade as the gold played out. Every ounce of gold men took from the gulches brought Virginia closer to that end, Lily Rae had said. Epiphany accepted the possibility. The town might fail, but she would not. Epiphany was sure she would reach her goals; she would persevere, she would succeed.

Epiphany thought again of Will Hunter. Where had he gone? Had some business venture called him away? Surely he would have told her if he had to leave; he would have said goodby. She remembered his kindness, his gentle touch. She recalled his shy smile, his loping walk, and the mysterious sadness deep in his eyes.

The shadow of a fast-moving cloud rippled across the valley, stealing the day's brightness and bringing a sudden chill to the air. Epiphany turned away from the open doorway and drew her woolen shawl more tightly about her shoulders. "Oh, Will," she thought, "where are you?"

———

Epiphany heard the clatter of the horse's hooves on the rocky street outside and knew it was Hunter's horse before she saw or heard him. She caught her breath, her heart racing. Quickly, she crossed to the open door. She heard the soft ring of spur, heard his footfall on the gravel outside, and then he was ducking beneath the lintel of the doorway, entering the cabin. "Will!" she cried, "I've missed you so!" and then she rushed into his arms. Eagerly, her lips sought his and found them. Her chaste kiss of greeting grew ardent, then abandoned. Epiphany felt him stiffen, resisting her embrace. Then suddenly his arms drew her hard against him and he gave himself to the kiss. She felt his mouth hard and hungry against hers, his strong arms close about her.

Abruptly, Hunter broke from the embrace. His hands gripped Epiphany's slim shoulders, pushing her away. Breathing heavily, he drew his head away from hers and stepped back. "I. . . I'm sorry, Piff," he said. "Forgive me. That was a mistake. I didn't mean for that to happen."

He saw her eyes widen, saw her smile fade, saw confusion and hurt pass over her face. Her body stiffened. Embarrassed, she turned away from him and slowly sat down at the table near the door. When at last she spoke, it was in a voice he'd never heard. "Perhaps," she said, "it would be better if you left now, Will."

He stumbled briefly at the doorway, watching her. He wanted to say something, do something, to change the moment. What could he say?

That it was his lust that had responded to her freely offered love? That he was crippled, incomplete, and that his one true love lay buried far away in a Missouri churchyard?

When she heard the hoofbeats carry him away, Epiphany laid her head down upon her arms and surrendered herself to weeping.

Tommy O'Flaherty had been a bartender for nearly as long as he could remember. His father had owned a tavern at a Kentucky crossroads that catered to travelers. The business had been a family affair. His older brother had managed the stables; his mother and sister had cooked, cleaned, and served meals; and Tommy had helped his dad run the bar.

He'd ended his apprenticeship at fifteen when the Old Man had gone to what the priest called His Great Reward. Tommy had ascended to management of the beer and whiskey end of the enterprise.

He had gone to the California gold fields during the great rush and had peddled Tanglefoot and Rookus Juice from Angel's Camp to

Whiskeytown. He had followed his customers to the placer strikes at Lewiston and Florence, to Bannack in '62, and Virginia City a year later. He had named his first establishment in Angel's Camp The Miners' Rest Saloon. The sign he'd had painted for that first saloon had hung above the front door of each successive enterprise, including the present one.

Tommy, an honest and amiable saloon keeper, had made his living from the gold fields without ever using pick or shovel. He had also come to be a good judge of men during his years behind the bar. When he saw the tall man stride through his front door that morning all the warning flags went up.

The stranger crossed the room like a storm, shouldered his way roughly between two miners at the bar, and leaned his elbows on the wood. "Whiskey," said Will Hunter, "and leave the bottle."

The men he'd jostled bristled, but one look at the tall man's face and the ivory-handled revolvers he wore persuaded them to let the insult pass. One of the miners shrugged and turned his eyes away. The other even mumbled an apology. Together, they moved on up the bar and left Will Hunter to himself.

Tommy maintained a calm demeanor, but the hairs on the back of his neck stood up. He felt as if a grizzly bear had just placed its paws upon the bartop and growled. The barman filled Hunter's glass, placed it and the bottle before him, and said nary a word. Tommy had no intention of going to *his* Great Reward any time soon.

Hunter emptied the glass, filled it again, and stared down at the amber liquid. "Whiskey is the last refuge of the hurting," he thought, "the great medicine that deadens pain and makes the world's madness bearable."

Oh my, yes, said his inner voice, *it helps a man avoid his problems, lets him persist in his folly, and makes every bad thing worse. It stands truth on its head, makes strong men weak, and fills the brave with self pity.*

"Just what I need," thought Hunter.

The Virginia Hotel stood stately and serene above the slapdash buildings that were her neighbors. Two stories tall, she rose like a queen above her subjects; and a raised veranda lifted her skirts above the common clay of Wallace Street. Setting her still further apart, the Virginia wore a dazzling coat of whitewash.

John Oakes stepped out onto the hotel's veranda and looked down the street toward Ulberg's Livery. His conversation that morning with Will Hunter hadn't gone as he'd hoped. Oakes, however, was a patient man—a man who knew how to wait.

Oakes took out his pocket watch and snapped open the case. The time read 11:44. "Time to be getting on the road back to Bannack," he thought. Hunter would not be coming—not today, at least. He stepped down onto the boardwalk, headed for Ulberg's.

He hadn't gone half a block before he saw Hunter. Miners and townsmen crowded the boardwalk at that hour, but there was no mistaking the lanky Missourian. Hunter strode toward Oakes in his loose, loping stride, his head held high, and his body unnaturally erect. Oakes smiled. "The son of a gun's been drinking," he thought. "Reckon he needed help coming to a decision."

"Looking for me?" Oakes asked as Hunter walked toward him. "I was just about to head out for Bannack."

Hunter stood, his shoulders stiff as a cadet's. His eyes were bright, and Oakes noted that his cheeks were flushed. "You said you'd be at the hotel 'til noon if I changed my mind," Hunter said. "Well, I have—changed my mind."

"Glad to hear it," Oakes said. "Let's get our horses and take a ride."

Will Hunter and John Oakes rode together along the rocky road to Summit, following Alder Creek. Prospectors hunkered at creekside, searching for the golden glint of flake, scad, or nugget in each dip and swirl of their pans. Beyond them, miners worked the waterless banks and bars, moving dirt by bucket and barrow down to the creek. Still farther out, men scoured the hilltops and ridges, seeking treasure that had perhaps once lain in the bed of an ancient stream. Piles of gravel stood alongside shaft holes, dust rose in plumes and swept away in the rising wind. Shacks, tents, and wakiups of the gold seekers—insubstantial and sloppy as magpie nests—lay scattered along the gulch.

Oakes nodded at the prospectors. "Those boys are all working on their 'six weeks,'" he said, "whether they've been in the diggings six days or six months. According to miners' lore, it's supposed to take six weeks to strike it rich and go back home to a hero's welcome. They all want to be out before winter sets in."

Hunter raised his eyes to the distant mountains. Already, new snow dusted their peaks. The wind blew down the gulch, cold and raw. "Most of them aren't going to make it," Hunter said.

Oakes tugged his hatbrim down and leaned into the wind. He nearly had to shout to be heard. "No, but the poor devils are long on hard work and hope. Each man figures he'll be the one who beats the odds; but those who strike it rich are few, and getting out with their gold gets harder every day."

"Everybody prospects the prospector," Hunter said.

Oakes shifted sideways in his saddle and studied Hunter. "Why did you change your mind about riding express?"

"My business," said Hunter, "a man does what he can."

How could he explain his decision to Oakes? The world was the same everywhere, Hunter thought. The cruel and powerful use their strength to exploit others; they take what they want because they can. What is there to stop them—the law? Not in Kansas and Missouri, where Lane and his Redlegs and Quantrill and his Raiders are the law. Not here, where the elected sheriff seems unable or unwilling to act, and may even be involved with the thieves and the killers himself.

"I was a fool to think it would be different here," he thought. "Ruthless men rule by force and terror in every time and place. There can be no peace, no law, and no order until good men stand together and make their voices heard. Win or lose, I'm drawing cards in this game, but I can't say all that to Oakes."

They passed Alder Creek's wide bend. Above the trail, hidden amid the pines, Hunter could just make out Thad Mitchell's cabin. Below, on the creek bank, he saw the young miner talking to another prospector as he cleaned the riffles of his sluice box. Hunter considered calling out a greeting, but thought better of the notion. "Another time," he thought.

John Oakes was talking again. "Those men I told you about—Albert Hess and Bill Fitzhugh—have a claim about a mile up the trail. I'd like for them to meet you."

The wind made talking difficult. Hunter answered with a nod, and the two men rode on.

On first meeting, Albert Hess and Bill Fitzhugh seemed to Hunter as different as two men could be. Stolid and humorless, Hess was a blonde, blue-eyed, Nordic youth. Fitzhugh was a lanky, fun-loving Irishman whose hair and beard were the blue-black color of a raven's wing. The two men had come to Alder Gulch in the first rush from Bannack and had made a rich strike. They had worked together as partners. They had forged a friendship in the hard-rock daily labor of the prospector.

"Albert, Bill, this is Will Hunter," Oakes had said, "Will, meet Albert Hess and Bill Fitzhugh."

Hunter shook the hands of the miners and liked them both on sight. Hess said nothing, but met Hunter with a broad, honest smile and a strong, work-hardened grip.

Fitzhugh had shaded his eyes as he squinted up into Hunter's face, and asked, "Do you know the poems of William Blake? He might have had you in mind when he wrote, 'Great things are done when men and mountains meet.' Sure, and don't you seem to be both man and mountain combined? How tall *are* you, Will Hunter?"

Hunter laughed. "I'm six-three, maybe six-five in my boots," he said, "but that's pretty short for a mountain. My dad was a great reader of Blake—if I remember right, the complete phrase is, 'Great things are done when men and mountains meet; This is not done by jostling in the street.'"

"So it is," said Fitzhugh, smiling, "and a sentiment I strongly support."

—◈—

The miners led Oakes and Hunter up a steep slope to their camp above Alder Creek. Like many other prospectors in the gulch, their dwelling was a wakiup—a rough, conical shelter made of alder logs, interlaced brush, and canvas. The structure contained no chairs, only a wooden box with a lid for groceries and two rude bunks with tow sacks stuffed with grass and sagebrush leaves for mattresses. The miners' one concession to comfort was a rusted woodstove that served both for cooking and heat. The men provided their guests a hearty dinner of beans, bacon, and cornbread, accompanied by some of the strongest coffee Hunter had tasted. As shadows lengthened along the gulch, Oakes and Fitzhugh filled and lit their pipes and the four men sat cross-legged on the ground in front of the wakiup.

"I told Will here about your need to get your dust out on the stage to Salt Lake," Oakes said. "I told him what I've told you—that no matter how you try to send it, the road agents will likely get word and intercept it. For the moment, your gold is safe at Dance and Stuart's. It will be safe once it leaves Bannack on a well-guarded coach for Salt Lake, but getting it from Virginia to Bannack won't be easy."

Fitzhugh looked thoughtful. He turned to Hunter, "I was at Lewiston last year when a man called Moses rode express to Salmon River. 'Twas seventy-five miles—a bit further than the distance from Virginia to Bannack—and the road agents planned to ambush him and steal the treasure he carried. Moses learned of their trap, took another way around, and got the gold safely through.

"They're good men, those express riders, bold as lions and skilled in the use of weapons. John Oakes says you may be one of the breed."

Fitzhugh's pipe had gone out. He studied it in silence for a moment, then raised his eyes to Hunter. "Would you then be willing to take our gold through? It would be worth five hundred to Albert and me."

"I'd need a good map of the ground between here and there," Hunter said, "and a place to change horses. Five hundred is too much. I'll make the ride for half that."

Fitzhugh's face turned grave. "You might not think five hundred is *enough*, by the time you reach Bannack." He spat into the palm of his hand and held it out to Hunter. "A bargain then, Will Hunter," he said, "and it's grateful we are."

Albert looked troubled. He had hardly spoken since Hunter and Oakes arrived, but now he spoke, his speech deliberate. "Just a minute," he said, "Vas. . . What. . . happens if those bad fellers kill you and take our gold?"

Hunter's smile was broad. "If *that* happens, I'll refund my *fee,* Albert," he said.

ELEVEN

Express Rider

E PIPHANY CURLED UP in the chair beside her window and stared outside at the darkening sky. A cold wind moaned through the camp, harrying the fallen leaves and gusting sand and grit against the walls of the boarding house. She listened as the building creaked and groaned under the buffeting. She imagined she heard grief and anger in the gathering storm and found it very like her own.

Epiphany had not bothered to light the lamp. In the twilight her room was as dark and cheerless as her mood. As her throat grew tight, she felt the ache inside her grow. Tears filled her eyes and overflowed. Silently, she wept in the gloom.

How could Will Hunter have treated her so badly? What had she done to cause him to reject her so? She had rushed into his arms, offering him all her love. She had kissed him. He had returned her kiss; but then he had pushed her away. He had *apologized*, for heaven's sake! Will Hunter had called their kiss a *mistake!*

She sobbed aloud, choked, and stifled her cries with her handkerchief. She heard a tapping on the door behind her. The door opened slowly, allowing a wedge of lamplight to enter. "Piff?" said Lily Rae. "Are you all right, hon?"

Epiphany blew her nose. She tried to control her voice. "Oh. Why, yes, Lily Rae," she said, "I. . . I'm fine."

Lily Rae stood in the open doorway, the lighted lamp in her hand. She came inside and set the lamp down on the table beside the bed. "Well, if you're fine," she said, "I hope I never see you when you're not. Your eyes and nose are red. You've been moping here in the dark, and you look terrible. What is *wrong*, Piff?"

Epiphany's attempt at control failed. She buried her face in her hands and wailed. "Everything!" she sobbed. "Everything!"

Then Lily Rae was beside her, gently patting her shoulder. "There, there," she said softly, "everything *can't* be wrong—I'm sure I'd have noticed. Come on now—tell me what has you so upset."

Epiphany dried her tears. Haltingly, she related the events of Hunter's visit to the cabin on Idaho Street. "I. . . I was so glad to see him," she said. "He took me in his arms and kissed me, and I kissed him back. . . but then he. . . he pushed me away! He said he was sorry, that he hadn't meant for it to happen. He. . . he said it was a *mistake!* Oh, Lily Rae, what did I do wrong? What's wrong with me?"

"Now, now," Lily Rae said, "nothing's wrong with you. You're a very attractive young woman, and a very special one. It may be no one's fault—it may just be that Will isn't able to return your love."

Hearing Hunter's name, Epiphany fell to weeping again. "But why not?" she cried. "I. . . I love him! I feel so. . . so foolish!"

Lily Rae held Epiphany at arm's length, her voice stern. "There could be a hundred reasons," she said. "He may be shy—afraid because of something in his past. He may love you—I'm sure he does—but perhaps not in the same way you love him. I can't believe he meant to hurt you."

There was sympathy and warmth in Lily Rae's eyes, and Epiphany clung to the kindness. "Men live in a different world," Lily Rae said. "They come, and they go. They leave, and sometimes they come back. Their love for us is only a part of their lives—our love for them is nearly all of ours. Maybe it's not fair, but that's the way it is.

"Right now, you need to get on with your life. Get that restaurant open and make it a success. Believe me, Piff, this hurt won't last forever."

"Lily Rae is a good, loving friend," Epiphany thought, "but she can't know how I feel. Everyone I've ever loved has left me, one way or the other. My father went away and never came back. When I was twelve, my mother hired me out to the Playfairs, then she died the next spring. The Playfairs were kind, but Indians killed them in that horrible raid at The Meadows. Now Will Hunter has rejected the love I offered him and walked away.

Lily Rae says there's nothing wrong with me. If that's so, why does everyone leave me? She says my hurt won't last forever. How can she know? Lily Rae says she's my friend. I know that she is, but I can't help wondering when *she* will go away."

Will Hunter led his black gelding out of the sunlight and into the dim quiet of the livery stable. He slid the big door closed behind him and stood in the warm semi-darkness of the barn's interior as his eyes adjusted to the gloom. The familiar smells of horse, leather, and hay calmed him. There was a comfortable, down-to-earth quality about a stable that soothed and centered a man.

Across the way, a stocky figure stepped out of the shadows and spoke his name. "Hello, Will," said John Oakes. "You're right on time."

"Yes. How are you, John?"

"A mite nervous, if the truth be told. A man never knows these days who might be listening."

Hunter said nothing. His eyes scanned the stable's interior and came back to Oakes. "Place looks empty," he said.

"Yes," Oakes agreed, "I'm just spookin' at shadows, I guess."

Oakes moved closer. His voice was almost a whisper when he spoke. "Everything's arranged. Judge Dance will give you Bill and Albert's goods tonight when he closes the store.

"That bay horse in the stall yonder is mine, the best horse I own. He'll take you as far as Stone's roadhouse on the Beaverhead. I'll be waiting there with your black gelding, and you can ride him the rest of the way in to Bannack."

Oakes fell silent. Nervously, he stroked his white beard stubble, his eyes restless. "It's the damnedest thing, Will," he said, "I'm the one who talked you into this express rider business, and now I'm the one who's turned goosey. I hope neither of us will be sorry."

"You didn't talk me into anything," Hunter said. "I guess I talked myself into it. I'm tired of the road agents having it all their own way."

He stripped his saddle from the black gelding and replaced his bridle with a halter and lead rope. Handing the rope to Oakes, he crossed the stable and saddled the bay. "I'll head out at first light tomorrow," he said. "See you at Stone's." The men shook hands. Having exchanged horses, they both left the stable and went their separate ways.

The barn was silent in the aftermath of their leaving. Sunshine filtered in through cracks in the boards, painting bright strips along the dirt floor. Dust motes danced in the sunlight. Somewhere, a mouse skittered.

Beyond the stalls, in a dark corner near the stable's back wall, the figure of a man stirred. The form rose stealthily from behind a pile of feed sacks and tarpaulins, hesitated, and hobbled jerkily to a small door in the rear. Moments later, "Clubfoot" George Lane, chief spy for the "Innocents," was limping hurriedly toward Cy Skinner's saloon.

Hunter was awake an hour before first light. He lay fully clothed inside his blankets beneath the wagon and waited for sunrise. He was impatient to be up and riding. During the long night he had slept fitfully, his hand on his revolver, alert to every sound. Next to his body, beneath the canvas tarpaulin and bedding that covered him, Hunter felt the five heavy buckskin pouches and smiled. "Five thousand dollars in gold makes for a lumpy bed," he mused, "but I can't say it was the lumps that kept me awake."

Hunter sat up, leaving the warmth of his blankets. He found his hat and donned it, then stood and pulled his boots on. It was the coldest hour of the day. He shivered as he shrugged into his greatcoat. Quickly, he built a small fire and put the coffee on. Soon, he'd breakfasted on beans, salt pork, and bakery bread. He washed and dried his dishes, drank two cups of coffee, and poured water on his cookfire.

Swiftly, he saddled the bay and retrieved the gold from his bedroll. He packed two of the heavy pouches on each side in the pockets of his saddlebags, wrapped the fifth pouch in his slicker, and tied the bundle behind the saddle's cantle. He checked the loads and percussion caps of his revolvers, slid the rifle into its scabbard, and swung up into the saddle. With a touch of his spurs, he turned the bay out on the road to Bannack.

There were travelers on the road even at that early hour. Hunter held the bay to a steady, ground-covering trot all the way to Junction. The horse was smooth-gaited and strong, and he kept the pace until the road dropped into the narrow, shadowed canyon beyond the settlement.

As the sun exploded above the Madisons, Hunter held to the shadows and brushy bottoms until he reached Pete Daly's roadhouse. At Daly's, smoke drifted up from the chimney into the clear morning sky. There were wagons in the yard and more than a dozen saddle horses at the hitchrack, but Hunter saw no one outside. Quietly, and keeping to the shadows, he rode past, then kicked the bay into a fast lope as he left the roadhouse behind him.

Beyond Daly's the road crossed the low and grassy valley of the Stinkingwater. Hunter put the bay into a pace that alternated between a run and a trot, making good speed but conserving the animal's strength. He met freight wagons, high-sided and lumbering, as the teams pulled their heavy loads up the grade toward Virginia. Three miles further on he met a small party of gold seekers, their new picks and shovels—tools as bright as their hopes— lashed to their packhorses.

As the sun climbed above the mountains, the morning grew warmer, Hunter stopped atop a low hill to give the bay a breather, carefully scanning his backtrail. The valley was still and silent. A hawk rode the thermals, slowly circling. Deer browsed at the edge of a cottonwood grove. Swallows flew in close order over the creek. "So far, so good," said Hunter, and turned the bay downhill.

He passed Cold Springs Ranch and then Baker's, crossed the creek, and headed west through low, rolling hills. He felt the sun's heat on his shoulders and felt his eyelids grow heavy. He had slept poorly the night before, in fits and starts. Hunter found his mind drifting as he rode. He thought of the prospectors whose gold he carried and of their trust in him. He thought about John Oakes, who had been bold and confident when he first proposed the idea of riding express, then nervous and edgy during their meeting in the livery stable. Oakes was no coward, Hunter was sure, but his enthusiasm tended to lead him to grand proposals and plans before he'd fully thought them through.

Hunter's thoughts went to Epiphany and their meeting at her cabin. He recalled her sudden, bright smile at the sight of him and her eager rush into his arms. He remembered their kiss, tender and warm at first, then bold and hungry with the stirring of his blood. He saw again Epiphany's stunned look as he broke off their embrace. He heard again the hurt and the dull, flat anger in her voice as she said, "Perhaps it would be better if you left now, Will."

He relived the moment in his mind, trying to think how he might have handled things better, some way he might have spared her the pain he'd caused. He knew he could not have handled the situation differently. There was nothing to do now but go forward. Looking back with regret was futile.

Too bad, observed the voice inside his mind, *looking back with regret is one of the things you do best.*

He passed the long, low buildings and corrals that marked Copeland's ranch and pushed on to his meeting with Oakes at Stone's Roadhouse. A relay point for the A. J. Oliver and Conover stage line, Stone's occupied a spot at the roadside beneath towering cottonwood trees. As Hunter pulled up at the roadhouse bar, a hound near the door stood, barked balefully, and lay down again. A moment later, John Oakes stepped quickly out, his broad smile a far better welcome.

Oakes walked close to Hunter, his voice low. "Man, I sure am glad to see you!" he said. "Any trouble?"

Hunter dismounted and loose-tied the bay. "No trouble," he said, "that bay is a good horse."

"Your black is in the corral yonder," Oakes said, "grain-fed and rarin' to go. I'll buy you lunch."

Hunter shook his head. "Much obliged, John, but I won't rest easy until I have this dust locked in the stage office at Bannack. I'm burning daylight."

Oakes nodded. "Then let's get the saddle off my horse and onto yours." He looked troubled. There was a pause before he spoke again. "There's been talk among the boys inside at the bar," he said. "Rumor has it that an express rider is coming through from Virginia, carrying gold." Oakes met Hunter's eyes, worry plain on his face and in his voice. "According to the bar-flies, the road agents figure to take it from him between here and Bannack."

"That's quite a rumor," Hunter said grimly, "but I never put much stock in rumors." Oakes smiled a nervous smile. "Yeah, me, neither. But watch yourself, anyway."

Moments later, Hunter had changed horses. Oakes swung open the corral gate and Hunter led the black out. "Want me to ride along with you?" Oakes asked.

Hunter set foot in the stirrup and swung into the saddle. "Appreciate the offer, John," he said, "but no. I expect I'll run a hole in the wind between here and Bannack."

Oakes looked rueful. "I don't expect I could keep up with that black tornado anyway," he said. "All right. I'll see you this evening in Bannack."

"Until then," Hunter said, and jumped the thoroughbred out on the road at a full gallop.

The black gelding scarcely paused at the Beaverhead crossing. The animal plunged into the river, splashed across, and lunged out onto the road again. Hunter felt the wind buffet his face. He felt the surging power of the thoroughbred beneath him, and his spirits rose. He'd ridden the long-legged black all the way from Missouri to the Northern Rockies. The horse had carried him through skirmishes with Federal troops and Kansas Militia and with the Bannocks at the Meadows. Whatever dangers lay ahead this day, he knew he would face them astride this courageous horse. Hunter eased the gelding back to a trot, alternating—as he'd done with the bay earlier—between that gait and a lope. Three hours later, he passed Bunton's ranch and began the final ten-mile ride to Bannack.

The road now meandered through a vast, open stretch of dry gulches, sagebrush, and rolling hills, relieved by patches of scrub cedar and pine. Three miles from Bannack on the stage road, a wooded outcropping called Road Agent Rock stood on a hilltop. Oakes had told Hunter the promontory was a favorite hangout for the roughs because it offered an excellent view of the country for miles in every direction. It also provided good cover among the trees for the robbers and their horses. There had been several holdups at the site, Oakes said. Hunter planned to avoid passing the rock, but he knew it was likely he'd be observed from the promontory if there were eyes to see.

Ahead, to the west, the sun blazed low over the mountains. Hunter squinted against the brightness, straining to see the land before him. Sixty yards ahead, the road dropped abruptly off into an old stream bed and rose sharply around a low hill on the other side. A deep coulee, marked by fallen boulders and a cedar patch, opened on the left.

Hunter shifted in the saddle, anticipating the turn and drop. Suddenly, he felt the choppy sidestep of the thoroughbred. Hunter stood hard in the stirrups to maintain his balance. His gaze flashed to the coulee's mouth where he saw three riders move out of the shadows and into the light. Two of the men wore long canvas dusters over their clothing, while the third, a big man on a gray horse, wore a faded blue overcoat. Beneath the shadow of their hatbrims black kerchiefs covered their faces to the eyes. They held their weapons ready as they rode out to block the road.

"Stop that horse and throw up your damn hands!" shouted the man on the gray.

Hunter's revolver was already in his right hand. "Not today," he said. He spurred the gelding toward the horsemen and reined it sharply to the right, leaning low over the animal's side. The big thoroughbred lunged sharply away from the riders, whose horses now jostled nervously in the dust.

Hunter leaned low across the withers of the black and fired his Colt's Navy from beneath the gelding's neck. The closest rider jerked upright as the ball struck him, then jack-knifed forward and fell dying onto the roadway. Reacting to Hunter's shot, the big man in the overcoat swung a sawed-off shotgun up and fired, the charge ripping through the air just behind Hunter's head.

Hunter reined the black sharply to the left and shot the third rider at point blank range. The man sailed backward out of his saddle and fell heavily to the ground. Frightened by the gunfire, the big man's horse began bucking wildly, nearly unseating him. Struggling to control the horse, the bandit could not control his second shot, and the shotgun exploded harmlessly into the air. Hunter spurred the thoroughbred past him, dropped into the dry wash and swept up the other side, racing for Bannack.

The sun had dropped beyond the mountains, but the skies above Bannack were still bright as Hunter rode into the busy camp and drew rein at the Stage Office. Lamplight burned in the windows and cast yellow squares out onto the rutted street. The smell of woodsmoke drifted on the wind. Will Hunter dismounted, looped the reins around the hitchrail, and took the five heavy pouches from his saddle.

Inside the office, a young clerk sat on a stool behind the counter, making entries in a ledger. He watched Hunter come into the office and smiled. "Evenin,' mister," he said, "what can I do for you?"

"Got some gold for shipment to Salt Lake," Hunter told him. "Five thousand in clean Virginia dust."

The clerk glanced at the bundles in Hunter's arms, then out at the black horse standing at the hitchrail. He looked at Hunter with new interest. "Five thousand in gold," he said, "and you brought it from Virginia City on a saddle horse? Alone? You must be new to the diggings, mister."

Hunter ignored the remark. "The gold belongs to Albert Hess and Bill Fitzhugh of Virginia City," he said. "Make the receipt out to them."

The clerk weighed the bags, made an entry in his ledger, and locked the gold in the safe behind the counter.

The clerk handed the receipt to Hunter. "Stage for Salt Lake leaves tomorrow afternoon, under heavy guard. Anything else I can do for you?"

"You don't happen to know where the sheriff is, do you? I need to talk to him."

"Sheriff Plummer? He lives over in Yankee Flat with his in-laws," the clerk said, "but he's generally at the Elkhorn Saloon this time of night."

Hunter had left the door to the street ajar when he'd carried the gold into the building. Now, from behind him, he heard the soft voice of Henry Plummer himself. Hunter turned.

"Generally, but not always, Frank," the sheriff said to the clerk. He shifted his gaze to Hunter and smiled a thin smile. "I saw that handsome thoroughbred outside and knew you must be in town, Will. You said you were looking for me?"

"Yes," Hunter said, "I was jumped by road agents on the stage road this afternoon. Three men, wearing masks. I shot two of them out of the saddle. The third was fighting his horse, last I saw."

Plummer's cold, gray eyes widened slightly, but they revealed no expression at all. The sheriff returned Hunter's gaze, a slight smile on his lips. "That was good shooting," he said, "and even better luck."

The sheriff looked tired, Hunter thought. He wore a day's growth of beard, and there were dark circles under his eyes. Beneath a travel-stained duster, his usually immaculate suit was wrinkled and dusty at the cuffs of his trousers.

Hunter continued his story. "I brought gold over from Virginia for some miners," he said. "The road agents rode out of a coulee about six miles back and threw down on me with shotguns and revolvers.

The two I shot wore dusters, like yours. The third was big, stocky man. He wore a blue Army coat and rode a glass-eyed gray horse."

Plummer looked thoughtful. "I'll round up some deputies and go out there," he said, "but I don't expect we'll find very much. I'm glad you're all right, Will."

The sheriff fixed Hunter with his cold stare. "I said when we met it was clear to me you're a man of action and boldness. I also said I can always use a good man. The offer is still open."

"I appreciate the offer, but I'm still a freighter."

"Too bad," said Plummer, and walked out onto the street.

TWELVE

Partners

SEVEN MEN OCCUPIED the bar room at Rattlesnake Ranch that evening, five living and two dead. The corpses lay sprawled against the room's back wall, still dressed in the dusters they had worn earlier in the day. Bill Bunton, Plummer's second in command, and Frank Parish, horse thief and roadster, sat playing cards at a round-topped table. Bravo Santee stood alone at the bar, his thumbs hooked in his gunbelt. Boone Helm sat on a chair in the center of the room, his beefy face red, his battered hat in his hand. Sitting beneath a smoky, coal-oil ceiling lamp, he glowered sullenly at the floor between his feet. He was perspiring heavily. Standing before him, Henry Plummer fixed the man with his cold stare and demanded an accounting.

"What happened out there?" Plummer asked.

Helm scowled. His chief was calling him on the carpet like a school-boy. What had happened on the road had not been his fault. How could he have known Hunter would fight back? One man against three, and yet he—

"Damn you!" Plummer said. "What *happened* out there?"

Helm's massive hands crumpled his hat. He squirmed in his chair. "There wasn't nothin' I could do, Henry! We pulled our guns and braced him on the road like always, but that sum'bitch Hunter put spurs to his horse and blowed Foley and Hanks away!"

"What were you doing while he was killing two of our men?"

"Shootin' at him! When he gunned Foley, I cut loose with my scattergun—but that horse he rides is quick!"

"You *missed* him—with a sawed-off ten-guage?"

"Hell, yes! Hunter dropped to his horse's offside like a damn Injun—shot Foley from under his horse's neck! I was fixin' to cut him down with my second barrel when he gunned Hanks!

"Then my horse fell to pitchin' with me, and my shot went wild! By the time I got that switch-tail settled, Hunter had slipped past and was ridin' hell-bound for Bannack!"

"With five thousand in gold, and leaving two good men dying in the dirt!" Plummer said, his tone heavy with contempt.

Plummer's gray eyes blazed. He stared at the hulking giant in the chair before him. His left hand closed on the grips of the revolver at his waist and held it. "I ought to put you down with those other two," he said, nodding toward the dead men. "You've cost us plenty this day. Get out of my sight, Helm—I'm tired of looking at you."

Boone Helm got to his feet. He nodded, shuffled to the door, and went outside. Plummer moved to the bar and poured himself two fingers of whiskey. He seldom drank—always in moderation when he did drink—but this had been a trying day. "When word of this gets out," he muttered, "we'll be lucky if the *next* man we rob doesn't laugh in our faces."

Abruptly, he turned away from the bar to face his men. "Well? Do any of *you* have anything to say?"

At the poker table, Parish and Bunton lowered their eyes and studied their cards. Santee stepped away from the bar and turned toward Plummer.

"Yes, by god, I reckon I do," he said. "You told me I could take Hunter when the time came. If you'd sent *me* out them boys might not be dead."

Plummer's eyes narrowed. "You certainly have a high opinion of yourself," he said. "What makes you think you could have done better than Helm?"

"I know Hunter—fought beside him in Missouri and Kansas—know how he fights. He's good, but so am I. Quantrill led the best damn horseback revolver fighters anybody's ever saw."

"Maybe. You think you can run this outfit better than me?" Plummer's voice had a flat, metallic sound. His hand caressed the grips of his holstered gun.

"No, sir, I don't. You're the boss, and I'll do what you say. I've took the oath, and I've took your word. Wouldn't have said nothin' now, except you asked. I still want Hunter—I want that long-legged bastard like a drownin' man wants dry."

Plummer took his hand off his revolver. He tossed back the whiskey and refilled his glass. "He's still yours," he said, "but not yet."

The next morning found Henry Plummer in a somber mood. As the mild weather of Indian Summer stretched into November, the day dawned clear and bright. Ordinarily, the sheriff would have found pleasure in the sunny morning. On this day, however, depression rode him with its spurs on; and it was no kind master.

Plummer headed into the rising sun, bound for Virginia City. The events of recent days troubled his mind and brought dark worry to the morning. The botched holdup of Will Hunter was particularly vexing. The news would spread like wildfire. The mishap would weaken his grip on the district and give comfort to the growing law and order element.

Plummer's rise to power had been swift. Born in Connecticut, he ran run away from home at the age of fifteen to the gold fields of California. At nineteen, he was elected town marshal of Nevada City, California. That same year, he began an adulterous affair in that town with a married woman.

When confronted by her husband, Plummer shot and killed the man. Sentenced to ten years in prison for the killing, Plummer petitioned for release on medical grounds—he claimed he was consumptive. With the support of influential friends in the area, he received a pardon by the governor and returned to Nevada City.

Upon his return, Plummer took up with a prostitute and nearly killed another man in a bawdy house brawl. In Washoe, California, he joined an outlaw band and was involved in the failed robbery of the Wells Fargo bullion express. He shot another man in Nevada City, was arrested and jailed, but escaped. Moving to Oregon in the company of another killer, Plummer sent word back to the California newspapers that he and his comrade had been hanged in Washington Territory for a double murder there. Later, he seduced another married woman in Walla Walla and helped murder a man in Orofino.

Plummer followed the rush to the booming gold town of Lewiston, Idaho, where he organized his first gang of thieves and road agents. When a band of vigilantes formed to deal with the outlaws, Plummer joined their ranks and ordered the murder of one of the vigilante leaders.

In 1862, he'd moved his operations to the gold rush at Bannack. He organized a small army of desperadoes and highwaymen, including many of his former associates from California, Washington and Idaho. With their help, he campaigned for and was elected to the office of sheriff of the mining district that included the town of Bannack. When prospectors discovered the new, even richer bonanza at Alder Gulch, Plummer got himself elected sheriff of that district, too.

He appointed deputies and assigned key men to both districts. Now, through a system that included misuse of his office and a network of spies, Plummer virtually controlled the movement of gold out of the area.

Plummer slowed his horse to a walk as he neared the site of the failed robbery. He circled the low hill, dropped into the old stream bed, and rode up its opposite bank to the cedar patch that marked the coulee's mouth. Clouds blocked the sun. The morning's brightness went abruptly into shadow, and so did the sheriff's mood.

Henry Plummer was a gambler. He rode a winning streak that could set him up for life, but everything depended on a delicate balance. He and his men must keep the miners intimidated and divided, but they must never be pushed so far that they were provoked to organized resistance. Plummer had seen vigilante justice before, and he feared it.

Always, it began with an incident—a spark—and built to a fire that could sweep away everything in its path. Lynch law admitted no negotiation, no compromise.

He knew that Hunter's victory would make the man a hero to the miners. His first reaction had been to strike back, to show them all that no man could stand up to the "Innocents" and live. He could take the leash off Bravo Santee. He could let the yellow-eyed runt kill Hunter, as he so clearly wished to do. As satisfying as that prospect seemed, the risks it carried were greater. Killing Hunter could prove to be the very spark that Plummer feared.

Galling as it was, there was nothing to do but wait, he decided. Hunter's death would come, but it would come later at a more opportune time. Softly, the sheriff spoke aloud. His horse cocked an ear back to listen, but the words were not directed to the animal. "Damn *you*, Will Hunter," Plummer said.

In Virginia City, Epiphany Baker stood beside Lily Rae Bliss on Idaho Street and cast a critical eye on the cabin she would soon open as her restaurant. Above the door, on a clean pine board, Epiphany had painted a sign: *Orphan Girl Cafe – Epiphany Baker, Prop.*

"Orphan Girl?" asked Lily Rae.

"Well," said Epiphany, "I am an orphan, and I am a girl. I think the name has a certain ring."

There was impatience in her voice, thought Lily Rae, and nervousness as well. Since her painful parting from Will Hunter, Epiphany seemed to have withdrawn into some private sanctuary deep inside herself. No longer did she share her hopes and dreams over tea in Lily Rae's kitchen. The girlish enthusiasm she'd brought to their friendship was gone now, replaced by a cautious reserve. "Epiphany is cordial enough," Lily Rae thought, "but she's turned brittle. She's gone into a shell and has taken her trust in with her. The young feel deeply, but they heal quickly—mostly, they do."

Every day for the past week, Lily Rae had watched from her kitchen window as Epiphany left the boarding house at first light and walked the three blocks west to her cabin. There she had worked throughout the day, returning at sunset to supper at the boarding house. Epiphany was usually too tired for much conversation, but she had kept Lily Rae apprised of the restaurant's progress.

Epiphany hired the cabin's former owner, hapless gambler Cootie Blake, as dishwasher, waiter, and handyman. Blake built shelves and bins and began work on a pie safe. Epiphany made curtains for the windows and bought oilcloths for the tables. She scrubbed, swept, and polished. She ordered supplies, baked bread, and made pies. Tomorrow, at noon, the Orphan Girl Cafe would open for business.

A fresh morning wind gusted along busy Wallace Street, scattering and tumbling the saloons' discarded playing cards like dry leaves. The wind had teeth in it. To the north, new snow capped the peaks of the Tobacco Roots and gave mute warning of winter's onset. Miners, freighters, and townsfolk were striding quickly along the boardwalks, weaving in and out among the wagons and bull teams that crowded the street.

Tall and straight-backed in the saddle, Will Hunter turned his thoroughbred off Wallace and and over onto less-traveled Jackson. At the corner, he drew rein in front of the Miners' Rest Saloon and stepped down. He had spent the night at Dempsey's ranch, twenty miles west on the road to Bannack. He had slept poorly and the long ride had left him feeling trail-weary and stiff. He wanted a drink, food, and a bed. Hunter tied the gelding to the hitchrail and pushed open the door.

After the brightness of the street the saloon was dark and warm, away from the bitter wind. Hunter paused, unbuttoning his greatcoat as he waited for his eyes to adjust. He then made his way toward the silhouetted men who lined the bar. As he approached, a man turned to look at him, smiled, and spoke. "Good morning, Will," said Thad Mitchell, "I hoped I'd run into you."

"Thad! What's a hard-working gold-seeker like you doing in the Miners' Rest?"

Thad smiled. "Well," he said, "I'm a miner, and I'm in need of rest. Where else would a gold-seeker go but The Miners' Rest?"

Hunter laughed. Speaking to the bartender, he said, "Give this tired miner another beer and bring me a double shot of Valley Tan. We'll be at that table yonder."

The two men moved to a table near the stove and sat down. Across the room, Tommy O'Flaherty came out from behind the bar, crossed the room, and set the drinks down before them.

Thad lifted his stein and looked at Hunter. "Here's how," he said, then drank.

"How," said Hunter, raising his glass.

For a moment Thad seemed to study the table before him. Then he cleared his throat and raised his eyes. "I'm glad our paths crossed," Thad said. "I wanted to see you before I left."

"You're leaving?"

"Sold my claim yesterday, cabin and all. I'm a placer man, and the free gold on my claim has about played out. The new owner is a hard rock man, a quartz miner, with time and patience. I'm on to new prospects."

"I'll be sorry to see you go," Hunter said. "You and John Oakes are just about the only friends I have in the district."

Thad looked thoughtful. He spoke hesitantly. "Rumor has it you rode express this week for Albert Hess and Bill Fitzhugh–took their dust over to Bannack for them."

"For once, rumor is right," Hunter said, "Guess I just got tired of the roughs running the show. Three of them jumped me on the road. I shot two and took the gold on in to the stage office."

Thad whistled softly. "Dangerous business," he said, "snatching meat from a lion's mouth. The road agents will be gunning for you now."

"I expect so."

The two men drank. For a moment, neither spoke. It was Hunter who broke the silence. "I've decided to go into the freight business," he said. "Nothing big right now, just some local hauling. I have two wagons and a third that only needs a front axle. I have harness and pasture and ten good mules. I could use a partner."

"I don't think so, Will. I'm a miner. I've never hauled freight before."

Hunter smiled. "Nothing to it," he said, "all you need is a weak mind, a strong back, and a few dozen cuss-words for the mules. Winter's coming on fast. You won't have time to develop another claim before the snow flies. Besides, if the freight hauling business doesn't pan out, you can always go prospecting again in the spring."

"I guess maybe I could at that," Thad said. "All right," he said, smiling, "I'll give it a try, partner."

◈

The line of hungry men extended nearly half a block the day the Orphan Girl Cafe opened for business. Along Idaho Street, miners and townsmen stood in groups of two, three, and four, sharing news and gossip under the noonday sun. In a camp ruled by hard work and rumor, men craved novelty. A new restaurant attracted both the hungry and the curious.

Many of the cafe's patrons had heard of Miss Epiphany, its young proprietress. They had heard about the raid at The Meadows. They had told and re-told the story of the slim girl with the flaxen hair, rescued from marauding Indians.

"Do you remember?" a man asked. "She's the pretty one who came to the gulch awhile back with Will Hunter."

"Who's Will Hunter?" another asked.

"Why, man, haven't you heard about Hunter?" the first man replied. "I'm talkin' about the tall man with the wild look of the wolf about him—"Lobo" Hunter! You know, the man who whipped Jack Gallagher!"

"Oh, him! Hell, yes, I know about Hunter—my partner was at the Mother Lode that day! Didn't actually *see* the fight, but was there right after—said they fought over the girl."

A third man spoke up. "I guess you boys ain't heard the latest. This man we're talkin' about, this "Lobo" Hunter, well, he rode express for Albert Hess and Bill Fitzhugh last week. Took their gold over to Bannack on that leggy black he rides. Road agents tried to stop him, and damned if he didn't *kill* two of them!"

"Two?" said another man, "I heard it was *four!* Each man shot right between the eyes!"

So the talk went, until a lanky miner mentioned a new strike beyond the mountains. "Gold at the grass roots! A richer strike even than Alder! Where? Beyond the mountains, somewhere to the east—or maybe it was the west, don't know exactly. Talked to a teamster who heard about it from a man who knew a man who'd been there."

From time to time, men would emerge from the cafe, picking their teeth, patting their bellies, talking about the fine food and the beautiful Miss Epiphany, who ran the place. Then Cootie Blake, or Miss Epiphany herself, would grant entry to two or three more of the patient and fortunate few as the lunch hour progressed.

Inside, the cafe bustled with activity. Customers sat crowded around the three tables and lined the counter while Epiphany stood in her apron at the stove, filling bowls from a huge kettle with the rich venison stew that was the featured lunch for the day. With each of the brimming crockery bowls, Epiphany served two feather-light biscuits, made fresh that morning. Through Lily Rae, Epiphany had found a farmer on Daylight Creek who kept bees and two milk cows. Each table—and the counter—held bowls of fresh-churned butter and honey.

Coffee and a generous wedge of mock-apple pie came with the price of the meal, which was either a dollar in coin or a pinch of dust from the customer's poke. Many a miner, settling his account in the light of Epiphany's brown eyes and bright smile, found himself giving more—even double or triple the amount of his bill. He paid, not only for his lunch, but for the pleasure of a few moments' conversation with the Orphan Girl's proprietor.

Epiphany made it a point to pay particular attention to each customer. She smiled often. With eyes lowered, she acknowledged each compliment. Later, when the men had been fed and the lunch "hour" had passed—on this opening day not until three in the afternoon—Epiphany took the opportunity to sit down. She poured herself a cup of coffee and enjoyed a moment or two of quiet. As she rested at a table, she planned the next day's menu. Then she and Cootie washed and dried the dishes, swept the floor, and scrubbed the table tops and counters. Finally, while Cootie replenished the wood supply for the ravenous stove, Epiphany counted her day's receipts. After she had placed the gold dust and coin in a small leather satchel, she locked the front and back doors.

On the street outside, she bade Cootie good afternoon. With all the talk about road agents and robbers in the gulch, she had worried about walking the streets alone with the satchel, but Cootie had been adamant about her safety. "Lordamighty, Miss Epiphany," he had said, "the worst man in Virginia City wouldn't harm you! Why, the entire gulch would turn out and hang him from the tallest tree!"

As she turned downhill toward the bank on Wallace Street, Epiphany felt the pride of accomplishment. She had worked hard to open The Orphan Girl, and this, her first day, had been successful beyond her expectations. She savored the feeling of triumph that now lifted her spirits and the solid weight of the satchel that gave tangible proof of her success. Despite her day's success, however, her triumph was incomplete. She had hoped to share this day with the man she believed she loved. A familiar sadness assailed her, as it did each time she allowed memories of Will Hunter to occupy her thoughts. Deliberately, she turned her mind to other matters.

Epiphany crossed Wallace Street and made her way along the crowded boardwalk to the Merchants' Bank. Miners stepped aside to allow her passage, some tipping their hats and others paying homage with a glance. Entering the bank, Epiphany made her deposit and accepted the banker's good wishes. She then re-crossed the bustling street and climbed the hill again to Idaho Street and home.

The Boarding House stood in the distance. Epiphany thought she would have time for a long, hot bath before supper. After the meal, she would relive the day's events with Lily Rae and then take her weary body to bed. She would enjoy a good night's sleep and be ready for tomorrow.

If she should dream, she prayed, please God, let it not be of him. If it should be of him, let it not be of a warm mountain evening and an old violin sweetly playing *Little Annie Laurie*.

THIRTEEN

A Stove for Epiphany

B Y NOVEMBER, many of the gold seekers along Alder Gulch had already begun to leave the diggings. Having prospered in the rich placers of the Fairweather District, looking ahead to hardship and idleness with the advent of winter, and facing the threat of robbery and murder at the hands of the road agents, many turned their eyes toward home.

Some miners had begun their exodus as far back as early autumn. Now, the trickle of departing gold-seekers became a steady stream. Most of these left the way they had come—by wagon, on horseback, and even on foot—but a number of them took passage on the coaches of the two new stage lines to Bannack and on to Salt Lake City.

The roughs grew stronger and more bold. Their successes made them arrogant. Their robberies became more brazen. Many of the men who left the diggings with their hard-won gold never arrived at their destinations. They fell to the guns of the road agents in dry gulches and shadowed canyons on the road from Virginia to Bannack, or from Bannack to Salt Lake.

As winter neared, Will Hunter and Thad Mitchell continued to haul freight from John Oakes' warehouse in Bannack. They delivered lumber and supplies to the other six settlements of Alder Gulch. From a departing miner, the partners bought a small cabin above Daylight Creek and laid in a supply of firewood. Both men kept a careful watch for trouble, but days passed and the expected retaliation by the roughs against Hunter failed to materialize. The partners kept their eyes open, their weapons close at hand, and went about their business.

———◈———

Early one November morning, Hunter delivered a shipment of winter clothing and flour to Dance and Stuart's store. When Hunter turned his mules toward home, the gray and windy sky was filled with spitting snow and sleet. Wallace Street had become even more congested than usual. Because Idaho Street ran parallel to Wallace, Hunter turned north a block, then swung the team east on his way out of town. The hour was still early. As the wagon rumbled along the rutted street, Hunter saw only an occasional rider.

He passed Epiphany's Orphan Girl Cafe, not yet open at that hour of the morning. Behind its windows, yellow lamplight glowed. Smoke billowed from the stovepipe and swept away on the wind. Seeing the lamplight and the smoke, Hunter knew the cafe was preparing for the lunch crowd. He wondered whether Epiphany was inside.

Driving his mules two blocks further, he found his answer. Epiphany walked toward him, her hands thrust deep into the pockets of the sheepskin coat she'd brought from The Meadows. Her head was covered by a woolen scarf, and her face was nestled deep within the coat's upturned collar. She walked into the wind, her eyes on the frozen ground before her. Hunter slowed the team as she drew near, then reined the animals to a stop.

"Good morning, Piff," he said. "A good day to be in out of the weather."

She stopped, shielding her eyes against the snow, and recognized him. "Hello, Will," she said. "Yes. . . I'm on my way to open the cafe. How have you been?"

"Better than I deserve," he said. "You're looking well."

Epiphany laughed. "You pay compliments on scant evidence," she said, "I'm so bundled in Tom's old coat that all you can see are my watery eyes and red nose, but thank you."

"I hear the cafe's doing well," Hunter said, "and I like the name. I'll have to come by one day."

"Yes," she said, no emotion at all in the word. "Not so long ago," she thought, "just seeing him would have filled me with excitement and joy. All I feel now is sadness. Even the anger is gone."

"The freight business is keeping me busy," Hunter said. "I've even taken on a partner—young miner named Thad Mitchell. We're doing all right. Everyone's stocking up for winter."

"That's good. I wish you well."

"And I, you. It was good to see you, Piff."

"Yes. Don't be a stranger, Will."

Hunter smiled and tipped his hat. He clucked to the team and drove up the street, sitting tall upon the wagon seat.

Two days later, at Ulberg's Livery, Hunter ran into John Oakes. "Just the teamster I was looking for," said the older man. "I need someone to make a delivery up on Idaho Street. Your friend, Miss Baker, has wanted a good restaurant range since she opened her place; and I finally found one for her. Eating house down on Cover Street closed up, and I bought the stove."

"Where is it now?" asked Hunter.

"Still down on Cover Street."

"I'm hauling lumber from Langford's sawmill up to Summit this afternoon. I'm already loaded. I'll ask Thad if he can do it."

Oakes stroked his jaw, trying to read Hunter's face. "Sure, if that's what you want," he said. "I just thought you might want to do it yourself, you and her being friends and all."

Hunter's smile was cool. "Don't think so much, John."

Oakes took the reproof as a joke. "I don't think *enough*, as a rule," he said, chuckling.

Hunter rode down to the cabin he shared with Thad Mitchell just at dusk. Nearly ten inches of snow blanketed the valley. Low and leaden, clouds still hung over the hills, obscuring the mountains and dimming the sunset. Hunter unsaddled at the lean-to beside the corral and turned his horse out. From the cabin door, Thad watched Hunter come striding through the drifts.

"It's not a fit night out for man or beast," Hunter said, stamping his feet at the threshhold, "so I came home and brought my beast with me. What's for supper?"

Thad grinned. "Same thing as last night—Perpetual Stew."

Hunter removed his greatcoat, shook it, and hung it on a peg. "One more week of that stew and I'm liable to get used to it," Hunter said. "It's a good thing, too. The only way we're ever going to get rid of it is to eat more than we add to the pot."

"That's a fact," Thad said. "We're mere mortals, but that stew just might live forever."

He poured a cup of coffee and handed it to Hunter. "I see you left the wagon in town," he said. "Did you take that load up to Summit?"

"No. Snow's even heavier up that way—maybe tomorrow."

Hunter sipped the coffee and set the cup down. "Ran into John Oakes over at Ulberg's. He's got a stove he wants delivered. I told him my outfit was loaded for Summit, but that maybe you'd do it."

"Sure. Where does this stove go?"

"Orphan Girl Cafe. Seems Miss Epiphany's been looking for a restaurant range and John found her one. You'll need to pick it up at the Blue Pony Lunch Room on Cover Street and take it over to the Orphan Girl. You'll have help at both ends, loading and unloading. Tobe Willis, from Ulberg's, said he'd help you get it on the wagon. Cootie Blake, Miss Epiphany's hired man, will help you unload it."

"Well," Thad said, "if I'm going to be tossing a 700-pound cookstove around tomorrow, I guess I'd better have some of that immortal stew. What about you?"

Will Hunter shrugged. "I can stand it if you can," he said.

Will Hunter left the cabin at first light. He rode his black gelding, bucking the drifts along the Virginia City road. An hour later, Thad harnessed the four-mule team, hitched them to the empty wagon, and set out for the same destination.

Overhead, tattered gray clouds brooded above the hills. Gusting winds swept the new snow back, stinging the eyes of mules and driver alike. Cautious on the icy slope, Thad applied the brake as he felt the wagon fishtail and slide ominously toward the steep shoulder of the road. The mules rolled their eyes, nervously quick-stepping on the slippery surface. With a sense of foreboding, Thad squinted into the blowing snow as he struggled to control the team.

Abruptly, the nigh lead mule kicked over the traces, creating a general insurrection. The wagon slewed precariously and dropped off the road with a crash into a deep, snow-filled washout. Thad urged the team onward in vain; the mules either could not or would not pull the wagon out of the drift. Taking a shovel from the wagon, Thad stepped out into waist-deep snow and started digging.

The day Thad Mitchell would later count as his best day was starting badly. The day was going to continue downhill from here.

Thirty minutes later, with the wheels and undercarriage cleared, Thad found himself winded and sweat-drenched. He tossed the shovel back into the wagon and plunged through the drifts until he reached the lead mules. Minutes later, exhaling vapor and curses, he had readjusted the traces and was urging the team on again. The mules, however, had apparently made their own decision regarding their ability to move the wagon. The vote was unanimous; they could not. After a half-hearted attempt, they ignored Thad's curses and blows and sank into a mystic mule meditation that admitted no outside information at all. Wearied by the struggle, his mule-persuading vocabulary exhausted, Thad passed into a sulk that equalled, if not surpassed, that of the animals.

Finally, nearly an hour after leaving the cabin, Thad achieved a victory of sorts. Soaked through by wet snow and perspiration, disheveled and angry, he unhitched the team and moved it to the rear of the wagon. Apparently, pulling the wagon backward was a concept just contrary enough to appeal to the mules. They lunged into the traces with a will and soon freed the stalled wagon. Thad re-hitched the team to the front of the wagon, took a minute or two to catch his breath, and took to the road again. The wagon was stuck twice more before he reached the settlement, but Thad shoveled free each time. He found consolation by telling himself the worst of the day had passed. He was wrong.

Tobe Willis looked cold and grumpy when Thad drove up to the Blue Pony. The sun had broken through the clouds. The brightness reflecting off the new snow dazzled the eye and caused both men to squint.

"Morning, Tobe," Thad said. "Nice of you to lend a hand."

"Nice, my ass," Tobe growled, "Ulberg told me I had to. They's about four thousand things I druther do than help you load a cookstove. And it ain't morning, by god, it's afternoon. Where the hell have you been?"

"Got stuck once or twice," Thad said amiably, "but I'm here now. Brought bridge planks for a ramp, and a block and tackle. Lead me to that cast-iron cooker."

"You're mighty damn cheerful for a man about to load a stove," Tobe grumbled.

"Look at the bright side," Thad said. "Once we get it on the wagon, your work's done. Mine won't be finished until it's delivered and unloaded."

"Somehow that don't cheer me a whole hell of a lot," Tobe said. "Drive your wagon around back and we'll let the fun begin."

———◆———

Thad drove the team around to the rear of the Blue Pony and backed the wagon up to the door. He stepped down, set the brake, and opened the tailgate. Sliding the bridge planks out to form a ramp, he attached the block and tackle inside the wagon box. Meanwhile, inside the building, Tobe Willis, to lighten the load, removed the stove lids, warming oven, doors, and grates. Straining, the men hefted and slid the massive range inches at a time toward the door and outside.

That short trip did little to improve Tobe's disposition. As soon as he began to catch his breath, he used it to discuss—in grunts and gasps—the improbable ancestry of the stove, and of John Ulberg, his employer. Thad attached the block and tackle and began inching the heavy range up the ramp. The planks bowed ominously under the weight as Thad eased the stove upward. Tobe Willis continued to mutter, now including Thad in his general cursing of the weather, his luck, the day of his birth, the stove's designer, its manufacturer, and the whole idea of cookstoves in general.

The two men nearly had the range loaded when one of the planks snapped with a sound like a rifle shot. The stove fell sideways into the street and onto the toes of Thad's left foot. Because Thad Mitchell had been born to, and reared by, church-going parents he took seriously the commandment against profanity; however, when the full weight of the range drove his foot into the snow-covered earth he gave vent to such creative swearing that even Tobe Willis was impressed.

Pushing with all their might, the two men managed to tip the heavy range enough to free Thad's foot. Thad sat down in the snow, pulled his boot off, and examined the throbbing digits of his foot. Finding all five toes present and unbroken, he apologized to the Almighty, wiped the tears from his eyes, and returned to the task at hand. After a brief search, Tobe Willis produced a replacement plank from a nearby storage shed. Forty-three minutes later, the ponderous stove finally rested four-square and solid in the wagon bed. "Now you have yourself a good time unloadin' that stove, Thaddeus," Tobe Willis said. "As for me, I wouldn't touch that man-killin' sum'bitch again for all the gold in the gulches."

———◈———

The lunch crowd at the Orphan Girl Cafe had eaten long since and gone their way by the time Thad pulled up to the restaurant's back door. His injured foot still throbbed, and an icy wind penetrated his clothing and gripped his sweated body in a frigid embrace. Cootie Blake stepped out through the doorway, peered up at Thad, and asked, "You the feller that's bringin' Miss 'Piphany's new stove?"

Thad's injured foot sent a streak of pain through his body as he stepped down from the wagon, but he managed a smile. "Sure am," he said. "Glad you're around to help unload—it's a mite heavy."

Cootie rubbed his chin and looked wistful. His long face and sad, red-rimmed eyes reminded Thad of an old bloodhound. "Well, now," he said, "I ain't sure how much he'p I'll be. Hurt my back Tuesday week, and can't do much liftin.'"

"Somehow that doesn't surprise me," Thad said wearily. "Is there anyone else around who can help me unload this thing?"

Cootie shook his head. "There was, half an hour ago. Lunch crowd's gone now. Nobody here but Miss 'Piphany and me."

Thad sighed. "Maybe I can round up some men over at the Miner's Rest," he said, "Where do you want the stove?"

"Well, Miss 'Piphany wants it inside, o' course. Trouble is, the old stove is still in there, too hot to move. Reckon you'll just have to put 'er here by the door. I'll throw a tarp over it once you get 'er off the wagon."

"You figure you can handle that all right?" Thad said, his voice rich with sarcasm. "Sure wouldn't want to see you strain yourself."

———◈———

Twenty minutes and ten dollars later, Thad had hired four burly drinkers from the Miner's Rest Saloon. He came limping back through the drifting snow to the Orphan Girl, leading his semi-sober work crew toward the wagon and its cargo. Arranging his planks and the block and tackle, Thad directed the men in the unloading process. Now, however, he found his problem to be too much help, rather than too little. Each of the men—including Cootie Blake, who was careful to lift nothing heavier than his eyebrows—had his own idea about how to best unload the stove. Thad soon found himself working against his helpers. One man slipped on the ice, bloodied his nose on the plank, and slid underneath the wagon. A second got into a shouting match with a third, each trying to move the stove in a different and opposite direction. Finally, with only the aid of his last remaining hired hand, Thad managed to get the stove off the wagon and onto the planks.

Suddenly, the block and tackle broke free and the massive range lurched down the ramp like a runaway locomotive. Desperately, Thad and his wide-eyed helper threw their weight against the plummeting stove, trying to slow its descent, but without noticeable effect. Leaping aside at the last possible moment, the two men watched as the range plowed into the drifted snow, belched an enormous quantity of soot from its interior, and came to rest in an upright position.

The silence that followed was profound. Black soot peppered the snowdrifts and begrimed the laborers. The worker who slipped on the ice sat beneath the wagon, dabbing at his bleeding nose with a bandanna. The two who had so recently been arguing stood wide-eyed and mute. The man who had helped Thad get the stove on the ramp lay sprawled and speechless on his back in a snowdrift. Thad, standing beside the stove, caught up a handful of snow and wiped his soot-streaked face. Cootie Blake kept raising his eyebrows and opening his mouth as if to speak, but no sound came out. From the eave of the cabin an icicle fell to earth with a soft, tinkling sound. Thad laughed.

Artesian mirth rose within him and erupted in hearty laughter. The day had been a series of disasters since he'd set out that morning, problems and mishaps piling upon each other in mad profusion. There was nothing left to do but laugh. Laugh he did, falling on his back and roaring into the chill mountain air with a giddy, contagious hilarity. A chuckle rose in the throat of the fallen worker and worked its way up to a guffaw. A second man joined the raucous laughter, then a third. Soon, all six men were rolling in the snow, convulsed with glee.

As the merriment reached full crescendo, Epiphany Baker opened the door and looked out. She clutched her shawl about her slim shoulders and stared, confusion plain on her face. "What in the world. . . ?" she began.

The laughter stopped abruptly as the men scrambled to their feet. Thad stood up and snatched his hat off. His eyes met Epiphany's. In that moment, his young life changed forever.

She was tall and slender, Thad saw, fair of skin, with flaxen hair and full lips. Her eyes were large, soft, and deep. Beneath a starched apron, she wore a blue-checked gingham dress, close-fitting at waist and bodice, the skirts full and flaring. She stood outside the door, hands on hips, her brown eyes now flashing. "What," she demanded, "is going on here?"

Her tone, Thad thought, was exactly like that of a teacher speaking to a group of mischievous boys. Further suggesting that image, the workmen brushed snow off their clothing, lowered their eyes, and looked guilty. Cootie Blake jammed his hands into his pockets and hung his head. Only Thad met Epiphany's eyes. He found himself lost in their depths, captured by her glance. "I. . . I'm Thad Mitchell, ma'm," he stammered, "delivering this range for John Eyes. I mean *Oakes*."

Her appraisal was cool. Thad suddenly had a clear image of how he must appear to her. Abashed, he lowered his eyes. He felt his face grow hot and knew he was blushing. Soot smudged his face and clothing. His overcoat was dirty and ragged. He ran the fingers of his left hand through his tangled hair and raised his eyes to hers again.

"Block and tackle gave way, ma'am," he said. "Dropped the range fast down the ramp. We tried to stop it, but—"

"Forgive me, Mr. Mitchell," Epiphany said, "but you seem unusually clumsy for a freighter. Are you new at the work?"

"Yes, ma'am. Until recently, I worked a claim up the gulch. Will Hunter offered me a partnership in his freight business, and I accepted. I have to admit this is the worst day I've had since I started, ma'am."

"I'm not a 'ma'am,' Mr. Mitchell," Epiphany said coolly. "I am an unmarried woman, thus, a 'Miss.' My name is Miss Epiphany Baker, and that stove you and your men have handled so roughly belongs to me."

"Yes, ma'am. . . miss. It was an accident. I apologize."

The commotion outside her cafe had at first startled Epiphany, but the stove seemed undamaged. Epiphany found herself enjoying the confrontation with the men. Their chagrin amused her. The four workmen slipped quietly away, walking back toward Wallace Street. The young freighter still stood, hat in hand, his eyes on hers. His smile was honest, open. Epiphany had the clear impression he was laughing at his own folly.

She tried to maintain a commanding pose, but found herself trying to contain her own smile. Turning away, she said, "Your apology is accepted. Good day, Mr. Mitchell." She closed the door behind her.

Thad turned the team out onto the road that led back to the cabin above Daylight Creek. The bitter wind seemed to knife through his clothing, penetrating his vitals and chilling him to the bone. His injured foot throbbed painfully. He felt a sharp tug in his lower back that bespoke a pulled muscle. Fixed on the memory of a slender girl with warm brown eyes and straw-colored hair, his physical discomfort seemed to vanish like smoke in a whirlwind.

During the winter he had spent in the Idaho diggings, Thad had traded an extra horse for a copy of *A Tale of Two Cities* by Charles Dickens. As he turned his four-mule team up the grade that led home to his cabin, he smiled, remembering. The novel's opening line seemed to perfectly describe the past 12 hours of his own life: *"It was the best of times, it was the worst of times."*

FOURTEEN
Venus and Eros

G EORGE IVES was drunk. He was not mean drunk, maudlin drunk, or falling-down drunk. Henry Plummer's associate in crime had consumed just enough whiskey to feel rowdy, reckless, and full of the Devil. He had spent the night—and the last of his ready cash—with a whore called Mexican Alice, and he was not yet ready to end his debauch.

Late morning found him astride a handsome sorrel horse on the snow-swept streets of Virginia with an empty purse and the urge to continue his binge. Ives reined the horse to a stop, inhaled the cold morning air, and looked around.

A hundred yards down the street, lamplight glowed in the windows of the Square Deal Saloon. Ives grinned and turned the horse toward the saloon. The Square Deal was a log building, low and long, with a large 20-pane window on each side of its recessed front door. Inside, men played poker beneath a hanging lamp, and a bartender in a brocade vest dozed standing up behind the bar. Ives turned the sorrel around facing the street and backed the animal up onto the boardwalk. The window to the right of the door shattered with a resounding crash as the sorrel's rump breached the glass. Ives stepped down and strode into the saloon.

Behind the bar, Bud Pettigrew, owner of the Square Deal, tried to hide his anger. "Damn, George," he said, "it's a cold day to be without a window."

Ives put a foot on the rail and both hands on the polished hardwood. "A man runnin' a business has to deal with all manner of risks," he said, "fire, flood, cyclones—even horses' asses." He tossed his empty purse on the bar. "I think you need some insurance, Bud—about forty dollars worth ought to cover you."

George Ives pulled his revolver and glanced about the room. "I wouldn't wait too long to pay for it, neither," he said. "Somethin' *else* is liable to get broke."

"Here," Pettigrew said, placing two double eagles on the bar, "and your drinks are on the house."

Ives put the coins in the purse and pocketed it. He leaned on an elbow, looking back toward the shattered window, as Pettigrew poured whiskey into a glass, "I'd get that window fixed soon if I was you, Bud," he said. "This cold weather could hang on awhile."

Thirty minutes later, Ives left the Square Deal and rode his sorrel down to a barbershop on Cover Street. Once there, he treated himself to a shave, haircut, and bath, and then had his suit brushed. He walked into Cy Skinner's saloon at 11:15. Henry Plummer was waiting, drinking coffee at the bar.

"Good morning, George," the sheriff said. "Your eyes look like two burned holes in a blanket. When did you sleep last?"

Ives grinned. "I'll catch up on my snoozin' when I'm dead, but I am hungry. Right now I could eat a raw skunk."

"There's a new cafe up on Idaho, the Orphan Girl. Epiphany Baker runs the place. You can buy me lunch."

"Baker? That wouldn't be the sweet little piece Will Hunter brought to the gulch, would it?"

"None other."

"I've only seen her from a distance. If she looks as good up close as she does from afar I just may have to make a run at her."

Plummer's smile was cold and thin. "I suppose that's the very *least* you could do," he said.

———◈———

At the Orphan Girl, Epiphany Baker sprinkled salt, pepper, and flour over the elk steaks and pounded the mixture well into the meat. Deftly, she fried the fat she'd trimmed earlier, added shortening, and fried each steak five minutes per side. With a fork, she put each steak on a thick china plate, added fried potatoes, biscuits, gravy, and green beans, and then placed the dishes on the worktable beside her new restaurant range. Catching the eye of Cootie Blake, she called out, "Order for the Murchison brothers," and watched as Cootie carried the steaks to a table near the front door.

The kitchen was hot and smoky. Epiphany swung open the back door, blocking it ajar with the brick she used as a doorstop. She watched the smoke clear. She felt the chill, entering air, and breathed deeply. As usual, customers nearly filled The Orphan Girl. Epiphany allowed herself a moment of self-congratulation. She had worked hard, kept her eye on details, and had prepared a variety of dishes. She had listened to her customers' suggestions; she'd sought Lily Rae's advice. She tried to find ways to surprise her clientele with special delicacies and desserts.

Epiphany smiled. One of her regulars, an older man who had been among the early Forty-Niners in California, told her, "You surely have struck a rich vein with this shebang, girl. Your cookin' is high grade and fillin', but it wouldn't make no never-mind if it wasn't. Most of these boys," he said, indicating the room full of diners, "would eat sagebrush and wood chips just for the chance to look at you while they're doin' it."

Three miners at a table near the door slid their chairs back and stood up. From beneath their hatbrims they glanced shyly at Epiphany. She rewarded them with a smile. At the front counter the men paid their bill in gold dust, offering their pokes to Cootie Blake. Cootie took a pinch from each poke, dropped the dust in a metal box, and the miners went outside.

Epiphany smiled. When she had first opened the cafe she had acted as her own cashier. Cootie's thumbs, however, were twice the size of hers and the pinches he took brought in more revenue. Epiphany turned back to her stove. Cootie was already clearing the just-vacated table.

The tinkle of the bell above the front door caught Epiphany's attention. Looking up from her cooking, she saw two men, both wearing black hats and overcoats, enter and take chairs at a table near the west wall. The men doffed their coats and hung them on pegs, though they kept their hats on. Both were well-dressed, she noted, wearing dark business suits and white shirts. There was something familiar about the smaller man. Epiphany was certain she'd seen him before, but at the moment she could not think where.

The man seated himself with his back against the wall. He looked across the room at Epiphany, touched his hatbrim in salute, and nodded. The other man placed his elbows on the table, leaned on them, and smiled. He, too, was watching her.

Abruptly, recognition came to Epiphany. She had met the smaller man in Bannack when she and Will Hunter had first come to the diggings.

She realized that he was Henry Plummer, sheriff of both the Bannack and Fairweather districts. Smiling, she approached the table.

"Sheriff Plummer," she said, extending her hand, "Epiphany Baker. It's good to see you again. Welcome to the Orphan Girl." Plummer and his companion got to their feet. The sheriff bowed over Epiphany's hand. "A delight to see you, Miss Baker," he said. Indicating his companion, he said, "May I present my friend, George Ives? George, this is Miss Baker, proprietress of this cafe."

"Henry said you were well-favored," Ives told her, "but you're much more than that. You're a beautiful woman, Miss Baker."

"Why, thank you," Epiphany said. "Please, gentlemen, be seated."

She was strangely disturbed by the compliment. Warily, she took a closer look at the stranger. George Ives was handsome, she decided.

There was an air of confidence, almost of insolence, in his pose as he sat smiling up at her. His blue eyes seemed to hold a secret mischief in their depths. His gaze was bold and knowing.

The frankness in his glance disturbed her. Most men regarded her either with quiet respect or a diffidence that bordered on worship. There had been a few—one or two—who had looked at her with naked lust, undressing her with their eyes. Ives' look, however, was not like that. His eyes were fixed on hers, seeming to invite her to share in some wild and exciting adventure.

With an effort, Epiphany broke away from his glance, but almost immediately looked back again. Ives's hat was tipped back on his head, exposing a tousled shock of blonde hair that fell low across his brow. Epiphany's hand trembled. Astonished at her own reaction, Epiphany felt a nearly overwhelming impulse to reach out and smooth the man's disheveled hair.

Plummer's voice broke her trance. "We'll each have the steak dinner, Miss Baker, with coffee and—what kind of pie do you have?"

"Uh. . . pumpkin and mince today, Sheriff."

"I'll have the pumpkin. What about you, George?"

"Haven't had mince in a long while," Ives said. "Mince, if you please."

Back in the kitchen, Epiphany returned to the familiar routine of meal preparation. She liked the busy rush of the lunch hour and the way work made the time pass. On this day she found her glance returning often to the table where the sheriff and his friend sat. Each time she looked their way, Epiphany found the intense blue eyes of George Ives looking back.

The men finished their meal, stood, and donned their overcoats. George Ives offered his poke for Cootie's commercial thumb. At the door, Henry Plummer tipped his hat to Epiphany and nodded before stepping out onto the street. Ives looked at her for a long moment, smiled, and followed the sheriff outside. Epiphany was still thinking about Ives' smile, and his lively blue eyes, when sleep finally came to her later that night.

Epiphany Baker was not the only person on the gulch to lose sleep that night. Three miles west of Virginia City, in the cabin above Daylight Creek, Thad Mitchell sat late over his work on the accounts of the Hunter-Mitchell Freight Company. He found himself letting his thoughts drift to Epiphany Baker.

Since their meeting on the day he had delivered her stove, she had seldom been out of his thoughts. He recalled how when the stove fell she had come out the cafe's back door to find him soot-covered and convulsed by laughter. She may have been perplexed, but she certainly had not been at a loss for words. "Forgive me, Mr. Mitchell," she'd said, "but you seem unusually clumsy for a freighter. Are you new at the work?"

He remembered the way she had looked—her warm brown eyes, the tiny freckles, her expressive, full-lipped mouth. He remembered the way her hair had shone in the sunlight. He recalled the lithe, sure way she'd carried herself—she had been as graceful as he had been clumsy. One by one, like treasured keepsakes, Thad took out the images of Epiphany Baker and reviewed them, like a miser counting money.

He closed the ledger, laid his pen on the table beside it, and wiped his ink-stained fingers. He awoke from his reverie with a start.

Will Hunter, his partner, was speaking to him. "Thad? I asked what do you think?"

"What? I'm sorry, Will—I guess I was wool-gathering. What were you saying?"

Hunter sat across the cabin on the edge of his bunk, cleaning his revolvers by lamplight. He replaced the cylinder, barrel, and wedge key on the second of his two .36 Navies and looked thoughtfully at his young partner. "I was *saying*," Hunter drawled, "that Walter Dance told me there's a great deal of freight on the levee at Fort Benton awaiting shipment to Bannack and Virginia. Most of it is just stacked in piles along the river. I think it might be worth our time to make a trip over there and pick some of it up. This open weather can't hold forever."

Thad looked at his hands. "Yes," he said, "The merchants and storekeepers will need that merchandise."

Hunter slid the revolvers back into their holsters and hung his gunbelt over a chair. Thad continued to look at his hands.

"I don't quite know how to ask this, Will," Thad said, "but do you. . . that is, are you and Miss Baker. . . I mean, I know you rescued her from the war party at The Meadows and that you brought her here to Virginia, but. . ."

"So that's it," Hunter said softly. "Epiphany and I traveled together, that's all. I'm fond of her, the way a man might be fond of a daughter."

"There's. . . nothing more? Not on either side?"

"Not on either side. So, you met Epiphany."

Thad nodded. "The day I delivered her cookstove. She took me for a prize fool, I'm afraid. My block and tackle broke and dumped her stove off the wagon. When she came out to see what all the ruckus was about, I was soaked through from sweat and snow, and covered with soot. I had a limp from dropping the stove on my foot, and I was laughing like an idiot. Whatever could go wrong that day *had* gone wrong. It was either sit down and bawl, go crazy, or laugh. I was laughing when I met her."

Hunter smiled. "At least she knows you have a sense of humor."

Thad rubbed the hair at the back of his head, chagrin plain on his face.

"The thing is, Will—I can't stop thinking about her. I've never felt this way about a woman before. I mean, I had only just that minute met her, but I felt. . . I felt. . ."

Hunter's voice was soft, his expression serious. "—as if you had always known her. As if you *recognized* her."

"That's right! How did you know—?"

"Felt that way myself once. I don't expect I will again."

Hunter closed his eyes, remembering. Then he said, "If you're asking my opinion, I think you two might be good for each other. But if you're looking for a stay-at-home, darn-your-stockin's and mind-the-house kind of woman, I don't think you'll find that in Piff Baker. She's ambitious and she has big dreams. I expect she'll do whatever it takes to realize them."

"Maybe she could use some help," Thad said hopefully.

"I suppose *everybody* can use help," Hunter replied.

On Monday of the following week, Thad Mitchell arranged to eat his lunch at the Orphan Girl Cafe. He was among the first in line when the cafe opened. When Epiphany swung the door wide to admit the waiting customers, Thad felt his heart skip a beat at the sight of her. Riding into Virginia City that morning, he had practiced the words he would speak when he saw her. He would remind her of their meeting. He would joke in a self-deprecating manner about his clumsiness that day. He would be clever, witty, and charming.

When his chance came, he was none of those things. He looked into Epiphany's deep brown eyes and lost his voice. The clever jests, the compliments, the charming speeches he had rehearsed were all forgotten. His throat grew tight. He stammered foolishly.

Somehow, he did find the words to remind her he was the teamster who had delivered her stove. Epiphany poured him a cup of coffee. He did place his order for lunch, but even that was not an unqualified success. Under the warmth of her gaze, Thad looked down at his hands, fumbling with his coffee and spilling it. Epiphany wiped up the spill with a dish cloth and smiled—tolerantly, Thad thought—as she might have done with a child, or an old and senile aunt.

Thad finished his meal, though he did not recall what it was he had eaten. He paid his bill, offering his buckskin poke for Cootie Blake's pinch.

His eyes remained fixed on Epiphany. Cootie could have taken half the gold he carried. Thad would neither have known nor cared.

Outside, on the street, he inhaled the crisp air, mounted his mule, and rode back to the cabin. His heart was light. Sweet confusion ruled his mind. Thad Mitchell was a man in love.

There was another customer at the Orphan Girl that week whose mind was fixed, not on the bill of fare, but on the cafe's proprietress.

George Ives entered the restaurant each day just before closing time. He stood inside the door, waiting as his eyes adjusted to the dimness. He smiled his bold smile when he caught Epiphany's eye. Ives wanted a table to himself. If the cafe was busy, he waited until one became available. Always, he ordered the daily special, coffee, and dessert, watching Epiphany as he ate. Always, he was among the last to finish, nodding at acquaintances as they left, staying until the lunchroom emptied.

The first day set the pattern. Epiphany left the kitchen, smiling as she approached his table. Ives stood up to his full six feet as she came near, returning her smile. He asked her to sit with him while he finished his coffee. Epiphany poured herself a cup and joined him. She sat across from him, glad to be off her feet. His eyes held her. Epiphany had the same odd sensation she had the day she met Ives; his gaze seemed to invite her to a special place of adventure and danger.

He talked about his job. He told her that he worked for a rancher outside the town who boarded horses. Whenever a traveler wished to take a journey, Ives would find and deliver the traveler's horse to him. Ives spoke of places he'd been—cities, towns and mountain vistas. He told her stories of people he had known. He imitated their voices and mannerisms, exaggerating for comic effect. Epiphany's laughter rewarded him.

From time to time, as he built upon a story with gestures and pantomime, his hand lightly touched hers or rested briefly on her arm. Once, as she laughed with delight at an especially vivid description he gave of a flirtatious dowager, his fingers lightly brushed her thigh, lingered, and quickly withdrew.

At first, Epiphany found this touching invasive and slightly unsettling. Later, she decided it was unintentional, merely a result of George Ives's enthusiasm. There was something more, although she could scarcely admit it even to herself. Ives's touches were also, well— strangely *exciting*.

Eventually, Ives would take his watch from his vest pocket, snap open the case, and look at its face. "Lord, where does the time go?" he would say, "I have to be getting back to work." Then he'd offer his poke to Cootie, saying, "Take another pinch, old hoss—for Miss Epiphany." He would open the door, stand briefly in the opening as if reluctant to leave her, and say, "Until tomorrow then. Good afternoon, Miss." Then he was gone, riding away up the street on his handsome sorrel horse. If Epiphany remained at the open door, Ives would turn in the saddle and wave his hat before turning down toward Wallace Street.

◈

Nearly three weeks after George Ives began stopping daily at the Orphan Girl, he was passing the doorway of Dance and Stuart's store when "Clubfoot" George Lane hobbled out onto the boardwalk and waved him down. "Henry wants to see you, George," Lane said. "He's waitin' for you down at the Elephant Pen."

The Elephant Pen Livery Stable and wagon yard stood at the bottom of Daylight Gulch, just west of town. A large adjacent corral held stacks of loose hay and was a favorite playground for the children of Virginia City. George Ives rode down off the bench into the gulch and drew rein at the corral. Inside the barn, Henry Plummer smoked a cigar and watched as Ives loose-tied the sorrel and walked toward him.

"Afternoon, George," Plummer said.

"Clubfoot said you wanted to see me, Henry," Ives said. "I came as soon as I heard."

Plummer smiled his careful smile and exhaled a thin stream of tobacco smoke. "I hope I didn't take you away from your romantic campaign, George."

Ives grinned. "No," he said. "I just fanned her sweet, young fire—same as always—and left the coals a-glowin'. I've seen her every day for three weeks. I've got her to where she looks forward to my coming. Now I'll make myself scarce for three or four days."

"So that when you come back, those coals may burst into flame?"

Ives laughed aloud. "Couldn't have put it better myself. What did you want, Henry?"

Plummer studied the ash on his cigar. He raised his eyes to Ives and said, "A miners' court at Nevada City flogged a certain man recently and let him go. You know who I'm talking about."

"Yeah," Ives said, "I heard about it. So?"

"This man seems to have made some kind of bargain with the court. Apparently, he's agreed to give them times and places of certain *transactions* of ours."

Ives swore. "That damn lick-finger! Where is he now?"

"I understand he'll be on the road between Virginia and Dempsey's ranch today. Close his mouth, George."

Ives was already striding toward his horse. "You can count on it, Henry," he said.

George Ives sat beneath a wind-twisted pine on a ridge overlooking the Virginia City road. Behind him, tied short to a another tree, his sorrel gelding dozed in the shadows. The view from the ridge was a good one. Ives could see the road stretching out for miles across the broken country. Several teams and wagons, as well as men on horseback, were moving on the trail that day, but Ives was looking for one particular rider.

Cloud shadows rippled over the valley and a fresh breeze brought a chill to Ives, even there in the shelter of the pines. Briskly, he rubbed his hands together, blowing on his fingers. Crossing his arms, he placed his hands beneath his armpits and huddled deeper into his heavy overcoat.

"Damned informer!" he muttered. "There was no call for a man to spill his guts," he thought. "We organized the "Innocents" to protect our people. All the yellow bastard had to do was repeat the password, 'I am innocent,' and Henry and the boys would have helped him. Instead, he ran his mouth and put every man in the outfit at risk."

Ives broke open the double-barreled shotgun he had brought and checked its loads. "The damned rat has spilled his guts," Ives thought darkly. "Now I'll spill his blood."

The rider came slowly around a bend in the road astride a spavined brown mare. He wore a dirty felt hat, pulled low over restless eyes. He rode slumped in the saddle as if apologizing for being alive. The man huddled beneath a heavy woolen coat that seemed two sizes too large for his small frame, and his head made short jerky motions as he glanced nervously about him.

Despite his apparent vigilance, the rider didn't see George Ives until he was almost upon him. From a patch of scrub cedar, Ives stepped silently out of the shadows and faced the horseman. Sunlight glinted off the barrels of the shotgun in Ives' hands. He raised the weapon and pointed it at the sad-eyed rider. "You're dead meat, you loose-lipped bastard!" Ives said, and pulled both triggers.

A wall of buckshot struck the man's chest. His body rocked backward with the impact, and pieces of fabric flew in the sunlight. The rider swayed forward and sat upright again, seemingly unhurt. He looked at his attacker and knew his death had come, yet there was no fear in his eyes. There was only a great sadness, and a kind of weary resignation.

"Not enough damn powder," Ives said, as if apologizing to his victim. Ives pulled his revolver and shot the rider through the head.

Slowly, the man slipped sideways from the saddle and fell heavily to the ground. Ives spurred the sorrel forward and caught the reins of the mare. Then, with a contemptuous glance at the dead man in the road, Ives led the animal away into the hills.

FIFTEEN

Visitors and Vandals

N OVEMBER'S DAYS GREW fewer, falling away like the yellow leaves of the cottonwoods along the gulch. Miners lifted their eyes to the mountains and saw winter already settled among the peaks. They inhaled the brisk air and tasted an urgent melancholy. Those who had determined to leave the diggings had already gone, returning to their homes in the east. Only a few had struck it rich. Others had done well enough to consider their enterprise a success. Some, their great adventure behind them, returned empty-handed to loved ones who cared only that they returned alive.

In Virginia City and the other settlements, saloon keepers, prostitutes, and cardsharps continued to harvest the miners who remained. Nearly every third building in the towns was either a saloon, hurdy-gurdy house, or gambling hall. The prospector who entered those establishments usually left with an empty purse and an aching head. Drunkenness, street fights, and killings were common. Bowie knives flashed in the lamplight and gunfire exploded in the smoky saloons and dance halls. Seeking entertainment and the company of others, miners were drawn to the temptations of the gulch like moths to flame.

East of the Mississippi, Sunday was a quiet day of rest designed for worship, reflection, and family life. In the mining camps of the west, Sunday was the wildest day of the week. Every store was open, with hucksters on each street corner hawking their wares. Horse racing was popular. There were bowling alleys and billiard parlors. Prize fights attracted hundreds of onlookers. Each spectator cheered his favorite bare-knuckle battler as the fighters pounded each other bloody inside the squared circle. Cock fights, dog fights, bull fights, shooting competitions, as well as amateur and professional plays, recitals, and musicals, provided further opportunities for diversion.

The last to pan the tailings of the prospector's purse were the bunco artists and flim-flam men who sold hokum on the half-shell. Mediums, phrenologists, and fortune tellers promised knowledge of the unknowable. Medical quacks and snake-oil salesmen peddled cures for every ailment known to man or beast. Anyone able to offer a new novelty could quickly draw a crowd in a mining camp.

Beyond the excesses of Sunday in the mining camps were a people and a way of life that had nothing to do with drunkenness, gambling, and violence. Decent, hardworking men and women, merchants and professionals, tradesmen and artisans, lived in the settlements as well. Their goals were prosperity, progress, and permanence. They attended worship services, improved their homes and business places, and established schools and hospitals.

They met in groups small and large. They met in homes, lodge halls, and social clubs. The men gathered together in the ritual and fraternal assembly of Freemasonry. They discussed the rise of lawlessness and they decried the absence of protection by law. They agreed on the need for peace, justice, and order. They watched. They waited. As their outrage grew, their resolve became stronger.

Near the end of November, George Ives and two other road agents, Whiskey Bill Graves and Bob Zachary, robbed the Salt Lake mail coach between Virginia City and Bannack. The robbers were masked, and each wore a blanket over his clothing in an attempt to conceal his identity. They even attempted to disguise their horses by covering them with blankets. However, all these efforts were futile. Their victims were well acquainted with the three men and easily recognized them.

Later, in a Virginia City bordello, a drunken George Ives boasted that he had been one of the robbers. "I am the bamboo chief that committed that robbery," Ives said. While the precise meaning of "bamboo chief" has been lost to history, nobody at the bordello disputed his claim.

Meanwhile, Sheriff Henry Plummer, secret leader of the stage robbers, hosted a grand Thanksgiving Day dinner in Bannack for Chief Justice Sidney and Mrs. Edgerton, Colonel and Mrs. Wilbur Sanders, and other prominent citizens. The turkey, shipped in by stagecoach from Salt Lake City, cost the sheriff $40 in gold.

———◈———

As December began, snow drifted softly out of the gunmetal clouds that scowled above the gulch. Huge, wet flakes descended in the stillness of late afternoon. A blanket of white covered the rough camp and the displaced rock that scarred the banks of Alder Creek. On Idaho Street, horses huddled at the hitchrail outside the Orphan Girl, awaiting their riders. Lamplight glowed in the windows of the cafe. The smoke from the cafe's stovepipe swirled downward, toward the ground, and disappeared.

Inside, only a handful of diners remained. Four bearded prospectors sat together at a single table, lingering over their coffee in the cafe's warmth. Cootie Blake cleared the other tables and swept the floors, impatient for closing time. Epiphany poured water from the copper boiler atop the stove into a dishpan and began washing the dishes left by earlier customers. From time to time, she glanced expectantly toward the front entry; but the bell above the door remained silent.

Where *was* George Ives? Epiphany had grown accustomed to his daily visits. Ives had said nothing about leaving the gulch, but for the past four days he had not made his usual stop at the cafe. Epiphany missed him. She missed his reckless smile and dancing eyes. She missed sitting with him and drinking coffee after the other diners had gone.

She missed his conversation. Ives was a handsome man, Epiphany thought, an interesting blend of manly poise and boyish charm. She found him exciting, in much the same way she might have found being close to a dangerous wild animal exciting, or standing near the edge of a cliff. She enjoyed being with him.

Had something happened to him? She knew accidents were common in the diggings. Men fell in pits and mine shafts, and were injured. Horses proved fractious and skittish at inopportune times. Road agents prowled the trails around the camp, robbing and killing travelers. Had a highwayman waylaid him? Maybe he lay dead or wounded even now in some remote canyon. Epiphany imagined his lifeless body lying sprawled amid downed timber and deadfall, saw the falling snow covering his body.

Epiphany shook her head, forcing her thoughts to return to the practical. "Silly goose!" she thought. "It's not like you to deal in morbid fancies." The miners, she saw, had finished their coffee. They stood, pulling on their overcoats, preparing to leave the cafe. Cootie propped his broom against the wall and shuffled over behind the counter to receive their payment. One of the miners tipped his hat to Epiphany and smiled. She returned the smile. "Thank you, gentlemen," she said, "I do hope you'll come back."

"Yes'm. We surely will," said the prospector as he stepped out onto the street. Epiphany was just moving to bar the door behind them when she saw George Ives pull up in a top buggy. He was dressed for the weather in a heavy blue overcoat, a red woolen muffler, and a wide-brimmed black felt hat.

He smiled his bold smile at Epiphany and reined the carriage horse to a stop facing the door. "I would not have thought it possible," he said, "but you have grown even more lovely since I saw you last."

Epiphany felt a warm glow flood through her. She returned Ives's smile and reached up to smooth her hair. She was surprised to note that her hand trembled. "It's good to see you again, George," she said.

Beneath the buggy's canopy, Ives features were illuminated by light from the cafe door. His eyes looked directly into Epiphany's. "I can't believe how much I've missed you, Piff," he said. "Now it appears I've missed lunch, too. Well, no matter."

Behind him, Epiphany saw that the snowfall was ending. Sunlight broke through the dark clouds. "The storm has passed," Ives said, "and the country will soon be full of light and glory. Come for a drive with me."

"I should decline with thanks," Epiphany thought, "I should tell him I appreciate the offer, but that I cannot accept." What she said was, "That would be lovely, George. I'll get my coat."

George Ives drove the carriage horse at a brisk trot along the road that led to Summit. Close beside him, Epiphany nestled beneath the lap robe and watched the passing scene. New-fallen snow adorned the gravel piles and shaft holes along Alder Creek, but the stream remained clear of ice. A few prospectors continued to work their claims with a single-minded concentration on the work at hand.

Epiphany breathed in the winter air, glad to be away for a time from the smoke and stifling heat of her kitchen. She closed her eyes, feeling the cold wind on her face, savoring the clean scents of pine and sage.

As the road climbed upward, Epiphany became increasingly aware of Ives's body on the seat beside her. Her breathing quickened. Furtively, she glanced at his face. Ives looked straight ahead, his attention fixed on the rocky, winding road. Epiphany studied his profile—the strong jawline, the sun-wrinkles at the corners of his eyes, the tousled blonde hair that tumbled from beneath his hatbrim and curled about his ears and collar. She felt again that strange urge to reach out and smooth his hair. What would he do if she really did reach out?

At the top of the grade, the road turned back down the ridge briefly before climbing again. Instead of following the road, Ives turned the buggy off to the right and drew rein at a point overlooking the valley. To the northwest, beyond the peaks of the Ruby Mountains, the Pioneer and Highland ranges loomed. Close at hand, the slopes fell away in a jumble of timbered ridges, where jackpine and scrub cedar trees cast blue shadows against the snow's brightness. High overhead, a red-tailed hawk circled in a smooth glide. As the hawk turned above them, its tailfeathers glowed red against the sun.

For a moment, Ives gazed at the panorama below. Then he said, "I wanted you to see this view because I knew you'd appreciate it. There's a beauty here that can't be found in towns and cities."

"It's magnificent, George," Epiphany said softly, "thank you."

Ives turned, his face close to hers. "You didn't even hesitate when I asked you to come out with me," he said. "Aren't you worried about what people might think?"

Epiphany met his gaze and held it. Again, she had the odd sensation that she had at their first meeting. Ives' intense gaze once more seemed to invite her to join him in some secret and thrilling adventure. She felt a stirring in her blood, and her heartbeat quickened. She crossed her gloved hands in her lap and dropped her eyes. "People will think what they will," she said, "I won't live my life according to the opinion of others."

Ives' smiled. "I sensed that about you," he said. "I knew the day we met that you were different. You're like no woman I've ever known."

His smile warmed her. She had remembered that smile, thought of it each night in her bed before sleep took her. Once, she had dreamed of it. "I love this land," she said. "It's wild and free, and it promises success to those strong enough to take it. I intend to have that success."

"The world belongs to men," she continued. "Men make the rules. Men tell women what they may do, what they may say, what their work may be. They try to tell us who we may love, and how. Women are supposed to stay at home, be submissive and supportive, and contentedly live their lives through their men. That will never be my way."

Ives took her hand in his. "I would not expect it to be, dear Piff," he said. "As I said, you're not like other women."

She looked into his eyes again and lost her way. Desperately, she tried to lighten the moment. "Have you known. . . so *many* women, George?" she asked.

"Yes, many," he said, "but none like you."

He took her in his arms then and kissed her. His lips lightly brushed hers, then grew more fervent. Epiphany felt his hands against her back, drawing her to him. She felt his beard stubble, tasted traces of tobacco and whiskey. She had wanted this moment, even longed for it. Now she thrilled to the fire it kindled in her blood. She returned Ives's kiss, caught in an abandon so great it dizzied her. His lips moved to her cheek, her eyelids, her neck. She felt his breath hot in her ear. Suddenly frightened, she brought her hands to Ives's chest, pushing against him. She drew back, her hands gripping his arms, the pounding of her heart loud in her ears. Epiphany turned her head away, shaken and breathing hard, her fear no longer of Ives but of herself. "No, George," she said. "Please. . . not now, not like this."

His eyes held her. Slowly, he withdrew, his hands no longer demanding, but gently holding hers. His face was composed now, his voice measured and serious. "I'm not sorry I kissed you, Piff," he said. "I'd be a damned liar if I said I was. I am sorry if I frightened you, sorry if I rushed you."

Epiphany turned away, disturbed by the depth of her passion. "Please, George," she said, "take me home now."

Ives turned the buggy back onto the road. "Of course, Piff," he said. His expression was properly contrite, but his heart rejoiced. He had tasted the ardor in her kiss, and he exulted. She would give herself to him, he was sure. It was only a matter of time.

The snow was already melting when Thad Mitchell turned the mud-spattered freight wagon up the slope above Daylight Creek. The road had turned greasy and slick from the snowmelt, and the four-mule team leaned into their collars as they struggled to keep their footing. When he reached the turn-off that led to the cabin, Thad reined the animals off the road and down through the trees. Pulling the mules in and applying the brake, he slowed the wagon's descent. It was as he broke out of the shadows and into the brightness of the yard that he first noticed the tracks.

Hoofprints and the tracks of booted men were clear and sharp in the new-fallen snow. Footprints were all around the corral, the lean-to, and the cabin. His heart pounding, Thad reined the team to a stop, set the brake, and stepped down. From beneath the wagon seat, he drew the heavy ten-guage shotgun he kept there. Thad held the gun ready as he stepped quickly through the snow and muck toward the cabin.

Broken and battered, the cabin door hung by a hinge. Beside the entry, split wood from the woodpile lay scattered about the yard. A blanket from Will Hunter's bed lay sodden in the melting snow, and canned goods littered the ground. Thad cocked the hammers on the shotgun, took a deep breath, and stepped through the doorway.

Inside the cabin, havoc reigned. Bedding was strewn around the cabin. The contents of shelves and boxes were scattered about the floor. Dried beans and flour mixed with mud from the boots of the raiders. Even the floor boards had been pried up. Thad let the scattergun's hammers down and exhaled. A quick first look about the cabin's interior revealed nothing missing. Whoever had broken into the cabin had apparently not found what they were looking for, but it wasn't for lack of trying.

Who had done this? What, Thad asked himself, were they looking for? Even as he asked the question, he knew. They had been looking for gold, of course, the ten thousand dollars in dust and nuggets he'd taken from Alder Creek, another ten thousand he had received from selling his claim, and almost twelve thousand belonging to Hunter! Thad rushed outside, his eyes fixed on the corral and lean-to. Please, God, he prayed as he dashed through the yard, let it still be there!

The lean-to was a three-sided shed that Thad and Will Hunter had built in the trees behind the corral to serve as a storage place for harness, saddles, and other equipment incidental to their freight-hauling business. Against the back wall, a large wooden barrel containing oats for the livestock lay on its side, the grain spilled and scattered. Harness was strewn beneath the trees. The double-ratchet forge used for working horseshoes and light blacksmithing lay tipped on its side.

A massive anvil stood bolted to the cross-section of a large cottonwood log. Heavier than needed—nearly three hundred pounds—the anvil had been accepted by Hunter as part payment for a hauling job. Thad held his breath. Hands trembling, he swung the block and tackle into place from the rafter overhead, raised anvil and base together off the ground, and thrust his arm into the hole beneath. At first, his fingers touched only the sides of the nail keg he had buried when they built the shed. Then, reaching deeper, he felt the buckskin pokes that held the glittering gold. Thad closed his eyes and breathed a sigh of relief.

Twice, he counted the pokes, handling each one to assure himself that the treasure was still intact. Convinced at last, Thad returned the heavy pokes to the barrel, lowered the anvil back to its place, and took down the block and tackle. Whoever the thieves were, they had not found the cache. Working quickly, Thad began to put the lean-to back in order.

He was nearly finished when he heard the hoofbeats. Someone was coming down from the road. Thad picked up his shotgun. The hoofbeats were closer now, approaching the lean-to and corral. Thad took a deep breath and stepped out into the light, bringing the gun to his shoulder and aiming it toward the opening in the trees.

The black gelding tossed its head high, hindquarters dropping as it slid to a stop. Will Hunter swung his Colt's Navy sharply toward Thad, the sound of its cocking clear in the stillness. For the briefest moment the two men faced each other over the barrels of their leveled weapons. Then Hunter raised his revolver, eased the hammer down, and grinned. Nodding toward the cabin, he asked, "What happened here, partner? Did you have bears in for dinner?"

Thad lowered the shotgun. "Bears in gum boots," he said, "prospecting for gold, I expect. *Our* gold."

Dismounting, Hunter asked, "Did they find it?"

"No. Too big a hurry. Too lazy to move the anvil."

"Don't blame them. No point in stealing if it involves work."

Hunter was studying the tracks. "Looks like two men. Bummers from town, most likely. Anything missing from the cabin?"

"Doesn't seem to be," Thad said, frowning, "but they sure made a mess."

Hunter grinned. "Nothing worse than a messy thief," he said. "You'd think the least they could do is rob a man neatly."

"The damn lawbreakers are getting worse all the time, Will! I've prospected from California to Colorado to Idaho, and I've never seen it this bad. Back in those camps a hungry man might rob a sluice for the price of a meal or a bottle, but I always felt safe leaving my cabin open. I can't recall a time when the road agents and thieves were as bad as they are here."

Hunter lifted his soggy blanket from the snow and slung it across the stretched rope he and Thad used as a clothesline. "I expect the problem will get worse before it gets better," he said. "Up to now the miners have been too busy working their claims to take a stand. As long as they aren't robbed personally they figure everything is all right. The time for good men to stand together against the thieves and killers is long overdue."

Thad picked up a spare shirt from the wet snow, wrung it out, and added it to the clothesline. "Well," he said, "at least they didn't find our dust this time. Let's clean up the mess and get supper on the stove. Being ransacked by thieves makes me cranky, but being hungry makes me even worse."

———◈———

Henry Plummer was sitting at his usual table in Cy Skinner's Virginia City saloon when Jack Gallagher and Boone Helm walked in. When the men saw Plummer they walked directly across the room and stopped at his table. Standing like truants before a schoolmaster, the road agents waited as the sheriff poured coffee into a delicate porcelain cup.

"Afternoon, boys," said Plummer. "How did your treasure hunt go?"

Boone Helm scowled. "Not so good. We went through everything them bastards owned, but we never found a damn thing."

Gallagher agreed. "That's right, Henry. Wherever Mitchell and Hunter have hid their dust, we sure couldn't locate it."

Plummer sipped his coffee. "That's too bad," he said. "Word is, Thad Mitchell took ten thousand out of his claim and got another ten when he sold it. What Hunter has is anybody's guess."

Plummer placed the cup carefully back in its saucer. "It's a cinch they haven't shipped their gold out—we'd have heard about it if they had. So it's still out there somewhere."

The sheriff raised his eyes to his henchmen and smiled his careful smile. "Cheer up," he said. "Now that you've stirred up the nest, I have a feeling they'll try to move their eggs to a safer basket. We'll be watching when they do."

Plummer nodded toward the bar. "You did well, boys," he said, "Tell Cy I said to give both you boys a whiskey on me."

———◈———

At the cabin above Daylight Creek, Will and Thad stood out beneath the clearing sky and watched evening come. In the west, a scatter of bright clouds blazed red, then turned ash-gray as the sun dropped behind the mountains. Most of the snow that had fallen earlier had melted, and the ground between the cabin and corral had turned into a sea of black mud.

The partners had eaten supper in silence, their thoughts on the men who had ransacked their cabin. Later, they had spent the better part of an hour taking inventory, repairing the damage, and setting things right. Now, as they watched the first pale stars appear, it was Will Hunter who spoke.

"You still heading for Bannack tomorrow?" he asked.

"Expect so," Thad said. "I'm picking up a mixed load at Ulberg's in the morning. Why?"

Will grinned. "You may be taking more of a mixed load than you figured on. Storekeeper named Ed Schwartz passed away yesterday over in Virginia City. Heart attack, I understand. His family lives in Bannack, and they want him buried there."

"Don't tell me—you want me to deliver his corpse to Bannack?"

Hunter's grin widened. "That's about the size of it. After all, we're freighters, and the late Mr. Schwartz has just become freight. About a hundred and sixty pounds, I'd judge, plus a handsome walnut coffin. You're to pick him up tomorrow at his place on South Jackson."

Thad stuck his hands in his pockets and leaned heavily against the cabin wall. "I was a happy young prospector before I let you talk me into becoming a teamster," he said. "All I had to worry about then was rheumatism, starvation, and the occasional claim-jumper. Now you want to turn me into an undertaker!"

Hunter laughed. "Look at the bright side, Thad," he said. "At least, Schwartz isn't likely to talk your ear off on the ride over."

SIXTEEN
The Late Mr. Schwartz

B RAVO SANTEE opened his eyes and stared up into the gloom. Overhead, the tangled brush and canvas that formed the roof and ceiling of the wakiup stared back. For a moment or two, he had no idea where he was. Santee closed his eyes again. Behind them, a dull ache throbbed, reminding him of the whiskey he had drunk the night before and the reason he had drunk it.

Time was, whiskey had been a way to untie the knots in his mind, a way to loosen up and take the hobbles off. Time was, he had drunk to celebrate life, and to just raise Billy Hell. Now and again he had drunk to ease his sorrows and to comfort himself. Some men used whiskey to boost their courage, but he had never been one of those. The Santee brothers, he told himself, had always been lion bold and wolverine mean, with no quarter given or asked. They had needed no brave-maker in a bottle to give *them* sand. No, he had begun last night's drunk for the poorest of reasons; he had drunk simply to kill the *boredom*.

Santee frowned. Thinking of his brother Rufus made his headache worse. He lived with the memory of Rufus, shot dead back there in Lawrence; gunned down in the bedroom of an abolitionist bitch for no crime but being a natural man! Santee threw the bed tarp back and sat up.

The wakiup was a marvel of disarray, dirt, and clutter. Ancient grease and charred food clung to the surface of a rusty box stove in the center of the room. Above the stove, a smoke-blackened lantern hung suspended from a wire. Whiskey bottles lay scattered beneath a stand that held a water bucket and basin. Faded playing cards littered the dirt floor. Rifles, belted revolvers, skillets, tin plates, boots, hats, and overcoats lay scattered in random piles.

Three other men slept beneath the stained canvas and quilts of their bedrolls. Jim Mosely and Corey McClure, Rebs like himself, were skedaddlers from the War. They were good men with a gun and game for anything—except, he thought, fighting Yankee regulars on an empty stomach. The third man, Goliath Pettigrew, was easy-going, loyal to Plummer and Santee, and completely devoid of fear. At three hundred and twenty pounds, he was strong as an ox and nearly as big.

The four of them had begun their binge to relieve the tedium, Santee supposed. It had been two weeks since they had killed the prospector and stolen his dust. The old man had come out of the timber above Bunton's ranch, on foot and carrying a pack on his back. Seeing a man walking in that country was not all that unusual. Prospectors traveled the road on foot almost every day, but that was exactly what had caught Santee's attention. The old man was not walking the road. He was avoiding other travelers, drifting in and out of the trees, trying hard not to be noticed.

Santee and the boys had ridden him down on horseback, running him until he was played out. Santee had shot him as he lay gasping for breath. They found barely eighty dollars in dust when they searched his body. In their disappointment and rage, Jim and Corey had taken turns shooting at the old man's corpse until Santee made them quit it. Goliath had carried the body to a ridge overlooking a narrow canyon and had thrown it into the tangled brush and deadfall below. Dividing the old man's gold between them, they found their violent crime had brought them exactly twenty dollars apiece.

Outside the wakiup, Santee squinted at the brightness and inhaled the crisp mountain air. From the position of the sun, he judged the time to be around eight-thirty in the morning. As they frequently did,

Santee's thoughts turned to Will Hunter, and his anger flared. "I came more than two thousand miles to find that Judas bastard," he thought, "only to be put on a chain by that slick-talkin' Henry Plummer. He says I can kill Hunter, but only when he tells me I can. I have to wait, says he. Well, by god I've had a bellyful of waitin' and I ain't sure how much longer I'm gonna do it."

In the trees behind the rude shelter, four saddlehorses drowsed on a picket line. As Santee watched, the animals became suddenly alert, heads erect. Standing stock still, the horses directed their eyes and ears toward a point west of the camp. Santee turned, hands resting on his holstered revolvers. He strained to see what the horses saw. The highway from Virginia City wound through jackpine and cedar before dropping down past Bunton's ranch. Santee could see no movement anywhere on the road.

He held his breath, the better to listen, but he heard only the wind sighing through the treetops. He glanced again at the horses. Still they stood, heads high, tasting the wind. Again, Santee tried to see what they saw. "Prob'ly jes' a damn deer or somethin'," he muttered. He had just bent to enter the low door of the wakiup when he heard the sound of hoofbeats. "No mistake," he thought. "There's someone coming this way, riding hard." "Rider comin', boys," he said quietly.

The horseman burst through the trees at a high lope just as Mosely, McClure, and Pettigrew stumbled out of the wakiup. "I am innocent," the rider called, slowing his lathered horse to a trot. Santee's hands still rested on the butts of his revolvers, but he felt the tension leave his shoulders on hearing the password of Plummer's men.

The rider reined the horse to a stop before Santee and looked down at the four outlaws. "Lookin' for Bravo Santee. I've got a message for him from Plummer himself."

"I'm Santee. Get down and rest your arse."

"Obliged, but I'm goin' down to Bunton's after. If I get down now, I might be too stiff to get back on."

"All right. What's the message?"

"Freighter name of Mitchell is comin' through today, bound for Bannack. Plummer thinks he might be carryin' gold."

"Never heard of him. How much gold?"

"Damned if I know. Might not be carryin' any—but if he is, Plummer says it could be from ten to twenty thousand."

Corey McClure whistled softly. Santee said nothing, but his yellow eyes glowed. Suddenly, the morning's hangover and the frustration he had felt all but vanished. "Sounds like it's worth lookin' into, all right. How do we spot this Mitchell?"

"He'll be drivin' a four-mule team, pullin' a light emigrant wagon. The boys at Virginia painted a red 'X' on the canvas top."

"'X' marks the spot, huh? Sure hope he's carryin' gold. It's been a long dry spell."

The rider turned his horse away, in the direction of Bunton's ranch. "Twenty thousand would end the drought," he said. "Luck to you boys."

Seated on the spring seat of the wagon, Thad Mitchell topped a rise on the road to Bannack and reined in his mules. He had spent the night at Dempsey's Cottonwood Ranch, twenty miles below Virginia; and he had been traveling again well before dawn. Now, late in the day, he saw Bunton's ranch in the distance and started the mules down the steep grade.

Thad had seen a number of wagons and horsemen throughout the morning. Now, as the afternoon sun dropped lower, the road was deserted. With his foot on the brake and his hands firmly grasping the reins, Thad turned the team toward the valley floor, riding the wagon as it jolted and swayed along the rocky track. The late sun was in Thad's eyes, blinding him to the trail ahead. Squinting against the glare, he slowed the wagon's descent as best he could, trusting the mules to keep to the road.

At the bottom of the grade the road narrowed, entering a shaded grove that seemed even darker after the sun's brightness. As Thad's vision cleared, he looked at the road ahead and saw the horsemen. They sat their mounts in the middle of the trail—four men in overcoats, their neckerchiefs pulled up over their faces, and their hats low over their eyes. Two of the men seemed to be about average size, while the one nearest the wagon was small, scarcely five feet four or so in height. Behind the three was a huge man astride a big, rawboned gelding. All four held shotguns at the ready, Thad noted; and all four were looking directly at him.

The small man rode forward a few paces and leveled the shotgun at Thad. "Throw up your hands, you mule-pushin' bastard!" he shouted.

Thad reined the mules to a stop, wrapped the reins around the brake handle, and raised his hands high. "Don't shoot, boys," he said. "I'm just a poor teamster, tryin' to make my way."

"You'll by god be a *dead* teamster if you give us any trouble," snapped the small man. "Get down off o' that wagon!"

Thad stepped down quickly and stood at the roadside. Corey McClure dismounted and strode quickly to cover Thad with his shotgun. He was keyed up and nervous, Santee noticed, making short, jerky motions with the gun, prodding and pushing at Thad. "Give us your damn gold, you sum'bitch!" he shouted. "Get it up right now!"

"I'm just a workin' man," Thad said. "Only gold I've got is two double eagles, but you're welcome to 'em." Keeping his right hand raised, Thad produced a buckskin purse and handed it to the robber.

"Damn you!" McClure shouted, his voice high-pitched and tight, "You've got more than that—*get it up!*" Savagely, he clubbed Thad with the barrel of his gun.

"Let him be, damn you!" Santee said. "He wouldn't be carryin' it on him—search the wagon!"

Pettigrew and Mosely were already obeying the command. The big man threw back the canvas cover as Mosely climbed up into the wagon box. "Gawdamighty, Santee!" Mosely bawled. "They's a damn coffin back here!"

Santee exploded. "You stupid bastard! Didn't I say never to call me by name? What do you mean, they's a coffin back there?"

Santee climbed up onto the wagon seat and looked inside. Together with assorted pieces of furniture and some boxed dry goods, a handsome coffin of varnished walnut did indeed occupy the wagon bed. "Damn!" Santee said. "Who's that coffin for, teamster?"

"It's not 'for' anyone," Thad said. "That casket is occupied. Store-keeper from Virginia named Schwartz passed away this week. I'm takin' his body to Bannack so his family can bury him there."

"We supposed to take your word for that?" Mosely said. "Hand me that pry bar, Pettigrew—I'll open that damn box."

"I'm not tryin' to tell you boys your business," Thad said, "but it might be better all around if you didn't. I'm told the man died of smallpox."

Beneath his mask, Mosely turned ashen. "Smallpox? Gawdamighty! I don't want nothin' to do with smallpox! That can *kill* a man!"

"It killed Schwartz," Thad observed.

Mosely scrambled out of the wagon and took several steps back. McClure was so nervous he almost seemed to be vibrating. Even Santee seemed uncertain. Only Pettigrew seemed undeterred. The giant crouched over the coffin and pried the lid up with a harsh screeching sound.

The late Mr. Schwartz lay face up in a bed of white satin, dressed in a dark suit and starched shirt, with his hands crossed over his chest. The eyes were closed. Thin wisps of white hair curled over the bald-ing head and ears. The dead man was a quite ordinary corpse, except in one regard. His face and hands were covered with what appeared to be small white scabs, plainly visible even in the dim light!

"The hell with this!" McClure said, making a rush for his horse. Startled, the animal backed away in alarm, but the outlaw caught the bridle reins and managed to swing into the saddle. Pettigrew stared dumbly at the corpse, like a child looking at a doll.

Mosely was tugging on Santee's sleeve. "Let's go," he urged. "Plummer got it wrong—there ain't no gold in that wagon, there's only the damn plague!"

Santee wavered. The outlaws had not expected to find a corpse in the wagon. The planned robbery had gone suddenly wrong. Mosely was right; there was no sign of gold on board, and exposure to small-pox could be deadly. Santee made his decision. "Pettigrew!" he shouted, "get away from that stiff and get on your horse—we're ridin' out!" Swiftly, he caught and mounted his own horse. Turning to Thad, he said, "Take that cadaver and go your way, teamster," he said. "There's nothin' on your goddam death wagon we want any part of."

With that, the four masked outlaws rode into the trees and disappeared in the twilight. Thad listened for a time to the receding hoofbeats, then he chuckled softly. "I guess I can put my hands down now," he said.

It was early evening when Thad turned the mules onto Bannack's main street. Already, street lamps cast their smoky glow along the boardwalks, and the day's last light clung to the summit of Bannack Peak. Music drifted out of saloons and hurdy houses as Thad drove past. Miners and townspeople thronged the muddy street. As the wagon passed the Goodrich Hotel, a gaunt man in top hat and overcoat stepped into the street and trotted nervously up to the wagon.

"Mitchell? Thad Mitchell?" he asked, "Obadiah Ottinger, Mortician—I certainly am glad to see you!"

"Sorry I'm late," Thad said, drawing rein. "I had a little trouble on the road."

Ottinger scrambled up onto the seat beside Thad. "Trouble? I'm sorry to hear that. Is the late Mr. Schwartz—"

"Oh, he's back there, all right," Thad said. "Still dead, I'm afraid."

The joke went over Ottinger's head. "Heavenly days," the undertaker said, peering back into the wagon. "The casket seems to be open!"

"Yes," Thad said, "there are a few things I need to explain. Where's your place?"

"I'm newly arrived in Bannack City. I have no regular mortuary yet, but I have rented a building. I have men working there this evening. Turn right at the corner."

Minutes later, Thad drew rein at a weathered building a block off Main. Ottinger went inside and returned with two burly laborers. With Thad's help, the men removed the casket from the wagon bed, carried it inside the building, and placed it atop two sawhorses. Ottinger glanced apprehensively at the coffin's open top. Raising a lighted lantern above the casket, he peered inside.

"Heavenly days!" the undertaker exclaimed. "What are all those spots?"

"Nothing to be alarmed about," Thad said. "That's window putty. Just a little something I added for reasons of my own. I figured Mr. Schwartz wouldn't mind."

"I fail to see the purpose—"

"I had reason to believe I might be stopped by road agents on my way here. I was right. Those spots on Mr. Schwartz helped save the day."

"Road agents!" Ottinger said, clearly bewildered. "Heavenly days! What do road agents have to do with—"

"Let me put it this way," Thad said with a grin, "Mr. Schwartz did one last good deed. He enabled me to transport my gold beneath the satin lining of his casket and saved me from highway robbery. The man deserves a medal—posthumous, of course."

Ottinger was a humorless man. "*Allowed* you to—it seems to me he had very little choice in the matter! But you, sir, have desecrated the departed in a most unseemly manner—*Most* unseemly, sir."

"I'll deposit my gold at the stage office tonight," Thad said. "As for the spots, they're easily removed. And the lid can be repaired. I'll take ten dollars off the freight bill to cover the 'unseemly.'" Thad placed his hat over his heart and leaned over the open casket. "Thank you for your help, Mr. Schwartz," he told the dead man. "Have a good eternity."

Two days later, after supper in the cabin above Daylight Creek, Thad told Hunter the story of the gold, the corpse, and the road agents for at least the third time. Weak from laughter, Hunter slumped in his chair, wiped a tear from his eye, and choked, "Has to be the first time—a man came down with smallpox—after his death!" Both men fell into another round of convulsive laughter.

When they finally caught their breath, Hunter poured them both a second cup of coffee and considered Thad's accomplishment. "Hard to believe our gold is safely out of the gulch and in a Salt Lake City bank," he said, "but you took a hell of a chance with those road agents."

"I wasn't even scared all that much 'til afterward," Thad said, "when I realized what *could* have happened. Then I got the shakes so bad I was afraid the mules would have to drive themselves to Bannack."

"Did you get a good look at the robbers?"

"Pretty good. It was getting dark, and they wore masks. There were four of them—two about average height and weight, one a big man maybe three hundred pounds or better. The gent that seemed to be the leader was a runt, not much over five foot three or four."

"Did you notice anything else? Maybe something they said?"

"Leader called the big one 'Pettigrew' at one point. I remember that especially because he'd just lit into one of the boys for using *his* name. One of them called him 'Santee.'"

"*Santee?* You sure he said Santee?"

There had been something in Hunter's tone of voice that caused Thad to look at him sharply. "Why, yes—I think so. What is it, Will? You're white as a sheet."

Hunter frowned, his eyes on his hands. "Probably nothing. I knew some brothers back in Missouri named Santee. Skulkers and cowards they were. Seems a long time ago."

Thad raised his coffee to his lips and drank, carefully observing his partner over the cup's rim. Hunter rarely spoke about his life before coming to the gulch, but there were times—like now—when hints of a violent and painful past broke through. Thad placed his cup down on the table. "There was one other thing, Will," he said. "Just before they rode out, one of the men said, 'Plummer got it wrong—there ain't no gold in that wagon.'"

"*Plummer?* You sure?"

"Dead sure. And how many men named Plummer do you know?"

Fresh snow had dusted the streets and buildings of Alder Gulch overnight, but by mid-morning the clouds were gone. The December sky shone luminous and blue as paint. In Virginia City, merchants cleared the boardwalks with shovel and broom, the vapor of their puffing visible in the still, chill air. Blue in the shadows and diamond bright in the sunlight, the snow overlaid rooftops and covered the litter of alley and street with a blanket of white.

Epiphany Baker turned her rented buggy onto Wallace Street and drove past freight wagons and pack animals until she drew rein at Dance and Stuart's store. On the days she conducted business or did her shopping for the cafe, Epiphany made it a point to dress well. This day was no exception. She wore her best dress—the blue satin—with a crinoline, a cabriolet bonnet, and her heavy cloak. Gingerly, she stepped out of the carriage into the ankle-deep snow, smiling as a passing miner tipped his hat and scuffled past in heavy gum boots. Epiphany's smile turned wry. Her high-topped shoes were fashionable enough, but the miner's rubber footwear was far more practical.

The small bell inside Dance and Stuart's door tinkled cheerfully as she entered. As always, the odors of spice, oiled wood, and tobacco filled the room. The potbelly stove at the store's center filled the space with dry heat, warming the room and steaming the windows. In the corner, astride his cobbler's bench, "Clubfoot" George Lane was stitching a miner's boot. He nodded shyly and turned his eyes back to his work.

Behind the counter, in vest and shirtsleeves, Walter Dance smiled a greeting. "Miss Epiphany," he said, "what can I do for you this snowy morning?"

Epiphany liked Judge Dance. More than a storekeeper, he served as banker, business advisor, miner's judge, and civic leader. Before opening his store that fall, he had also been a prospector. He was strong, honest, and fearless. He had the respect of both the roughs and the law and order crowd. Epiphany returned his smile, drawing a list from her reticule. "I need more supplies, Walter," she said. "Business continues to flourish."

"Delighted to hear it," Dance said, taking her list. Quickly, he scanned the paper. "You're in luck," he said. "I have most of these things in stock. I am out of potatoes and raisins, but I expect a shipment from Salt Lake any day now."

"I still have one sack of potatoes," Epiphany said, "but that won't last long. Starting next week I'm expanding my cafe from lunch only to three meals a day. I'm adding two more tables, and I've hired another cook."

"Excellent!" Dance said, smiling, "May both our houses prosper."

Dance handed Epiphany's list to a clerk in apron and sleeve protectors.

"Peter will fill your order and load it in your buggy for you," he said. "Feel free to look around while you're waiting. If I can do anything else, just call."

"Thank you, Walter," she said. "I may look at your yard goods. I'll be needing tablecloths."

Epiphany heard the tinkle of the door bell and turned to see Will Hunter and Thad Mitchell come in. They were laughing at some shared joke as they entered, but stopped when they saw her. Hunter tipped his hat and smiled. "Good morning, Piff," he said. "You grow more beautiful each time I see you."

He wore his Army greatcoat and a black silk scarf. The cold had brought color to his cheeks. "Good morning, Will," Epiphany said, giving him her hand. "Good morning, Thad. How is the firm of Hunter and Mitchell this snowy day?"

Thad stammered, adoration in his eyes. "Uh. . . Good morning, Miss Epiphany. . . I. . . we're doing fine."

"I haven't seen you at the cafe for almost a week," Epiphany said. "Have you been away?"

Thad lowered his eyes. "Uh. . . yeah. *Yes.* Had to deliver some furniture to Bannack. Just got back day before yesterday."

Mentally, he cursed himself for his clumsiness. "Fool! Why do you turn into a tongue-tied idiot whenever she's around? Why can't you be easy, natural?" Then hope lifted his despair. "Wait a minute! She missed me! She remembers how long it's been since she's seen me!"

Epiphany was speaking to Hunter now, studying his face. "He still has the look of the wolf about him," she thought, "and that old and secret pain is still there in his eyes. But he does seem easier in his mind, more calm. He's been too long alone with his grief, whatever it is. Taking the young miner Thad in as a partner has been good for him."

Out on the street, Dance's clerk loaded Epiphany's order onto the buggy and hurried back inside the store. Hunter touched his hatbrim and said, "Put a good T-bone aside for me, Piff. I'll be in for dinner next week."

"I'll do that, Will. It has been good to see you."

Turning to Thad, she smiled. "You, too, Thad. Nice seeing you again."

"Uh. . . You bet," said Thad, "Nice seeing me. I mean nice seeing *you*."

Epiphany turned the carriage onto Wallace and drove up the street. Thad watched until she disappeared around the corner. When he turned back, Hunter was smiling, watching him. Thad felt his ears grow hot, and knew he was blushing. Hunter chuckled. "I have to say one thing for you, Thad," he drawled. "You are a sweet-talkin' devil."

SEVENTEEN
Sanders Calls a Meeting

WILL HUNTER dreamed of Rachel. He dreamed he was camped
on the shore of a quiet lake, alone and lonely, grieving for the
woman who had been his wife.

In the dream the skies were dark, obscured by clouds. A strange,
gloomy light revealed a spectral landscape that was both unreal and
familiar. Across the lake, gentle foothills led to imposing mountains
whose peaks were lost in gray mist. As he watched, Hunter became
aware of a growing radiance in the sky above the water. The brightness seemed to descend from the mountaintops with the sound of
singing. Hunter thought he had never heard music so glorious.

Looking across the lake, he saw the radiance approaching and observed that it was made up of many beautiful, singing spirits. The
music swelled, and Hunter fell back in awe. Then the brightness
stopped, hovering over the lake as the music soared and reached a
crescendo. As he watched, one spirit separated from the others, drifting serenely toward him, and he saw that it was Rachel.

Gracefully, Rachel touched the earth and approached him. She
smiled as she came, her fine, blonde hair flowing about her shoulders and her eyes deep and warm as he remembered them. Gently,
she stretched out her hand. Hunter grasped it with his own. He lowered his head. Shame and guilt overwhelmed him. He felt unclean,

unworthy to be in her presence, yet desperate to hold her. After a time, he raised his head and looked into her face. He expected to see anger and sadness, but he saw only love and peace.

Then, as he watched, she looked back at the shining multitude above the lake. The spirits were smiling and singing as they beckoned her to rejoin them. Rachel's gaze returned to Hunter. He saw a wistful longing in her eyes. As he held her hand, the music grew louder and its tempo more urgent. Rachel began to pull against his grasp, but he held her tightly. She struggled, looking toward the calling spirits, but still he held her. She looked into Hunter's eyes and spoke. "Please, Will," she said, "let me go. You must let me go."

The voice was Rachel's, yet otherworldly, filled with ineffable wisdom and peace. It spoke not with words alone but in song, like the music he had heard when the spirits first appeared. He clung to her hand, and felt the old pain fill him.

"Forgive me, Rachel," he said. "Oh, please, forgive."

Gently, she raised her other hand and placed it upon his head. "There is no need for my forgiveness," she said. "All is well, as you see."

"But what about my guilt? What about my pain?"

"*You* must forgive," the Rachel spirit said. "Yes, you must be forgiven, but not by me. You must forgive *yourself*, Will."

His voice was a moan. "How can I?"

"You must *find* the way," she said.

His grip relaxed. Rachel withdrew her hand. Glowing brightly, she ascended into the dark sky and became one with the cloud of spirits. The music swelled again, and Hunter was bathed in its beauty. Then, abruptly, the light and the singing were gone. Overhead, the clouds were darker than before. Loneliness fell upon Hunter like a weight. Rain began to sweep across the lake toward him. He turned into the storm, felt the rain warm upon his face.

He awoke, breathing hard, staring up into the darkness of the cabin. He raised his hand to his eyes. The dream had ended, but the raindrops remained.

For a time, Hunter lay in his bunk and thought about his dream. He dreamed but seldom, or at any rate seldom recalled his dreams.

This one, however, remained sharp and clear, long after he had awakened. He remembered the spirits, and Rachel his wife among them. He recalled the sound of their singing and their joy. Most of all, he remembered Rachel and the touch of her hand. She had looked so serene, so peaceful. "All is well," she had said, and so it seemed to be.

How was that possible? He had failed her when she needed him most. He had left her to go drinking with his friends. He was absent when the raiders came. He was at a tavern in Harrisonville when they burned their home, when they abused her and murdered her. The guilt was his, and his the fault. *Mea culpa, mea culpa, mea maxima culpa*, the Catholics said, my fault, my fault, my most grievous fault. It was his fault, he believed, to the very depths of his soul.

How, then, could Rachel say there was no need for her forgiveness? She had said he must forgive himself. In the dream, he had answered, "How can I?" Rachel had answered, "You must find the way."

"Let me go," she had said. "You must let me go." Now awake, no longer dreaming, Hunter's words were the same: "How *can* I? How *can* I, Rachel?"

Later that morning, as Hunter rode out of the trees above the cabin, he met John Oakes riding up the slope toward him. The day was bitter cold. The older man sat bundled to the eyes in a heavy buffalo coat as his glass-eyed roan picked its way over the frozen ground.

"Morning, John," Hunter said. "Nice day for a picnic."

Oakes grinned above the turned-up collar of his coat. "For polar bears, maybe," he said. "How are you, Will?"

"Ready for spring," Hunter said, "and winter has scarcely begun. You looking for me?"

"I was. There's a meeting at Wil Sander's law office today. Figured you might want to be there."

"Why's that?"

"There's some men coming that think the way we do. Men you should meet."

"I don't know, John. I've never been much for meetings."

Oakes grinned. "You wouldn't want to make me out a liar, would you? I told them you'd come."

Hunter shook his head. "You've got more brass than a wagonload of doorknobs," he said. "All right—I guess it won't hurt me to listen. Lead on."

Wilbur Fisk Sanders was an honorable man and a fighter. A lawyer since the age of 22, he had served as first lieutenant on the staff of Union General James Forsyth during the early part of the War. He had resigned his commission because of poor health. He had come to the gold fields in the summer just past with a party of his relatives and had settled in Bannack with his wife and two small sons. Later in the year, he established a law practice in bustling Virginia City, where his services were much in demand.

When John Oakes and Will Hunter entered the tent that served as Sanders's office, they found him seated behind his desk. Other men sat in chairs around the potbellied stove. A short, stumpy man with careful eyes and a flowing moustache added wood to the fire. Sanders stood, smiling, as Oakes and Hunter came in.

"It's good to see you, John," he said. "There are cups on the cabinet and coffee on the stove. Help yourself." He remained standing, his eyes on Will Hunter, and extended his hand. "You must be Will Hunter," he said. "I'm glad you could come. I'm Wilbur Sanders."

Hunter noted with approval that Sanders's grip was firm and dry, and that his eyes met his own. He liked the lawyer on sight. Sanders turned to the other men. "That's X. Beidler there at the stove," he said, "and I think you know Judge Dance." Nodding, Hunter shook hands with both men. "And this," Sanders said, indicating a third man, "is Neil Howie, prospector. We're still waiting for Nat Langford."

Returning to his desk, Sanders glanced at his guests. "I guess you all know John Oakes."

"Hell," Beidler said, "*everybody* knows John." The other men grinned as Oakes poured himself a cup of coffee. Oakes's grin was a sheepish one. He had many friends, but he was well aware that his curious and amiable nature had given him the reputation of being something of a busybody.

Judge Dance smiled. "And John knows everybody," he said, and they all laughed.

Nat Langford entered the tent during the laughter. He wore a heavy canvas duster over a sheepskin coat and leggings. He knocked the snow off his hat and held his hands out to the stove's warmth. "Never fails," he said, "be the last to arrive, and find your friends laughing at you behind your back."

X. Beidler's eyes shone. He spat a stream of tobacco juice into a gallon can beside the stove. "That's not true, Nat," he said, wiping his moustache. "Some of us laugh at you in *front* of your back."

"Glad you're here, Nat," Sanders said. Langford was part owner of a small sawmill and was Sanders's closest friend. They were brothers in freemasonry, as were most of the men in the room, and had been active in establishing Masonic lodges both in Bannack and Virginia City. "You know Will Hunter?" Sanders asked.

"I do indeed," Langford replied. "He's hauled a good deal of lumber from our mill this past month. How are you, Will?"

"Good, Nat," Hunter said.

Sanders leaned against his desk. He nodded at Hunter. "I'm glad you could be with us today, Will," he said. "We're here to talk about the road agent problem."

"Again," said Langford wearily.

Sanders ignored his friend's comment. He kept his eyes on Hunter. "Your reputation precedes you, Will," he said. "You've become known as a man of action—a man who's not intimidated by the roughs."

"They're only men, like the rest of us," Hunter said.

"Not quite like the rest of us," Sanders said, "they're damnable thieves and murderers, and a menace to society."

"I'm looking for a peaceful life," Hunter said. "I don't bother them unless they bother me."

Sanders eyes brightened. "Ah, but they have bothered you, haven't they? Your first week in town you whipped Jack Gallagher on the gallery of the Mother Lode."

"He insulted a young lady."

"Something he's done quite often, I imagine, but on that occasion you called him to account."

Sanders sipped his coffee and set the cup back on his desk. "Then you rode express for Albert Hess and Bill Fitzhugh and took their dust to the stage office in Bannack. Shot two road agents when they tried to stop you."

Langford spoke up. "Some of us—the men in this room and others—have had a bellyful of the damned spoilers. We feel it's time to establish law and order."

"Past time, I'd say," Hunter said.

Beidler broke in. "Yes, but whose law? Henry Plummer is the law hereabouts, and most of us figure he's behind the thieves and killers as well."

"A *definite* conflict of interest," Langford drawled.

"And not Federal law," Sanders added. "The government has its hands full trying to preserve the Union, and the territorial government is hundreds of miles away, across the mountains in Lewiston. Nobody seems to care about our troubles."

Langford broke in. "This past August, the territorial government at Lewiston finally sent a U.S. Marshal out here, after Sanders and I both made trips there to ask for help. He took the matter under advisement and high-tailed it back to Lewiston. Apparently, he's still studying the problem—we haven't heard from him since."

"Nat's right," Sanders said. "The fact is, we're on our own. Whatever is to be done here is up to us. Are you with us, Will?"

Hunter was silent for a long moment. Thoughtfully, he studied the contents of his coffee cup. At last, he placed the cup on Sanders's desk and raised his eyes to the lawyer. "I appreciate your asking," he said. "I have no argument with what you say, but I play a lone hand. I mean no offense to anyone here, but I've heard all this before—from the miners in their wakiups to the idlers in the saloons. Everyone talks—some talk very well, but it's action that's required."

He stood up. "When that time comes, you can count on me. Until then, I guess I'll go on playing a lone hand."

The men were silent. John Oakes seemed disappointed. Nat Langford and Wil Sanders looked at Hunter with what seemed to be a kind of grudging admiration. Neil Howie sipped his coffee. X. Beidler studied the tall man thoughtfully.

Will Hunter turned, ducked his head at the tent's door, and went out onto the snowy street.

Josie Mulhare sat at the small table in her rented cabin, remembering her meeting with George Ives the night before. The hour was early, scarcely seven o'clock in the morning. Josie frowned, fighting a growing feeling of panic. Her hand trembled as she raised the small, brown bottle of laudanum to her lips and drank.

Usually, a visit by George Ives left Josie Mulhare in rare high spirits. After days or weeks, Ives would make his way to her door and knock softly.

Always, distinct from all the others, Josie recognized George's knock. Always, his soft rapping made her heart leap. She would rush to open the cabin door and throw herself into his arms, desire rising within her like a flame. Then would come the shared laughter, perhaps a drink or two, and the swift, clumsy undressing.

They would come together in her white-painted iron bed. Only with Ives was Josie's passion real. For a time she would forget the nameless men, the shabby crib in which she lived, the merciless passage of time, and the depression that could lead to death. Josie would give herself to Ives, drawing frail hope in return, and lose herself in the act of loving.

After weeks away, George Ives had come to her door the night before. His soft knock had been the same, and her rush to the door, but after that everything was different. There had been no laughter, no drink together—Ives was drunk and sullen when he arrived. There had been no gentleness in his touch, no kisses, none of the fumbling, endearing caresses Josie loved because they were his. Ives had taken her roughly, cruelly, without a word. Only the creaking of the bed and Ives's labored breathing broke the stillness. When she had tried to speak, he had covered her mouth with his hand. He had taken her and turned away, sitting up on the bed, his back to her. "Clearly," Josie thought, "he did not come to be with me—he doesn't want to see me or hear my voice."

Then, at once, she knew. Josie's heart seemed to stop. She felt suddenly cold and alone. Someone else, another woman, occupied Ives's mind and heart. It was that woman's body he desired even while he was in her arms. Josie had lain very still, feeling Ives' nearness. After what seemed a long time, he spoke. His voice sounded flat, impersonal.

"What do I owe you?" he said.

"Be careful now," she told herself. "Don't get mad. Keep it light."

After a moment, she said, "Why don't you just pay me what you think it was worth, lover?"

Ives stood. He turned, really looking at her for the first time. In the dim light of the cabin, his cruel eyes glittered like ice. He smiled a hard smile. "Hell, Josie," he said, "I can't do that. I *have* to give you *somethin.*"

Josie felt as if he had struck her. Hot anger rose like bile in her throat. "Damned if I know *why*, darlin'," she snapped. "You sure as hell weren't with *me.*"

"That's right," Ives said, "and I never will be again."

The sound of the closing door was loud. The silence that followed seemed louder still.

Josie sat at her table, her anxiety rising. She tried to convince herself that this was only another of George's moods. He would be back, of course he would. Some late night, a week or a month from now, she would hear his soft knock and rush to open her door. He would take her in his arms again, and everything would be as it had been. Josie tried to hold onto the thought, but doubt crept in and took away her peace. Somehow, she knew, this time was different. Another woman had stolen George's heart and her hope.

Josie had never been the jealous sort. The very idea seemed absurd.

She had known envy, certainly—envy of women who were younger or prettier, women who commanded higher prices or who seemed to have a special gift when it came to pleasing men. Seldom, if ever, had she known the emotion that people called jealousy.

She was a hurdy-gurdy dancer, a soiled dove, a woman of the night, a whore. Her profession was entertaining men for money, the more men the merrier. She'd never been able to see a nickel's worth of difference between them. They were customers, made foolish by their lust. They were a claim to be worked, sheep for the shearing, and nothing more.

She had not even been jealous of George Ives. She knew he visited other women in the brothels and cribs of the camps—that was to be expected because that was the way men were. Never before, though, at least to her knowledge, had he had special feelings for any particular woman. Now she sensed with a cold certainty that she was losing him, that he was already lost, and the pain of the loss nearly overwhelmed her.

Suddenly, the small rented cabin seemed incredibly drab. She looked at her tiny bedroom, separated from the parlor by a curtain on a wire, and found it cheap and tawdry. Her iron bed, its paint chipped and flaking, stood sadly on its rickety legs. The stained and lumpy mattress, cheap cotton sheets, and the hand-made quilt George had given her spoke of countless encounters she had no wish to remember.

Her eyes took in the pathetic attempts she had made to decorate her crib—a faded tintype of her parents, a framed needlepoint sampler extolling the virtues of home and family, a dusty peacock feather, her name carved above the door to let the world know she had lived. How far she had fallen! As tears came unbidden to her eyes, self-pity choked her. An empty, lost feeling held her in its cold grip. The walls seemed to be closing in. She had to get out, get away. Dressing hurriedly, she left the cabin and walked quickly up the street toward Hallie Kinkade's parlor house.

Hallie Kinkade's "Boarding House" was a two-story brothel on Jackson Street on the road to Summit. Josie had worked for Hallie in California and still knew several of Hallie's girls. She considered one of them, Cat O'Leary, her closest friend. It was Cat she had come to see. Josie climbed the back stairs and rang the bell. A moment later, a frizzy-haired slattern in a silk wrapper opened the door. Her painted mouth formed a pout as she looked at Josie with dull, hostile eyes. "Yeah? Whad'ja want?" she asked.

"I'm Josie Mulhare—a friend of Cat O'Leary's. She here?"

The eyes lost their hostile look, but the girl kept her pout. Stepping back, she swung the door open. "Yeah, she's here," the girl said. "Come in, before we let all the warm out."

The room opened onto a spacious kitchen, dominated by a large woodstove and a circular dining table. Two of Hallie's girls sat at the table drinking coffee, and a third concentrated on trimming her toenails. All three stared at Josie curiously. She did not recognize any of them.

The frizzy-haired doorkeeper disappeared down a hallway off the kitchen and returned shortly, followed by Josie's friend. Taller than Josie and two years younger, Cat O'Leary was a striking brunette with milk-white skin and green eyes. Christened Catherine O'Leary as an infant in Limerick's slums, she had been called Cat as long as Josie had known her. Cat and Josie had met in Angel's Camp back in '59 and had been friends ever since.

Seeing Cat, Josie's eyes brimmed with tears. She managed a brave but shaky smile. "Hello, Cat," she said, "longtime, no see."

Cat's smile was bright, and honest. "Too damn long, Josie," she said. "Where have you been keepin' yourself, girl?"

Josie looked down at the rug beneath her feet. "Oh, I'm still working days at the hurdy on Wallace," she said, "You know. . . time slips by." The smell of fresh coffee drifted across the room to her. She glanced quickly at the pot atop the stove, then back at Cat. "I. . . I need to talk to somebody, Cat," she said. "I need a friend."

Cat read her mind. "You've got one," she said. "I'll fetch a wee pot of coffee and some cakes up to my room and we'll have us a goddam *tête-á-tête.*"

Josie couldn't help comparing Cat's comfortable bedroom with her own spare crib. At one end of the room, a handsome oak bed, commode, and wardrobe stood atop a rich carpet of oriental design. A small, marble-topped table occupied a place by the window, flanked by two upholstered parlor chairs. Cat set the tray down on the table and took Josie's coat.

Not until the women were seated across from each other drinking coffee and eating cakes, did Cat break the silence. Then she looked across at her friend, smiled, and said, "Whatever it is, it isn't that bad, Josie. You look like you've lost your best friend, but that can't be. I'm still here."

Josie looked away. "It's a man I've lost, Cat. I've lost George."

"George Ives? Best thing that could happen to you. Somebody should lose that arrogant bastard permanently."

Tears welled again in Josie's eyes. Seeing this, Cat reached out and touched her hand. "Sorry, Josie. Sometimes I talk without thinkin'. Now what do you mean, you've lost him?"

"There's another woman. I know it."

"Josie, Josie—with George, there's likely to be a *hundred* women."

"No. Not a woman like that. This is a woman he loves."

Cat thought about that. "Then it wouldn't be one of us," she said. "It would have to be one of the decent ones. It would be a *lady*."

Josie picked up her coffee cup. Her hand trembled as she brought it to her lips. "Yes," she said sadly, "that's what I thought."

Cat sipped her coffee. For a moment she gazed out the window, her face troubled. "I'll tell you what I know," she said. "George came to see Mexican Alice last week. According to her, George told her he was keepin' company with that fair-haired kid that runs the Orphan Girl Cafe. Alice said he sounded like a lovesick schoolboy—like he wanted to carry her damn books home from school or somethin'."

"This girl. . . do you know her name?"

"Some kind of holy, mother church type name, like Easter or Pentecost, or—no, wait! *Epiphany*, that's her name—Epiphany Baker! Ain't that a pisser?"

Josie looked even more miserable than before. "George told Alice about her? What else did he say?"

Cat shrugged. "Not much, I guess. Men are a stupid lot, Josie. Sons o'bitches like George take to decent young girls like cats to catnip. Hell, Henry Plummer even *married* one last summer—and she's left him already."

Cat took her friend's hand. "Don't worry about it too much," she said. "Chances are, he'll get tired of the game and come back to you. You two have quite a history together."

The hope that lit Josie's face was painful to see. "Do you think so, Cat?" she asked. "Do you really think so?"

It was a lie for a friend. "Hell, yes," Cat said.

EIGHTEEN
The Trouble with George

T HE SKY ABOVE Daylight Gulch had cleared by early evening, leaving only a thin scatter of clouds to catch the last of the day's brightness. Thad Mitchell turned the mule he called Shadrach downhill to the cabin and dismounted. In the corral, Hunter's black gelding raised its head and whinnied. Shadrach brayed a reply. Lamplight glowed in the cabin's window and a thin wisp of smoke drifted up from the chimney. Thad stripped the saddle and blanket from the mule, turned the animal in with the gelding, and forked hay into the feed trough. Then he picked his way over the frozen ground to the cabin.

Will Hunter was stirring the contents of a heavy iron skillet when Thad came in. Will nodded toward the skillet, grinned, and said, "Liver and onions. You're a braver man than I thought. You knew I was cooking tonight, but you came home anyway."

Thad shrugged out of his sheepskin coat and hung it on the peg beside the door. He returned Hunter's grin. "Eating your cooking is how I stay so slim," he said. "How about a drink before supper to bolster our courage?"

"Jug's on the shelf. You'll have to pour, though–I'm a chef, not a bartender."

Thad poured two fingers of whiskey each into tin cups and handed one to Hunter. "Here's how," Thad said, raising his cup.

"How," Hunter replied, and the partners drank.

"Spent most of the day in town," Thad said. "Had that loose tire on the big wagon re-set and got Shadrach sharp-shod for winter. Hauled some planed board siding in from Langford's for that new place on Cover Street."

"That's a relief. If you spent the day in town, I know you had at least one good meal. How was the attractive Miss Baker today?"

"As always, perfect. You know me too well."

"Met John Oakes as I was heading out this morning. He took me to a meeting at Wil Sanders's office—some of the leaders of the law and order movement."

"Anything new?"

"Not really. They've had a bellyful of the road agents. They know they need to take action, but haven't spelled out what it will be."

Thad's expression grew serious. "Vigilantes?"

Hunter nodded. "That's what they're talking about, but nobody wants to put a name to it yet."

Thad sipped the whiskey and sat down. "Serious business, that. I've seen it before—in Colorado and Idaho. Rough justice may fill the gap where there is no law, but it's risky. Vigilantes are men, and men make mistakes."

Hunter nodded. "And when they do, the mistakes are hard to fix. It's pretty hard to un-hang a man."

Hunter carried the skillet to the table and scooped a generous helping onto each man's plate. "It's come down to a test of strength between good men and bad. The old quote from Burke comes to mind: 'The only thing necessary for the triumph of evil is for good men to do nothing.'"

Thad looked somber, remembering. "There's another old quote, Will—something about choosing the lesser of two evils. Except a man doesn't always know which is the lesser until afterward."

"This talk is getting too serious," Hunter said. "Let's eat this grub before we lose our nerve."

At a small table in the kitchen of the Orphan Girl Cafe, Epiphany made a final entry in her ledger and looked at the page with satisfaction. The neat, precise rows of figures told the story. Her restaurant was a success. The bills were paid, the improvements completed, and her business was in the black.

For a moment, Epiphany basked in the pride of her accomplishment. The busy supper hour rush had ended. Silence replaced the clatter of pots and pans and the hum of conversation. The last of her customers had gone their way. At the counter inside the back door, Cootie Blake washed dishes. Wong Lee Fat, the new cook, rested at the counter, drinking tea. His daughter, Lo Toy, cleared the tables and swept the floors. Expanding from lunch to three meals a day had been a risk, as had her decision to hire the Blue Pony's former cook and waitresss. The increased business, however, had more than justified the expense.

Epiphany had not seen George Ives in nearly a week, and she missed him. She remembered those first days when he had come daily to the cafe, staying to talk with her after the other patrons had gone. His stories had amused and entertained her. His compliments had warmed her. She recalled sitting close beside him as they took the road to Summit in the rented buggy. She remembered the fresh snow and the way it covered the prospect holes the miners had made along the gulch. She remembered the red-tailed hawk, gliding out across the valley. Most of all, she remembered George Ives.

Epiphany closed her eyes, the better to recall his face. She saw again the unruly hair, the bold blue eyes and the reckless smile that stirred her. She had hoped—she had expected—him to proclaim his love for her that day; but it had been his kiss, not his words, that had spoken. Parked high on the hilltop above the valley, he had taken her in his arms and kissed her. Her body had responded as though it had a will of its own. She had given herself freely to the embrace, lost in an abandon she had neither known nor imagined. She had felt his passion, strong and demanding; however, it was her own fervor that had frightened her and caused her to break away from his embrace.

Had her panic lost him? Had he taken her attempt to regain control of her emotions as rejection? Why had he not come again to see her? Epiphany pushed her chair back from the small table that served as her desk and stood. "I'm going home now," she told her staff. "Please lock up when you leave."

Outside, Epiphany turned the collar of her cloak up around her face and walked slowly over the frozen ground toward the boarding house. Behind her, the day's last light hugged the horizon. Overhead, the evening star heralded the coming darkness.

"If I wished upon a star," Epiphany thought, "would that cause George to come again?" She smiled at the fancy and shook her head. She was a child no longer, she reminded herself. She no longer believed in wishing on the first star of evening. Having thus declared her maturity, she raised her eyes to the heavens. "Star light, star bright, first star I've seen tonight," she began.

The woman was waiting when Epiphany reached the front steps of the boarding house. She stood in the shadows, huddled against the chill night air. When she spoke her voice was hesitant, almost apologetic. "Miss Baker?" she asked, "Epiphany Baker?"

"Yes," Epiphany said. "Can I help you?"

The woman smiled nervously, then lowered her eyes. She took a halting step forward, into the light from the parlor window. "I . . . I just wanted to talk to you, Miss. If you can spare a minute."

In the lamplight, the woman looked tired and worn. Her heavy makeup revealed more than it concealed, Epiphany thought. Her face seemed even more pale and drawn than it was. She wore a stained red crinoline under a pelerine of beaver fur. Beneath her bonnet, her dark hair showed streaks of gray.

"You must be freezing," Epiphany said, taking the woman's arm, "Please—come inside. I'll make us some tea, and you can warm yourself."

The woman's smile was a nervous flash that came and disappeared quickly. Epiphany caught the raw odor of whiskey when the woman spoke. "I'd be obliged, Miss," she said. "I do have a bit of a chill."

Inside, Epiphany led the woman into the parlor and to an upholstered chair near the Sunshine stove. "Wait here, and warm yourself," she said. "I'll bring the tea."

As she approached the kitchen, Epiphany saw Lily Rae scowling in the direction of the seated woman. "Christian charity is one thing," she huffed, "but that woman has no business in my parlor."

"No," Epiphany said, "I expect she conducts her business in a *different* parlor, but she's come to see me here. I can't very well leave her out on the street to freeze."

"Well, who is she?" asked Lily Rae. "It's pretty obvious *what* she is, but who is she, and what does she want with you?"

"I'm sure I can't say," Epiphany said, pouring hot water into a teapot. "I'll let you know when I do, all right?"

"Oh, for goodness sake," said Lily Rae, "I didn't mean to pry. Take the poor thing some cookies to go with that tea."

Back in the parlor, Epiphany set the tea service down on a table between the woman and herself and filled two cups. Handing one to her visitor, she lifted the other and said, "Now, then. What did you want to see me about?"

The woman fidgeted nervously in her chair. She raised her eyes to Epiphany's, then lowered them. "My name is Josie Mulhare," she said, "and I don't hardly know how to begin."

Lifting cup and saucer together, Josie sipped the tea. She looked across the cup's rim at Epiphany and sighed. Her expression was one of despair, and sadness tinged her voice. "Oh, my," she said, "you are a pretty one, and so young."

She seemed to steel herself then. Her tone became earnest and purposeful. "Now see here, Miss—it has been brought to my attention that you've been keeping company with George Ives." Josie took a deep breath and continued, her words coming in a rush. "I surely kin see how a lady like yourself might be taken with a man like him, but he ain't exactly all he seems to be. I mean, George ain't ever going to be what you could call faithful. He tends to be a triflin' man, and Lord knows he can be a cruel sonofabitch sometimes, excuse my French."

Epiphany's eyes widened; anger made her voice tight. "I don't know who you think you are, Miss Mulhare," she said, "but my relationship with George Ives is really none of your concern."

"Oh, hell," Josie said, "I knew I'd make a botch of this. I should have just come out and told you the god's honest truth. I've come to ask you to let George go. I expect he's made you think he loves you— maybe he even believes it himself—but it ain't true, Miss. George don't *give* love; he *takes* it.

"For better than five years now, I've been the closest thing to a full time woman he's had. We've been together in damn near every gold camp this side of California. George and me—well, that's how it is. It's George and me. George Ives is the only man I've ever loved, and I'm asking you not to take him from me."

Epiphany struggled to keep her voice steady. "I don't wish to insult you, Miss Mulhare," she said, "but I have no reason to believe anything you've said. To be frank, I find it hard to believe George Ives could have had any kind of romantic interest in a woman like you."

Epiphany stood up. "I'm afraid I'm going to have to ask you to leave now," she said.

Josie seemed to grow smaller, weaker where she sat. Unsteadily, she got to her feet. She drew her pelerine close about her shoulders and walked across the room to the vestibule. At the door, she hesitated, then turned back to Epiphany.

"You're a sweet little thing," she said, "pure as spring water and green as new grass. But you've got no idea what you're dealin' with here. A lamb may sometime run with a wolf, but not for long." Then she was out the door and walking away into the night.

The silence that followed the front door's closing seemed ominous and heavy. In the stillness, Epiphany heard the rapid beating of her heart and fought to control her breathing. She felt outrage, anger, and something more.

Deep within her, beyond her indignation and denial, the feeling began to grow that there might be truth in the strange woman's words. Could she have been so wrong about George Ives? Had she once again allowed her heart to blind her to the truth?

There was only one thing to do, she decided. She must confront George. She must ask him directly about his intentions, and about the woman, Josie Mulhare. She would seek him out in the morning and settle the matter. She prayed that Josie Mulhare was a liar.

———🔷———

By the time she reached the cafe the next morning, Epiphany had already put her plans into motion. Formidable in her earnestness, she trapped Cootie Blake in a corner of the kitchen and made her request. "I want you to find George Ives," she said, "and ask him to call on me at his earliest convenience."

Cootie assumed his best hangdog expression and tried to avoid his employer's gaze. "I ain't real sure I can find him, Miss 'Piphany," he grumbled. "He might not be in town today."

"You know where he lives, don't you?"

"Well, yes. I hear tell he's got a place up yonder on Daylight Creek, on the divide—but he might not be there, either."

"Besides, Miss 'Piphany," he pleaded, "I've got chores to do here at the cafe—wood to split for the stove and what-not. I don't—"

Epiphany placed her fists on her hips and straightened to her full five feet ten inches. "Cootie Blake," she scolded, "it is important to me that you find Mr. Ives and convey my message. You *will* do that for me, won't you?"

Cootie surrendered. "Yes'm, I will. I'll try," he sighed. He tugged on his gum boots, shrugged into his sheepskin, and opened the back door. Just before he stepped outside, he turned and looked at Epiphany with his sad, blood-hound eyes. "But you sure do *surround* a man some-times," he said.

George Ives had stayed late in a high-stakes poker game at Skinner's saloon. His losses and his frustration had mounted through the night in direct proportion to the whiskey he'd drunk, but somehow he'd failed to see the connection.

When the horse-faced gambler who ran the stud game—and who drank nothing stronger than cold tea during working hours—cleaned him out with a baby straight, Ives had pulled his revolver, fumbled it, and dropped it to the floor. By the time he picked it up again and tried to find his target, the gambler had produced a cut-down Army .44 and had aimed it at a spot exactly between Ives's bloodshot eyes. It was Cy Skinner himself who saved Ives's life. He dropped his friend with a well-placed blow from a bung-starter and hauled him off to the back room to sleep it off.

It was just past 8:15 the next morning when George Ives stumbled out of the storeroom and staggered up to the bar. Skinner poured three fingers of whiskey into a glass, pushed it over to Ives, and stood by, ready to provide a refill. Skinner's greeting was amiable in the extreme. "Good morning, George," he said. "Have a little hair of the dog that bit you."

Ives raised the glass with a shaky hand and downed the contents. "Damn you, Cy," he rasped. "Wasn't no damn dog bit me—it was you hit me from behind."

"And a good thing, too," Skinner said, filling the glass again. "You were tryin' to shoot my stud dealer, but booze had turned you clumsy. You were bettin' the farm against a pat hand with a .44 in it."

"Didn't have to hit me so hard," Ives grumbled.

"If I hadn't, demons would be roastin' your ass in Hell right now. You need to play poker or drink, but not both at the same time."

The front door opened. A sad-eyed man in winter cap and sheep-skin coat shuffled in, stamping his feet.

"Hey, you!" Skinner said. "We ain't open yet. Come back at nine."

Cootie Blake stopped where he stood. "'Scuse me, Mr. Skinner," he said, "but I got a message for George Ives. That's him there at the bar, ain't it?"

It was Ives who answered. "Yeah—I'm George Ives. What the hell do you want? Message from who?"

"Miss Epiphany, from over to the Orphan Girl. Said I was to find you and ask you to call on her at your earliest convenience."

Ives straightened, interest plain on his handsome face. "Miss Epiphany, huh? Come on over here, pardner—let me buy you a drink."

"Mr. Skinner just told me he ain't open yet."

"He's changed his mind. Come here."

Cootie's approach was a half-hearted shuffle. When he reached the bar, Skinner had already poured whiskey into a shot glass.

"I know you," said Ives. "I've seen you at the Orphan Girl. You work for Miss Epiphany, don't you?"

"Yessir. Like I said, she sent me to find you."

Ives looked thoughtful. "You know what she wants to see me about?" he asked.

Cootie studied the whiskey like a jeweler examining a ruby. "No, sir, I don't. She just said I was to find you and tell you what she said. It seemed mighty important to her."

Ives downed his whiskey and ran his fingers through his hair. "Tell Miss Epiphany I'll pick her up at noon," he said. "Tell her I will be delighted to call upon her."

Cootie tossed back the drink and wiped his mouth with his sleeve. "Yessir. I surely will," he said. "Much obliged for the whiskey." Carefully, he placed the glass back on the bar, walked to the door, and went outside.

Skinner's expression was a knowing leer. "So you're still workin' on that big-eyed young'un from the cafe. Sort of like shootin' fish in a barrel, ain't it?"

"Go to hell, Cy. What would you know about it? You've never had a decent woman in your life."

Cy Skinner picked up Cootie's shot-glass and wiped the bar. "Don't intend to, either," he said. "Decent women are more damn trouble than they're worth. Ask Henry Plummer."

"Put that watered whiskey on my tab," Ives said. "I'm off to see the barber."

Skinner laughed. "Tell him to comb the sawdust out of your hair," he said.

———◈———

Promptly at noon, George Ives drove the rented buggy up to the front door of the Orphan Girl Cafe and drew rein. He had prepared for the occasion by obtaining a shave, haircut, and bath at a barbershop on Wallace Street. He had also bought enough "hairs of the dog" at the saloon next door to ease his pain and settle his nerves.

For a time, he waited in the street for Epiphany to appear, wondering at the reason for her summons. Had she heard tales about his life in the saloons and brothels of Virginia? Or had his strategy of allowing time to build her longing for him borne fruit? Overhead, the ragged clouds, like torn, wet cotton, obscured the peaks. Tendrils drifted among the hills and valleys like cold smoke. The wind grew stronger, scattering crystals of sleet across the camp.

Where *was* she? Epiphany had asked him to call on her. Well, damn it, here he was. Then, abruptly, he realized the truth. She was inside the cafe, playing the lady, waiting for him to come to the door. Ives grinned, mocking himself. "She *is* a lady, you fool," he told himself. "That's one reason you want her." He wrapped the reins around the whipsocket at the dashboard, stepped down, and made his way to the doorway.

Epiphany, lovely in a street dress of green silk, was waiting when he entered. Her hair shone like spun gold in the cafe's lamplight. Customers sat, busy at their meals. The Chinese girl who waited tables hurried between the kitchen and dining room to serve them.

Ives smiled his practiced smile and nodded. "Dearest Piff," he said, "how lovely you look!" Epiphany donned her woolen cloak and her dark cabriolet bonnet, deftly tying the ribbons beneath her chin. She studied his face, her expression serious and reserved. "Thank you for coming," she said. "Shall we go?"

"No smile of greeting," George thought. "So she has heard stories about my wicked ways. No matter—she wants to be reassured. Women are excited by scoundrels. They all believe they alone can reform him. I'll thaw the ice in those brown eyes and make them warm again."

Ives opened the door. "Your carriage awaits," he said. He helped Epiphany into the seat and spread the thick buffalo robe across her lap. Then he walked around to the other side, stepped up, and started the horse with a crack of the whip. As snow gusted out of the north, he swung the buggy onto the Bannack road.

"You seem troubled, Piff," Ives said. "What is it? If it's something I've done—"

Epiphany made no reply. She sat beside him on the buggy seat, her eyes straight ahead.

Ives spoke carefully, watching her from the corner of his eye. "I've missed you so, Piff," he said. "I'm sorry I haven't come to see you sooner, but I've been away on business down at Bannack, buying mules."

The snowfall grew thicker. Behind them, buildings faded into the whiteness.

Epiphany looked down at her gloved hands. "Is there someplace nearby where we can talk privately?" she asked.

"A friend of mine is away on business at Fort Benton. He has a cabin about four miles from here. We could go there."

She turned, looking at him. Her voice sounded hesitant, uncertain. "So far?" she asked. "Isn't there someplace nearer?"

"It's a good cabin, Piff. Dry, and comfortable. I'll build a fire."

"I. . . I'm not sure that I. . . that we. . . "

"It's only a few more miles, Piff. And it *is* private."

Nervously, Epiphany looked back toward Virginia City. The town had disappeared behind a blanket of falling, blowing snow. She said nothing, but nodded. The die was cast.

---◈---

The cabin stood five hundred feet above the road in a clearing, surrounded by stands of pine and aspen. Behind the cabin, in a small pasture, two saddlehorses watched the buggy leave the road and climb the steep slope.

The snowfall had grown heavier during the short drive; and there, back among the trees, the wind had died to a whisper.

George Ives stopped the buggy and sat for a moment, listening. Only the labored breathing of the carriage horse broke the stillness. Ives stepped down and tramped through the drifted snow to the cabin door. Grasping the latchstring, he lifted the bar and shouldered the door open. Moments later, he had found and lighted the cabin's oil lamp and had returned to the carriage for Epiphany. When he reached to help her down, she shook her head and dismounted unassisted.

Inside, Ives stacked dry wood in the fireplace and struck it alight. Soon, the fire was blazing, sending heat and flickering light into the darkened room. As the cabin warmed, Epiphany took off her bonnet and cloak and seated herself near the fire on a log section cut to serve as a stool.

The cabin's furnishings were sparse—a rough plank table, cut logs that served as chairs, a few boxes to hold supplies, and a canvas-covered bedroll laid out on pine boughs. Cooking utensils lay scattered about the fireplace—tin plates and cups, a dutch oven, a cast-iron skillet. The flames flickered, projecting dark, dancing shadows across the room. George Ives moved a log section closer to Epiphany and sat, facing her.

"Now, then," he asked, "what is all this fuss about?"

Epiphany met his gaze, trying to read answers to her questions in Ives's face, but she found none. There were only his strong, handsome features, just as she remembered them. The bold, blue eyes still carried their invitation, his smile still caused her heart to beat faster. He had removed his hat, and the unruly blonde hair shone warm in the firelight, inviting her touch.

"I. . . had a visitor last night," Epiphany said, "a woman of the streets named Josie Mulhare. Apparently, an old friend of yours."

Ives' expression did not change. He had played enough poker to learn how to conceal his feelings. He said nothing, but reached into his overcoat pocket and took out a silver brandy flask.

"She told me she was your woman," Epiphany continued, "and asked me to stop seeing you. Apparently, she believes she has a prior claim."

George Ives drank from the flask and replaced the cap. Rage exploded within his mind, but he forced himself to remain outwardly calm. "Damn that Josie Mulhare!" he thought. "The pathetic bitch has gone too far this time!" He shook his head, then said sadly, "That poor woman—*again*."

He leaned toward Epiphany, taking her hands in his. "Dearest Piff," he said, "Josie Mulhare has been a thorn in my side since I first met her five years ago in California. For some reason—and who knows how a woman like her thinks—she has convinced herself that she and I are lovers!

"It's not true, of course—not a word of it. You know I could never be with a woman like that. She's followed me from one camp to another, sending me notes and letters, approaching me in the street—making up a history and a link between us that never was!"

Ives' shoulders slumped. He lowered his eyes, and spoke in a weary, resigned tone. "I swear, I feel sorry for her, Piff. I can't imagine what it must be like to live with such a sad, false notion."

Epiphany reached out and touched his hair. There had been nothing in his words that disproved Josie's story, but Epiphany desperately wanted to believe him. "Thank you, George," she said, "I. . . I knew it couldn't be true."

Ives raised his head, gratitude written upon his face. "Thank you, dearest," he said. "You are the kindest, sweetest woman in the world!" His fingers grasped her arms, and when he stood he raised her as well. "Forgive my boldness," he said, "but I must speak my heart—I can't hide my feelings for you no longer. I love you, dearest Piff."

She raised her face to his and found his lips waiting. Epiphany cast her doubts aside and gave herself fully to his embrace. Her arms encircled his neck. She clung to him, lost in the passion of their closeness. She felt his arms compass her waist, drawing her still nearer and holding her so tightly she struggled to catch her breath.

His eager mouth moved to her eyelids, her ears, and her throat. His hands were on her, caressing her hair, her back, the curve of her hips. Fear began to sound its alarm far back in her mind. The tender flame she had kindled had grown into a raging fire. Epiphany struggled against his embrace, turning her face away, pushing against him. "Please, darling," she gasped. "No, George—we mustn't—"

Again, rage flared in George Ives's mind. His head had begun to throb painfully. "Damn that Cy Skinner," he thought. "He *did* hit me too hard!" He felt the whiskey and the brandy fogging his brain, burning away the veneer of his assumed gentility. "Damn that two-bit whore Josie Mulhare, as well," he thought. "I'll pay the bitch a visit one night and teach her to mind her own business!" Dimly, he felt Epiphany's resistance through the hot storm of his passion—she was pushing against him and trying to break away, *rejecting* him.

Angrily, he caught her by her hair and pulled her roughly to him. "Not *this* time!" he said, and tore open her dress. Hot and demanding, his mouth found her again. He kissed her throat and her naked shoulder. He turned her, backing her toward the pine boughs and the bedroll. Epiphany tripped and fell. Ives fell with her and pinned her with his body. His hands groped, clawing at her clothing and at his own. "No!" she shouted. "Stop it, George!" He was deaf to her words, heedless of her struggles.

They rolled off the bed, toward the fire. Epiphany struck him with her fists and tore at him with her fingernails. Her flailing hands upset the coffee pot and scattered the plates and cups along the floor. She knocked over the dutch oven. Touching the heavy, iron skillet, her fingers found the handle and grasped it. With strength born of desperation, she swung the skillet hard against Ives's head—once, twice, a third time.

He swore and tried to dodge the blows. He swung at her face, but Epiphany was moving, writhing beneath him. His knuckles only grazed her cheek. He moved back, away from her, and reached for the hand that struck at him. When he did, she grasped the skillet's handle with both hands and hit him with all her strength just above his right temple. Stunned, Ives fell back, blood flowing from his wounded head.

Epiphany found her feet and ran for the door. She swung it wide, and dashed out into the storm. Seconds later, she had stepped up into the buggy and had grasped the whip and the reins. Another moment, and the buggy was sweeping downhill through the falling snow toward Virginia City.

NINETEEN

Runaway

W ITH HER FEET BRACED against the buggy's floorboards and her hands tightly grasping the reins, Epiphany drove the carriage horse out of the trees and into the teeth of the storm. The buggy careened off the bench, struck the drifted roadway, and slewed across its surface in a spray of snow. The frightened horse, nearly blinded by the driven snow, raced into the wind. The horse was fighting to keep its footing. Ahead, above a boulder-strewn gully, the road turned sharply to the left. Half-standing in the buggy, Epiphany pulled back on the reins with all her strength, attempting to slow the racing animal and to swing the rig around the curve.

Too late, the horse sensed danger. Desperately, the animal attempted to slow its pace and negotiate the turn; but it lost its footing and fell heavily on its side in an explosion of snow and rock. Legs flailing, the horse hurtled over the steep embankment, taking the light buggy along with it.

The impact was shocking. Epiphany gasped, too stunned by the force of the fall even to scream. The buggy was on its side now, tumbling and turning in a jumble of twisting, breaking wood, tangled traces, and snow. Still holding the reins in a death-grip, Epiphany felt herself tossed about as if by a giant hand. Abruptly, she flew free of the buggy and hurtled into space. She felt a sharp, blinding pain as her head struck something hard. Snow muffled her face, packed against her neck and shoulders, A glaring crimson curtain flared behind her eyes, and then darkness fell over her like a blanket of mercy.

George Ives came awake slowly, prodded back to consciousness by a pulsing, insistent ache that throbbed through his head. He lay face down, eyes tightly closed, trying to remember where he was, but without success. Only the pounding in his head seemed real.

Slowly, he raised himself on his arms and looked around. A cabin—he was sprawled full length on the floor of a cabin. But whose? Where in the hell–? With an effort, Ives pulled himself up to a sitting position. *Cold.* He shivered and pulled his overcoat closely about his shoulders.

Across the room, the door stood open wide. Blowing snow had drifted into the cabin. Atop a rough table, an oil lamp guttered in the breeze.

Ives could see his breath, explosions of vapor in the lamplight. He raised a trembling hand to his right temple, felt the sticky wetness of his hair, and the pain. He stared, baffled, at the bright blood on his fingers. He saw that he sat beside a stone fireplace, amid scattered cooking utensils. Wisps of smoke rose from charred wood. The wind through the open door stirred the ashes and brought new life to the embers.

Beside a section of log near the fireplace lay a woman's cloak and bonnet. For a moment Ives stared at the articles, uncomprehending. Then, abruptly, memory returned with a rush. Epiphany had struggled against his embrace, resisting him, fighting him. He recalled his passion and his anger—damned, teasing woman! How the bitches loved to lead a man on, get his blood up, and then say no! He had fallen with her, she struggling still, clawing at his face, striking at him. Then had come the sudden pain and the falling away into blackness.

Ives got to his feet and stumbled to the open door. Epiphany's footprints, nearly filled by the falling snow, led to where he had parked the rig. He saw the tracks of horse and buggy where they swept down the hill and away toward Virginia City!

George Ives swore, his mind clear now. Once she got back to town and told her story, men would be coming for him. A man could bull or bluff his way through most accusations and avoid the consequences, but being accused of trying to force a good woman could get him hanged!

Ives snatched his hat from the floor and rushed outside. From a lean-to behind the cabin, he took a saddle, blanket, and bridle from their pegs.

Bucking snow, he made his way to the small corral in the trees where the saddlehorses stood. Moments later, he was riding away from the Virginia City road, toward his ranch beyond the divide.

Earlier that day, at the cabin above Daylight Gulch, Will Hunter cleaned and loaded his revolvers. He had spent the morning at shooting practice in a clearing above the creek. He had returned to the cabin only when the snowstorm had made it difficult to see the target. Back inside the cabin, he disassembled the twin Navy Colts and scrubbed their barrels and cylinders. Once cleaned of their black powder residue, he rinsed them in boiling water and set them out on an old blanket to dry by their own heat. He oiled the cylinders and barrels, coated the base pins with gun grease, and replaced both barrels and cylinders. He blew through each of the nipples to clear them, filled the chambers with powder from his flask, and rammed the greased felt wads and lead balls home. Hunter loaded all six chambers of each revolver, affixed percussion caps to five, and rested the hammers on the uncapped chambers for safety.

Hunter was constantly surprised by the way most men along the gulch cared for their weapons, or rather failed to care for them. In a time and place where nearly every man went armed, relatively few seemed to spend time making sure their weapons were clean, loaded, and in proper working order. Revolvers and shotguns were constantly misfiring or falling apart when their owners needed them most. To Hunter, the lack of proper maintenance seemed foolish at best and suicidal at worst. From his first days with Quantrill, back in Missouri, he had learned to keep his weapons cleaned, loaded, and ready for action at a moment's notice.

Because the cap and ball revolvers loaded slowly, Hunter had picked up the habit of carrying extra cylinders which he could quickly trade for spent ones. From his coat pockets he produced two extras and reloaded them as well.

He had expected trouble after his run-in with the road agents outside Bannack, but so far none had come. Still, he thought, it was well to be ready. Trouble chose its own time. In his experience, it usually came suddenly and when a man least expected it.

He slid the revolvers back into their holsters and secured their hammer thongs. He put the extra loaded cylinders back in the pockets of his greatcoat and put away his cleaning equipment. Pouring himself a cup of coffee from the pot atop the stove, he sipped the steaming brew as he looked out the window at the worsening storm.

Thad had left for Virginia City early that morning, saying he had a load of tools and supplies to haul to the hard-rock miners at Summit. Hunter smiled. His young partner was painfully honest. There was no doubt that he planned to make such a delivery, but Hunter knew the real reason for his early departure was the hope of seeing Epiphany Baker at the Orphan Girl Cafe.

Thad's love for Epiphany was painfully obvious, but he had apparently said nothing about it to her. Hunter understood why. Recalling the first days with Rachel, he remembered his own shyness and his reluctance to declare himself. He'd been a young man who feared nothing, yet he had feared to tell Rachel of his feelings. "If she should turn me down," he had thought, "I could not bear the pain." Only when Rachel had encouraged him through her smile and her touch, when she had made him believe she might welcome his declaration, had he dared to speak his heart. It would be the same for Thad and Epiphany.

Hunter marveled. He realized that for the first time the memory of Rachel had not brought the old, familiar anguish that had assailed him since her death. He had dropped his guard, he had uncorked the bottle and released the genie, but this time the guilt and the grief had not come. He recalled his dream of Rachel and the spirits. In the dream Rachel had told him he must find the way to forgive himself. Looking out at the falling snow, Hunter dared to hope. Maybe he was beginning, at last, to find the way.

It was nearly noon that day by the time Thad Mitchell had the big wagon loaded and the mules harnessed for his trip to Summit. Overhead, steel-gray clouds scowled down on Virginia City and a cold north wind chased ice crystals across Ulberg's wagon yard. For the second time that morning, Thad checked the bill of lading against his load and made sure his axe, snow shovel, and blankets were at hand.

"I still have time for a hot meal at the Orphan Girl," he thought. Immediately felt the quick rush of pleasure the possibility of seeing Epiphany always brought him. Turning up the collar of his sheepskin coat, he walked briskly to the corner of Van Buren and turned south up the hill to Idaho Street.

The snow was beginning to fall in earnest as he came in sight of the Orphan Girl. A half-dozen saddlehorses huddled at the cafe's hitchrack. A chestnut horse stood hitched to a buggy at the restaurant's front door. As Thad drew nearer, the driver of the rig stepped down, looked both ways, and went inside. He wore a heavy blue overcoat and a wide-brimmed black hat.

Something in the sure, lithe way he moved seemed familiar to Thad. He had seen the man before, he was certain, but it had not been behind the reins of a carriage horse. The man was a horseman, certainly, but he was a rider—yes, one of the finest riders in the district —*George Ives!*

For a moment, Thad stood still. Ives was a familiar, even notorious, figure in the camp. Ives was wild and reckless, and a terror to the town's saloon keepers and merchants. When he was in need of funds, Ives would simply toss his empty purse on the bar or store counter and demand a "loan." No one ever refused him, and of course he never repaid the "loans." Ives was belligerent, quick-tempered, and dangerous. He was widely reputed to be a leader of the road agents.

Thad had never seen him at the Orphan Girl before, and there was certainly nothing unusual in his being there. Still, seeing Ives enter the cafe gave Thad a strange, apprehensive feeling he could not explain.

Thad did not believe in intuition. In his judgment, hunches and premonition were colored by what people hoped for or feared. Thus, he was surprised by his reaction. A feeling of dread had come over him so strong that he felt his breathing quicken and his heart beat faster. Thad refused to indulge the feeling. "You're spooking at shadows, like a moon-eyed horse," he told himself, and walked on toward the cafe.

The door swung open, and George Ives came out with Epiphany on his arm. He helped her into the buggy, covered her with the lap robe, and they drove away together. Thad was stunned. Epiphany— with George Ives! It could not be true, he told himself. Yet he had just seen them together. Was it his imagination, or had there been a familiarity between them that spoke of a prior closeness?

Jealousy tormented him. Thad felt a sense of loss, of betrayal and of broken trust. He knew these feelings were baseless. There had been no understanding between himself and Epiphany. She did not even know of his feelings for her, and she certainly seemed to have none for him. His emotions defied reason. Still, realizing all that did little to relieve the lost, hollow feeling in his chest. Thad swallowed hard and began the long walk downhill to the wagon yard.

— ◈ —

It was a freighter from Bannack who found Epiphany. Nels Pedersen, one of John Oakes's teamsters, was driving a wagon-load of flour, whiskey, and dry goods to Virginia City just after ten o'clock the next morning when he came to the sharp turn in the road. The storm had passed through during the night, and the day had dawned cold and still under cloudless skies. Nearly six inches of new snow had fallen. It sparkled in the sunlight, dazzling the eye, and lay pristine and blue in the shadows.

Nels saw the carriage horse first. The animal lay tangled in the traces, its neck broken, in deep snow below the road. Already, magpies had found its body. The long-tailed scavengers scolded and chattered at their feast. Behind the horse, the shattered buggy lay on its side. Its leather top was torn and one wheel was partly visible above the drifted snow. Nels shaded his eyes against the brightness, squinting into the hollow. It was then he saw the woman.

Nearly invisible beneath the snow, she lay at the foot of a large boulder, perhaps twenty feet from the wreckage of the buggy. A corner of her skirt protruded from the snow, green silk bright against the whiteness. One shoulder and part of her head were visible, blood staining her hair and the nearby snow.

The teamster did not hesitate. Nels Pedersen plunged off the roadway, sinking nearly hip-deep into the snowbound hollow. Half wading, half swimming, he slipped on the hidden boulders and tripped over buried deadfall. He plunged ahead until he reached the silent figure. Falling on his knees beside her, Nels burrowed into the drift with his hands, clearing the snow from her face.

Lifting her head and shoulders from the snow, he saw the woman was young and pretty. A jagged wound marked her left temple, and her skin was cold and clammy to the touch. Her dress had been ripped away from her neck and shoulders. The teamster laid his head upon her cold flesh and held his breath, listening for a heartbeat.

"Please, little lady, don't be dead," he whispered, raising his head. "Poor little lady. Poor thing." Again, he laid his ear upon her breast, listening. Faintly, he heard the slow pulsing that meant life. Quickly, he removed the heavy, buffalo coat he wore and bundled the woman inside. Then he took her in his arms and plowed his way back up to the road.

News of Nels Pedersen finding the "poor little lady" swept through Alder Gulch like the rumor of a new gold strike. When he arrived in Virginia City, the burly teamster carried the unconscious young woman into the lobby of the Fairweather Inn and demanded help. Help came swiftly. John Oakes, Pedersen's employer, was on hand to greet him. He identified the "poor little lady" as Miss Epiphany Baker, owner and proprietor of the Orphan Girl Cafe. Oakes not only knew her, but he knew where she lived. Epiphany was quickly taken to Lily Rae's boarding house and ensconced in her own feather bed.

John Oakes, who made it his business to keep well informed, and who seemed to know virtually everything that transpired in the district, had heard that Dr. Glick was in town treating an injured miner. Oakes summoned the good doctor, and the physician arrived promptly at Epiphany's bedside.

Onlookers crowded her small room, from the desk clerk at the Fairweather Inn and a clutch of out of work miners to Lily Rae Bliss, John Oakes, and the hero of the hour, Nels Pedersen.

"It was me that found her, Doc," said Nels. "Looked like her horse ran away and took her buggy off the road during the storm. The poor thing was buried under the snow, colder'n a carp! I thought sure she was a goner!"

Dr. Glick removed his coat and rolled up his shirtsleeves. "Struck her head in the fall, too, apparently," he said. "The cold helped slow the bleeding."

One of only two physicians in the Beaverhead and Fairweather mining districts, Dr. Jerome Glick had the confidence of the people. At the time, the other doctor, a man named Leavitt, was on a gold-seeking sabbatical from the medical profession. Dr. Glick was a dedicated practitioner who served his patients with impartiality and skill. His practice included calls to treat the bullet wounds and other occupational injuries of the road agents and killers of the region. He had treated Henry Plummer, among others. Dr. Glick was a man of influence in the camps. He exercised that authority as soon as he arrived at Lily Rae's boarding house.

"I want everyone out of this room," he said, "except Mrs. Bliss."

Turning to Lily Rae, he asked, "Madam, will you assist me?"

Lily Rae had been weeping over Epiphany while she bustled about trying to see to her young friend's comfort. The doctor's call to service seemed to focus her energies. "Yes, doctor," she said, "of course I will."

The doctor was a stout man of medium height with a full beard and a kindly manner. Seated at Epiphany's bedside, he leaned forward and began his examination. "See this ridge on the young woman's scalp?" he asked. "It would appear at first glance to indicate a fractured skull. That is not the case, I'm happy to say. What seems to be the edge of a broken bone is instead a blood clot beneath the scalp.

"We shall need to treat her both for her head wound and for exposure to the cold," he said. "Her hands, feet, face, and upper body must be slowly warmed by bathing in moderately warm water. Will you see to that while I attend her wound?"

"Yes, doctor, right away," said Lily Rae. "Will. . . will she be all right?"

"We have every reason to hope so," the doctor replied. "She's young and strong, and she seems to be remarkably fit."

Lily Rae wiped her eyes and blew her nose. "A body feels so helpless at a time like this. I wish there was something more I could do."

"There's always prayer," said the doctor. "I've always believed in calling in a qualified consultant when one is available."

<hr />

Will Hunter was splitting wood behind the cabin on Daylight Creek when he heard the fast-running horse coming through the trees. He heard the clatter of hooves on loose rock, sunk his axe into the chopping block, and drew his revolvers.

John Oakes burst suddenly into view astride his roan, yelling as he came. "It's Miss Epiphany, Will! She's hurt bad!"

Oakes pulled the roan to a sliding stop, dismounting even as the animal struggled to find its footing. Hunter was already rushing to meet him. Oakes' voice had been strained, the words indistinct, but Hunter had heard three of them clearly: *Epiphany, hurt,* and *bad.*

He holstered his pistols and caught Oakes's arm. "Epiphany's hurt?" he asked. "Damn it, John—what happened?"

Oakes struggled to catch his breath. "She—had a runaway. Went off the Bannack road in a buggy. Horse was killed."

Hunter gripped Oakes's shoulders, his eyes intent on his friend's face. "How bad is it?" he asked. "Where is she now?"

Oakes's expression was somber. "Pretty bad, Will," he said. "Struck her head on a rock. She laid out all night in the snow."

"Where is she *now?*" Will asked again.

Oakes moved the axe and sat down on the chopping block. His hands were shaking, his face pale. "At Lily Rae's," he said, "Doc Glick is with her."

Hunter was already striding toward the corral. Both his black gelding and Thad's mule Shadrach stood watching, their ears erect, as he approached. "Thad got back from Summit late last night," he said, "He's still asleep. Wake him, John, and tell him I'm saddling his mule and my horse. There's coffee on the stove, and whiskey on the shelf. Help yourself."

Twenty minutes later, the three men were in the saddle and riding fast on the road to Virginia City.

◈

Lily Rae met Hunter and Thad at the front door of the boarding house. Her eyes and nose were red from weeping. There was a tremor in her voice as she led the two men into her parlor. "I'm glad you've come," she said. "Our girl is in a bad way, I'm afraid."

"What happened, Lily Rae?" Hunter asked, "John Oakes said something about a runaway and a wrecked buggy."

"We really don't know very much, Will," Lily Rae said. "Apparently, Epiphany was driving back to Virginia last night in that storm when her horse ran off the road with her. She was thrown from the buggy and struck her head when she fell." Lily Rae's eyes brimmed with tears. "Poor thing still hasn't come to her senses."

Down the hallway, Hunter saw Dr. Glick emerge from Epiphany's room and softly close the door. The doctor carried his coat and medical bag. He nodded at the two men as he came into the parlor. "Members of the young woman's family?" he asked.

"As close as she has," Hunter said. "How is she?"

"Well," said the doctor, "I'd say she's doing rather well, considering what she's been through in the past twenty-four hours. There seems to be no permanent damage due to the cold, and her vital signs are good. Her head injury is severe, but there is no evidence of a skull fracture. With rest, quiet, and the tender care I know she'll receive at the hands of Mrs. Bliss, I would expect a full recovery."

"Can I . . . can we. . . see her?" Thad asked.

Dr. Glick had a gift for reading faces. His perceptiveness had made him an effective physician. They had also made him a successful poker player. He looked at Thad Mitchell's honest young face and read Thad's concern and love there. "I don't see why not," the doctor said, "but she must be kept perfectly quiet at all times. There must be no noise and no disturbances. Her head must be kept low—no pillows—and her bandage should be changed every few hours."

He removed a small bottle from his bag and handed it to Thad. "This is tincture of aconite, a very powerful remedy. Give her one drop every half hour. If her pulse weakens, try one drop every hour. I'll stop by again tomorrow."

Dr. Glick smiled. "Do you think you can handle all that, young sir?"

Gratitude lit Thad's face. "I'm your man, doctor," he said.

"Yes," said Dr. Glick, smiling, "and *hers,* apparently."

Behind drawn shades in her room, Epiphany lay pallid and still beneath the bedcovers. The bandage that encircled her head was stark white in the dim light. Hunter and Thad stood together at her bedside, each man lost in his own thoughts.

"I love you, Piff," thought Thad. "I'm here for you, and I'm not leaving."

"I'm sorry, Piff," Will Hunter thought. "Whatever happened out there, I wasn't there to protect you. In my damn fool pride I had promised myself I would be."

After a few minutes, the partners left the room and closed the door behind them. "I'm staying, Will," Thad said. "I have to."

Hunter nodded. "I know," he said. "I'll take care of the business. There isn't much going on right now, anyway."

Thad frowned. "There is one other thing," he said, "something no one else knows. I stopped by the Orphan Girl at noon yesterday to see Piff. There was a horse and buggy outside the cafe when I got there, and the driver seemed to be waiting for someone. As I came up, he stepped down from the buggy. I saw it was George Ives. He looked around and went inside the cafe.

"I don't know why I didn't go in. I just stood there as the snow began to fall. A few minutes later, Ives came back out—with Piff on his arm! He helped her into the buggy, and they drove away toward the Bannack road."

"George Ives!" Hunter said. "Are you sure it was Ives?"

"Dead sure. I don't know what they were doing together, or where they were going. All I know is what I saw. Something happened out there last night. Now Epiphany's hurt and fighting for her life. All I want to do is stay with her."

Hunter's face was hard as flint, and his pale blue eyes had turned to ice. "I understand, partner," he said, "I think I'll go pay a call on George Ives."

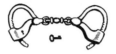

TWENTY
Murder Most Foul

IT WAS LATE in the afternoon when Will Hunter rode his black gelding out on the road to Bannack. Swiftly, he passed Nevada City and Junction, moving on into the canyon beyond. Snow from the previous night's storm had settled, melting during the day, but there were still patches on the roadway and deep drifts down through the shaded canyon. Hunter rode at a steady trot. He watched the rutted ground for tracks left by the horse and buggy, but the fresh snow and wagon traffic had obliterated every sign.

Not quite four miles from Junction, Hunter came upon the sharp turn overlooking the hollow below the road. He drew rein at the brink, looking down into the boulder-strewn gulch. In the bloody snow below, a dozen magpies scolded and chattered as they fed on the carcass of the carriage horse. Coyote tracks led out of the trees to the dead animal and back again. Behind the horse, the buggy lay half buried beneath the snow, shattered and forlorn.

As Hunter surveyed the scene, he marveled that Epiphany had survived at all. The distance from the roadway to the wreck told him the carriage had been travelling at a breakneck pace when it left the road. Had the horse run away with her, as some believed? Or had she been desperately driving the animal, fleeing something—or someone—she believed threatened her life?

Hunter turned the gelding back up the road, riding slowly on beyond the scene of the wreck. Heavy brush and deep snow marked the edge of the roadway. Stands of pine and aspen stood tall on the slopes above. From time to time, Hunter scanned the hillside. For the most part, he leaned low in the saddle, carefully studying the shoulder of the road.

Less than a mile away, he found what he had been searching for. A short, steep trail swung up from the road to the bench above. There, beneath the new snow that covered the tracks, were the indentations that told the story: a horse and buggy had climbed up from the road and descended again. Epiphany had driven the carriage down from somewhere above!

The gelding lunged up the trail, spraying snow with each leap, while Hunter leaned forward over the horse's withers to aid its progress. Then horse and rider were atop a long bench beneath dark pines. There, in the shadow of the trees, stood a small cabin.

The door was ajar, and snow had drifted inside. In front of the cabin, tracks of the horse and carriage were clearly visible beneath a dusting of new snow. Hunter drew rein and dismounted. Silently, he walked toward the cabin, paused, and stepped through the doorway.

Inside, the room was cold and empty. Hunter waited, allowing his eyes to adjust to the gloom. Then he carefully studied the interior. A cabin like a hundred others, he thought—stone fireplace, a rude plank table, a bedroll atop a base of pine boughs. Water bucket, wood pile, pots, pans, and supplies.

Then his gaze fell on two items that made the cabin decidedly unlike the others he had seen. On the floor, beside the fireplace, lay a woman's heavy wool cloak and a dark cabriolet bonnet! Hunter had seen the cloak and bonnet before. They were Epiphany's and no mistake. Hunter bent down and picked up the clothing.

She had left this place in a hurry—in such a hurry that she dashed out into a snowstorm and left her warm cloak and bonnet behind. She had run to the buggy and dashed down to the road, desperate to get away from this place. She had risked her life to escape a threat that terrified her, he thought. She had risked her life to escape George Ives!

226

Outside again, Hunter found Ives' tracks. The tracks were clearer than Epiphany's, which meant they'd been made later, as the storm was ending. Ives had walked to the corral in the trees. There he had saddled and mounted one horse, put a second one on a lead rope, and had raced away toward Bannack.

Hunter's eyes narrowed. He recalled the passage from the Book of Proverbs: *The wicked flee when no man pursueth.* "Yes, they do indeed," he thought, "but you may depend on one thing, George Ives—*this* time a pursuer *is* coming."

Back in Virginia City, Hunter rode directly to the boarding house. When Lily Rae opened the door to admit him, the expression on her face brought him a measure of hope.

"Epiphany's resting comfortably, Will," she said. "We've been giving her the medicine Dr. Glick left for her every half hour, but she still hasn't really regained consciousness. Thad hasn't left her side for a moment."

Hunter handed her the cloak and bonnet he'd recovered from the cabin. "Found these out near where the accident happened," he said. "Thought I'd best bring them here."

Lily Rae nodded. She took the clothes and led him into her parlor.

"I'm glad she's resting easy," Hunter said. "I had hoped she could tell us more about what happened out there, but getting her strength back is more important. Would you tell Thad I need to see him?"

"Certainly. Have a chair, Will. I've made fresh coffee, and I'll bring you a cup."

Thad emerged from Ephiphany's room and walked down the hallway to the parlor. He took a chair opposite Hunter and ran his fingers through his hair. He looked tired. "Did you find Ives?" he asked.

"Not yet, but I think I know where he's gone. I tracked the buggy to a cabin the other side of Junction. Whatever happened there last night caused Piff to make a run for it alone. She was going too fast when she hit that sharp turn on the way back, and she didn't make it. Horse, buggy, and Piff went off the road and into the hollow below."

"What about George Ives?"

"He left the cabin sometime later. There were two horses in a corral behind the cabin. He rode one and led the other, headed toward Bannack."

Thad was silent for a moment. "Ives has a place on Wisconsin Creek, near Dempsey's ranch. Named the stream for his home state, I hear. A rag-tag collection of brush wakiups, shacks, and corrals. If he's there, it's likely there will be a half-dozen or so other hardcases with him."

"More than likely," Hunter said pleasantly.

Thad studied his friend's face for a long moment in silence. There was nothing in its expression to reveal Hunter's thoughts. Thad nodded.

"Take care of yourself, partner," he said.

"Take care of Piff," Hunter replied.

Hunter had just descended the boarding house steps when John Oakes thundered up on his roan. His face was flushed, and his eyes were bright with excitement. "I saw your horse and figured you were here," he said. "I've got big news, Will—judgment day has come at last! Twenty-five men rode out at ten o'clock last night to arrest George Ives!"

"Arrest him? Why?"

"Robbery, and murder most foul! Come down to the Miner's Rest with me, and I'll tell you all about it!"

———◈———

Prospectors and townsmen nearly filled the Miner's Rest as Hunter and Oakes walked in. In the crowded saloon smoke drifted in layers beneath the low ceiling. Men were two deep at the bar, and saloon-keeper Tommy O'Flaherty and two bartenders were busy keeping the glasses filled. Oakes caught Tommy's eye, gesturing toward the rear of the building where a muslin curtain separated the back rooms from the saloon proper. "Tommy's got a private room in back he lets me use," Oakes said. "We can go there if it's available." Across the room, Tommy nodded, and Oakes parted the curtain and led Hunter inside.

A deal table with six chairs sat beneath an oil lamp near the back door. Oakes struck a match and lit the wick of the lamp. "High-rollers use this table sometimes for their private games," he said. "It's a good place to talk and be free of interruptions."

One of Tommy's barkeeps came in through the curtain, carrying a tray with two glasses and a full quart of Valley Tan. He placed the tray on the table, took Oakes's money, and went back into the bar. Hunter pulled out a chair and sat down. "All right," he said. "What's all this about a posse going out to arrest Ives?"

Oakes poured three fingers of whiskey in each of the glasses and sat down across from Hunter. "Let me start at the beginning," he said.

"I don't know if you ever met Nick Tbalt—big, good-natured kid some called 'The Dutchman?' Worked for Nevada City claim owners Burtchey and Clark. No? Well, anyway, Nick owned a span of mules he kept pastured with George Ives at Dempsey's place over on the Stinkingwater. Burtchey and Clark wanted to buy the animals, so the kid took their money and set out to pick up the mules.

"That's the last his employers ever heard from him. As time passed and he didn't come back, they came to think he'd absquatulated with both their money *and* the mules. The thought distressed them considerable."

Oakes raised his glass and took a long sip. "Yesterday, nine days after the kid left, Bill Palmer—saloon keeper from Nevada City—was out hunting on the Stinkingwater in his wagon when a grouse flew up in front of him. Palmer made a lucky shot and saw the grouse drop. When he rushed over to pick up the bird he found it lying smack on top of the dead, frozen body of Nick Tbalt!"

Oakes paused. He seemed to be seeing the grisly scene in his imagination. Then he continued. "The body lay on its face in a patch of heavy sagebrush. There were rope marks on its neck, and a bullet hole just above the left eye. The corpse had pieces of sagebrush and grass clenched in its hands. Nick Tbalt had been shot, and dragged—still living—through the brush by his neck!

"Bill saw a wakiup about a quarter mile below the body, and went down there. Turned out to be "Long John" Franke's place. Bill told Long John and George Hilderman, who were there, about the body. He asked them if they'd help him load it in his wagon.

"The sons o' bitches *laughed* at him, Will! Said a dead man was nothing—that men were killed every day in Virginia City and nobody gave a damn. Told him they wanted no part of it.

"Well, their attitude sure stuck in Bill's craw, but there wasn't much he could do about it. He went back and somehow managed to load the corpse by himself, then he set out for Nevada City. Bill showed Nick's body to every man he met on the way back and told each man what Long John and Hilderman had said. Back at Nevada City, Bill let the corpse lay out in his wagon for half a day while some of the boys built a coffin.

"Hundreds of men from the gulch came by to see the corpse, and late yesterday they buried the kid above Nevada. You know Jim Williams? Runs a livery stable in Nevada City? Well, Old Man Clark went to Jim, all fired up to start a vigilance committee. Said it was high time somebody put a stop to the thieves and killers. Jim told him he had 50 or 60 head of saddle horses and 25 or 30 saddles and bridles—he offered them to outfit a posse. Some of the boys, including Jim Williams, Elk Morse, and X. Beidler, raised a war party. At ten o'clock last night they set out in force for the valley of the Stinkingwater."

Hunter lifted his whiskey, drank, and placed the glass carefully on the table. "You said they rode out to arrest George Ives," he said. "How do they know he did the killing?"

"I suppose they don't. I guess they'll question Long John, Hilderman, and any other roughs they find out there, but there's no doubt in *my* mind who did it," Oakes said. "Nothing much happens down at Dempsey's that George Ives doesn't do or order done. Besides, it was Ives the dead kid was going to see."

Hunter made no reply. He sat, looking down at his empty glass, an amused smile on his lips.

"What's so funny?" Oakes asked.

"I was just thinking," Hunter said. "Back in Missouri when I was a kid, I had to haul water some distance from the creek to irrigate our family garden. I hated that job. Spent most of one night fretting and fussing about all the water I was going to have to carry the next day. Finally fell asleep, still fretting.

"When I woke up next morning, I found a hard rain had come in the night and I wouldn't have to carry water after all. I was relieved, but in a strange kind of way, disappointed. I feel like that now."

"What? Sometimes I don't have the slightest idea of what you're talking about, Will," John Oakes complained.

When the citizens' posse from Nevada City rode out at ten o'clock the night before, they were bound for the valley of the Stinkingwater.

At midnight, they stopped briefly at a ranch house on the way where they warmed themselves and picked up another volunteer, a man named Jack Reynolds. Then they rode on, avoiding the road and circling the bluff in order to stay clear of Dempsey's ranch.

At three-thirty in the morning the riders found Wisconsin Creek frozen over and decided to cross it on horseback. The ice, however, was not thick enough to hold the weight of a horse and rider. One after another the horsemen broke through, saddlehorses plunging, half-swimming, thrashing through the ice-filled waters. When the posse reached the other bank, most of the men were wet through and chilled to the bone. The company had elected Elk Morse captain. About a mile beyond the crossing, he called a halt. The posse was then about six miles from Dempsey's and near the place where Nick Tbalt's body had been found.

"Get down, boys, and hold your horses by the bridle," Captain Morse said. "Keep quiet and stand easy 'til daybreak."

The men obeyed. There, in the gray light, they waited. Huddled in their blankets, stamping their feet to keep them from freezing, their thoughts had remained focused on the capture and arrest of the person or persons who had killed Nick Tbalt.

Ninety minutes later, the day's first light painted the mountain peaks.

"Mount your horses," Morse commanded. "Don't say a word 'til we're in sight of Long John's wakiup."

They had nearly reached the camp when the barking of a dog sounded the alarm. The riders spurred their horses into a run across the frozen ground. When they reached the wakiup, they surrounded it, their shotguns cocked and leveled. The raid was a complete surprise. Several men slept in their bedrolls at the entrance to the rude shelter. They stirred, suddenly awake.

Jim Williams dismounted quickly, his shotgun trained on the men, and shouted, "Don't move! The first man that raises will get a quart of buckshot in him!"

Overhead, the skies went from gray to rose. Dawn touched the eastern slopes with light, but darkness clung to the wakiup just as sleep clung to the men in their beds. "Is Long John here?" Williams asked.

"Yes," said Long John, from inside the wakiup.

"Come out here," Williams ordered, "I want you."

Long John Franke stepped out into the chill morning. He squinted against the brightening sky, taking note of the armed men surrounding the shelter. Captain Morse, Williams, and two others took Franke some distance away to question him. They left the rest of the posse to guard the others.

Williams and Morse then accused Long John of the murder. "I didn't do it, boys," Long John said. "As God shall judge me, I did not."

"Well, if you didn't," said Morse, "you damn well know who did."

"You refused to help me load the body in my wagon," Bill Palmer accused.

"That's right," Williams said. "You knew of a man lying dead for nine days near your house, and you didn't report his murder. You deserve to hang for that alone. Why didn't you come to Virginia and tell someone?"

"I. . . I was afraid," Long John said.

"Afraid of what?" Williams asked.

"Afraid of the men hereabouts. They'll kill me if I talk."

"You'll hang if you don't."

Long John hesitated. "There's one of 'em back at the wakiup. He's the one killed Nick."

"Who is he?"

For a moment, Long John hesitated. He glanced nervously about, as if pleading for someone to help him. At length he said, "George Ives."

Leaving Palmer and the other three men to guard Long John, Williams strode toward the camp. Finding Ives there, he said, "I want you."

"What do you want me for?" asked Ives.

"To go to Virginia City."

"All right," Ives said, "then I expect I'll have to go."

A long-time associate of Henry Plummer and George Ives, an outlaw known only as "Old Tex," stood near the wakiup, pulling on his dirty undershirt.

When Williams saw him, he said, "I believe we shall want you, too." Tex tossed the shirt toward one of the possemen with a sneer. "There's my old shirt and plenty of graybacks. You'd better arrest them, too."

At first, both Tex and Ives appeared confident and unworried about their arrests. Ives professed complete innocence of the murder, using the password of the roughs. "I'm innocent, boys," he said, "you know— I'm *innocent.*" However, when Tex and Ives approached the men who held Long John prisoner, their attitude changed. Seeming to realize the gravity of their situation, they remained silent and said nothing more.

The prisoners were directed to saddle and mount their own horses. When they had done so, the entire party moved on down to Dempsey's ranch. As the posse approached the ranch with the arrested men, the two lead riders saw a man working on a new bridge across a small stream. Posse member Bill Palmer recognized him as George Hilderman, the man who had been with Long John on the day they had refused to help load Nicholas Tbalt's corpse. Hilderman, too, was taken into custody. The party had then continued toward Nevada City.

The posse had foolishly allowed George Ives to ride without restraints. Ives had been cordial and friendly, and for a time the possemen nearly forgot that he was also a dangerous man. Talking and joking with his captors, Ives had turned the conversation to the subject of horse racing. He had boasted to some of the posse members about the speed of the bobtailed gelding he rode. The posse members had in turn boasted of their own horses. Soon, Ives had talked these men into competing against him in an impromptu horse race.

Ives allowed himself to lose two short scrub races, and a general spirit of racing fever seemed to ignite among the members of the posse. As the party neared Pete Daly's ranch, Ives urged his gelding to its top speed. He raced away from his captors in what he knew was a life-or-death contest.

Meanwhile, some of Ives's friends had witnessed his arrest. They rode ahead of the posse and its prisoners to Pete Daly's ranch. Once there, they saddled and made ready George Ives' favorite horse, a fleet-footed mare. Their intent had been to help Ives to escape by providing him with a fast, fresh horse. However, in spite of his substantial lead over most of the posse, Ives found himself too closely pursued to stop for the animal.

However, two members of the posse—George Burtchey and Jack Reynolds—had stopped. They obtained fresh mounts at Daly's and had rapidly narrowed the gap between themselves and Ives. While still ahead of the pursuing riders, Ives jumped off his exhausted mount and took refuge in a canyon. Burtchey and Reynolds also dismounted and pursued him on foot. It was Burtchey who found Ives, crouching behind a large boulder. He commanded the desperado to come out and surrender. Laughing, Ives did so.

Sobered by Ives's near escape, the posse restrained their prisoners securely and proceeded on toward Nevada City.

At ten-thirty the following morning, Epiphany awakened to full consciousness. She had been awake for brief periods during the day and night since her accident, but she had no clear memory of what had happened. She lay in the dark room and tried to recall where she was and how she had come to be there. Her head throbbed with a dull, persistent ache. She struggled with the nausea that accompanied her waking. She tried to speak, but the words escaped her lips, jumbled and unintelligible.

Someone moved in the darkness—a man, seated at the foot of her bed! Frightened, she tried to move, to call out. Her heart beat faster. She stared at the man. Who *was* he?

The man stood up. He smiled. Slowly, Epiphany felt her fear subside. Somehow, she seemed to recognize the man. "He is the man in the chair," she thought. "The man who cares for me." How did she know him? She couldn't think. All she knew was that the man was there to help, not harm her. He was beside her now, placing his hand cool upon her brow. He held the basin beside her head and she grasped it, retching until the spasms stopped. She then fell gasping back upon the bed. The man wiped her face, her eyes, her lips with the cool, wet cloth again. His touch was surprisingly gentle.

During her brief periods of wakefulness, Epiphany had learned to lie very still and to control her breathing so as not to provoke the pain, and she did so now. Moments passed. Like a great prowling predator, the pain worried at her and mauled her, then withdrew as Epiphany continued to breathe deeply. Again, she tried to speak. "Who—who are you?" she whispered.

"It's Thad, Miss Epiphany—Thad Mitchell," the man said. "You're safe now, Miss. Everything's going to be all right."

"The man has a kind voice," she thought, "gentle, like his touch. He speaks as though he thought I should know who 'Thad Mitchell' is, but I can't remember. Something happened, something bad, and now I am here in this dark place with my pain and my sickness. I should be able to recall what happened. Why can't I?" She closed her eyes again. "I'll try again later," she thought, "when my head doesn't hurt so bad."

The man in the chair was saying something, talking to her. "I must try to pay attention," she thought. "I must try to concentrate."

"I have to go away for awhile, Miss," the man said. "Just for a moment. Mrs. Bliss will be in directly."

She heard the chair scuff against the floor as the man got to his feet. The door opened, briefly admitting lamplight into the dark room, then closed with the click of a latch. Epiphany heard the man's footsteps going away, then the darkness gathered around her like a blanket and covered her.

Thad found Lily Rae in her kitchen, stirring a pot of rich-smelling broth that simmered on the stove. "She's awake again," Thad said, "but still confused. She vomited again."

"Poor child," Lily Rae said, "how is she ever to get better if she can keep nothing down?"

She ladled a dipperful of the broth into a soup bowl and placed it on a tray. Her gaze searched the young man's face. "You look tired, Thad," she said. "You've been wonderful with her, but you need rest yourself."

Thad shrugged off the suggestion. "I'm all right," he said, "but I was thinking. Somebody should go down to the Orphan Girl–tell Cootie and Wong Fat that she has regained her senses. I could do that–maybe stay and help out some."

"Yes, I suppose you could," Lily Rae said. Thad's face was haggard, she noted, stamped with sadness and worry. His eyes were red, and he needed a shave.

"We feel helpless when we see someone we care about in pain," Lily Rae said. "Love makes us hurt on their behalf."

"*Love?* I never said–"

"There was no need," she said softly. "The way you look at her, the gentle way you touch her–those things say it for you."

Thad looked away. When he spoke, his voice was tight, and full of longing. "She doesn't even know I'm alive," he said.

Lily Rae laughed, her hazel eyes merry. "Well, then," she said, "one of these days you must let her know. Now get along with you–I have a patient to care for."

In the darkened bedroom, Epiphany lay on her back and stared at the ceiling. Memories–or fragments of memories–formed in her mind. Now she recalled that each time she had awakened, the quiet man had been there. He had given her water and medicine. He had bathed her face and had held her hand. Moments before, when he had left her, the man had mentioned his name as if she should know who he was.

Who was "Thad Mitchell" and who was "Mrs. Bliss"? The answers continued to elude her.

"It is as though there is a great dam inside my mind," she thought, "holding back a sea of memories. All the thoughts, all the names of people and places I should know, are caught in that dark flood and I can't bring them to mind."

"I must be patient," she thought. "My head will stop hurting, and I'll remember names and places again. The dam will break, and memories will flood my mind. I won't be sick or confused any longer. I'll know all the things I'm supposed to know, good and bad."

Epiphany shuddered. Fear whispered strange names and places in her ears. Her heart began to race; she felt her breathing quicken. "What if the memories are bad?" she thought. "What if they're ugly and frightening? What if the memories come and break my heart? *Will I be strong enough?*"

The sound of her voice echoed in the small room. Epiphany realized she had spoken the last question aloud.

The door swung open. Lily Rae stood in the doorway with the light behind her, a serving tray in her hands. The rich aroma of chicken broth filled the room.

"Hello, Piff," said Lily Rae. "I heard that last question as I stopped outside your door." Her smile was warm. "The answer is yes, honey," she said. "You'll be *plenty* strong enough."

TWENTY=ONE
A Jury of His Peers

NEWS OF GEORGE IVES'S arrest reached Nevada City a good two hours ahead of the posse's arrival and galvanized the camp. Borne by a hard-riding horseman on a lathered mount, the report swept the town—a citizen's posse had arrested George Ives for the robbery and murder of Nicholas Tbalt! By sundown on the evening of December 18, hundreds of miners and townsmen thronged the streets and waited for the posse's return. Will Hunter and John Oakes were among the crowd.

The sun set. A chill wind swept the streets. An expectant hush fell over the waiting men. Then someone at the edge of the crowd shouted, "Here they come!" as the posse and their prisoners came riding out of the west and up the camp's main street.

Jim Williams and Elk Morse rode at the column's head, X. Beidler close beside them. Behind them, surrounded by posse, came the captives—George Ives, his hands now securely tied behind him and his feet roped together beneath his horses belly, Long Johns Franke, his expression apprehensive and downcast, and George Hilderman, shoulders hunched, his jaw set, only his eyes moving. The procession drew rein in front of Lott Brothers store, where John Lott asked, "What are you going to do with them?"

Jim Williams replied, "Take them to Virginia City."

"No," said Lott. "The roughs have too many friends there. If we try them there, we'll have the same kind of mess we had at the Dillingham trial. Let's try them here in Nevada City."

John Lott's brother Mortimer came out of the store and vigorously supported his brother's suggestion. He stood on a dry goods box and spoke to the crowd, forcefully arguing against a Virginia City trial. His brother was right, he said—the prisoners had too many friends in Virginia City. Besides, he went on, long-established tradition held that accused criminals should be tried at a place nearest the scene of the crime.

He closed his remarks with a formal motion to keep the men in Nevada City. Only posse members voted. The vote carried. "We will hold them here in Nevada City," Williams announced. Shackled and bound with chains, Ives, Franke, and Hilderman were placed under guard in a nearby house.

"Clubfoot" George Lane knew a crisis when he saw one. He was devoted to Henry Plummer and to the "Innocents." He was certain Plummer would use his legal authority as sheriff to protect Ives and the others from trial. Lane arranged to have fresh horses waiting at key stops along the road and set out at a gallop to carry the news to his chief at Bannack.

As he swept through Junction and dropped into the narrow canyon that led to Daly's roadhouse, a nameless man stood waiting in the shadows of a low barn with a fresh mount, saddled and ready. Lane drew rein, jumped off his spent and faltering horse, and mounted the new one with a bound.

Soon he was out of the gulch and into the Stinkingwater valley, racing past Baker's ranch. A cold moon rose above the Bitterroots, lighting the way across the snow-covered ground. Ungainly and clumsy on foot because of his deformity, George Lane was a master horseman. Realizing the imminent danger to the "Innocents," he pushed his mount to its limits. Dog-like in his devotion to Plummer, Lane's admiration of his chief bordered on worship. "The fat is in the fire now," he thought, "but Henry will make it right. Henry's smart, he knows the law. He'll get the boys off. He'll rescue Ives and the others."

Twice more, Lane changed horses, sweeping into Bannack on the fourth horse just short of daybreak. Hot and dripping lather, the animal slowed, steam rising from its body in the chill morning air. The horse's breath came in great, racking gasps, and its limbs trembled. Clubfoot lashed at the struggling animal, spurring it viciously. "Just a little farther, damn you," he said. "We're almost there!"

The horse stumbled and fell, dying in that part of Bannack called Yankee Flat. Lane left the animal in the road and hobbled up the slope toward the cabin where Plummer lived.

Henry Plummer lay in his bed and stared up into the pre-dawn gloom. He had stayed late at the faro tables the night before, and Lady Luck had once again proven herself to be a treacherous bitch. She had dealt him a losing streak that darkened his mood while it lightened his purse. Unfortunately, his pride would not let him cut his losses and quit. Faro was his game, he had told himself. Damn it, he was Henry Plummer! He was a winner, not a loser! So he had stubbornly gone on bucking the tiger like any greenhorn from the mines, hoping his luck would change. It had not.

He remembered the sweating dealer at Skinner's, nervous and nearly apologetic as the house won bet after bet. He remembered the onlookers, their expressions carefully neutral as the play continued to go against him. Were they laughing behind his back? "To hell with them," he thought. "One bad night doesn't make me a loser. A man is a loser only when he thinks himself so."

Plummer swung his legs over the side of the bed and sat up. He shivered, pulling the bedclothes closely around himself. He had neglected to bank the fire when he came in early that morning, and the cabin was now cold as a crypt. Still wrapped in his blankets, he shivered as he piled kindling into the sheet iron stove and struck it alight. He washed his face in the icy water from the basin beside the door, toweled himself dry, and dressed quickly. As the stove began to make pinging sounds with the growing heat of the fire, the sheriff stood close, waiting for the warmth.

The sudden pounding on the cabin door startled him. Plummer spun, his revolver cocked and ready in his left hand. "Who's there?" he demanded.

"It's me, Henry—George Lane!" came the reply. "Let me in!"

The sheriff swung open the cabin door and frowned. "George!" he said. "What the hell—?"

"I been ridin' all night," Lane said. "Killed a horse gettin' here. The news is bad, Henry, awful bad!"

"Damn you," Plummer said. "What is it?"

"They've arrested George Ives! A miner's court is fixin' to try him for murder in Nevada City!"

"So," Plummer thought, "it begins."

"Who arrested him?" he asked. "Quick—tell me everything."

Clubfoot George recounted the facts as he knew them. He told of the murder of Tbalt and the discovery of the body by Palmer. He described Palmer's return and the anger of the crowds.

"It was men from Nevada City who brought him in," said the cripple. "Elk Morse and Jim Williams led a posse over to Dempsey's and jumped the boys right at sunup! Arrested Ives, and brought Long John and Hilderman in, too. You got to get up there, Henry—you got to save the boys!"

Plummer's voice was calm. "Yes," he said, "I'll have to do that. My extra horse is in the barn, down at the livery stable. Take her and get back to Nevada City. Tell Ives I'm on my way."

"I'll wait and ride with you, Henry," said Lane.

"No. I have some important business here first. You go ahead. I'll be along directly."

Lane looked worried. "It. . . it is gonna be all right, ain't it, Henry?"

"Yes. You did well, George. Those men made an unlawful arrest. I'll straighten everything out when I get there."

For a time, Plummer stood outside the cabin, watching as Clubfoot George hobbled away toward the livery stable. Henry Plummer had never been a superstitious man, but on that cold December morning his losing run at the faro tables the night before now seemed very much like an omen.

He had no intention of going to Nevada City. "George Ives has dug his grave," he thought. "Now he can try it on for size." Ives had become ever more reckless and arrogant over the past month or so, drinking heavily, even boasting publicly about the crimes he had committed. Plummer considered Ives a danger to the very existence of the Innocents. "Robbing and killing the young Dutchman was foolish," Plummer thought. "I will not provoke the law and order crowd by taking a hand on Ives' behalf."

"Ives finally did it," the sheriff thought. "He played with fire until he lit the fuse. We'll be lucky if this whole territory doesn't blow up in our faces."

That evening in Virginia City, Thad Mitchell walked in the back door of the Orphan Girl Cafe at the height of the supper hour. Customers filled the tables and counter in the dining area to capacity, and the arrest of George Ives seemed to be the only topic of conversation. Amid the smoke and steam of the kitchen, Wong Lee Fat moved quickly. His face was shiny with sweat as he filled plates and placed them on the sideboard above the stove. His daughter, Lo Toy, hurried the orders to the diners and refilled their coffee cups.

Cootie Blake stood behind the counter near the front door, greeting new arrivals and accepting payment from the departing patrons. Customers no longer offered their pokes for Cootie's big-thumbed pinch because the Orphan Girl now boasted an accurate gold scales that provided a more consistent standard for payment.

"Howdy, Thad," Cootie said. "How's Miss Epiphany doin'?"

"She's resting. Doctor Glick says she needs peace and quiet."

Cootie's face was somber. "Surely was a terrible thing, that horse runnin' away with her," he said.

"Yes," Thad said. He glanced around the crowded room. At the tables and counter, diners spoke earnestly, gesturing with their hands. "What's going on, Cootie?" Thad asked.

"Ain't you heard? Some boys from Nevada City arrested George Ives for killin' Nick Tbalt. They aim to put him on trial tomorrow."

Four miners stood up at a nearby table and pulled on their overcoats.

One, a burly man with bright red hair and a florid face, settled the bill with glittering dust from his poke. The four men went out into the night, still talking excitedly.

Thad hung his coat on a peg and rolled up his sleeves. Cootie was already clearing the recently vacated table, stacking dishes and flatware on a tray. Thad offered his help. "Who arrested Ives?" he asked. "Surely not Plummer's deputies?"

Cootie gave Thad a scornful look. "Not hardly," he said, "it was men from the gulch who've had a bellyful of robbery and murder. They say Jim Williams led the posse, and X. Beidler was with 'em, too."

Cootie hefted the heavy tray and started back to the kitchen. "Appreciate the help," he said. "You here for supper?"

Thad shook his head. "No. I just thought I'd lend a hand."

Cootie's sad-eyed face looked yellow under the lamplight. "We can always use an extra hand," he said. "I sure hope Miss Epiphany's gonna be all right."

"She will be," Thad assured him. "Please, God," he prayed, "let it be so."

The morning of December 19 dawned clear and mild. The snow had all but disappeared from the gulch. Even the rutted mud of Nevada City's main street had softened under the rays of a benign sun. Standing in the bright sunshine, a crowd estimated at between 1500 and 2000 men stood silent and watchful as the proceedings began.

The trial was held outdoors, and took up the better part of Saturday the 19th and all of the following two days. Four lawyers formed the defense team, while Colonel Wilbur F. Sanders was chief prosecutor. Judge Don L. Byam, of the Nevada mining district, was named presiding judge, assisted by Judge Wilson of the Junction district. The trial was held before all the miners of the gulch as a body, who reserved to themselves the final decision on guilt or innocence, as well as all other matters which might arise. A twenty-four man jury—

twelve men from each mining district—was also appointed to advise the miners.

George Ives was the first of the prisoners to be tried. He sat, secured by chains, in a chair beside his attorneys. The judges sat nearby in the bed of a wagon. Spectators crowded the street, some climbing to the roofs of nearby buildings for a better view. When the weather turned cold, heat was provided by bonfires.

Ives' friends had responded to the threat posed by his arrest. From the monent the trial began, they made their presence known with loud threats, insults, and interruptions, but Judge Byam and prosecutor Sanders refused to be intimidated. Sanders stood up to the threats of the roughs, countered the perjured testimony of defense witnesses, and relentlessly built a solid and convincing case against the defendant.

Long John Franke testified that Ives had boasted about Tbalt's murder. Ives had told them, "When I told the Dutchman I was going to kill him, he asked me for time to pray. I told him, 'All right, kneel down then.' When he did so, I shot him through the head just as he started his prayer."

Throughout the trial, George Ives maintained a confident, calm demeanor as prosecutor Sanders built the people's case against him. The evidence presented was not limited to the murder of Nicholas Tbalt, but also included testimony by witnesses of other murders and thefts commited in the region.

Feelings ran high, both among the hard-working miners and Ives's friends. The roughs threatened Sanders, Judge Byam, and those who dared testify against Ives. The miners' newly appointed sheriffs did their best to maintain order during the trial; one hundred armed men under the command of Jim Williams formed a protective circle around members of the court, the witnesses, and the accused, George Ives.

Late on Monday afternoon, December 21, the presentation of evidence ended. The attorneys for both sides then delivered their closing arguments. Ives sat in a chair near the bonfire that warmed and lit the outdoor court. He sat poised and assured as the jury left to deliberate.

At about six o'clock in the evening, the jury returned from an adjacent cabin and announced a verdict of guilty.

Anticipating a demonstration by the roughs in the crowd and a possible attempt to intimidate the jury and the court, Wilbur Sanders took a bold step. He stood in the wagon box that served as the court's bench and moved that whereas the jury had found George Ives guilty of murder, that he be "forthwith hanged by the neck until he is dead."

The majority of the miners who crowded the street approved the motion, but there were angry shouts of disagreement from Ives's friends in the crowd. The confident countenance that Ives had maintained throughout the trial vanished. He seemed suddenly to realize the seriousness of the situation. Plummer had not come, nor had there been any deliverance on the basis of legal technicality, intimidation, or force. Ives jumped to his feet and climbed into the wagon with Wilbur Sanders. Taking the chief prosecutor by the hand, he pleaded for a delay. "For god's sake, Sanders," he said, "give me time to settle my affairs! I want to write my mother and sister back in the States! Give me just until morning, Colonel—I give you my word of honor I won't try to escape!"

Across the street, X. Beidler stood guard on top of the sod roof of a low cabin. Beidler, who was a short, stocky man, held a shotgun that was nearly as tall as he was. He stood on the roof and called out, "Sanders, ask him how long a time he gave the Dutchman."

Rough laughter rippled through the crowd. Sanders firmly denied Ives's request, telling him he might have time to write a short note if he hurried. Ives' request had largely been a stalling tactic; he declined the opportunity to write his relatives.

Across the street stood an unfinished log building, and the miners chose the site as Ives's place of execution. The roofless building stood open to the night sky, only the walls in place. The top log of the structure was thrown down inside the walls and its butt secured against the rear of the building.

The other end of the secured log slanted outward at a 45-degree angle above the street. A length of rope was brought from a nearby store. An agile young miner shinnied up the pole and tied it to the unsecured end of the log.

George Ives stood on top a dry goods box and X. Beidler tightened the noose about his neck.

Jim Williams and his hundred-man cordon surrounded the prisoner. Judge Byam asked the condemned man if he had anything to say. "I am innocent of this crime," Ives declared. "Alec Carter killed the Dutchman."

The voices of his friends and sympathizers grew louder, more strident. A number of the roughs, made bold by whiskey and angered by the defiance of the miners' court, made a threatening move toward the men surrounding Ives. The guards leveled their weapons and, in a rattle of sound, cocked them. The would-be rescuers quickly fell back. Sanders gave the order "Men, do your duty." Guards kicked the box away. The sentence had been carried out. George Ives' body now swung at rope's end.

"He is dead," said Judge Byam. "His neck is broken."

After Byam's announcement, silence ruled. The angry voices and the righteous voices all fell silent. Every eye was fixed on the still form that twisted slowly above the street in the chill night air. High overhead, the moon cast its pale light upon the scene. A winter moon, aloof and cold—it would, in the days ahead, light the paths of both fugitives and manhunters. A moon of pursuit, capture, and retribution—it would be a vigilante moon.

On the night of George Ives's execution Epiphany slept fitfully in her bed at Lily Rae's. Nameless terrors troubled her rest, and menace seemed to be a part of the air she breathed. She tossed restlessly in her sleep, cried out, and suddenly awoke.

At first, she had no idea where she was. The small room seemed as strange and forbidding as a prison cell. Her nightdress was wet with perspiration. Her breathing was rapid and irregular. Epiphany touched the bandage at her temple. Then, glancing about the room, her memory returned.

She remembered sitting beside George Ives in the buggy, the snow falling heavily as they set out on the Bannack road. She recalled her confusion, her doubt, as she told him of her visit from Josie Mulhare. She had told Ives what Josie had said, the claim that she and Ives were long-time lovers. Please, Josie had asked, would Epiphany not take him from her?

Epiphany remembered that she had believed Ives's denial because she so desperately wanted to. Gratefully, she had given herself to his embrace. Ives had held her, kissed her, and then—

The scene in the cabin returned to Epiphany in a rush of images and sensations. Epiphany saw the shadows cast by the flickering firelight. She felt Ives's arms, his hands, his mouth—no longer loving, no longer content to accept the tenderness she offered, but demanding and rapacious. She heard again Ives's labored breathing and felt her dress tear. She remembered fighting against his strength, resisting, trying to break free.

She recalled the falling and the struggle on the cabin floor. She felt her panic and her fingers grasping the heavy iron skillet. She had struck George Ives again and again; she had struck the hard, two-handed blow that caused him to fall away. She recalled her desperate dash outside to the waiting buggy. She re-lived her reckless ride through the storm to the road. She remembered the curve coming up fast—too fast—and the crash, the pain, and the darkness.

Epiphany turned onto her side and drew her knees up toward her chest. What a fool she had been! She had let her attraction to Ives blind her; and she had thrown herself at the man! How could she have been so stupid?

The door to the room opened slowly. Epiphany heard a concerned voice. "Piff? Are you all right?"

Blinded by her tears, she turned toward the sound. "Oh, Lily Rae," she sobbed, "I'm too foolish to live!"

Lily Rae sat down at the edge of the bed and took Epiphany in her arms.

"So am I," she said softly, "but I try not to think about it."

For the next hour and forty minutes, Lily Rae's other boarders waited impatiently for their breakfast. Finally, they gave up and went out to find a restaurant. Epiphany and Lily Rae sat together as the room grew lighter, Epiphany propped up on her pillows and Lily Rae seated beside her. Epiphany told Lily Rae about her meeting with George Ives at the restaurant and of their subsequent encounters. She spoke of her meeting with Josie Mulhare and described the events that occurred the night of the accident. "Oh, Lily Rae," she wailed, "what is the matter with me?"

Lily Rae smiled, stroking Epiphany's hair. "Nothing time won't cure," she said. "It's just that you're young, and there are still one or two things you don't know. Everything that glitters isn't gold, Piff. Sometimes even the worst of men can seem like the answer to a maiden's prayer.

"You've been working your guardian angel overtime, honey; but that's all right, that's what he's for. He fetched you back from the Valley of the Shadow, and you're going to be all right now."

Lily Rae was silent for a moment as she framed her next words. "You are mighty fortunate to have escaped from the dashing Mr. Ives," she said. "He was even worse than you know." Holding Epiphany's hands in her own, she then recounted, simply and directly, all that she knew about the trial and execution of George Ives.

Epiphany leaned back on the pillows and closed her eyes. For a time, she wept silently as Lily Rae held her hands. Then she dried her eyes and looked away, toward the window. "I'm not crying for him," she said. "I'm grieving the loss of what I thought he might be."

Lily Rae had just left Epiphany's room when she heard the doorbell's brisk ring. Hastening to answer it, she found Dr. Glick waiting, his medical bag in his hand. "Good day, Mrs. Bliss," he said, "how is our patient today?"

"Good morning, doctor," Lily Rae said. "Come in, please—I think you'll find her much improved."

Dr. Glick walked over to the parlor stove and briskly rubbed his hands together before its warmth. "I meant to be here earlier," he said, "but I was intercepted en route by the owner of a hurdy house on Wallace. One of his dancers committed suicide last night by consuming a bottle of laudanum. Nothing I could do—the woman was quite dead when I arrived at her cabin.

"Life and death, Mrs. Bliss—who can understand their mysteries? Last night George Ives, desperately desiring to live, was hanged for his crimes. Later that same night, a prostitute named Josie Mulhare, desperately desiring to die, took her own life. As I asked, who can understand such things?"

TWENTY-TWO
The Wrath of Honest Men

O
N TUESDAY, December 22, the day after Ives's execution, morning dawned sunny and calm under scattered clouds. Alder Creek rippled over its rocky bed, steam rising from its surface. A light snow had fallen during the night, but only traces remained in shaded places. Miners were at their claims, merchants in their stores, and a strange silence had settled along the gulch.

In Nevada City, the street that had witnessed such high drama during the past three days was empty. The log used to hang George Ives still extended from the unfinished cabin out over the street. The dry goods box beneath the log sat frozen in the mud. The wagon that had served as judge's bench stood deserted now. All that remained of the bonfire was charred wood and cold ashes. The muddy street, trampled the previous day by thousands of booted feet, held only the litter left behind by the crowd—scattered bits of paper, cigar butts, and an empty whiskey bottle.

The cabin that had served as a jail was empty as well. In the judgment of the court, there had been insufficient evidence to hold the other prisoners, and Long John, Hilderman, and the outlaw called "Tex" had been released.

George Ives's corpse had hung above the street for an hour. It was then cut down and carried into a wheelbarrow shop where it was laid out on a workbench. The cadaver remained there overnight. That morning on December 22, Ives's friends claimed the body and buried it on a hill overlooking Nevada City, not far from the grave of Nicholas Tbalt.

Will Hunter had been among the crowd throughout most of the three-day trial. He had observed the flow of events, from the testimony of the witnesses to Ives's execution. He had watched the roughs attempt the tactics of intimidation that had served them so well in the past. He had admired the courage of prosecutor Sanders, assistant prosecutor Baggs, and judges Byam and Wilson as they stood firm in the face of threats and abuse. There had, Hunter thought, been a new resolve among the men of the gulch and a determination that justice would prevail this time.

What had caused the change? Had the excesses of the roughs finally become too great? Had the murder of young Tbalt shamed the men who by their failure to act had allowed the desperados to flourish?

Throughout the past summer, miners had heard reports of robbery and murder. They had sympathized with the victims and gone back to work. Such things happen in a new camp, they had told themselves. It was a damn shame, but at least it hadn't happened to any of them—not yet, anyway.

Then, on a cold December day they learned of one more robbery, one more killing. The miners had liked Nick Tbalt. His murder had kindled a sense of outrage too strong to deny. They had arrested his killer, and they had brought him to trial. When they had found him guilty, they had put him to death. Decent men had challenged the spoilers. They had at last embarked on a course of action. Hunter wondered if they would have the courage to follow that course to its end.

Bravo Santee witnessed George Ives's execution by chance. He awoke early Sunday morning, December 20, at the wakiup above Bunton's ranch with a hankering for good whiskey, bad women, and smoky saloons.

Henry Plummer had ordered Santee to stay away from Alder Gulch in general and from Will Hunter in particular, but Bravo was tired of wearing Plummer's hobbles. "I am a rake and a rounder," he declared to his comrades at Bunton's, "and a spirit of defiance is upon me. Henry Plummer can kiss my rebel ass."

Santee had mounted his blue roan and set out for the settlements on Alder Creek.

Resentment ruled Santee's mind as he rode. He was not like the other members of Plummer's band. He had not come to these mountains for gold but for vengeance. He had come to avenge the death of Rufus, his brother.

He had come to kill Will Hunter.

Wherever Santee had been, there had been a leader, a man in charge. In Missouri, that man had been William Clarke Quantrill. Santee had given Quantrill his loyalty. He had obeyed his orders. Here, in these mountains, the man in charge was Sheriff Henry Plummer. As Santee had done with Quantrill, he had done with Plummer. He had offered his allegiance. Plummer had told Santee he would permit him to kill Hunter, but only at an opportune time. Plummer would let him know when that time had come. Until then, Plummer expected Santee to be patient. Santee's patience, however, was wearing thin.

When he drew rein in Virginia City, Santee was inundated by the news. In the saloons and on the streets, there was but one topic of conversation. George Ives had been arrested by a citizens' posse for the murder of young Nick Tbalt. He was on trial by a miners' court in nearby Nevada City. Thousands of men had come from the gulches to see justice done. Ives's friends were trying to intimidate the court. The law and order crowd were standing firm. The sheriff had been informed and was expected at any time. He had not come yet. Things looked dark for George Ives.

Santee arrived in Nevada City just as the trial was concluding. His short stature made it impossible for him to see above the heads of the crowd, so he climbed to the roof of a building across the street. From there, he heard the jury's verdict announced—Ives had been found guilty. He heard Wilbur Sanders the prosecutor move that Ives be executed by hanging forthwith. He heard the motion approved with a roar from the crowd. Santee watched Ives's friends surge forward in an attempt to intervene. He saw them turned back by the armed sheriffs. He heard Ives appeal for mercy and he heard him refused. Fifty-eight minutes after the verdict was announced, George Ives was executed by hanging.

Santee had cancelled his planned debauch and had turned his horse back onto the Bannack road with more questions on his mind than answers.

Where was Plummer? After all the talk of loyalty by members of the "Innocents," why had its leader failed to rescue George Ives? Had the sheriff turned yellow? No, Santee decided, for all his faults Henry Plummer was no coward. Why, then, had he failed to appear at the trial?

The answer came suddenly to Santee. At once, he knew the reason as surely as if he could read Plummer's thoughts. Henry Plummer had seen the writing on the wall. The reign of the "Innocents" and of Plummer as their chief had ended with the execution of George Ives.

The law and order crowd had prevailed. They had stood against the "Innocents" and they had won the day. They would move swiftly now. They would follow up their victory.

As he approached Bunton's ranch, Santee left the road, spurring his horse up a steep, snow-covered hill and drawing rein at its crest. He sat his saddle easily as he allowed the roan a breather. "Vigilantes will come next," Santee thought. "Fat bankers, miners, and merchants in masks with killing on their mind. They'll raise hell for awhile and then quit. Mostly, they'll go after the leaders of Plummer's outfit. They won't bother much with the rest of us, except to try to bluff us out of the territory."

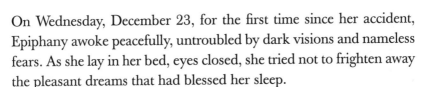

On the ridge, wind had blown the snow clear, revealing patches of cured bunchgrass. Santee's gray stretched out its neck and began to graze.

Santee jerked its head up. "If you can eat, you can travel," Santee said. He tightened the reins and spurred the horse on through the trees toward the wakiup above Bunton's.

"There will be time enough for me to do what I came to do," Santee thought, "and no man can tell me I can't, by god! Will Hunter is a dead man."

On Wednesday, December 23, for the first time since her accident, Epiphany awoke peacefully, untroubled by dark visions and nameless fears. As she lay in her bed, eyes closed, she tried not to frighten away the pleasant dreams that had blessed her sleep.

With wakefulness came the sense that she was not alone. She knew that another person was with her in the room. Slowly, Epiphany opened her eyes. She lay on her side, facing the bedside table and the window. The shade was pulled down and the room was dim. The bright light at the edge of the sill told her the time of day was mid-morning. She turned, looking toward the door, and saw him.

He stood just inside the doorway, his hat in his hands, watching her. Epiphany smiled when she saw him. She would have recognized his tall, lanky form among a hundred men. "Hello, Will," she said.

Will Hunter smiled. "Hello, Piff. I didn't mean to disturb you."

"It's high time I woke up. All I seem to do these days is sleep."

"That's good. Shakespeare called sleep 'nature's soft nurse.'"

"Please. Come, sit by me."

Hunter crossed the room and eased himself into the chair beside her bed. "How are you feeling?" he asked.

"Much better," Epiphany said, smiling, "Lily Rae won't have it any other way."

She studied his sun-bronzed face. He needed a haircut, she decided, and his beard showed more gray than she remembered. Otherwise, he looked much as he had on the day he had rescued her from the Bannocks. His eyes met hers. He looked away.

"You heard about George Ives?" he asked.

Epiphany lowered her eyes. "Yes. Lily Rae told me."

"I was about to go after him when the posse beat me to it," he said. "I let you down, Piff."

Epiphany looked up, surprised. Hunter's head was bowed, his mouth a bitter line. "Why, Will Hunter!" she exclaimed. "How can you say that? What could you have done?"

"I promised myself I'd look after you, and I failed. I knew the kind of man Ives was. I could have warned you, but I didn't know you were seeing him."

Epiphany frowned. "You take too much on yourself, Will. I'm a grown woman. I'm responsible for my own choices, even the bad ones."

Hunter looked down at his hands. It was as if he had not heard her. "I have a habit of letting women down," he said. "It cost the last one her life."

Epiphany heard the pain behind his words. Her hand found Hunter's and held it. "Tell me about her, Will," she said simply.

Hunter shook his head. "Some day, maybe—it's not a thing to bother you with now," he said.

"I believe you need to tell someone," Epiphany said. "Let me be that someone."

Hunter looked into Epiphany's earnest brown eyes and let himself remember. Later, he would wonder what it was that led him to tell his story that afternoon. Since the terrible day at his Missouri farm he had told no one. He had borne his pain and his guilt alone, as he believed a man should. Surely, this idealistic young woman was the very last person he should tell!

Something about Epiphany, the kindness in her voice the compassion in her touch, reminded him so very much of his wife Rachel. Haltingly, slowly at first, he began to speak. The years fell away, and the memories returned, sharp-etched and deep-rooted. There, in Epiphany's room, Will Hunter told his story.

He spoke of Missouri, of summer nights and fireflies, and of the scent of blooming dogwood outside the cabin door. He spoke of Rachel and the way they had met. He described their wedding and the happiness they had found in each other. He told of their joy when they learned Rachel was with child, and of the hopes and dreams they had shared.

He spoke of his farm which was Eden because Rachel was there, and he spoke of the Serpent that was hatred and blood and border war. Hunter's voice deepened as he spoke of Harrisonville and of Rachel's fears, which prompted her to beg him not to go but to remain at home with her.

He had gone anyway, he said, and Epiphany heard the self-reproach in his tone as he described his ride to the tavern where he had met his friends Lem and Buck. The three friends had sung brave songs and drunk corn whiskey, sharing the fear that hides beneath the bravado of young men going to war.

Hunter paused. When he spoke again there was self-hatred and emptiness in his voice. He told of seeing flames from a distance, of his desperate ride to his farm, and of the horror and chaos he had found there. "A part of me died with her that night," he told Epiphany, "and the part that went on living can never forget how I failed her."

"You didn't fail, Will," Epiphany said. "Even if you'd stayed with her, the results would have been the same, except the raiders would have killed you, too."

"At least she wouldn't have died alone."

Hunter stood. "I don't know why I told you all that," he said. "Maybe you're right—maybe I did need to tell someone. I'm glad it was you, Piff."

She smiled. "So am I."

At the door, Hunter put on his hat and smiled shyly. "Be well, youngster," he said. Then he was gone.

Epiphany listened to the soft ring of his spurs as he strode away down the corridor. She lay back against her pillows and closed her eyes. "It's not for me to grant you absolution, Will Hunter," she thought, "but I wish I could."

Hunter had descended the front stairs of Lily Rae's boarding house and was untying the reins of his black gelding from the hitching post when he saw John Oakes riding toward him. Hunter swung up into the saddle and waited for the older man to arrive. "You're a hard man to hide from," he said as Oakes rode up. "Wherever I go, you manage to track me down."

Oakes drew rein and studied Hunter with a one-eyed squint. "Nothing to it," he said, "I just look for that flashy thoroughbred. When I find him, I know you'll not be far away."

Oakes nodded toward the boarding house. "How's the patient?" he asked.

"On the mend," Hunter said. "The young heal quickly."

Oakes got directly to the point. "Some men are meeting down at the Fox house this morning," he said. "Sanders asked for you by name."

"I'm not much for meetings."

"That's what I told him you'd say. Sanders said I was to remind you of the last meeting you attended, the one he held at his office. You told him then that when the time for action came, he could count on you."

"Damn lawyers," Hunter said ruefully, "they remember everything."

The small house was crowded when Will Hunter and John Oakes walked in. Men sat talking, their conversations subdued. Paris Pfouts, Virginia City merchant, and attorney Wilbur Sanders sat behind a long table near the back wall. Near them, at the end of the table, was a strongly built man with unruly black hair and deepset blue eyes. He wore a full moustache and chin whiskers. He seemed restless and faintly ill at ease.

Hunter recognized a kindred soul. "That man doesn't like meetings, either," he thought. Hunter remembered him from the trial. He was Jim Williams, the Nevada City stable owner and stockman who had provided horses for, and later assumed leadership of, the posse that brought Ives in. He had also helped keep order at gunpoint during the trial and execution of Ives.

Nat Langford was there, and John Lott from Nevada City. Hunter recognized Elkanah "Elk" Morse, who, with Jim Williams, had led the posse on the trip to arrest Ives. Hunter knew many of the men in the room by sight if not by name. Others were strangers to him. In all, he counted twenty men, including John Oakes and himself.

Sanders stood, and the room grew quiet. The lawyer looked slowly about the room, his gaze lingering briefly on each man. "Good afternoon, gentlemen," he said. "Thank you for coming."

"Last night," Sanders began, "four men in Bannack, and five here in Virginia, met to form the nucleus of a Vigilance Committee. We pledged our sacred honor to that purpose so that in the struggle between order and crime, order might prevail. We are determined that it shall."

Sanders paused. Only the ticking of the Regulator clock on the wall behind him disturbed the silence. His voice firm, Sanders continued. "At that meeting, Paris Pfouts was named President of the Committee; Captain James Williams, Executive Officer; and myself, Special Prosecutor. Also present were John X. Beidler and William Clark."

"We have long discussed the need to act," Sanders said, his gaze fixed meaningfully on Hunter, "and we are determined to do so. Too long has an organized band of thieves and brigands ruled the people of this territory. Too long has justice been a prisoner of corrupt officials and violent men. At least fifteen hundred men have just expended four days in order to try, convict, and execute George Ives. Many good men have questioned whether each criminal will require that much attention. They have expressed the concern that there will be little time left to pursue their ordinary vocations if the pursuit of justice requires so much time.

"In addition, friends of the miscreants have threatened the lives of those who took part in the trial, and those good men deserve protection. This meeting, and the meetings to follow, will address those concerns.

"The settlements of Summit, Highland, Virginia, Adobetown, Junction, Nevada, and Bannack are presently forming Vigilante companies. You gentlemen have been invited here this evening to join our cause because you are honorable, courageous, and trustworthy. I have said enough. If you are in agreement with our purpose, I ask you now to stand and I will administer the oath."

Weeks before, when Hunter had attended the meeting at Sanders' office, he had expressed the belief that action, not talk, was required to end the rule of the lawless. "When that time comes," he had told Sanders, "you can count on me." Now the time had come. With the others, Hunter was on his feet. He raised his hand with the other men, and with them he recited the oath:

"We, the undersigned, uniting ourselves together for the laudable purpose of arresting thieves and murderers and recovering stolen property, do pledge ourselves on our sacred honor, each to all others, and solemnly swear that we will reveal no secrets, violate no laws of right, and never desert each other, or our standard of justice, so help us God."

Hunter had donned his overcoat and was preparing to leave when Nat Langford approached. "Glad you're with us, Will," he said. He offered his hand, and Hunter took it. "By the way," Langford said, "do you travel?"

Hunter studied Langford's face, trying to discern the meaning behind the question. "Why, I expect I do sometimes, Nat," he said lightly. "Why do you ask?"

Langford chuckled. "I perceive that you are not a member of the Masonic Lodge. Neither is Captain Williams, but most of the men in this room are brothers, bound together in the spirit of Freemasonry, committed to a common cause. You can rely on the men in this room."

"That's good to know," said Hunter, "now that I've bet my life on it."

A frigid wind from the north swept snow across the frozen ruts of Idaho Street as Will Hunter drew rein in front of the Orphan Girl. Two other horses huddled at the hitchrail, heads down and eyes closed.

Hunter watched the wind ripple the animals' winter hair. He tied his thoroughbred beside them, opened the cafe's front door, and stepped inside.

Out of the wind, he paused as the room's warmth washed over him. Two miners sat together at the counter, and a pallid gambler breakfasted on soft-boiled eggs and oatmeal at a table near the back. Other than that the cafe was devoid of customers. "The early crowd has come and gone," Hunter thought, "and it's too soon for the lunch trade." Hanging his greatcoat on a peg, Hunter sat down at an empty table just as Thad Mitchell came out of the back room.

"It never fails," Thad said, smiling broadly, "no sooner do we try to upgrade our clientele than a rangy old wolf like you comes in! How are you, Will?"

Hunter returned the smile. "Not bad, partner," he said. "I just came by because my belly's been misbehaving, and I thought I'd punish it. Do you have anything decent to eat, or just the usual?"

"Tell you what," Thad said, enjoying the banter, "I'll bring you a cup of our fine coffee. It that doesn't kill you, we can try something else."

A moment later, Thad brought two steaming mugs to the table and sat down across from Hunter. "It's good to see you, Will," he said. "What have you been up to?"

Hunter lowered his eyes. "Took in Ives' trial with John Oakes," he said, "and went to a meeting this morning."

Thad looked up sharply. Hunter sipped his coffee, his face without expression. "We all know how you love going to meetings," Thad said slowly. "What kind of meeting?"

Hunter looked into Thad's eyes and smiled thinly. When he spoke, his voice was low, barely audible. "Something to do with hunting and tracking, seeking and finding, and about being—vigilant."

For a moment, Thad said nothing. Then he nodded, comprehending.

"Yes," he said softly, "I heard that was in the wind."

"I'm leaving town this afternoon," Hunter said. "Not sure when I'll be back. Our freighting business—"

"Can wait. The weather has slowed things down anyway."

"Good of you to take a hand here at the cafe for Piff," Hunter said. "I saw her this morning. She's doing well."

"Yes," Thad said.

Amazing, the way he comes alive when he hears her name, Hunter thought, even the sound of his voice changes. "Well," Hunter said, looking at his empty cup, "it appears I survived your coffee. Better bring me a stack of hotcakes and some ham, if you have some—I'm in a mood to push my luck."

Twenty minutes later, Hunter paid for his breakfast and shook his partner's hand. Thad followed him outside and watched as he untracked the thoroughbred and swung into the saddle. "Watch your back, partner," Thad said.

Hunter smiled. "Watch your *heart*," he replied.

Once formed, the vigilantes wasted no time. Later that afternoon, under the command of Captain Jim Williams, twenty-four men set out to capture an outlaw named Alec Carter. Carter was a known associate of the late George Ives and a suspected accomplice in the murder of Nick Tbalt. Most of the volunteers were armed with two revolvers and a rifle or shotgun. Each volunteer rode a horse provided by Captain Williams. Each man also carried a blanket roll. A coiled rope hung from the pommel of each saddle. The men carried provisions, but no whiskey or brandy.

Because most of the riders had been called directly from their work, many had neglected to dress for the freezing temperatures and deep snow they would encounter. To prevent warning the roughs of their approach, they built no warming fires when they stopped at night. They made their beds atop the snow or, if they were trail-wise, beneath the snow. They suffered from weariness and cold, but they persisted. Not a single man turned back.

The vigilantes visited all the old haunts of the road agents, but found no one. Warned by their friends, the "Innocents" had taken flight.

On Christmas Day, the riders found and arrested Erastus "Red" Yeager, a known associate of Alec Carter. At Dempsey's ranch, they found George Ives' ranch manager George Brown and took him into custody. That night, calmly accepting his fate and admitting his guilt, "Red" Yeager astonished his captors by naming Sheriff Henry Plummer as leader and organizer of the road agents. He provided his captors with the organizational plan of the gang. He told of the password, "I am innocent." He described and demonstrated the sailor's knot the gang members wore in their kerchiefs. He told of the secret marks used to identify gold shipments on the road to Bannack. He also gave details of specific crimes committed and provided a list of the gang's chief members.

Told of Yeager's confession, George Brown confirmed Plummer's leadership and added additional names. When the questioning of Yeager and Brown had ended, the vigilantes' list included the names of twenty-three "Innocents."

The vigilantes held a meeting, and took a vote. They sentenced Yeager and Brown to death for capital crimes. A half-hour before midnight, the vigilantes hanged the two outlaws from a big cottonwood tree just outside the ranch house. Papers identifying each man and his office in the gang were pinned to their clothing. The papers read: "Brown! Corresponding Secretary" and "Red! Road Agent and Messenger."

Back in Virginia City, Captain Williams and John Lott gave their report to a full meeting of the captains and lieutenants of the vigilante companies. At the meeting, the movement's leaders offered congratulations to Williams and his men and gave formal approval to the organization's selection of officers. Paris Pfouts was confirmed as President, Wilbur Sanders as Prosecutor, James Williams as Executive Officer, and John Lott as Secretary and Treasurer.

Williams's report was a sobering one. The detailed revelations given by "Red" Yeager and George Brown clearly meant that the task of the vigilantes would be more daunting than anyone had thought. The men had originally believed the capture and execution of Alec Carter would be a sufficient warning to the roughs—get out or be hanged. Now, everything had changed. There were an additional twenty-three criminals to track down.

The vigilantes' work had only begun.

On Saturday, January 9, Bannack City lay frigid and still, locked in the grip of a cold snap. Under a brilliant blue sky, hoarfrost clung to the giant sagebrush along the town's rutted streets. Fresh snow sparkled in the sunlight and drew a white blanket over the camp. At Cy Skinner's Elkhorn Saloon, Henry Plummer leaned his elbows on the bar and thoughtfully studied the whiskey in his glass.

Behind the bar, Skinner filled his own glass and raised it. "The game is played out, Henry," Skinner said. "We've had us one hell of a run, but it's over. It's time to cash in our checks and move on."

"Losing your nerve, Cy?" Plummer drawled.

"You know better than that," Skinner said. "I'm no coward, but I ain't a damn fool, neither. When them stranglin' sons o' bitches hung George Ives, I seen the writin' on the wall."

Skinner sipped the whiskey, his eyes on Plummer. "Now they're callin' themselves vigilantes, and they've hung Red Yeager and George Brown. I tell you, Henry, it's time to dust for healthier climes."

Plummer shrugged. "There are no vigilantes in Bannack. There's still time."

Skinner shook his head. "You and me have come a long way since we shared that cell at Quentin. We've made us a pile of money, and we've stayed alive. No reason we can't do it again someplace else."

Plummer looked thoughtful. "When are you leaving?"

"This afternoon. Takin' my best whore Nellie and one packhorse."

"Any idea where you'll go?"

"Away from here is all you need to know. You ought to leave, too."

"Yes. maybe."

The two men shook hands. Skinner buttoned his heavy overcoat and turned down the ear flaps on his winter cap. He walked across the room, turned, and looked around the nearly empty saloon. "We sure had us some wild old times in here, didn't we?"

Plummer didn't reply. He tossed back the whiskey and carefully placed the glass back on the bar.

Cold air rushed inside as Skinner opened the door for the last time. For a moment he stood in the open door, silhouetted against the brightness outside. Then he said, "Don't wait too long, Henry," and was gone.

TWENTY-THREE
The Deer Lodge Scout

O N SUNDAY MORNING, January 10, 1864, cold sunlight filtered
through sullen clouds and revealed a camp besieged by winter.
Snow stood two feet deep on the level and drifted to five and better on
the windward side of the buildings. Grasshopper Creek rippled beneath thick ice in a world without color, the snow along its banks
disturbed only by the tracks of deer and rabbit.

The delegation from Virginia City had arrived about midnight and
sought out those key men known to be in sympathy with the movement. John Lott presented a letter from the executive committee
requesting support and encouraging trustworthy men to join the
organization. The letter also ordered the execution of Sheriff Henry
Plummer and his two deputies, Buck Stinson and Ned Ray.

Men left their beds to meet with the delegates, and by daybreak a
branch organization had been formed. They spent the rest of the day
in recruiting and equipping the new members. At dusk, the report
came that three saddlehorses, owned respectively by Plummer, Stinson,
and Ray, had been brought into town. It seemed apparent that Plummer
and his deputies were preparing to leave the country. The Vigilance
Committee put plans in motion to arrest them promptly.

The vigilantes divided themselves into three companies, each
responsible for the capture of one of the wanted men. Vigilantes

arrested Buck Stinson at a friend's house where he was spending the night. John Lott and his company found Henry Plummer at the house he shared with his sister-in-law, Martha Vail. The sheriff was standing at a basin inside the door, washing his face and hands.

"Look, boys," one of the men quipped, "the sheriff is washin' both his faces."

"You'll have to come with us, Henry," said John Lott.

Plummer's expression was one of total unconcern. "Be right with you, boys," he said, drying his hands on the towel. "What seems to be the problem?"

"Just come along, if you please."

Plummer dropped the towel, smoothing his shirtsleeves as he walked toward a nearby chair where his coat lay. "I'll be with you as soon as I can put my coat on," he said.

One of the vigilantes moved quickly to the chair. "I'll hand it to you," he said. Lifting the coat, he saw that a loaded revolver lay beneath it.

Plummer's face turned pale. Outwardly, he maintained his calm, confident manner. Inwardly, he cursed his overconfidence. He had waited too long.

The third company of vigilantes found Ned Ray passed out on a gaming table at a Yankee Flat Saloon and took him into custody. Then, as twilight faded into evening, the vigilantes marched their prisoners up the road to the place of execution. A rough-hewn gallows measuring about ten feet high by twelve feet wide loomed atop a low hill. Plummer had erected the gallows the previous summer to hang a horse thief. Now, with cruel irony, it was to be the place of his own execution.

Stinson and Ray were defiant, swearing and struggling against their bonds. Henry Plummer begged and bargained, pleading for mercy and using every argument he could think of in the hope of swaying his captors. He asked for a jury trial. He begged for time to settle his business affairs. He promised to leave the country forever. He asked to see his sister-in-law, and begged the vigilantes to let him live for the sake of his absent wife. Finally, he fell on his knees in the snow and confessed to a variety of crimes, sobbing to the Almighty that he was "too wicked to die."

The first rope sailed up and over the crossbeam. From beneath the gallows came the order to bring up Ned Ray. Still cursing, Ray struggled as one of the men tightened the noose about his neck. Then, suddenly, the vigilantes siezed the rope and jerked the deputy off his feet.

Buck Stinson was brought forward and made to stand beneath the crossbar. His curses ceased. Facing death, he fell silent. His last words were the perverse password of the gang. As he uttered "I am innocent," the vigilantes pulled him abruptly into space. Stinson died quickly, twisting at rope's end in the cold, night air.

Plummer was last. When his executioners approached, he made one final request. "For God's sake, at least give a man time to pray!"

The vigilante leader spoke from beneath the gallows. "Certainly," he said, "but say your prayers up here."

In the end, Henry Plummer accepted his fate. There was no further talk of prayer. He calmly approached the gallows and stood tall as the vigilante leader adjusted the noose. "Now, men," he said, "as a last favor, give me a good drop."

Several of the strongest men among the company complied. Raising the sheriff's body as high as they could reach, they suddenly let it fall. Plummer died almost instantly, without a struggle. Only the creaking of the rope broke the stillness. Somewhere, high in the hills above Bannack, a coyote sang a lament.

The following day, Monday, January 11, the vigilantes executed two more road agents and murderers in Bannack—"Dutch John" Wagner and Joe "The Greaser" Pizanthia. The rule of Bannack by the corrupt and the lawless was over.

Three days later, on January 14, in Virginia City, vigilantes surrounded the town, then rounded up road agents Boone Helm, Jack Gallagher, Frank Parish, Haze Lyons, and Clubfoot George Lane. The five bandits were hanged from the main beam of an unfinished building at the corner of Wallace and Van Buren streets. A sixth man, desperado Bill Hunter, managed to escape by crawling away through a drainage ditch and eluding the men that guarded the town.

Five days after vigilantes hanged Henry Plummer and his deputies at Bannack, Epiphany sat by the sunshine stove in the parlor when Thad came into Lily Rae's Virginia City boarding house. Outside the window, Epiphany could see snowflakes drifting straight down in the still afternoon air as if on invisible wires. A blanket of silence muffled the camp. When Epiphany heard the solid thump of Thad's feet as he stamped snow off his boots in the foyer, she turned in her wing chair to greet him.

She wore her blue street dress and carpet slippers. She had arranged her hair, concealing the scar on her forehead that marked her injury. She had only that morning recovered sufficiently to leave her bed, and she was glad to be up and about once again. Thad came into the parlor, smiling as he approached her chair.

"Good afternoon, Miss," he said. "It's good to see you looking so well."

Epiphany returned his smile. "Thank you, Thad," she said. "It's even better to be feeling well." She patted the arm of the chair beside hers. "Sit down, please," she said, "and tell me all the news."

"The Orphan Girl is thriving," Thad said, "although the business misses your guiding hand. I brought the account books. Thought you might like to look them over."

"Later," she said. "I expect to be back at work in another week. I can't thank you enough for lending a hand."

Thad lowered his eyes, color flushing his cheeks. "No thanks needed," he said. "It was a thing I could do. A way I could help."

"His blush makes him look like a schoolboy," Epiphany thought, "that and his tousled blonde hair. I never really noticed before but he really is quite handsome."

Her expression turned serious. "Lily Rae told me about the hangings," she said, "Plummer, Stinson, and Ray at Bannack, and five more yesterday here in Virginia City. Any word from Will?"

"No," Thad said, "not for more than a week now. I expect he'll be riding with the vigilantes until the job's done."

"It's a brutal business, but they're dealing with brutal men."

"Yes. The vigilantes feel they have to do the job, and do it right. If they stop too soon, the roughs will strike back—try to take revenge."

"Lily Rae says criminals are leaving the territory like rats from a sinking ship," Epiphany said. "I do hope Alder Gulch isn't sinking."

Thad laughed. "It isn't," he said, "just getting rid of the rats."

They fell silent then, neither of them feeling the need to speak. Orange flame flickered behind the tempered glass windows of the parlor stove. Thad sat, listening to the burning wood. He heard the measured ticking of the cabinet clock down the hall. Outside, the snowfall grew heavier. Thad felt a deep sense of well-being and a quiet happiness. He breathed in the warm air and the floral scent of Epiphany's perfume. He closed his eyes, savoring the moment.

As she sat quietly, Epiphany watched Thad, seeing him anew. Usually, he seemed nervous, restless in her presence. Now he sat, relaxed and motionless, his hands folded before him. Curious, she glanced at Thad's hands, seeking clues to the man who sat beside her.

His hands were nearly twice the size of her own, and wider by half. His fingers tapered slightly to square ends. His nails were clean and cut short. He had been a miner, she knew. She imagined his hands at work with pick and shovel, pan and rocker, separating the fine gold from the sand and gravel. She smiled, remembering the day he had delivered her stove to the cafe. She recalled hearing the crash and rushing outside to find Thad and the workmen he'd hired laughing uncontrollably, undamaged. Soot had peppered Thad from head to foot.

Covered in soot, he had met her glance that day, and doffed his hat, running blackened fingers through his tousled, yellow hair. His smile had been without self-consciousness, and he had laughed at himself. Epiphany had liked him for his laughter, and she smiled now as she remembered.

Her smile faded. Her expression grew serious as she recalled the confusion and pain that had followed her accident. Lying helplessly in her bed, she had been aware of someone in her darkened room who had soothed and comforted her. That someone had been Thad. His strong hands, now folded quietly in his lap, had nursed her. They had awakened her gently, they had spoon-fed her medicine. His hands had changed her bandages and held the basin for her as nausea racked her fevered body. His hands had smoothed her hair, wiped her face with a cool, wet cloth.

Now he sat, apparently content just to be in the parlor with her. During the difficult days of her recovery, his voice had been kind, reassuring. "You're safe now, Miss," he had said. "Everything's going to be all right."

Sitting with Thad that winter afternoon in the parlor, Epiphany believed it.

On January 15, the same day Epiphany and Thad shared their quiet afternoon at Virginia City, the manhunt entered a new stage. Most of the remaining outlaws from Plummer's gang had fled north to Deer Lodge and the Bitterroot Valley, many intending to move on from there to the gold camps of Idaho. On that Friday, Captain Jim Williams led a party of 20 men out of Nevada City, determined to intercept and arrest the fugitives. The weather was cold and the snow deep, but the men were well-mounted and equipped. Each rider had a revolver; and some, like Will Hunter, carried two.

On January 16, a troop of vigilantes captured and executed Steve Marshland, a young desperado wounded in the recent robbery of a wagon train. After burying the outlaw, the men rejoined the main party and continued on to the town of Deer Lodge. There they found, arrested, and convicted Bill Bunton, Plummer's second in command.

Only two weeks before, Bunton had acquired an interest in a local saloon. Facing death by hanging, he gave his gold watch to his business partner. He told the vigilantes his remaining property should pay his debts. He also told them that he would give the signal for his execution himself. Counting to three, he jumped from the makeshift platform and died instantly.

"Old Tex," the outlaw captured with George Ives and released with Long John Franke at the time of Ives' trial, was discovered with Bunton at Deer Lodge. He, too, was tried by the committee. Finding the evidence against "Old Tex" to be inconclusive, the vigilantes let him go.

Ninety miles upriver was a small settlement called Hellgate. Guided by a rancher named Allen, the manhunters set out for Hellgate. The weather was bitterly cold. Men huddled into their overcoats, bowed their heads against the wind, and rode on. The light faded. Darkness fell. While crossing the frozen surface of Deer Lodge Creek, men and horses broke through the ice and into the water. Weary and cold, the men and animals managed to reach Allen's ranch. At eleven o'clock, after caring for their horses, the men fell into a sound sleep before a roaring fire in the rancher's fireplace.

Although he was as weary as his companions, Will Hunter lay awake for a long while. He watched the flickering shadows on the log walls and rafters overhead. As he listened to the snoring of his sleeping comrades, he gave thought to the killing of men.

He had killed his first man in 1862, after a skirmish with Federal troops on the road near Harrisonville, Missouri. Quantrill's men had ambushed a Union supply train, and for a time the fighting had been at close quarters.

Then the Federals had broken, scattering like quail, chased by the Missouri raiders. Hunter had pursued a young Federal lieutenant for nearly a half-mile into the woods when the officer abruptly drew rein and dismounted. Raising his hands, he had turned to face Hunter. "I surrender, Reb," he had said. "Don't shoot me!"

Foolishly, Hunter had holstered his revolver and stepped down to take the man prisoner. Suddenly, he heard the gunshot and felt the wind from the passing ball brush his cheek. The young officer had drawn his pistol while Hunter was dismounting and had fired point-blank.

Cursing his carelessness, Hunter had drawn his own revolver, fumbling the weapon out of the leather as the young officer fired at him and missed a second time. Hunter's aim was true. His first shot struck the Federal high in the chest. His second shot put him down and dying into the high grass of the woodland floor.

Hunter closed his eyes, remembering his enemy's face. He saw the blue eyes wide and staring, the mouth open slightly, the thin, downy beard. It was a frightened face, a face too young. The killing had stunned and sickened Hunter. Whatever the lieutenant's life had been to that hour, all was ended now. "Whatever the man's life might have been, would have been, would not be now," Hunter thought, "because of me." Hunter killed other men in the bitter fighting of the Missouri-Kansas border war, more than he cared to recall, but he never forgot that first Federal and the woods beyond the Harrisonville road.

Hunter remembered his father reading from the Bible: "Thou Shalt Not Kill." The ancient command had made sense to Hunter as a child. Men should not kill each other. The Book was clear about that. Cain had murdered his brother Abel out of jealousy. Cain had fled to another land, a fugitive and a scandal forever.

Some of the stories from the Book had confused Hunter. Moses the law giver had been a killer. He killed the Egyptian overseer and, like Cain, became a fugitive. Saul, Israel's first king, had slain his thousands, said the Book. David, whom the Lord loveth, had slain his tens of thousands.

Now Will Hunter, son of a country preacher, has killed his share and then some. "Let me count the ways," he thought. "I killed to avenge the murder of my wife and to ease the pain of my guilt. I killed in time of war, defending my homeland. I killed in self-defense because others were trying to kill me. I killed to protect others. I killed in obedience to orders. And killing, may God forgive me, has become easier over time. I've learned to be more proficient, a *better* killer.

"We tell ourselves our killing is different because our reasons are better. We tell ourselves we are not murderers, and I pray we are not. Now I'm tracking men down with a group of other men. When we find them we kill them by hanging. They deserve it, or at least I hope they do. It must be done, but God I am weary of killing.

"Good morning, Missouri."

Will Hunter awoke to find X. Beidler standing over him with a cup of coffee in hand and a smile on his face. Scarcely 5' 6" and slight of build, Beidler's appearance concealed his true nature. During his days with the vigilantes, Hunter had learned that Beidler was a fearless, dogged manhunter who neither quit nor forgave the outlaws and spoilers he pursued. "The Lord said he would make us fishers of men, but I would rather hunt them," he once told Hunter. "I gave up prospecting for gold so that I might prospect for human fiends." X. had become, Hunter knew, chief hangman for the vigilantes.

Hunter sat up in his blankets and put his hat on. "Morning, X," he said. "What makes you so cheerful this cold January day?"

"Why, I just learned you're on the list of men we're looking for," Beidler said. "I always did think you had a shady look."

"If that's a joke, it's a poor one," Hunter said.

Beidler removed a folded list from an inside pocket, studied it, and showed Hunter the top name. "There you are, Missouri," he said. "Bill Hunter, telegraph man and roadster for the Plummer gang. Crawled out of Virginia through a drainage ditch the day we hung those other five. You may as well confess."

Hunter grinned. "The man's a thief, obviously," he said. "Among other things, it seems he stole my name."

Beidler chuckled, enjoying the joke. "Not quite," he said. "He's *Bill* Hunter, and you're *Will* Hunter, or 'Lobo' Hunter, or 'Missouri.'" He put the list back in his pocket and assumed an expression of disappointment. "I guess you're not him after all." Then he brightened. "Could be he's kinfolk, though—maybe your daddy or your brother."

"No relation, X," said Hunter, laughing, "and the poor devil's probably not nearly as good-looking as I am, either."

Beidler sipped coffee from his cup. "Nor as modest," he said. "Let's go wolf down some breakfast before the other boys eat it all."

The vigilantes left Allen's ranch at sunup, bound downriver for the settlement of Hellgate. The snow was deeper than before, varying from two to three feet; and the weather continued cold. Vapor from the breaths of men and horses bloomed white and faded in the sunlight as the column proceeded. There was ice on the horses' bridle bits and the moustaches and beards of the riders.

By day's end, the manhunters had completed nearly sixteen miles of hard travel. They decided to stop for the night. They built fires and began to prepare meals. The horses were set out to paw for the bunch grass beneath the snow.

The next morning, January 18, dawned frigid and still. The men crossed the river and rode on to the workmen's quarters on the Mullan wagon road where they camped for the night. Accidents plagued them. Some of the men had frostbitten fingers and toes. While driving the horses into camp, one of the animals had stepped into a badger hole and had broken its leg. With no way to attend to the injury, one of the men shot the horse. A second horse had broken through the ice and had stripped all the skin from both hind legs from the hock down. The men turned the horse loose. They would pick the animal up on their return.

At first light, on the morning of January 19, the vigilantes were in their saddles and riding for Hellgate. Late afternoon found them about six miles from the settlement. Jim Williams halted the column on the bank of a small creek to wait for dark. "I need a man to ride on ahead and spy out the camp," he said.

"I'll go, captain," Hunter said.

Williams turned in his saddle and studied Hunter for a moment. "All right, Will," he said. "You're well-mounted and equipped. Try to find out who's in town and where they are, then get back here as soon as you can."

Hunter replied with a nod, touched his spurs to the thoroughbred, and rode off toward Hellgate.

As dusk fell across the valley, Williams led the troop ahead until they were only two hundred yards from the settlement. A short time later, Hunter returned, his black gelding nearly invisible in the gloom. Quickly, Hunter described the buildings and the layout of the settlement. His inquiries at Hellgate provided the vigilantes with important information. Cy Skinner was with his woman in a building he ran as a saloon. Alec Carter was in the building next door. George Shears and Johnny Cooper had been seen in the area.

Guns at the ready, the vigilantes thundered into the settlement at a gallop. Cy Skinner stood in the open doorway of his saloon beside the woman known as Nellie as the company surrounded the building.

"Throw up your hands!" ordered Williams.

Nellie's jest was ill-timed. "You must have learned that from the Bannack stage robbers," she remarked.

Two of the vigilantes dismounted, seized Skinner, and tied his hands behind his back. At the cabin next door, vigilantes found Alec Carter asleep on a lounge inside. They disarmed and bound him as well. They took Carter and Skinner to Higgins's store for questioning.

A short time later, Nellie came down to the store to argue on her man's behalf. Vigilantes turned her away and escorted her back to the saloon and living quarters she shared with Skinner. There, the vigilantes found Johnny Cooper, one of the lieutenants of the Plummer gang. Cooper was in a bad way. The outlaw had been wounded by Alec Carter in an argument over a stolen revolver, and was suffering from three bullet wounds. The manhunters promptly took him into custody.

Shortly before midnight, vigilantes hanged Carter and Skinner by torchlight at Higgins's corral. Before they died, both men recited the password of the gang: "I am innocent." Acting on information obtained during questioning of the prisoners, a detachment of eight men departed immediately after the executions and captured outlaws Bob Zachary and George Shears. Shears confessed his crimes, and vigilantes hanged him in a barn near the place they caught him. Three vigilantes, headed by "Old Man" Clark, rode on to Fort Owen in the Bitterroot Valley. There they arrested and hanged stagecoach robber "Whiskey Bill" Graves. The detachment that had captured Cooper and Zachary returned. The two outlaws were hanged at Hellgate the next morning.

After the hangings, Jim Williams gathered his men together, commended them for their faithful service, and the company began its long ride back to Nevada City.

TWENTY-FOUR
Raising the Stakes

T HAD CONTINUED to spend his days at the Orphan Girl Cafe. He arrived each morning promptly at five. He entered the previous day's receipts and expenses in the account books and helped the staff prepare for the breakfast trade. Wong Lee Fat occupied his place in the kitchen like an ancient emperor, proud of his exalted position as cook, and temperamental as a diva. His daughter, Lo Toy, provided him both professional and familial respect, and waited upon the customers swiftly and efficiently. Cootie Blake, despite a habitual tendency to look at the dark side of almost everything, managed to clear and set the tables; wash, dry, and put away the dishes; and keep the insatiable cookstove supplied with firewood.

Thad listened patiently to the staff's requests and complaints, accepted deliveries from the restaurant's suppliers, paid the bills, and responded to questions of staff and customers alike regarding Epiphany's health.

"Mornin', Thad," a grizzled prospector would say. "How's Miss 'Piphany doin'?"

"Better every day," Thad would reply. "She expects to be back here full time in a week."

"Glad to hear it," the prospector would respond. "Tell her Wild Horse Jack sends his regards." Then, with a chuckle and a wink, he would add, "A lot of us boys sure do love that little lady."

"Yes," Thad would say, "a lot of us."

———◈———

Tuesday, January 26, was a warm, sunny day along the gulch. After the lunch crowd had thinned, Thad stepped outside and squinted against the brightness. Snowmelt dripped from the cafe's roof, and the sky was a deep and brilliant blue. Thad kept a horse and sleigh out behind the cafe. He customarily weighed the gold dust and totaled the currency in the till at about four-thirty each afternoon. He would then drive the rig down to the Merchant's Bank and deposit the money. Afterward, he would drive up to Lily Rae's boarding house and spend an hour with Epiphany.

On this day, however, he changed his routine. The day was too fine to spend indoors, he told himself, and too fine not to share with Epiphany. He told the staff he had business downtown, took the deposit to the bank, and swept on up to Lily Rae's, sleighbells jangling.

At the window of the boarding house, Epiphany watched Thad step down from the sleigh. For a moment he stood on the boardwalk, looking up at the front door. Then, seeing her, he smiled broadly and came bounding up the steps two at a time. The sudden, warm glow Epiphany felt at seeing him surprised her. Quickly, she pinched her cheeks to give them color and met him at the door before he could ring the bell.

"My goodness!" she said, smiling. "You certainly seem happy today."

"Why not?" he said. "It's a beautiful day, and I'm coming to see you."

She blushed and lowered her eyes. "You don't usually come by until five," she said. "There's nothing wrong at the cafe, is there?"

"Not a thing," said Thad. "You have money in the bank, and all your regular customers are in love with you. Wong Lee Fat is almost as good a cook as he thinks he is, Lo Toy does the work of ten people, and it's getting harder all the time for Cootie to find something to complain about."

Facing her, Thad took both Epiphany's hands in his. "Piff," he said, "let's do something crazy. Let me take you for a sleigh ride."

Epiphany searched his face. Had he read her mind? She was tired of being cooped up in the house. "Oh, Thad," she said, "could we? Do you think we really could?"

Lily Rae appeared in the doorway of her kitchen. She had been baking, and flour smudged her apron, hands, and face. An accomplished eavesdropper, she had overheard Thad and Epiphany's exchange. Placing her hands on her hips, she struggled with mixed emotions. On the one hand, she liked Thad and was pleased to see Epiphany taking an interest in him. On the other hand, she considered it her responsibility to protect Epiphany's health. She assumed a stern frown, but her smile and the flour on her nose tended to dilute its effect.

"Sleigh riding! What are you two thinking of?" she scolded. "I really don't think you should—"

"*I* do, Lily Rae," Epiphany interrupted. "It's *exactly* what I should do! I need fresh air and sunshine! Besides, I'll dress ever so warmly, I promise!" Lifting her skirts off the floor, Epiphany swept down the hallway to her room. Thad stood, his thumbs hooked in the pockets of his vest, smiling broadly. "Don't worry," he told Lily Rae, "getting out for a spell will be good for her."

"Well," said Lily Rae, "Well, I suppose it might, at that—but don't you stay out too long, you hear?"

Thad answered with a grin. Lily Rae turned quickly away to hide her own smile and flounced back into the kitchen.

Thad and Epiphany dashed west on Idaho Street, past the Orphan Girl, and swung north onto Wallace and the road to Nevada City. Bundled in her heavy cloak and cabriolet bonnet, Epiphany nestled beneath a buffalo robe while Thad held the horse to a brisk trot, harness bells jangling with the rhythm of its gait.

As they swung past Adobetown, Epiphany noticed that many miners were also out enjoying the break in the weather, many in their shirtsleeves. A group of men were unloading logs from a wagon and bucking the wood into stove length sections with a crosscut saw. Two men, walking toward them on the slushy road, stepped aside as the sleigh approached. Both men reverently doffed their hats at the sight of Epiphany.

Beside a small cabin on the banks of Alder Creek, a prospector had taken advantage of the mild day to do his washing. A makeshift clothes-line contained his bedding and what must have been nearly his entire wardrobe. He waved at the sleigh as they passed, and Epiphany re-turned the wave with a smile. From somewhere in the settlement a black dog dashed frantically toward them, delighted to have some-thing to chase. Barking excitedly, the dog followed them all the way to the end of the settlement before it gave up the race.

They swung past Nevada City and turned west. The sun was low in the afternoon sky, blinding in its brightness and lighting the crusted snow with acres of diamonds. At Junction, Thad turned the sleigh north. He drove up a low hill and drew rein overlooking the valley. Only the labored breathing of the horse broke the stillness. To the north, the timbered slopes of the Tobacco Roots glistened in the late afternoon light. To the west, beyond the shining peaks of the Ruby Range, the Pioneers formed a rampart at the edge of the world. Tower-ing clouds billowed overhead, adrift on the deep sky like ships under sail, and slid their shadows over the land.

Epiphany inhaled the clean, sun-warmed air and closed her eyes. Beside her, she felt Thad's body shift. She knew he would be watch-ing her, his gaze admiring and warm. The knowledge stirred her and made her heartbeat quicken. She remembered Thad's strong, open face and the curious way his expression managed to be both respect-ful and ardent at the same time. She met his eyes briefly before he glanced away.

"Penny for your thoughts," she said, smiling.

Thad did not meet her gaze. He looked out across the valley, then down at his folded hands. For a moment he was silent. Then he turned in the sleigh's seat and looked into her eyes. "No charge for my thoughts. They're free," he said, "but my heart is not. I can't go an-other day without telling you. I love you, dearest Piff. I guess I've loved you since the first moment I saw you."

His voice was soft, filled with longing. Holding both her hands in his, he continued to gaze into her eyes. Now it was Epiphany's turn to look away. "Will Hunter once told me that the first time he saw his wife, he *recognized* her," Thad said. "That's how I felt when I first saw you."

"Thad, I. . ."

"Please let me say it all, Piff. I don't know if I can muster the courage a second time. I believe we were meant to be together. Above all, I want you to be my wife. I'm not asking anything of you, now or later. Of course, my hope is that someday you may come to love me, too; but even if that never happens it won't change the way I feel. Nothing can change that. I will love you, and only you, until the day I die."

There were tears in her eyes when Epiphany met his gaze. When she spoke, her voice was hesitant, uncertain. "I. . . I don't know what to say, Thad. I'm a little confused about my feelings these days. I do care about you, and I want you in my life. You are a dear, special friend, and I'm deeply honored by your words. . . but right now I don't know what I can offer you. . ."

Thad's chuckle was gentle. "I said I wasn't asking for anything, Piff. I want to give, not take."

The sun dropped behind the Pioneers, and the sky was ablaze with color. A cold breeze had risen with the setting sun. Epiphany pulled he cloak more closely about her. "Speaking of giving and taking," Thad said, "I think I'd better give this horse his head and take you home before Lily Rae calls out a posse."

Epiphany sat close beside Thad as he put the sleigh back on the road to Virginia City. Neither of them spoke, nor did they feel a need to.

On Monday, February 1, Epiphany returned to work. Wong Lee Fat greeted her with a deep bow, such as a regent might make to his sovereign. Lo Toy smiled sweetly and often, shimmering with happiness. Cootie Blake was so glad to see Epiphany that he actually volunteered for tasks he had not been ordered to perform.

Thad returned to his job as teamster, hauling supplies from Kiskadden's and Oakes's warehouses to destinations along the gulch. He continued to call on Epiphany nearly every evening at the boarding house.

Their conversation covered such varied topics as childhood dreams, adult goals, and gossip of the camps, but neither spoke of Thad's declaration on the day of their sleigh ride.

Will Hunter came at irregular times to the cabin he shared with Thad, seldom staying longer than a night. He was usually up and gone well before first light, sometimes remaining at the cabin only an hour or two before riding out again. He was the same as he had always been, Thad thought, but his face was wind-burned and haggard. There was an edgy, haunted look about his eyes that spoke of lonely trails and grim secrets.

Responding to reports that outlaw Bill Hunter had been seen by settlers along the Gallatin River, four vigilantes set out from Virginia City to overtake and capture the fugitive. They found their quarry in a cabin where he had taken refuge from a snowstorm. On February 3, 1864, the vigilantes hanged the outlaw on a lone tree overlooking the trail, some twenty miles above the mouth of the Gallatin. He was the last of the Plummer gang to be executed.

Bravo Santee was not yet drunk when he left Skinner's Bannack saloon, but he had stopped being anywhere near sober at least four drinks earlier. With Cy Skinner's departure and subsequent hanging by vigilantes at Hellgate, his saloon had come under new management. In Santee's opinion the whiskey had not improved, nor had its price. Despite his opinion, Santee bought two bottles of Rebel's Pride and left the saloon.

When Santee stepped onto Bannack's main street, an icy wind struck him like a cold fist as it swept new snow up the street toward Hangman's

Gulch. Santee's blue roan huddled at the hitchrack, head lowered and its eyes closed against the gale. Before he stepped into the saddle, Santee placed a bottle in each of his saddlebags and tightened the cinch. On that bitter day he wore a heavy canvas duster over his sheepskin coat, two pairs of wool pants, elk-hide mittens with wool liners, a shirt of cotton flannel beneath a woolen overshirt and vest, and gum boots over felt liners and thick German socks. He turned down the flaps of his Scotch cap and pulled his road agent's scarf up to cover his nose and mouth. Born and raised in southern Missouri, Santee had never known such unrelenting cold, and he hated it. Because vigilantes had hanged 24 members of the Plummer gang, including Henry Plummer himself, Santee often thought of leaving for safer, and warmer, climes. "Not yet," he thought, "not just yet."

He turned the roan up the gulch to the gallows where Plummer, Stinson, and Ray had died. He rode past the gallows to the shallow slope that held the bandit chief's mortal remains. Dry snow swirled like fine sand atop the crusted drifts, dancing through the sagebrush and sweeping across the hills. Santee drew rein, lowered the scarf that covered his face, and spat on Plummer's grave. "You ain't so high and mighty now, are you, by god?" Santee sneered. "Strung up on your own gallows and buried like a spud in the frozen dirt!"

"Well, I'm still alive," he continued, "and makin' my own decisions —without havin' to ask your damn permission. Keep an eye out in Hell for Will Hunter, Henry—I'll be sendin' that long-legged bastard down there directly."

Santee shivered, turning his horse away and into the wind. "If the fire's as hot down there as they say," he muttered, "both you sons o' bitches will be a hell of a lot warmer than me."

———— ⬧ ————

It was bitterly cold and snowing heavily the following day when Santee reached Jack Irwin's ranch on the Stinkingwater. Irwin had fled just ahead of the vigilantes, leaving a cabin, large barn, and corrals behind. Santee and his henchmen had promptly vacated their wakiup near Dempsey's and had taken up squatter's rights at Irwin's.

Santee's roan plunged through the drifts that marked the passage from the road down to the ranch, plodding wearily as it wove its way through the pines. At the corral, the horse stopped, its nose nearly touching the gate, and waited. Stiff from hours in the saddle and encumbered by heavy clothing, Santee sat for a long moment before he was able to slide from the saddle and lead the roan through the corral and into the barn. He put the horse in a stall, tossed a double fork-full of hay into the manger, and leaned against the stall's partition. The barn was dark and quiet. Santee stood, enjoying the shelter. He stripped the saddlebags from his saddle, removed one of his whiskey bottles, and drank deeply. Then he leaned back against the partition again, feeling the warmth spread through him.

A plan had come to Santee on the long ride from Bannack. He would lure Will Hunter here, to Irwin's ranch, and kill him. He would make sure Hunter came alone, without other guns to back him—without notifying the vigilantes. That would be a tall order, Santee realized, but he was convinced it could be done. He had thought of a way.

Santee had nearly reached the cabin when a huge man stepped out of the shadows and leveled a shotgun at him. "Who's there?" the man shouted. "Speak up, damn you!"

Santee's anger flared. He had made a long, hard ride, and he was in no mood to be kept from the warmth and shelter of the cabin. He had, however, ordered his men to be on guard. He could hardly blame them if they were doing what he had told them. "Damn you yourself, Goliath!" he snapped. "It's me, Bravo! Put up that scattergun and get the hell out of my way!"

The giant did as ordered. He grinned foolishly as he recognized Santee.

"Howdy, Bravo," he said. "Thought you was one o' them vigilanters, come to hang us."

"They'd have to hang you with a hawser, heavy as you are," Santee said. He opened the cabin door and stepped inside. His other men, Jim Mosely and Corey McClure, had been playing cards at a table near the stove. They jumped to their feet as he came into the room.

"Damn, Bravo," said Mosely, visibly frightened. "We never heard you ride in!"

Santee went directly to the stove, warming his hands above it. Snow fell from his sleeves, popping and hissing as it struck the stovetop. "You boys are a mite goosey, ain't you?" Santee sneered. "You got some reason to be afeared?"

"Reason enough, I reckon," Mosely said. "We came by our old wakiup yesterday. It had horse tracks all around it."

"Yeah," McClure added, "them damn vigilanters, more'n likely."

Santee poured coffee into a tin cup and let the cup's heat warm his hands. "Well, we ain't at the old place no more, now are we? Them stranglin' sons o' bitches will figure they already scared us out."

Mosely and McClure said nothing, but worry was plain on their faces. "When are we leavin' then?" Mosely asked. "This country's played out for the likes of us. There's dead men from here to the Bitterroot who stayed too long."

Santee sipped his coffee. "We'll be goin' soon," he said, "but I've got one more job to do. I came to this country to kill a man, but the bastard's still alive. We ain't leavin' until he's dead."

"Let's do it then," said Mosely. "We been here too goddam long already."

Santee pulled a chair up to the table and sat down. His yellow eyes glowed in the lamplight, and his lips formed a wolfish grin. "I like your attitude, Jim," he said. "I expect we'll have Will Hunter's scalp before the week is out."

By mid-afternoon of the following day the snowfall had stopped. In Virginia City, snow blanketed the streets and alleys of the camp. Overcast skies threatened more of the same. Along the main streets, the sounds of scraping shovels and genial talk echoed among the buildings as merchants and their minions cleared paths to their enterprises. The children of the gulch, accompanied by panting dogs of varied sizes and shapes, attacked the day with delight. Towing their sleds up to the hills above town, they coasted down in flurries of snow and laughter.

At the Orphan Girl, Epiphany counted the day's receipts, counted them a second time, and entered the sum in her ledger. She laid the pen aside, closed the ink bottle, carefully blotted the entries, and allowed herself a moment to savor her success. The small, neat rows of figures in her own hand and the clean, bold entries made by Thad during her absence told the story; the Orphan Girl was doing very well indeed.

Since her return, Epiphany had begun to think about expanding the cafe, perhaps in a larger building or a different location. There was no question about it; the vigilantes' victory over lawlessness had brought renewed confidence to the gulch. Freed from the threat of organized outlaws, both miner and merchant could look forward to a secure and prosperous future.

She glanced at the clock above the table. Four-fifteen, she read, time of the daily lull between dinner and supper. The cafe was empty at that hour. Wong Lee Fat sat on a high stool beside the stove, sipping tea as he waited for the evening's customers. Lo Toy, his daughter, fluttered about the dining room—cleaning, straightening, and polishing. Busy as a hummingbird, the girl went about her tasks with enthusiasm and good cheer. In the back of the kitchen, Cootie Blake was putting the clean dishes back on their shelves, a gloomy expression on his face. Epiphany caught his eye and smiled. He did not return the smile, but he gave her a curt, nervous nod as he went on with his work. For all his habitual worry, Cootie was becoming a willing and hard worker. Epiphany appreciated each one of her employees, and she let them know it. In return, they gave her their industry and their loyalty. It was a good bargain, she thought.

She placed the coins, bills, and buckskin pokes of gold dust that represented the day's receipts into one of the canvas bags she used for her bank deposits. She took her cloak and hat down from their peg. Donning overgaiters, muffler and mittens, she walked to the front door. "I'm off to the bank. See you tomorrow," she said as she stepped out into the bleak afternoon.

———◈———

Wallace Street was nearly deserted when Epiphany approached the Merchant's Bank. A canvas-topped emigrant wagon stood just up from the building, hitched to a four-mule team. Three doors away, a miner came out of a saloon and walked unsteadily toward the livery stable. At the upper end of the block, teamsters unloaded freight in front of Dance and Stuart's store.

Seeing the freighters made her think of Thad. When they had talked the night before, he had said he would be hauling a load of flour to Junction, but would meet her, as usual, at the boarding house around five o'clock.

She was thinking of Thad as the teller took her deposit and gave her the receipt. She was remembering Thad's warm, brown eyes and his honest smile as she stepped out in front of the mules. She did not notice the shadowy figure inside the emigrant wagon or the huge man in the alley beside the bank. She turned, stepped off the walk and into the street that would take her to the boarding house and her meeting with Thad.

Epiphany's nostrils flared as a strange, pungent scent caught her attention. She turned, saw the big man coming up fast, only inches away. His right arm encircled her, binding her tightly to him, as his left hand covered her mouth. Panic consumed her. She struggled, tried to scream.

That odor again—sickening, strange! Wait! Now a second man, small, with a cruel, sly face and yellow eyes, was pouring liquid from a bottle onto a cloth! The small man thrust the cloth into her face, covering her nose and mouth. The fumes were reeking, turbid and strong. "Can't breathe," she thought, "but I must! That smell!" The world faded, blurring, spinning. Then it fell away into darkness and a silence so deep it admitted no sound at all.

TWENTY-FIVE

Accounts Payable

P ROMPTLY AT FIVE O'CLOCK, Thad Mitchell drew rein at the front door of Lily Rae's and dismounted. He glanced up expectantly at the window that overlooked the street. Epiphany was usually there, waiting for him, but on this day the window was dark and empty. Thad's face fell and his eager grin faded. Then he stamped the snow from his boots and bounded up the stairs.

It was Lily Rae, not Epiphany, who answered the bell. "Come in, Thad," she said. "Piff isn't here yet, but I expect her any minute." She ushered him into the parlor, and Thad took a seat in his favorite chair. "Can I offer you a cup of coffee?" Lily Rae asked.

"If it's already made," Thad said. "Thank you, Lily Rae."

By five-thirty, Thad had begun to grow restless. By six, he had become concerned. Where *was* she? He finished his third cup of coffee and walked again to the window. Outside, darkness was falling fast across the gulch.

Thad's mule Shadrach dozed at the hitchrack. It had begun to snow again. Thad frowned. "I can't imagine what could be keeping her," said Lily Rae. "Did you stop by the cafe?"

"Yes," Thad said, "on my way here. Cootie said she left there for the bank about four-thirty. She was expecting to meet me here at five." He stared out at the deserted street, his body tense. Concern gave way to worry. "Something has happened," Thad thought, "otherwise, she'd be here. I know she would." He donned his cap and shrugged into his coat. "I'm going to look for her," he said.

Jefferson Brown was only ten. He was quick, bright, and a great favorite among the people of the camp. For fifty cents the boy would perform a lively tap dance or play a stirring quick-step on his battered harmonica, his ebony face gleaming, merriment behind his clever eyes. The boy spent his days among the shops, saloons, and brothels of the gulch. He was always eager to do an odd job or run an errand for a modest fee.

So, when the stranger with the yellow eyes offered him five dollars just to deliver a letter, Jefferson could hardly believe his ears. The instructions were simple enough: find Will Hunter and give him the letter. Give it to him personally, and to no one else. There would be no need to wait for a reply.

Jefferson found Hunter in the Miner's Rest Saloon. The tall man sat at a table near the back, drinking whiskey and talking with manhunter John X. Beidler. The boy approached the table, doffed his cap, and smiled at Hunter. He produced the letter from inside his ragged coat. "A man paid me to give you dis letter, mistuh Will. He say give it to you an' nobody else."

Hunter accepted the envelope and returned the boy's smile. He took a silver dollar from the change on the table and handed it to him. "Must be a mighty important letter," he said. "Worth at least a dollar, I expect."

Jefferson lowered his eyes. "Yessuh," he said, smiling, "maybe even mo'."

Hunter laughed. "The boy's a born businessman," he told Beidler, "getting paid on both ends of a deal. What are we going to do with this rascal?"

Beidler looked at Jefferson through narrowed eyes and thoughtfully stroked his moustache. "Turn him over to the committee on a charge of highway robbery," Beidler said.

Jefferson's smile turned shaky. He had heard about X. Beidler and the vigilantes. He was sure Beidler was joking, the way men did, but there was no point in tempting fate. "No, suh," he said, "I got's to be goin' now." He turned and scurried out the door.

When the boy had gone, Hunter laid the sealed envelope on the table and studied it for a time. Only his name appeared on the envelope, printed carefully in large block letters: WILL HUNTER. "I have no idea who'd be sending me a letter," he said.

Beidler sipped his whiskey and set the glass down. "There is a way to find out, Missouri," he said laconically, "a man might *open* it."

Hunter lifted the flap with a thumbnail. He removed the crudely folded paper inside and opened it. As he did so, a lock of golden hair fell to the table. The hair was silky soft, the color of straw. Hunter froze, staring at it. Slowly, he unfolded the paper and read:

HUNTER

YOU KILD MY BROTHR RUFUS. NOW IV CUM TO KIL YOU.

EYE FOR EYE. TOOTH FOR TOOTH. LIFE FOR LIFE.

I HAVE THE GIRL. MEET ME AT IRWIN RANCH. <u>CUM ALONE</u>! YOU DONT CUM, GIRL DIES. YOU DON'T CUM ALONE, GIRL DIES.

<u>CUM ALONE</u>! <u>NO DAM VIGILANTERS</u>!

BRAVO SANTEE

For a long moment, Hunter sat motionless, his eyes narrowed and fixed intently on the letter. Slowly, he reached out and gently touched the blonde hair that lay upon the table top. He felt Beidler's eyes upon him.

"Must be some letter," Beidler drawled, "your face has gone white as fresh snow."

Hunter did not reply, but slid the letter across to his companion. Beidler read the words, his expression controlled. When he had finished, he looked up at Hunter and pushed the paper back. There were questions in his eyes.

"A voice from my past," Hunter said wearily. "A banker from Hell, calling in my note."

"Did you kill his brother?"

There was old pain in Hunter's voice. "Yes. He needed killing."

Beidler nodded. "Who's the girl?"

"Epiphany Baker, owns the Orphan Girl Cafe. Appears he's taken her."

The vigilante looked thoughtful. "I'd be happy to go with you, Will," he said.

Hunter shook his head. "I know you would, X," he said, "but I can't take the chance. It's Santee's game, and I have to play his rules."

"A few good men and a length of stout rope—" Beidler began.

Hunter's voice was tense, his reply more firm than he intended. "No," he said, "I know Santee. He means what he says. He would kill the girl."

X. Beidler filled his glass and re-corked the bottle. "Old Man Clark told me once that men like Santee are all cowards at heart. Their courage is only whiskey courage, and they are only brave when they have the best of it."

"I expect he's right," Hunter said, "but it doesn't take much courage to kill a woman. I have to go, and I have to go alone."

"What makes you think *he'll* be alone? He could have a dozen guns backing his play."

"That doesn't change anything."

Beidler frowned. "You make it damned hard for a man to help you," he said.

Hunter smiled. "I'm obliged for the offer," he said. "Maybe you could come in after the party and clean up the mess."

Beidler's eyes were fixed on the front door of the saloon. "That young partner of yours just came in here like a sparrow in a whirlwind," he said. "He's spotted you, and he's headed this way."

Hunter turned in his chair as Thad came up to the table. "Hello, Thad," he said. "You've met X. Beidler, haven't you?"

Thad nodded curtly to Beidler and turned back to Hunter. Worry made his young face seem older. "Piff is missing," he said. "No one has seen her, Will—she's disappeared."

"Yes, I know," Hunter said. "Please, Thad—sit down."

"What? You *know?* Where *is* she?"

Hunter hesitated. Then, as he had done with Beidler, he slid the folded letter across the table. Thad drew out the table's third chair and sat down. His hand trembled as he reached for the paper. Hunter and Beidler sat in silence as the younger man read the letter and then touched the lock of flaxen hair.

Thad looked up, confusion and pain clouding his face. "What does this mean, Will?" he asked. "Who is Bravo Santee?"

"An old enemy," Hunter said. "It seems he has taken Piff to make sure I come to him."

"What are we waiting for? We have to bring her back!"

"We? You're not going, Thad."

Thad's eyes flashed. "The hell I'm not! You know what Piff means to me—I'm going!"

"At the risk of her life? Use your head, man."

"Seems to me it's your history with this Santee that's put her life at risk. I'm coming with you, Will. You'll have to kill me to stop me."

For a moment, time stopped and turned back. Hunter heard the anger and the fear in his young partner's voice, saw the reckless disregard for danger in his face, and recognized himself. He had loved a woman that way not so long ago. He loved her still. Hunter lowered his gaze, then raised his eyes to meet Beidler's. The little vigilante looked back at Hunter as if to say, *What now, Will? Your move.*

"I'm sorry, Thad," Hunter said. Getting to his feet, he nodded at Beidler. "This young fool is interfering with a lawful action of the Vigilance Committee."

Beidler smiled. "Indeed he is," he said. Drawing his revolver, he turned to Thad. "You're under arrest," he said. "I'm afraid I'll have to hold you for questioning."

Will Hunter turned his back on the men and made his way through the crowd to the saloon's front door. From behind him, he heard Thad

Mitchell's angry voice shouting, "Damn you, Will! You bring her back safely, you hear?"

It was, in its way, a kind of prayer, Hunter thought.

Epiphany struggled in darkness, rising toward consciousness in a kind of primal panic. It seemed to her she was drowning in some thick and stupefying sea as she fought for life and breath against the fumes that had robbed her of her senses. She came awake with a start, but the darkness remained. Attempting to move, she became conscious of a weight that held her down and bound her. She lay on a canvas-covered bedroll that smelled of mildew, dampness, and sweated bodies. Her hands, tied tightly behind her, had grown numb.

Epiphany breathed deeply, trying to clear her lungs and renew her mind. After a moment, she was able to identify the weight atop her—a buffalo robe, heavy and stifling. She heard the low murmur of voices from somewhere nearby. Men's voices, playing cards. Suddenly, she recalled the huge man who had siezed her outside the bank, and the small man with the cold, yellow eyes who had drugged her. Who were they? What did they want with her?

Nausea rose suddenly within her. Epiphany raised her head and vomited at the edge of the bedroll, gasping and choking until the spasms quieted.

"I believe your guest has woke from her beauty sleep," said Corey McClure. "She's pukin' on your bedroll, Bravo."

Bravo Santee kicked back his chair, slid his Bowie knife from its scabbard, and stood up from the table. "Then I expect I'd best cut her free so she can clean it up," he said.

Abruptly, Santee jerked the buffalo robe aside. He stood over her, knife in hand. Beyond him, she saw the big man and two others seated at a rough table, watching her. Santee grasped her hair with his left hand and forced her head up. The blade in his right hand caught lamplight. He held the knife close to her face, his voice flat and without emotion. "There's hot water on the stove," he said, "and a raggy old shirt on that nail yonder. Clean up your damn mess."

He threw her, face down, onto the bedroll and cut the cords that bound her hands with one quick slash of the knife. Epiphany sat up, rubbing her wrists to restore feeling to her hands. "Why. . . did you bring me here?" she asked.

"I'm fixin' to trap me a wolf," Santee said. "You get to be the bait."

Epiphany's brown eyes flashed in the lamplight. "You know you'll die for taking me," she said. "There's law in the district now."

Santee's smile was cold. "Vigilanters ain't law, missy," he said. "They're just killers with ropes. As for dyin,' everybody dies—even you."

He slid the knife back into its scabbard. "Thing is," he continued, "you get to choose. You can die here and now in this cabin with your throat cut, or some years down the road, after you've growed up enough to do a man some good."

Epiphany got unsteadily to her feet. The room seemed to spin and she thought she might faint. Her vision blurred, then cleared. She forced herself to concentrate on the small man who was her captor. He was short, she saw, barely five feet four. He stood before her, his hips thrust forward and his thumbs hooked in his gunbelt, watching her from beneath his hatbrim. There was a cold confidence about the man, she thought, an implacable determination that was frightening in its intensity. Haltingly, Epiphany moved toward the stove.

"They tell me you run a cafe over in Virginia," Santee said. "When you've cleaned up your mess you can make yourself useful and cook us up some grub."

Corey McClure laughed. "That's right," he said. "Then we'll cut the cards to see who gets to bed you first."

Santee's movement was too fast for the eye to follow. His hand caught the back of McClure's head and slammed the man's face hard onto the table top. McClure came up bleeding from his nose and mouth, reaching for the revolver at his waist, but Santee's knife was against his throat. "Go ahead," Santee said, "pull that pistol, and I'll cut your damned head off."

McClure slumped back in his chair and placed his hands on the table.

"I expect it maybe slipped your mind who's runnin' things around here," Santee said. "Nobody touches the girl 'til after we kill Hunter. Then we'll see."

Epiphany froze on hearing Hunter's name, her eyes wide. "I see you heard that," Santee said. "That's right, little Missy, that wolf I told you about is Will Hunter. Him and me have an old score to settle."

Santee pulled out a chair and straddled it backward. "I was in Virginia the day Hunter whipped Jack Gallagher over you. It occurred to me I might get him to come meet me if I let him know I had you. What do you think?"

"What I thought before," Epiphany said, "you're a dead man."

Santee answered with a low chuckle. "If that's so," he said, "I don't expect I'll be the only one."

It was just past seven in the evening when Hunter led the black thoroughbred out of Ulberg's Livery and set off for Daly's roadhouse. Snow was falling again. Icy needles of sleet stung Hunter's face, driven by a howling wind that seemed to be a lament for Epiphany. Images of the helpless girl in the hands of Bravo Santee tortured Hunter. He wrenched his mind away from the ugly thoughts by an act of will, focusing instead on the road and the task before him.

With a troop of vigilantes from Nevada City, he had visited Irwin's ranch some two weeks before and had found it abandoned. Now he tried to recall the location in detail. How did the land look? Where were the buildings? He recalled that the ranch lay just five miles from Daly's at a bend in the river. The road to Bannack turned due west at that point, moving on to Beaverhead Rock and Dempsey's stage station.

The land at Irwin's, he remembered, sloped down from the road through pines and aspens to a cabin, barn, and corrals. In memory he saw the cabin—small, sod-roofed, and low to the ground. Was there a fireplace or stove? He could not recall. Windows? He did not know. Inside the cabin, with Bravo Santee and how many others, would be Epiphany. She would be frightened, fighting panic, caught by the hatred of men in a scheme of vengeance and blood she could not possibly understand. "Oh, God," he prayed, "please don't let them hurt her."

Fifteen miles later, stiff with cold and weary from bucking the storm, Hunter drew rein at Daly's. Ice clung to his beard and eyelashes. He slid stiffly from the saddle, clinging to the gelding's side until he was able to catch his breath. He led the thoroughbred to a vacant stall in the barn and stripped the saddle from its steaming back. Pouring a double handful of oats into the feed box, he forked loose hay into the manger. He then took his saddlebags, rifle, and blankets and bulled his way against the wind to the door of the roadhouse.

Inside, he paused as the heat warmed his lungs and branded his cheeks. The smells of stew and coffee drifting from the kitchen nearly overwhelmed him. He focused his watering eyes and glanced around the room. Two teamsters sat eating together at a table while the cook poured them coffee from a blackened pot. Hunter knocked the snow from his hat, hung his greatcoat on a peg near the door, and took a place at the table.

"Supper, and a place to sleep," Hunter said.

The cook, a man in his fifties with a short, white beard, nodded. "Two dollars," he said, glancing at the rough-hewn stairway. "You can roll out your blankets up yonder."

When Hunter had eaten, weariness fell on him like an avalanche of sand. He took his possessions and climbed the narrow stairway to the second floor. A dim lantern lit the big open room, and Hunter could see that three other men slept sprawled against the room's north wall. He lay back in his blankets, basking in the warmth that rose from the lower level, and closed his eyes. Outside, the wind wailed, at times low and mournful, at other times keening like a banshee chorus. Hunter listened for a moment, glad to be inside, and fell into a deep and dreamless sleep.

At the Miner's Rest, Thad fidgeted in his chair, his frustration mounting. Across the table, X. Beidler watched the young man through half-closed eyes and pitied him.

Thad's tone was urgent. "For God's sake, Beidler, let me go! Will Hunter is riding into an ambush!"

"Very likely," said Beidler calmly.

"You don't understand! He's going because that man—those men—hold the woman I intend to marry! They plan to kill him!"

Beidler sipped his whiskey and nodded gravely. "Yes," he said, "I expect they do."

Thad felt himself growing desperate. His voice sounded nervous and shrill, even to himself. He took a deep breath, then spoke quietly and deliberately. "Then how could you let him leave without going with him?" Beidler fished his watch out of a vest pocket and snapped open the case.

"His choice," Beidler said, "I offered, and he turned me down. Didn't want to risk the woman's life. Seems he didn't want you to risk yours, either; so I agreed to keep you here until he was well on his way."

Thad said nothing. He listened to the men at the bar, laughing and swearing, their voices loud and raucous. Anger blinded him. How could those fools waste their time joking and drinking when just twenty-five miles away Epiphany and Will were in mortal danger?

X. Beidler glanced at his watch and closed the case. "But now that he *is* well on his way," he said, "I believe we might ride out and see if we can be of help. How does that strike you, Thad Mitchell?"

In the dim light that precedes dawn, Will Hunter awoke at Daly's. Across the room, the other men slept soundly, their bodies mounded beneath their blankets. Hunter donned his hat, boots, and greatcoat. He rolled his blankets, and descended the stairs. All was silent in the lower level. Hunter eased the door open and stepped outside.

The storm had passed during the night, and a thick blanket of new snow covered the land. Overhead, the skies were clear, resplendent with stars. From the position of the Big Dipper, Hunter judged the time to be about four o'clock. The morning was absolutely still. There was not a breath of wind. Inside the barn, Hunter brushed and saddled the thoroughbred and set his mind on the five-mile ride to Irwin's.

Bravo Santee had demanded he come alone, but Hunter was a realist. He knew he would almost certainly face more guns than Santee's at the ranch. He would use the element of surprise: a fast horseback attack, the way he had learned the tactic from Quantrill—and an assault on the cabin itself to drive his enemies into the open. He refused to consider the possibility of failure. Epiphany's life depended on him, and he would not let her down. He checked the loads in his revolvers, slid the Henry into its scabbard, and stepped up into the saddle. The thoroughbred danced an impatient quickstep in the snow, seeming to sense the coming clash. As Hunter touched the gelding's flanks with his spurs, the animal stepped boldly out onto the drifted roadway like the war-horse it once had been.

Dawn came grudgingly to the land. Above the silent valley, cold stars faded and vanished as sunlight staked its claim on the day. At Irwin's ranch, Bravo Santee opened the cabin door and stepped outside, taking the measure of the morning. Behind him, Epiphany stood at the stove, her cloak drawn tightly about her shoulders, and felt the chill air sweep in through the open door. Seated at the table, Santee's men wolfed down the breakfast she had prepared, measuring her with their eyes.

"That's enough," Santee said, closing the door and turning back to his men. "Daylight's comin' fast and so, I expect, is Hunter. You boys had best look to your weapons."

Reluctantly, Mosely turned his glance from Epiphany to Santee. "I don't know what all the fuss is about," he said. "This Hunter's only one man, and there's four of us—or don't you figure he'll be comin' alone?"

"He'll come alone, I expect," said Santee, "but he's a guerrilla fighter and a border ruffian, like me. We'll take him, all right, but by this evenin' some of you boys just might have got your hair mussed."

Goliath Pettigrew, the big man, donned a bulky buffalo coat and buttoned the garment across his barrel chest. He cradled a Sharp's carbine in the crook of his arm and stood, stolid as an ox, awaiting Santee's orders.

"Get on up to the road and keep your eyes open," Santee told him. "Lay quiet and let him get close. One shot's all the chance you're likely to have."

McClure and Mosley still sat at the table. As Pettigrew ducked under the doorway and went outside, Santee turned to the others. "Take the barn," he told McClure. "Lay up in the loft and watch. I expect Hunter will come in fast and a-horseback. Don't let him get past you."

Santee turned to Mosely. "I want you outside the cabin, but close by," he said. "There's no tellin' which way he'll come, but he'll figure the girl is in here. Call out if you see him."

Mosely pulled on his overcoat, covered his ears with his scarf, and pulled his battered hat down over it. "Where will you be?" he asked.

Santee's yellow eyes gleamed. "In here, keepin' my eye on the girl." He smiled his cold smile. "When Hunter comes, I may let the bitch scream, just to get his attention. Hell, I may just *cause* her to scream."

The cabin door closed behind the two men, and Epiphany found herself alone with Santee. "You're a coward," she said. "You talk of settling a score with Hunter, but you're afraid to face him alone."

Santee shrugged. "I aim to kill him," he said. "Don't matter how I do it. Them three boys are just weapons, like my gun or my knife. All I keer about is Will Hunter dead."

"He's a hundred times the man you are," Epiphany said. "Even if you kill him, you'll have to live with that."

Santee's fist caught Epiphany just below her rib cage. She doubled over, gasping for breath, and fell to the cabin floor as pain exploded from the point of impact. Santee followed up the blow with a kick, and Epiphany choked back a scream. "You're a feisty little bitch," the small man said. "Damned if I don't admire that in a female." Quickly, he tied her hands behind her back and threw a hitch about her feet. "When this is all over, missy, I may just tame you down some before I let the boys have their turn."

In the first light of day, the road west from Daly's was a ribbon of trackless white. As Will Hunter neared Irwin's ranch, he turned the thoroughbred off the road. Staying parallel to the road, he rode carefully among the trees. The drifted snow muffled the sound of his travel. The valley was a hushed world of beauty that gave no hint of danger.

Riding past the turn that would have taken him down to the ranch, Hunter guided the gelding through the tall pines, stopping frequently to listen before moving on. He avoided passing through or near the aspen groves, knowing that fallen trees and deadwood underfoot would hinder the silence of his passage. From time to time the snow-covered branches of the pines, warmed by the sunlight, would release their burden in a silent avalanche of white. From somewhere nearby, a squirrel scolded. High above the trees, a raven soared, calling raucously as it flew. Drawing his revolver, Hunter crossed the road and turned the thoroughbred back toward Irwin's.

Hunter saw the horse first. A moon-eyed roan stood, tied high to a pine branch some two hundred feet off the road. Below the horse, his eyes on the trail down to Irwin's, a big man sat behind a fallen log with the Sharp's across his knees. In his heavy buffalo coat, the man reminded Hunter of a huge, curious bear.

"Looking for me?" Hunter asked. Startled, Pettigrew jerked suddenly about, his eyes wide and staring. Desperately, he swung the carbine up, but he was too slow. Hunter's revolver bucked in his hand and the big man's body jerked as the ball struck him in the chest. Pettigrew grimaced, still trying to bring the carbine to bear, as Hunter's second shot took him in the throat. Eyes bulging, beefy face reddening, the big man struggled to his feet. He dropped the Sharp's carbine, unfired. Pettigrew swayed, both hands clutching his throat. A brute rage stamped his features. The giant took two halting steps, stumbled, and fell like a toppled tree into the deep snow.

In the barn loft, Corey McClure turned up the collar of his coat and studied the tree line beyond the cabin. He sat at the loft's opening, facing the cabin and clutching his Spencer carbine with mittened hands. The sun had risen, and its warm light spread over the clearing and cast blue shadows across the snow. McClure had never been good at waiting. He was nervous and edgy, anxious for the fight to begin. Again, he scanned the clearing; but the only movement was the smoke from the cabin's stovepipe drifting up into the cold, still air. McClure produced a pint whiskey bottle from a coat pocket and took a long pull, shuddering as the whiskey warmed and braced him. Re-corking the bottle, he stopped abruptly in mid-motion, listening. In the stillness the sound of the two revolver shots had been sharp and clear. McClure levered a cartridge into the Spencer and turned his eyes again to the tree line. The players were in their places. The game had begun.

TWENTY-SIX

Redemption

W ILL HUNTER lay beneath the spreading boughs of a massive pine and studied the clearing through his field glasses. The cabin was as he remembered it, a low, sod-roofed building perhaps twenty by thirty feet in size. The door faced east, and a small window on the north side provided the cabin's only outside light. Dry brush and kindling lay stacked against the cabin's north wall. A chopping block stood nearby.

Hunter lowered the glasses, his eyes still on the cabin. Epiphany would be inside, probably guarded by Santee himself. How many others were there? The big man had been sent to ambush him, he knew, but how many more? Where were they? Hunter brought the glasses back to his eyes and turned his attention to the barn lot.

Four horses and a span of mules stood together in the corral, and five more horses occupied the catch pen beyond. Between the barn and the river stood a canvas-topped wagon, looking bleak and forlorn in the snow. Again, Hunter lowered the glasses. The horses and mules told the story; two to three men, at least—maybe more. Yes, Santee was with Piff in the cabin.

Slowly, he eased back from beneath the tree and stood. From a patch of deadfall, he selected three sticks. Each stick was about two inches thick and three feet in length. He carried them back to where the thoroughbred stood waiting. From his saddlebags, Hunter removed a handful of rags and a quart bottle of kerosene. Tying the rags carefully to the ends of the sticks, he drenched them with the contents of the bottle. Then, holding all three makeshift torches, he mounted the gelding and set his feet firmly in the stirrups. He snapped a sulphur match to life, lit the torches, and gave the gelding its head.

Flaming torches held high, Hunter burst out of the trees and into the clearing. The thoroughbred plunged through the drifted snow, running hard toward the cabin. From the barn loft, Corey McClure opened fire. He levered the Spencer carbine and fired again, but his hurried shots missed the rider on the black horse racing across the clearing.

Gunfire exploded from the cabin's window, stabbing tongues of flame amid the white smoke. Hunter leaned low in the saddle as he came alongside the cabin. He tossed two of his burning brands into the dry brush and kindling against the building's north wall. Once past, Hunter turned the gelding sharply away and toward the barn, the horse zig-zagging as it ran. McClure fired rapidly, kneeling in the opening to the loft, cursing as horse and rider continued to elude his bullets.

Then Hunter swung sharply away, throwing the third torch into the barn and riding hard toward the tree line. At the cabin, the woodpile was ablaze, flames spreading to the cabin wall and licking along the eaves. From beyond the cabin came Mosley, mounted on a close-coupled bay. He reined up briefly, watching the fire spread. Then he kicked the horse into a run as he rode out after Hunter. He had nearly reached the trees when Hunter burst out of the woods directly in his path. Mosley jerked the bay hard to the left and felt the animal lose its footing. The horse fell heavily, throwing its rider, then lunged back up in an explosion of white. Mosely struggled to his feet, snow-dusted and hatless. He pulled his revolver out of the leather and brought it up. Coolly and deliberately, Hunter shot him twice and left him dying in the bloody snow.

Hunter returned then, racing across the clearing on the black, curving toward the barn. From the loft, Corey McClure watched as Hunter closed the distance. He swung the carbine in a smooth arc, leading his target. Then, as horse and rider reached the center of his field of vision, McClure squeezed the trigger. The bullet struck Hunter hard in the chest and blasted him out of the saddle. He fell, found his feet, and came up shooting. McClure ducked back, then knelt in the loft's opening, aiming the Spencer for a second shot.

Now the barn was burning, too. Woodsmoke billowed from the lower level and obscured the loft. Hunter pulled himself to his feet and ran not away from the barn as McClure expected, but toward it. As flames spread through the barn, the sound of the fire grew to a roar. Smoke drifted across the barn lot, blocking the rifleman's view. Hidden by the smoke, Hunter passed through the corral gate and went inside the barn. He met McClure as the rifleman was coming down from the loft and shot him off the ladder. McClure triggered the carbine as he fell. The bullet struck Hunter in the left shoulder and knocked him down. Hunter rolled, came up on one knee, and fired again. McClure slammed back against the wall, dropped the carbine, and fell lifeless to the floor.

Inside the cabin, Bravo Santee stood at the window, straining to see through the thickening smoke. He had watched Hunter come riding across the clearing on the thoroughbred, torches held high, and in that moment he had admired his enemy. There had been a boldness to Hunter's charge, a reckless courage that brought Santee memories of the wild days with Quantrill. "Best damn horseback revolver fighters in the world, we was. Look at that sum'bitch ride!"

He had heard McClure's shots from the barn loft and he had seen them gouge up spurts of snow as McClure missed his target. Santee had fired at Hunter himself, shooting from the cabin's window. He had watched the man come on. He had seen Hunter's face, determined and unafraid. He had seen him hurl the burning brands, move on to fire the barn, and then sharply turn and race back to the trees.

Mosley had ridden past the window then, intent on pursuing Hunter. Santee had yelled at him—had tried to stop him, but to no avail. Using another of the Raiders' old tactics, Hunter was retreating before the enemy and leading him into the wildwood. Santee knew he would then turn and kill him. When Santee heard the shots, he was certain Mosley would not be coming back.

A moment later, his judgment was confirmed. Hunter exploded out of the trees. The black horse crossed the clearing at a gallop, charging the barn. As smoke began to obscure Santee's view from the window, he had stepped outside to watch Hunter's attack. He had watched as McClure shot Hunter out of the saddle. He had seen his enemy fall, and then find his feet and rush the barn on foot. He had watched the frightened horses and mules flee the corral through the open gate as Hunter entered the barn. Then, he heard more shots, one the boom of McClure's Spencer, the others were revolver shots.

Now, Santee watched as Hunter stumbled back out through the gate, a revolver in his right hand, coming toward the cabin. His left arm hung loosely at his side, and the front of his greatcoat was bright red with blood. Twice, he fell in the drifted snow of the clearing, but each time he found his feet and continued toward the cabin. Then he fell a third time and sat slumped, facing Santee, a hundred yards from the cabin.

"It has come to this," Santee thought, "Will Hunter and me. The man who killed my brother sits wounded over yonder, waiting. He came, and he fought as well as a man can, but it's over now. I am obliged to go to him now and settle our accounts."

With a revolver in each hand, Santee stepped away from the cabin and stalked slowly across the snowy field.

Epiphany lay, tied hand and foot, on the bedroll where Santee had thrown her. She had heard the gunfire outside and had watched Santee fire his revolvers through the cabin window. She had heard him shouting to Mosley, "Don't follow him, damn you! It's a trap, Jim! You hear me?"

Now Santee had gone outside, leaving her alone. As frigid air rushed in through the open door, Epiphany felt its bite and its menace. Smoke poured in at the roof line, filling the room. Its bitter smell assailed her.

Coughing and choking, she struggled to free herself from her bonds. Flames flickered at the edges of the window and crept inside.

She continued to try to free herself, straining with all her strength against the ropes. Her wrists burned, rubbed raw by her efforts. Wait! Had the ropes loosened slightly, or was it only her desperate imagination? "Try again, try harder," she told herself. "Keep trying, Piff!"

Suddenly, a hand pulled free! Quickly, holding her breath against the smoke that burned her eyes and lungs, she untied the ropes that bound her. Half walking, half crawling, she rushed to the door and dashed out into the clean, cold air.

Will Hunter slumped in the snow, his long legs folded beneath him. He let the pain of his chest wound have its way. He felt the rapid beating of his heart and heard the quick shallow panting of his breath, as he stared dull-eyed across the clearing. Santee had stepped out of the burning cabin, a revolver in each hand, staring at him. "Come on, Santee, come closer—another twenty-five yards."

Hunter felt the cold of the snow upon his skin and the hot wetness beneath his shirt. There was a numbness spreading through his body. His eyelids fluttered and tried to close, as if they had a will of their own. "Not yet," he commanded. "The job isn't finished. Stay awake now, just a little bit longer."

His Navy revolver lay in his lap, its ivory grips clasped by the fingers of his right hand. There was blood on the ivory, blood on his fingers, and blood staining the snow. Hunter's eyes closed. He forced them open. He watched the steam of his breath puffing out into the cold air. "I must be alive. I'm still breathing."

Across the clearing, Santee continued to hesitate.

"He's afraid of me," Hunter thought. "I'm hard hit and down, and still the yellow bastard is afraid of me." Hunter shifted his position, cocking the revolver and sighting along its barrel. "Have to give you some encouragement, make you come closer."

Santee stopped and took a nervous step back. Hunter pulled the trigger and heard the hammer fall on an empty chamber with a dull click. He cocked the weapon, aimed, and triggered it twice more—each time with the same result. Hunter sagged back and let the revolver rest again in his lap. He groped beneath his greatcoat for his other revolver, and found the holster empty. "Must have lost it when I fell," he thought. He pushed back the wedge key on the empty Colts, removed the barrel, and let the cylinder drop into the snow. His trembling fingers found one of the loaded cylinders he carried in the greatcoat's pockets. He slid it onto the revolver's base pin, replaced the barrel, and pushed the key back in. Concentrating on keeping his hands steady, Hunter affixed percussion caps to the cylinder's nipples and fell back.

Now Santee was walking toward him again, made bold by Hunter's futile attempts to fire. Hunter watched him come, feeling consciousness dim and his strength fading. His mind began to drift, taking away his will and resolve. His eyes closed. Again, he forced them open. Santee continued to stride toward him, his knees rising and falling as he plunged through the snow. In the distance, Hunter saw the burning cabin. He saw the red-orange flames engulfing the structure and black smoke belching skyward as a dirty brown shadow of the smoke slid over the pristine snow. Sudden movement caught his attention. A woman, her flaxen hair catching sunlight, emerged from the cabin. She turned her face to him. Looking at the woman, Hunter was back in Harrisonville.

He had been drinking with Buck and Lem. Together, they had played the old songs, just as they had so many times before—fiddle, banjo, and guitar. They had celebrated their youth, and they had said their goodbys.

He was nearly home when he saw the flames rising high into the night sky. Redlegs! Jayhawkers had attacked his farm! Their home—his, and Rachel's—was on fire! He came riding fast up the lane. He saw the barn burning. He saw the milk cow dead on her side. Rachel! Where was Rachel? He saw her! Rachel—his Rachel—was alive and well, coming out of the cabin! He was not too late; he had arrived in time!

The last Jayhawker is walking toward me, coming closer, a revolver in each hand. Hate is twisting the man's face. His yellow eyes burn bright as the fire. He is talking to me but I can't hear him. Now he's raising his pistol.

He's aiming it at me, still talking. I wonder what he's saying.

------◈------

Twelve feet away, Santee stopped, breathing hard. He raised the heavy pistol and aimed it at the man slumped in the snow. "I have settled your flint, Will Hunter," said Bravo Santee. "You are a gone coon, by god!"

Hunter's revolver bucked in his hand. The last thing Bravo Santee saw was the bright belch of flame at its muzzle. A small black hole appeared above Santee's bulging eyes, and a pink mist exploded in the sunlight behind his head. Santee rocked backward, the Dragoon falling from his lifeless fingers. Then his knees buckled, and he fell face down into the snow.

Hunter saw the woman running toward him, her golden hair flying. *I found the way, Rachel. Everything's all right now.* Hunter lay back, closed his eyes, and died.

------◈------

Thad Mitchell and X. Beidler rode into the clearing just at moonrise. Above the distant mountains the pale moon ascended, aloof and beautiful in the morning sky.

Epiphany was sitting in the snow, holding Will Hunter. As she cradled his head in her arms, her soft crying was like the crooning of a lullaby. Beyond Epiphany and Hunter lay the body of Bravo Santee, sprawled in the bloody snow. Hunter's black thoroughbred stood nearby, its head high, watching their approach.

Thad rushed to Epiphany's side, his throat tight, relief making him light-headed. "Piff!" he said. "Thank God you're all right!"

Epiphany raised her head, tears filling her eyes. She rose from Hunter's side, her face wet from weeping. "Oh, Thad," she said simply, "Will is gone. Our great, brave friend is gone."

X. Beidler knelt in the snow beside Hunter, sadness plain on the manhunter's face. He met the young man's eyes and nodded curtly.

Thad held Epiphany close, grief and gratitude waring within him. "Yes," he said, his voice breaking. "Yes, Piff, he's gone."

She clung to Thad, eyes closed, her face against his chest. "Yes is *my* word, Thad," she said. "My answer is yes."

"Dearest Piff," he said, "I haven't *asked* you anything."

"Whatever you ask," Epiphany said, "my answer will be yes."